Never Enough Gold

A Chronicle of Sardis

By
David Phillips

HEARTBEATS OF COURAGE

Volume Two

Never Enough Gold

A Chronicle of Sardis

By
David Phillips

Century One Chronicles
Toronto, Ontario, Canada

NEVER ENOUGH GOLD: A CHRONICLE OF SARDIS
HEARTBEATS OF COURAGE, BOOK 2

©2020 David Kenneth Phillips
Published in the United States of America

Canadian Intellectual Property Office CIPO Registration Number: 1152521

ISBN 978-1-9994752-2-2
e-Book ISBN 978-1-9994752-3-9

The stories in this book are fictional. Some personages are based on historical fact; these are indicated in the list of characters, but resemblance to persons alive or dead is coincidental and unintended. All rights reserved solely by the author. The author guarantees all contents including poems and songs are original and do not infringe upon the legal rights of any other person or work.

No part of this book may be reproduced, stored in a retrieval system, or transmitted in any form or by any means - electronic, mechanical, digital, photographic, recording, or any other - except for brief quotations in printed reviews, without the prior permission of the author at:

Century One Chronicles, PO Box 25013 Morningside Avenue, 255 Morningside Avenue, Toronto, Ontario, Canada M1E 0A7

Unless otherwise indicated, scripture references are taken from the New International Version. Used by permission. All rights reserved. Copyright 1982-1996 by Zondervan Corporation, Grand Rapids, Michigan, 49530 USA

Credits:
Front Cover: "Anthony takes Miriam to visit needy people in Sardis"
Back Cover: "Miriam talks with family members near the slums"
Illustrations and composition by Dusan Arsenic
Map of Asia Minor and Map of Sardis: Anoosh Mubashar
Back Cover: Photo of the author by Sarah Grace Photography

For
Elizabeth and Robert,
Samuel and Aimee

For
those who
are misunderstood
or ignored because of
humble social standing
and for those who
come alongside with love,
care, and creative compassion,
finding means for others to discover
their value as human beings
because of the Name Above All Names.

Prologue

Ancient Sardis was known as one of the most influential and prosperous cities around the Mediterranean region. Gold was discovered in the stream flowing through the center of the city, and skilled men there were the first to mint gold coins. The city became the center of the Lydian Kingdom. Eventually, powerful troops from the Persian Empire overthrew a long reign of monarchs. Subsequently conquered by the Greeks, Sardis fell in standing as the Kingdom of Pergamum rose in importance. After Rome took control of Asia Minor, some people in Sardis yearned to return to the past glories of previous kingdoms.

One day Antipas, a businessman in Pergamum, was killed for his beliefs. Why his teaching and beliefs brought conflict to Sardis is the basis for this chronicle. The story is told as historical fiction. In this novel, Miriam, Antipas's granddaughter, and her husband, Anthony, a Roman soldier, have fled from Pergamum to Sardis. The first book in this series, *Through the Fire: A Chronicle of Pergamum,* reveals the events that forced them to move.

> *In this you greatly rejoice, though now for a little while you may have had to suffer grief in all kinds of trials. These have come so that your faith—of greater worth than gold, which perishes even though refined by fire—may be proved genuine. 1 Peter 1:6–7*

HEARTBEATS OF COURAGE

Book 1: Through the Fire: A Chronicle of Pergamum
AD 89–91

Book 2: Never Enough Gold: A Chronicle of Sardis
AD 91–92

Book 3: Purple Honors: A Chronicle of Thyatira
AD 92–93

Book 4: The Inn of the Open Door: A Chronicle of Philadelphia
AD 93-96

Book 5: Rich Me! A Chronicle of Laodicea
AD 96–97

Book 6: Fortress Shadows: A Chronicle of Smyrna
AD 97–111

Book 7: An Act of Grace: A Chronicle of Ephesus
AD 111

The Songs of Miriam: A Collection of Miriam's Songs

Characters in *Never Enough Gold*

* Indicates historical figures – Major personages are noted in bold.

Domitian,* Second son of Vespasian and Emperor of the Roman Empire: AD 81–96
King Decebalus,* King of Dacia (Bulgaria/Romania/Moldova), in opposition to Domitian
Lucius Ocrea,* Governor of Asia, in Ephesus, AD 91–92

<u>In Sardis</u>

Felicior Priscus, 37, Commanding Officer of the Garrison of Sardis
Prosperus, 38, Instructor in the Garrison of Sardis; previously served in Zeugma and Syria
Tymon Tmolus, 39, Mayor of Sardis, an "Asiarch"; a patriarch of an aristocratic Lydian family
Panthea Tmolus, 38, Wife of the mayor of Sardis
Cynthia Tmolus, 18, Daughter of Tymon and Panthea Tmolus
Diodotus, 39, Banker and Chief Manager of the Bank of Hermus
Delbin, 35, Wealthy woman in Sardis; the wife of banker Diodotus

Ankara, 47, High priest of the Temple of Artemis in Sardis
Alala, 45, High priestess of the Temple of Artemis in Sardis

Anthony Suros, 36, Legionary from Legion XXI, the Predators; a reservist and Miriam's husband
Miriam Bat Johanan, 26, Antipas's granddaughter
Chrysa Grace, Two months old, Anthony and Miriam's daughter

Simon Ben Shelah, 60, and **Judith**, 60, Businessman and his wife
Ezar, 39, and **Chenya** Ben Shelah, 36, Simon and Judith's elder son and daughter-in-law
Elaine, 15, **Tamir,** 14, and **Amath,** 7, Ezar and Chenya's children
Heber Ben Shelah, 37, Simon and Judith's second son; a widower
Nissa Ben Shelah, 28, and **Ravid**, 28 Simon and Judith's daughter and her husband

Lyris, 50, Widow working as a servant in Simon and Judith's home

Cleon, 32, Shop clerk in the Ben Shelah store

Ateas, 22, and **Arpoxa**, 21, Former slaves from Scythia, north of the Black Sea
Saulius, Three months old, Ateas and Arpoxa's son

Jakob, 45, Rabbi of the Synagogue of Sardis
Achim, 36, Elder and leader in the Synagogue of Sardis
Gaius,* 42, Leader and teacher of the God-fearers of Sardis

Eugene, 55, Widower and father of Kalonice
Jace, 36, Teacher of history and philosophy in the Gymnasium of Sardis
Kalonice, 35, Jace's wife and Miriam's friend
Isidoros, 15, Jace and Kalonice's elder son
Hector, 14, Jace and Kalonice's second son; an avid runner

Felix, 29, Stonemason
Gina, 29, Felix's wife and mother of five children
Cosmos, 8 Felix and Gina's son
Demetrius,* 47, Messenger sent by John at the church of Ephesus
Dares, 19, and Cohn, 17, Two recruits for the Roman army

In Forty Trees
Nikias, 35, Farmer working on Olive Grove Farm

In Pergamum
Antipas,* Deceased leader of the Household of Faith in Pergamum
Onias, 41, Antipas's steward

Quintus Rufus,* 46, Mayor of Pergamum
Cassius Flamininus Maro, 41, Commanding officer of the Garrison of Pergamum

Lydia-Naq Milon, 54, High priestess of the Altar of Zeus in Pergamum
Diotrephes Milon, 29, Son of Lydia-Naq, Head of Department of History at Gymnasium of Sardis
Zoticos Milon, 43, Chief Librarian of the Library of Pergamum; brother of Lydia-Naq Milon

Servius Callistratus, 31, Commanding officer of the Garrison of Soma

Marcos Pompeius, 37, Lawyer in Pergamum; new leader of the new House of Prayer
Marcella Aculiana, 38, Wife of Marcos
Florbella Pompeius, 10, Daughter of Marcos and Marcella

Diodorus Pasparos,* 40, Gymnasium Headmaster, elementary and high school of Pergamum

Horacio, 44, Civil servant in Pergamum
Cratia, 44, Wife of Horacio
Trifane, 25, Mother of Chrysa Grace; a former student of Zoticos

Yorick, 28, Previous employee of Antipas Ben Shelah

<u>In Laodicea</u>
Charmaine Memmius, 36, Widow; mother of four children, three of whom are dead
Titus Memmius, 18, Young man; also known as **"Little Lion"**

<u>Roman Army Deserters and Rebels</u>
Flavius Memucan Parshandatha, also known as Mithrida
Sesba Bartacus Sheshbazzar, also known as Sexta
Claudius Carshena Datis, also known as Craga

THE CITY OF SARDIS IN THE PROVINCE OF ASIA MINOR

1 Simon's Property
2 Western Gate
3 Outer Walls of Sardis
4 Western Marketplace
5 Temple of Hera
6 Hot Baths
7 Gymnasium/School
8 Synagogue of Sardis
9 Shops on Royal Road
10 Businesses/Guilds
11 Temple of Apollo
12 Eastern Marketplace
13 Eastern Gate
14 Homes of Poor People
15 Temples of Various Gods
16 Stadium
17 Theater
18 Storehouses/Supplies
19 Governor's Palace
20 Treasury
21 Garrison of Sardis
22 Mint and Gold Processing
23 Temple of Artemis
24 Pactolus River
25 Homes of Wealthy Families
26 Cemetery
27 Homes of Aristocrats
28 Aqueduct/Water Pipes
29 Military Training
30 Mount Tmolus

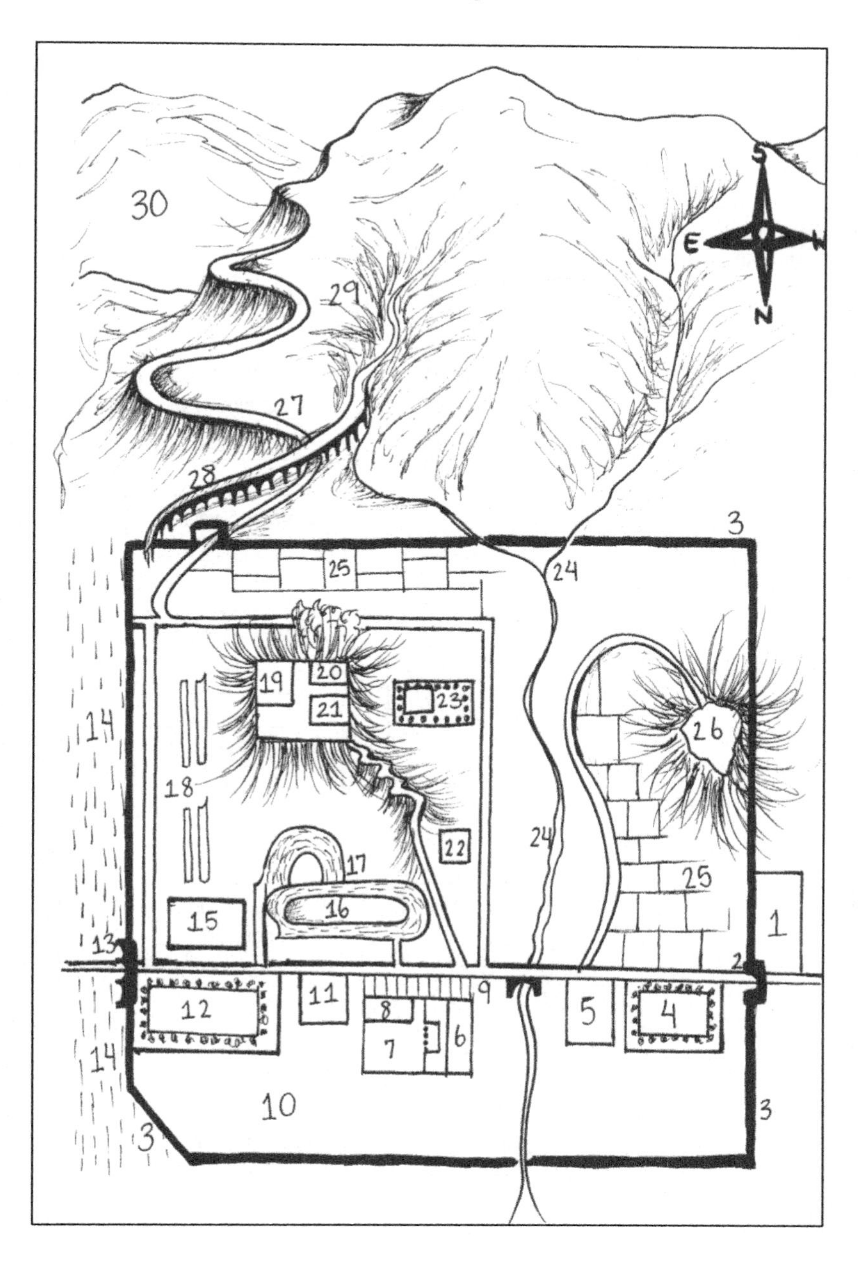
30
29
27
28
S
E
N
3
25
24
19
20
21
23
26
14
18
24
22
17
25
16
15
1
13
2
12
11
8
9
5
4
7
6
14
10
3
3

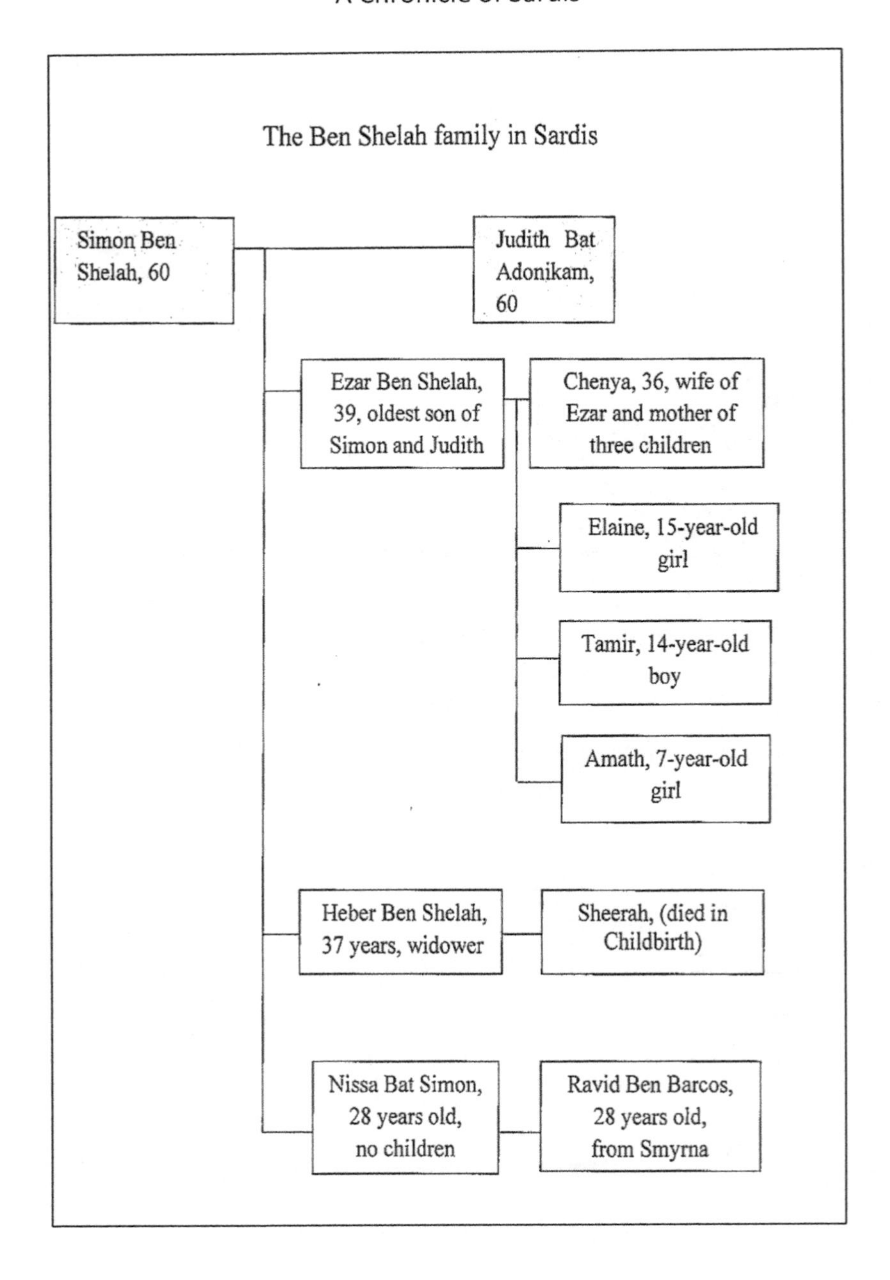
The Ben Shelah family in Sardis
Simon Ben Shelah, 60
Judith Bat Adonikam, 60
Ezar Ben Shelah, 39, oldest son of Simon and Judith
Chenya, 36, wife of Ezar and mother of three children
Elaine, 15-year-old girl
Tamir, 14-year-old boy
Amath, 7-year-old girl
Heber Ben Shelah, 37 years, widower
Sheerah, (died in Childbirth)
Nissa Bat Simon, 28 years old, no children
Ravid Ben Barcos, 28 years old, from Smyrna

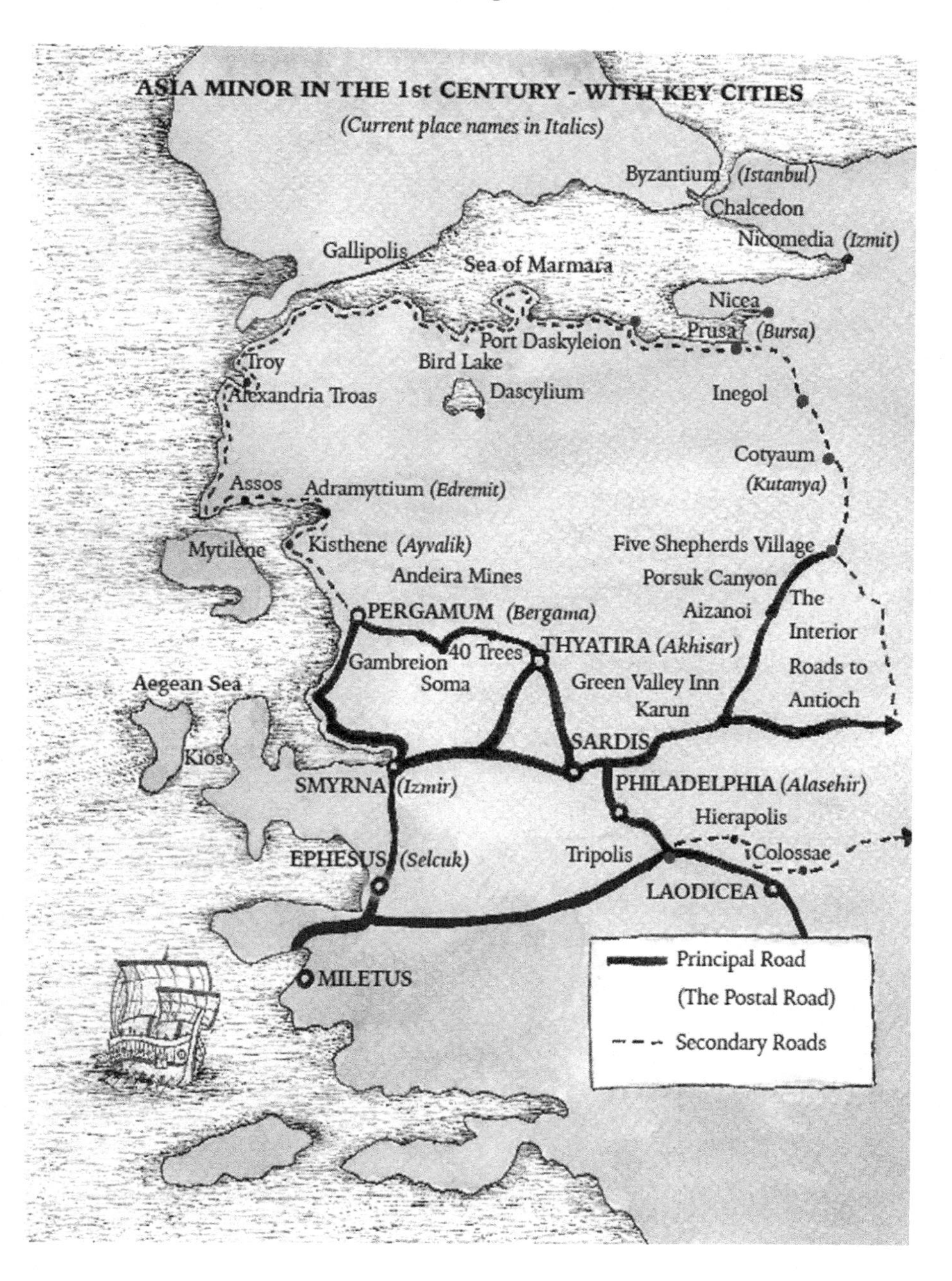
ASIA MINOR IN THE 1st CENTURY - WITH KEY CITIES
(Current place names in Italics)
Byzantium (Istanbul)
Chalcedon
Nicomedia (Izmit)
Gallipolis
Sea of Marmara
Nicea
Prusa (Bursa)
Port Daskyleion
Troy
Bird Lake
Alexandria Troas
Dascylium
Inegol
Cotyaum
(Kutanya)
Assos
Adramyttium (Edremit)
Mytilene
Kisthene (Ayvalik)
Andeira Mines
Five Shepherds Village
Porsuk Canyon
Aizanoi
PERGAMUM (Bergama)
The
Interior
Roads to
Antioch
Gambreion
40 Trees
THYATIRA (Akhisar)
Soma
Aegean Sea
Green Valley Inn
Karun
SARDIS
Kios
SMYRNA (Izmir)
PHILADELPHIA (Alasehir)
Hierapolis
Tripolis
Colossae
EPHESUS (Selcuk)
LAODICEA
MILETUS
Principal Road
(The Postal Road)
Secondary Roads

Never Enough Gold

A Chronicle of Sardis

Part 1

April AD 91

Strangers in Sardis

Chapter 1
Commander Felicior

THE GARRISON OF SARDIS, THE ACROPOLIS, SARDIS

Anthony wiped away the sweat pouring down his face as he dismounted from his horse at the gate leading into the Acropolis Garrison. Although he had rehearsed a dozen times what he would say in the next few moments, he was still fearful of the possible results. His heart beat wildly, not knowing if a soldier in the Roman army was permitted to do what he had planned.

Below him, in the early morning, the city of Sardis spread out across a level plain. Apple blossoms along the road up to the top of the acropolis gave off a sweet scent.

The gate to the acropolis opened, and he hoped the guard would not notice the nervous movements of his hands. He knew he was risking his life.

"I need to speak to the commanding officer," he said, controlling the panic rising in his throat.

"Why are you here?" demanded the guard. "Are you a courier?"

Anthony looked intently at the guard. "No, I am a reservist requesting a transfer from Pergamum. I have been training scouts for the impending battle in Dacia."

The city's four most prestigious institutions were visible from the entrance: the Temple of Athena, City Treasury, City Hall, and the Garrison of Sardis. The sun's early morning rays cast a golden glow on the city's cut stone walls.

"I think this is irregular," muttered the guard under his breath. Anthony watched the guard's eyes as he took in the scar on the right side of his face, his thick black hair, and his strong shoulders. "Tether your horse here, and come with me," the guard said.

Anthony was led along a path paved with cut granite stones and entered a sparsely furnished office. The commander sat at a table, examining a large map.

"Commander Felicior Priscus, a soldier is here to see you." The guard saluted and withdrew.

"Anthony Suros, Legion XXI, the Predators, instructor of scouts in Pergamum," the soldier began, keeping his voice controlled. He paused and quickly added, "Reporting for duty, sir!"

Commander Felicior raised thick black eyebrows. "I was not expecting, and I did not ask for, another instructor."

Anthony felt hairs standing on the back of his neck. He knew that no soldier could report for duty like this. What am I doing arriving at this office and saying I am offering myself for service?

"Where did you come from?"

"I have been serving in Pergamum."

"And last night? Were you in our barracks?"

"No, sir, I stayed at Green Valley Inn, halfway along the road from Thyatira. I left early and came alone. My wife and daughter are arriving later today or tomorrow."

A frown clouded Felicior's face. "Were you sent to Sardis by your former commander?"

Anthony saw unfriendliness rising in Commander Felicior's face, where a straight nose matched a long face. Anthony wondered if the officer's penetrating eyes left new recruits asking if their commander was a friend or a foe.

"The transfer from Pergamum is by my own request, sir."

"Under whose authority?" Felicior's voice rose sharply. Sudden irritation sounded. "Who transfers without orders from their commander?"

"This is a special circumstance, sir."

"In the army, nothing warrants the expression 'a special circumstance.' I should arrest you right now." He went to the door to call the guard.

Anthony felt panic overtaking him, so he looked around rapidly. The garrison's eagle standard stood in one corner. The flag of Sardis was a scarlet flag with a black eagle over a cluster of grapes, and it stood in another corner.

The unmistakable scent of a new parchment directed Anthony's attention to the map lying open on the table. *Hmm, Commander Felicior has been studying the army's coming invasion against Dacia. Emperor Domitian is going to attack the barbarians.*

"Guard!" called the commander. "Come here!"

Sweat trickled down his back. If Anthony did not present

something in his favor quickly, he would be arrested as a rebellious soldier.

“My arrival has to do with the invasion against Dacia, sir.”

“What could you possibly know about Dacia?”

Felicior turned to the door. The guard who had admitted Anthony into the acropolis was standing outside, waiting for orders.

Anthony fought to keep his voice calm. “Sir, I served with Legion XXI, the Predators. We fought successfully. Many tribes were subdued, and that region is now a province. I'm sure you have heard of Upper Germanica. I fought in terrain like that which the XXI is about to invade.”

Felicior walked from the office door back to the table. “Guard, you may leave. Stay close by in case I need you.” Turning to Anthony, he sneered. “And you were so successful that you are now a soldier without a garrison?”

“Sir, I am here because of a very unusual situation. I serve under Commander Cassius Flamininus Maro, but I am requesting permission to serve in this garrison. I'm on regular holiday leave from Pergamum during the Festival of Zeus, so I am not absent without leave. The holiday is for two weeks. If you refuse to accept me, I will immediately return to Pergamum. You will know what decision to make after you hear me speak.”

“All right, soldier, your story. Make it brief.”

“Thank you, sir. I enlisted at the age of seventeen to avenge the defeat of our legions in the Battle of Teutoburg Forest. Barbarians had wiped out Legions XVII, XVIII, and XIX.

“For the next twenty years, Legion XXI secured the high ground west of the Neckar River bit by bit. I was a scout, always on the forward edge. We wanted to save lives, so villages were given the choice of loyalty—to be part of a province and assured of a peaceful existence. Towns have emerged with taxes being paid, and laws are being learned. The region is now a province.”

The commander nodded, narrowing his eyes.

“I was good at archery. Being a scout is a dangerous job, sir. Every village has to be brought into submission one at a time.”

While Felicior turned to look out the window, Anthony studied the officer. Everything suggested someone who demanded immediate results. He looked at a smaller table and noticed that every scroll was lined up in perfect order, only an inch from the edge.

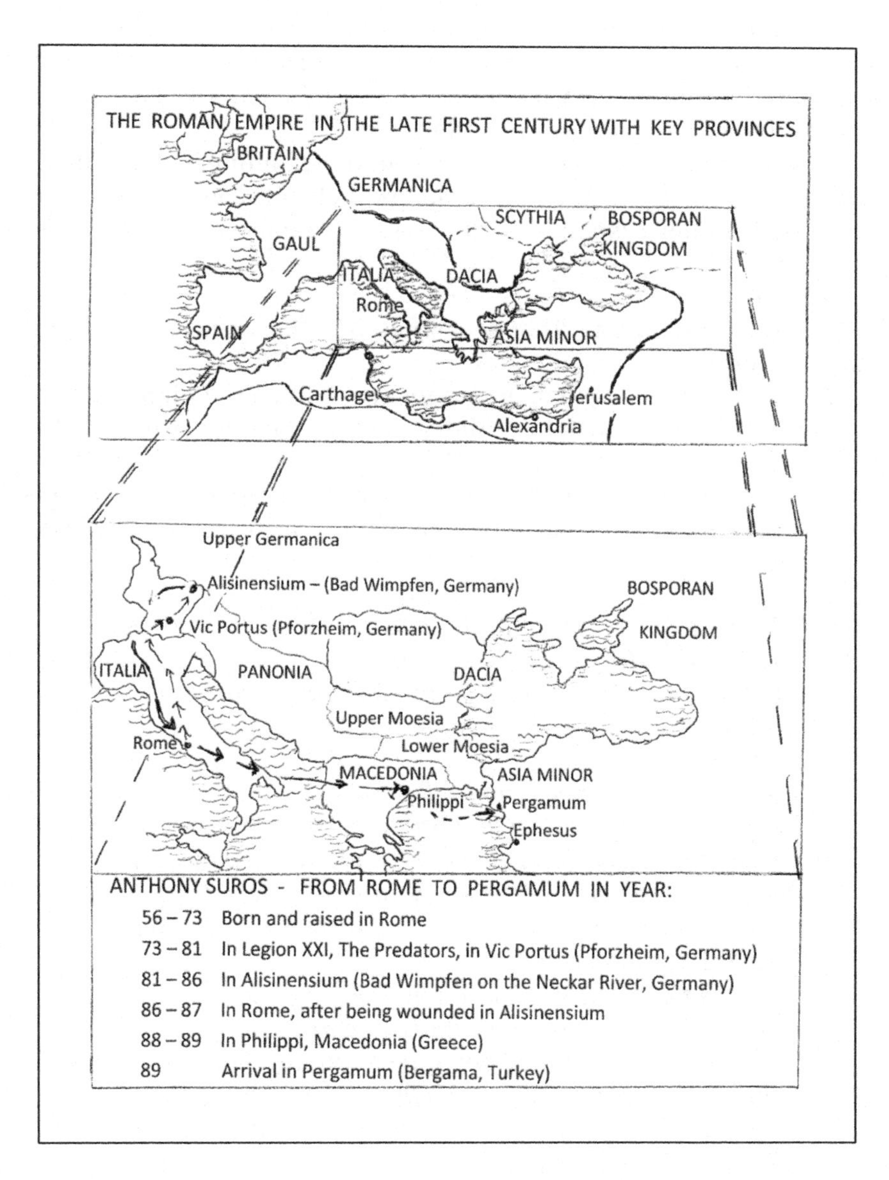

Turning suddenly, Felicior asked, “How did you get the wound on your face, soldier?”

The question almost took Anthony’s breath away. “I was wounded in an ambush. I survived, became a reservist, and was assigned to the Pergamum Garrison. For the past two years, I trained scouts for Dacia. Here is the assignment authorization issued by our superiors in Philippi." Anthony pulled a scroll from a small leather bag and handed it to the commander.

Outside the office, there was the sound of running feet and then two loud knocks on the door. Before Felicior could speak, an exhausted soldier rushed in with news: "Two more robberies have been reported, sir."

"Where?"

"In the same area, sir. The homes are the ones next to the mayor's home."

Felicior swore. "What is happening? Who's behind these robberies?" Turning back to Anthony, he said, "Soldier, I'm going to be busy for the next few days. We are facing a serious situation, having suffered several robberies. As for you, remain in the garrison barracks. I will discuss this with you further on Saturday, two days from now."

COMMANDER FELICIOR'S OFFICE, THE ACROPOLIS, SARDIS

April 25 in the 10th year of Domitian

From: Commander Felicior Priscus, Garrison of Sardis

To: Commander Cassius Flamininus Maro, Garrison of Pergamum

If you are well, then I am well.

I write to let you know that Anthony Suros, a reservist from your garrison, arrived here today. He carries an assignment to teach scouts for use in Dacia given by our superiors in Philippi. His orders are to train scouts for Legion XXI, the Predators.

He mentions a misunderstanding with the Garrison of Pergamum but has given no details, and he has requested duty at the Sardis Garrison. I understand that he is scheduled to return to Pergamum by the end of the month.

I have placed him under barracks detainment in Sardis and am awaiting your response. Kindly send me a report on this soldier.

THE HOT BATHS OF LAODICEA

In Laodicea, three days' travel east of Sardis, a young man named Little Lion arrived with a small pull-cart at the city bathhouse with another load of firewood. The wood was used for fires to heat the floor of the caldarium room of the bathhouse. After water was poured on the hot floor, steam filled the room. Little Lion was thankful for the daily payments he received for his labor.

"Titus, drop the wood over there!" one of the older men shouted. Little Lion tipped the cart, dumping the load. He piled the logs near the roaring furnace but cursed as a splinter dug into his right hand. He stopped to examine the puncture in his little finger.

At age eighteen, he hated his name, Titus Memmius. The manager of the hot baths would never call him by the name his friends had given him, the name he asked others to use.

He watched two city counselors as they approached the front steps of the bath house. Smelling of perfume to cover other scents, they had just arrived for their daily bath. Little Lion edged closer. He was always curious about other people's opinions, and he heard something in their conversation that he found exciting.

"I heard that Domitian has plans to invade Dacia again."[1]

The second counselor stopped on the first step and responded with a rapid nod, "Domitian needs brave men for the fight. King Decebalus is the wiliest barbarian that Rome has faced in many years—the worst in decades. Our armies trapped him once, but every effort so far has ended without a victory."

"Yes, Rome needs the best soldiers we can send," came the reply as the two continued up the steps and into the front entrance.

Little Lion could not hear the rest of their conversation, but he sat on the bottom step for a few minutes to catch his breath. A sweat-covered slave walked up the steps with a bucket of water to be poured onto the heated floor.

Wiping sweat from his eyes, Little Lion walked back to his cart, received his daily payment from the manager, and tucked it into a brown leather pouch. As he left the bathhouse, his imagination took

---

[1] Four invasions were made by the Roman military against King Decebalus. The ruler of the Kingdom of Dacia governed the area today known as Romania and Moldova and smaller portions of Ukraine, Slovakia, Poland, Hungary, Serbia, and Bulgaria.

wings. He saw himself dressed in armor, brandishing a sword, and facing King Decebalus, Rome's smartest opponent.

He thought, *Men describe the barbarian king of Dacia as intelligent and cunning. He can outsmart the best army general, but I will be there when the army conquers Rome's greatest enemy. I will be in the army that defeats the king of Dacia!*

Knowing the army would need more soldiers and believing it was a path to a better income, the young man pulled his cart out of the shadow of the bathhouse and into the bright sunlight. He stretched tall, and there was a new spring to his steps. All day he had been carting firewood, and he imagined what he would say when he returned home.

For years, Little Lion had attended the Laodicea Gymnasium. At age fourteen, his last year there, he won some unauthorized contests against fellow classmates. They sometimes ganged up on the youngster with a talent to mimic, but he wrestled skillfully although he was smaller than most.

That was when his best friend gave him his nickname. Since then, his friends said, "Little Lion never slinks away from difficulty. He runs toward danger."

But then came that dreadful week when four of the six people in his family died of a winter pestilence. That fever did not just affect Little Lion's family. It took many lives in Laodicea and left entire households destitute. Memories of days and nights without sleep still sent shivers down his back. He shut his eyes, sometimes unable to keep the worst memory away. The scene returned. In his neighborhood, bodies were piled on top of each other in the street, like slaughtered sheep ready for the marketplace. The corpse of a neighbor slipped off the four-wheeled wagon that was taking the dead to a cemetery. The driver's voice came back again. He was yelling, "Too many dead today. I'll come back in an hour to get it!"

Little Lion cringed at the thought of that moment. The driver, known for his surly attitude and smelly clothing, inched his way down to the cemetery.

After the death of his three sisters and his father, he and his mother barely survived. His pitiful daily wage rarely paid for anything more than rent and food. *What else can I do to keep my mother alive? I hate this menial work.*

Little Lion and his mother lived in a small, dingy, two-room apartment on the second floor of a dilapidated building. He vowed to get her away from the open sewer running under their window.

Still, every conversation he imagined ran up against the same problem. His mother, Charmaine, would never let him go to war.

Chapter 2
Simon's Choice

SIMON AND JUDITH'S HOME, SARDIS

Early the next day, Simon Ben Shelah sat down slowly at his workplace, and his gray head was soon bent over a ring he was polishing. The sixty-year-old man pondered his work for the day: to shape another gold ring or make a bracelet. On the bench next to his elbow lay a scroll he had received at daybreak by postal courier. He had already broken the red wax seals and scanned through the contents.

Usually Simon began the day by blowing on dull embers, gently bringing the fire back to life. He inhaled the smell as the flames grew, and he laid several small charcoal bricks in the furnace. Ample space at the back of his house held the tools necessary for his business.

Almost two decades before, shortly after coming to Sardis from Alexandria, Simon and Judith had purchased this house. The great earthquake, decades earlier, had left the building unlivable with the flat roof caved in. While most buildings on this side of the city had been rebuilt, this house remained in disrepair. The Greek family was living in rented quarters, and the owner happily accepted much less than the property was worth and took his family to Smyrna.

Positioned outside of the city's eastern entrance, the house overlooked the busy Postal Road linking Smyrna and Sardis to cities in the east. Behind the two-story house, a broad green pasture on the small farm was home to horses, cows, goats, and chickens. A shed built with timbers behind the main house provided more than ample covering over his three wagons.

Simon stood up and shook his head as if getting rid of a disturbing daydream. He again opened the scroll. This day was going to be different.

Simon sighed deeply and put his dark-stained apron aside. Reading the letter, he leaned his shoulder heavily against the door, running his fingers through his thinning black hair.

The day before, a brief message had arrived by carrier pigeon from Simon's brother, Jonathan Ben Shelah, in Thyatira. The note told of Antipas's death, but no details were known. To accompany their mourning, black coverings had been placed on all the couches, and the entire family would be wearing black prayer shawls of mourning another twenty-nine days.

Simon again read the letter from his brother, Antipas Ben Shelah, written on the day of his death five days before. He held his breath, wondering about the events that lay behind the words.

14 April, in the 10th year of Domitian
From: Antipas
To: My beloved brother Simon

Grace and peace. I long to see you, and there is much to discuss but my time is short. I must give you my family's news. My granddaughter, Miriam, married Anthony Suros this morning. He is a legionary, a reservist wounded on the inside and scarred on the outside. Perhaps you will meet him one day. If Anthony ever comes to your house, please show our best Jewish hospitality to Miriam and her new husband.

Anthony became a faithful follower of Yeshua Messiah and will face difficulties as a result. He has a thought-provoking story. I recommend him to you as a sincere God-fearer.

Tomorrow, Miriam and Anthony will adopt a baby girl, Chrysa Grace. I love this child. She is now part of our family. For her safety, Miriam will shortly leave Pergamum to stay with Jonathan in Thyatira. She is traveling with two ex-slaves, Ateas and Arpoxa. Their young son is four months old.

When I will write my next letter, I do not know. The powers of the acropolis have lined up against me.

Good health to you and Judith, along with my wishes and all my prayers.

Simon opened the door leading from his workshop into the home. "Judith, come!"

Simon's wife rose from the breakfast table, where she was enjoying the early morning with their family. "What is it?" she called, walking to his workshop.

"It's about that second note we received by carrier pigeon yesterday from my brother Jonathan. The first note said that my brother Antipas had been killed, and yesterday's note said we can expect our niece Miriam to arrive here this afternoon. Jonathan wasn't able to give us the whole story in the carrier pigeon note.

"Now, this morning, the letter arrived from my brother Antipas, in Pergamum. It was written before his death. He says that Miriam is traveling with a baby and two ex-slaves. But listen to these details: Miriam married a Roman. And not just any Roman man. Her husband is a legionary! How could my brother accept a soldier into the Ben Shelah family?"

In an instant, Judith's cheeks were tinged a bright red. She pulled her husband close and poked her finger into his chest, punctuating each word. "No soldier can ever be part of our family. Simon! Why did your brother permit this marriage? Think of the shame!"

Simon closed his eyes, trying to stop the pounding of his heart. "We'll announce this to the family and our servants during the noon meal. I'm going back to work. Ravid won't appreciate a single thing in Antipas's letter! My son-in-law has complained before. What's he going to say now?" Ravid was Simon's principal helper and did much of the detailed finish work on the jewelry.

"Check the condition of our spare rooms upstairs. From what this letter says, we'll be having more guests than we thought," he instructed.

Simon trudged back to his workshop. The bellows blew on the dull embers, and the charcoal soon shed a bright orange glow. His head was bent over a ring as he tapped the softened metal into the required shape around the mandrel. Calluses on his hands, formed from the constant pressure of the tools against his palms and fingers spoke of long, dedicated hours at his work.

Antipas's letter left Simon agitated. *If he ever comes to your house, please show our best Jewish hospitality to Miriam and Anthony.*

He spoke silently. "Lord, I control this fire with the bellows, and this jewelry is the result. This little fire is hot. I form rings and other jewelry in this place, so I can control things here. But uncontrolled fires...I fainted as the flames in Alexandria took the lives of my three older sisters. I was only eight years old when fires consumed our family home and my sisters. Those terrible scenes never leave me.[2]

"Greek young men were running along the road, yelling, 'Burn them! Burn the Jews!' I knew that day that we would have to leave Alexandria."

He realized that he had been daydreaming. "It's time to take a short break," he said to himself as he laid aside the unfinished ring.

He straightened his back, stood up, and stretched. Simon wanted to talk with his second son, Heber, but that was not possible right now. The thirty-seven-year-old was at work at the family's shop on Royal Road. Heber kept the business accounts, and he was preparing documents to share with Diodotus, the banker.

Ravid, Simon's son-in-law, knocked on the outside door. "Good morning, Father. What are we making today?"

Simon increasingly depended on his son-in-law's ability to shape and detail gold jewelry. "Ravid, I'm finishing up the batch of rings we started last week, and next we need to make a batch of shoulder brooches for togas and stolas. Sometime today we will meet with Diodotus. He wants to examine our business records. Of course I agreed. He wants me to join their bank as a director. I want you to come with me for this meeting. Heber will also meet Diodotus with us."

Simon was looking forward to this meeting with cautious optimism. To be accepted as a director of the Bank of Hermus would convey social acceptance like little else in Sardis.

THE WESTERN AGORA, MARKETPLACE IN SARDIS

Halfway through the morning, Judith came to his workshop. "Simon, a messenger is here from the Bank of Hermus. He's requesting you come to the Western Agora. In the marketplace, you will find their representative at the Golden Bowl Thermopolium, close to the temple."

"Thank you, Judith. Tell the man I will be there right away."

Simon covered up the fire in the small forge and locked the door to the workshop. Outside the West Gate to the city, Simon and Ravid stopped in front of his property. Beyond the highway, looking to the north, the Hermus River flowed rapidly toward the Aegean Sea. A

---

[2] Pogroms took place in Alexandria, Egypt, in AD 38 and 68, when tens of thousands of Jews were killed.

month earlier, it had been a gushing torrent as the snow melted. Behind them, the melting snowcap on the highest peak, Mount Tmolus, still sparkled, glistening like diamonds. The mountain filled the entire horizon, disappearing where it curved eastward and then south toward Philadelphia. Across the wide valley, fresh green leaves covered vineyards.

As they passed by the Ben Shelah store, they picked up Heber for the meeting. Diodotus, the banker, greeted them as they entered the marketplace. He was a rotund man, suggesting that he frequently enjoyed a second portion, and maybe more, at the thermopolium. The scent of a tasty stew drifted through the air.

"Thank you for coming right away, Simon Ben Shelah, Heber, Ravid. Let us sit down at the table, and we can have a short discussion of the next steps. I'll call a cook. He'll serve us after a cup of wine."

Ravid shook his head. "No. I am sorry, sir. I cannot sit at these tables. The cooks serve meat offered to an idol worshiped at the temple next door."

A strained look crossed the banker's face. "Well, Simon Ben Shelah...then we'll talk standing up." He forced a slight smile. "I'm sure my offer will not cause offense. On behalf of the directors of the Bank of Hermus, I asked for this preliminary contact. We note with satisfaction the growth of your business. If you agree to our terms, we will examine your financial records, and if all is satisfactory, you may be invited to join us as a director in the bank. Final arrangements could be made within six months."

Simon replied, "Yes, I am pleased by this. I will consult my family. We are Jews, and my sons, Heber and Ezar, and son-in-law Ravid will want to give their opinions. They are being trained to take over my business. Your financial examiners will be talking with Heber. He keeps our accounts, and he's in charge of my shop."

A handshake confirmed this initial step. They continued chatting for a few minutes, discussing business activities.

As they turned to go back to Simon's house, a loud noise came from one of the unfinished buildings. Workmen screamed, "Get out of the way! It's going to fall! Felix! Let go of the rope! Move away!"

The grating sound was caused by a stone crashing down from the top of a column to the pavement. It was followed by a loud cry.

"Giles, run to the workshop and get some water!" yelled an

overseer to a workman. "Felix's leg is broken! Stupid slaves! The scaffolding for the second floor was not properly attached!"

Diodotus shrugged, turned to Simon, and commented, "No matter how many times we tell them to be careful, there are so many ways to get hurt. Someone else will take that man's place."

Many workers rushed over to the worker bellowing with pain. The large block of stone had split in two. Felix's leg jutted out at a sharp angle between his knee and his ankle.

A small boy screamed in a loud voice and ran away, crying.

SIMON AND JUDITH'S HOME, SARDIS

Simon's family was reclining on three large couches placed in the form of a U as they began their noon meal. Judith reclined next to her husband. Ezar, Simon's son, was with Chenya, his wife. Their children, Elaine, Tamir, and Amath, were on one side of the table. Ravid and Nissa reclined on the other side.

"Blessed are you, O Lord our God, King of the Universe. You have supplied us with food, family, and community. We bless your name," he prayed.

"Now, I received news that you need to hear. First, a pigeon brought a message from Jonathan in Thyatira. He explained that my niece Miriam left his farm at Forty Trees, and she will be here this afternoon.

"Then a letter came this morning from my brother Antipas, written before his death. He says Miriam is married and wants me to offer hospitality to Miriam and her husband. Antipas's letter also tells us that there are two babies and two ex-slaves traveling with her."

Ravid sat straight up, his eyes wide open.

Ezar, the oldest of Simon and Judith's children, would not usually be the first to speak at a family meeting. He had never been given to many words. "What's happening, my father? I sense your spirit is disturbed."

"The letter tells us that Miriam is married. Her husband, Anthony, is a legionary...a soldier."

Judith clasped her chubby hands, shuddered, and looked away.

Ezar put his hand to his mouth, closed his eyes, and bowed his head. Ravid had his head in his hands, and then he stood up and marched out of the house without saying a word. Nissa followed him, trying to take hold of his hand.

Chenya, Ezar's wife and the mother of their three children, was the first to speak. "Well, if Miriam comes with two ex-slaves, then she can stay here with the child. We will find a place for her two ex-slaves. I am sure there must be an empty apartment in the poor part of the city. Ezar, you will do that for us, won't you? You will go to the insulae? Father, don't worry about the soldier. We'll take him to the barracks."

She turned to each one around the table, and with a flourish and a smile, she added, "There! Things will be fine with Miriam here. Now what's the problem?"

FELIX, GINA, AND COSMOS'S HOME, THE INSULAE OF SARDIS

In the Southeast Quarter of the city, where the most disadvantaged people lived, Gina was preparing a meal. She had only beans and barley for her five children, and she wiped away a tear. She had long ago stopped bowing down at the temple. The gods did not show her their favor. She wanted more space; in this small apartment, her children were always under her feet.

Gina heard her little boy running home before she saw him. She knew his voice above those of other children playing games outside. She listened to his panting at the base of the stairs and waited while he climbed the steps two at a time.

"Daddy was helping to raise blocks at the Western Agora!" sobbed Cosmos, the eight-year-old. "A big stone block fell. It's broken Daddy's leg! He's at the building site and can't come home without someone to help him!"

"Oh, Hera! O, Zeus!" Gina screamed. She fell to her knees, and a loud shriek expressed her fear and pain. "Help me, Demeter! What are we going to do? What will become of us if Felix can't work?"

SIMON'S FARM

Elaine, Ezar and Chenya's fifteen-year-old daughter, walked to the shed. Following her mother's pronouncement, little more was said around the table.

Brushing her favorite horse's neck, Elaine spoke into the horse's ear. "You know, Star, I've been noticing how good-looking boys are, especially Isidoros. Should I tell my mother? Isidoros is the son of a well-known teacher, Jace. At the gymnasium, boys speak well about him. His mother is Kalonice."

The scent of her horse's coat soothed her, and she fingered the pattern of hair on its flanks. "A couple months ago, Isidoros looked at me. Our eyes met for a long moment, and my heart started thumping. Since then, I'm been looking for someone to talk to. Nothing can come of my feelings, right? I'm afraid because a relationship with Isidoros would go against everything the adults talk about at home, especially Uncle Ravid!"

She brushed the horse's hindquarters, delighting in the patterns of tiny hairs, and she whispered, "Why did Isidoros have to be born a Gentile? What would Uncle Ravid say to me about such thoughts?"

SIMON AND JUDITH'S HOME

Heber sold a set of silver earrings to his newest customer, Delbin, the banker's wife. Pulling the door shut tightly, he closed the shop early and turned the lock. He wanted to be home when his cousin Miriam arrived. He smiled, happy to have a new client. Conversations with the chief manager of the Bank of Hermus earlier in the day were very satisfactory.

Ten minutes later, Heber was home, and Judith explained what Antipas's letter said.

Ravid was listening and exploded. "I deeply oppose that your mother and father would give hospitality to Gentiles. It's bad enough that Ezar, my brother-in-law, lets his son, Tamir, study and practice sports with Gentiles! Tomorrow evening, the Sabbath begins! Just thinking about the letter that came this morning makes me upset. And I don't want to begin the Sabbath with unkind thoughts."

Heber listened and wondered what to say. *No one is supporting Ravid in his outbursts. My brother-in-law is speaking out more and more these days. The safest thing for me to do when he becomes angry is to stay quiet.*

SIMON'S PROPERTY ON THE WESTERN EDGE OF SARDIS

Simon was the first person to see the wagon. The noon meal was over, and he was about to go back to his workshop. Hearing the noise of horses' hooves, he rushed to the front door.

"They're here!" he shouted. "Come, everyone!" Seeing his friend, the wagon driver, he called, "Hello, Nikias! I'll open the gate!"

Nikias was a farmer who worked for Simon's brother, Jonathan

Ben Shelah. The hard-working father of five children had taken goods back and forth between Sardis and Thyatira for many years. Today he did not bring new clothing or polished brass cups. Instead, five people were with him in the wagon.

Once through the wide gate, the wagon stopped. The Simon Ben Shelah family hurried out and stood in a semi-circle.

Simon stood with Judith. He already knew that Ravid and Nissa would not be present for Miriam's arrival. His son-in-law had prohibited Nissa from even being in the presence of a Roman soldier. He looked around the semi-circle. Chenya stood with Ezar, the oldest of Miriam's three cousins. With them were the three children: Elaine; Tamir, her fourteen-year-old brother; and seven-year-old Amath.

Miriam was the first one off the wagon. She looked down at her daughter. Grace was sleeping in her arms, and she rearranged the blanket around the baby girl.

Simon watched open mouthed as Nikias helped two young adults, Arpoxa and Ateas, down from the wagon. Ateas, the young man, used crutches. One leg hung down helplessly.

Arpoxa was about the same age as Ateas. Her blue eyes mirrored the afternoon sky, and her hair was the color of wheat at harvest. But Simon noted that she held onto her husband to stand. Both of her feet were deformed and twisted inward. She was unable to stand and hold her little boy, Saulius. Nikias, the farm hand, was holding their baby boy.

Miriam hurried to Uncle Simon, and he kissed her on both cheeks. "Welcome, Miriam," he said, giving her a hug. "It's two years since my father Eliab died. That's the last time I was with you in Pergamum. I'm happy to see you! Tell me about my dear brother. Jonathan wrote us three days ago telling us Antipas had died, but we know almost nothing else. I received a letter from Antipas this morning...."

Tears began pouring down her face. "It was horrible!" Miriam burst out between sobs. "Grandpa was killed by the authorities! He was tried and..." She could not finish her sentence.

A cloud of grief settled on the family. No one was prepared for this. "Come everyone, let's go inside," Simon urged.

Chenya, Ezar's wife, put her arm around Miriam's shoulder. "Please, tell us every detail! How terrible! What happened?"

Simon said, "We knew you were coming today. My brother Jonathan sent a note about you yesterday. But who are these other people?"

Miriam smiled through her tears. "This is Chrysa Grace! Anthony and I adopted her the day after we were married! Oh, my husband came ahead yesterday. He was going to check in with the garrison. Have you heard from him? No? Well, we were married two weeks ago."

Heber took Miriam's elbow and led her to a chair. "Dear cousin, it's been years since I saw you. Take a breath and tell us *everything*. We're here to listen."

Miriam laughed through her tears. "You will need an hour or more. It's a long story. These are my friends, Ateas and his wife, Arpoxa. They came with us from Pergamum so Chrysa Grace wouldn't starve from a lack of milk. Their little boy is one month older than our baby, so we call them the 'almost twins.'"

Arpoxa, the twenty-year-old woman, spoke Greek with a slight accent. Happiness shone through every word. "We are Scythians! Ateas and I were slaves, but Antipas gave us freedom. He bought us at the slave market and gave us a new life. He gave us our freedom papers and let us work for him, and now we have our baby boy, Saulius."

Simon asked a servant to bring water. Miriam's shoulders were shaking. Judith sat close to Miriam and put an arm around the young woman. "All this has happened so quickly, hasn't it?"

"Yes. Marcos, our family lawyer, knew that Grandpa was going to face the city's authorities in a trial. I don't know all that he knew, but he suspected it might end in tragedy. Apparently, Marcos knows what happens in the city council in Pergamum. Before Grandpa's trial, Marcos kept Anthony and me from going back to our village. We got married on my birthday, and the next day, we formally adopted Grace! She had been rejected. We do not know who her mother is. Then, before we knew what was happening, Marcos had us leave Pergamum in a convoy of four wagons. We were going to Thyatira to stay with Uncle Jonathan. I heard Marcos say to Marcella, his wife, that he was protecting us.

"Several young women from our village went with us in the other wagons, and Marcos told them to sing loudly. I realize now that he wanted the soldiers at the city gate to notice them and not Anthony and me. We were on the road when we were told by a messenger from Uncle Jonathan that we should not go to Thyatira but should stay at my uncle's farm near Forty Trees. That was where we decided it was safest to come to Sardis and ask you for hospitality. Anthony is requesting assignment to the garrison here.

"The young women went on to Thyatira, staying for a few days with Uncle Jonathan and Aunt Rebekah. They will go back to Pergamum at the end of the Festival of Zeus next week. And then they will be at the village again, but Grandpa won't be there.... Grandpa was killed after the second trial, and he..."

She began to sob again.

Simon ached to comfort his broken-hearted niece. Tears came to his eyes as he realized he would never see his brother again.

Chapter 3
Miriam

SIMON AND JUDITH'S HOME, SARDIS

Late Friday morning, Miriam lay in bed. She had been sure Anthony would come to Simon's house from the garrison, but the afternoon came and went. When he still had not arrived by evening, she walked restlessly back and forth across the room.

"Go ahead to the synagogue," she said to Judith. "I'm tired from yesterday's trip. I'll attend the service with you next week."

Deep lines crossed her face, and Miriam prayed. *What's gone wrong, Lord? Anthony was so confident he would be accepted as an instructor of new recruits! He said he would come and tell me all about it. Where is he? I couldn't stand for him to be sent back to Pergamum and for me to stay in Sardis.*

It was clear to Miriam that many people in Pergamum had not liked Antipas. After all, the previous year, she had watched as her grandfather had suffered exclusion from the synagogue. She had heard him say the real reason for the antagonism was not the kindness he showed to sick people and widows, although that had caused a stir. It was his teaching about Yeshua, the Messiah, that brought antipathy.

Instead of going to sleep, she rubbed her hand against her wet cheeks and turned over one more time. For months, her grandfather had opposed her marriage to a soldier. Suddenly, however, Antipas had agreed to their wedding. She knew he had been writing down his thoughts for months before going to bed, so there must have been a series of steps before coming to this decision.

Miriam spoke softly to herself. "I would love to see that scroll. What finally allowed Grandpa to agree with our marriage?" She picked Grace up and held her close, swaying back and forth. Miriam whispered her name in the dark of the night.

"Chrysa Grace Suros, I love you so much!"

She took the baby girl in her arms and rocked her gently. "If only

Grandfather Antipas could be with us here! You are only ten weeks old, and your arrival was sudden, so unexpected. You do not know this, but your mother is unknown to me. Somewhere outside of Pergamum, she brought you into the world. Afterward, a messenger came to my home to inform me that a baby was coming to our home, and you would be in my arms the next day! You, my precious bundle, were placed at the edge of that smelly old trash dump. Oh, I bent down, picked you up off the ground, and immediately claimed you!

"And then, in the following days, Grandfather decided our marriage should quickly be followed by your adoption."

In the unfamiliar darkness of Simon's house, she felt a sharp pain. It was a stabbing ache in her stomach. Miriam rose from the bed, just as she often did when conflicting emotions gripped her. The first time she suffered such distress was at the age of five. She had fallen face down on the ground while escaping from Jerusalem. Miriam shook her head, unwilling to think of it again, but she could not shake that memory. She closed her eyes.

Jewish soldiers upon the walls shook their fists. Arrows were falling around the people who were running. The small gate behind them was still open, and staunch defenders yelled, "You're traitors! Don't leave the city!"

Death, destruction, and fighting filled Jerusalem. Not having eaten for days, she was thin and weak from hunger, too weak to run. Her father, Johanan, had been holding her on his shoulder. "Daddy! The smell! It's terrible! I can't breathe!" she cried.

Trumpet calls, shouts from warriors, the rumble of army wagons, ladders being placed against walls, and worst of all...the stench. The images came once again.

"Put one hand over your nose! Breathe through your mouth. Do like I'm doing! Tens of thousands...bodies rotting...outside these walls." Her father was panting as he ran.

Amid all the noise, raucous voices called, "The Roman legions will kill you! Get back into the city! You are not permitted to leave!"

Now they were outside, past the gate, escaping, drawing near to the Roman army. Her father was shouting, begging for mercy. "Food! Please give us food! We're starving!"

There, close enough now to make out the details of Roman faces. Arrows kept falling all around. One of them left a hole as it passed through Miriam's dress. Her father was screaming, "Food! We are starving! Mercy, please, mer…"

But then Miriam was suddenly dropped to the ground. She fell on her back. She pushed herself up from the gray, dusty gravel and looked up. Her father's body lay lifeless behind her. His mouth was open, and his eyes were closed. He would never ask for mercy again. An arrow stuck in his back, and blood dripped from his mouth. Grandfather Antipas scooped her up as he ran and carried her to safety. A moment later, her mother also cried out. An arrow dangled from her leg as she ran toward the Romans.

In the dark of Simon's home, Miriam's hands were trembling with the dread of being alone. "Little one, I'll never see my grandfather again…or my mother or father." Miriam repeated her father's last words: "Mercy! Please have mercy!"

She kissed the sleeping child in the dark. "We are safe in Sardis, little one. Your daddy thinks the people who killed Grandfather want me back in Pergamum. Free me, Lord, from such fears!"

Miriam frequently hummed songs while working in the Ben Shelah shop in Pergamum. Children played on smooth paving stones in the marketplace, and while listening, she learned many tunes familiar across Asia Minor. The previous night, while staying at Green Valley Inn, Miriam had begun to compose a song while putting words to a tune she had heard. Words flowed together, falling into place.

I grasped Grandpa's hand, tracing small brown specks,
And then I wound a ribbon around his neck.
He told stories of our land. It seemed grand
To trace the veins upon his well-worn hand.

Daddy fell. In that instant, he was gone.
I was young, not yet knowing what went wrong.
Grandpa held me tight. "In God, we delight.
I'm here, close by, my child. No need for fright."

Grandpa taught about Abraham and Ruth.
He smiled, "God reveals justice and is truth.
He knows our needs. A loving home prepares,
He hears our thoughts as we repeat our prayers."

Grandpa wanted to throw away slaves' chains.
He gave them freedom, sensed their deepest pains.
Now free, singers strum with skillful fingers.
They still give thanks. Their gratitude lingers.

"Yeshua's kingdom is our goal," Grandpa said.
"Our expected king was rejected, led
From place to place. Some cursed him to his face.
He prayed for them, banishing shame through grace."

"Those hands," Grandpa taught, "were nailed to the tree.
His lifeblood spilled in love for you and me.
The grave could not hold him. By grace, we're saved.
His life transforms the timid into brave."

Where Anthony was, she did not know, but for tonight, she was content to leave that with Adonai, the Eternal One.

Chapter 4
Marcos and Marcella

THE ACROPOLIS, PERGAMUM

Marcos Pompeius, a prominent lawyer in Pergamum, walked up the steep steps of the street connecting the lower market area to the Lower Agora and then to the upper portion of the acropolis. As legal counsel for the city of Pergamum, he faced the hardest assignment of his life.

Thoughts tumbled around in his head. *Climbing this hill in a hurry, I can imagine someone saying to me, "Marcos, you're puffing! You must be getting old!" In June, I'll be thirty-seven and still am not used to ascending the acropolis every day! Fortunately, people are friendly. They stop me on my way up so I can catch my breath. But mounting these steep steps is nothing compared to what I must achieve today.*

He looked below him. The lower section of the city of Pergamum was now lit by the sun's direct rays. Spring leaves gleamed with a light green sheen, and the aroma of flowers spread everywhere. He stopped to look across the city, and he located his two new properties on the hill beyond the New Forum. If he was successful this morning, he would be able to put the houses to good use.

He stopped. *Hmm, if I'm unsuccessful...that new villa beside our family home, the one being remodeled as our new meeting place, will never be used the way I want. I rehearsed my speech for this morning with Marcella. Will I sway the nobility to my point of view? Can I survive the politics of Pergamum?*

He knew that ugly stories were circulating. Although his legal work was held in high regard, some of his activities might be seen as a threat by the city fathers and temple priests. Walking toward the Odeon, the building where the city council met, he rehearsed his speech again. This might be a troublesome meeting.

The men of the city council were gathering. The steep angle of the acropolis shaped the sharp slope of the seating inside the tall, narrow building, and the center aisle of white marble steps led to the top benches. The aisle divided each of the fifteen rows, with four men on each side of the aisle. About 120 men wore togas, some with a red stripe or other bright color woven into the right-hand portion to indicate status. The end of Marcos's toga was wrapped over his left shoulder and held with a bronze clasp. Entering the Odeon, he looked over the crowd to judge the difficulties he might face during the meeting. He saw men sitting forward with eager eyes, waiting for what he had to say.

He entered through the side door at the front, and immediately, voices became quiet.

Damon is here, the high priest of the Imperial Temple. And beside him is the high priest of the Altar of Zeus. Five nights ago, these men, and several others, were shouting their demands to make the fire hotter as they prepared to kill Antipas! Lord, you must give me the right words. This is your work, not mine. Three years ago, I didn't even know about the God of Abraham. But on this Friday morning, I must survive an angry crowd to continue his work in Pergamum!

In a loud voice, Mayor Quintus Rufus brought the meeting to order. "Caesar is lord and god!"

After the important men of the city echoed the phrase, Quintus turned to Marcos. "Today, we will hear a report from Counsel Marcos Aelius Pompeius regarding the area known as 'The Village.' Marcos, a rumor is going around saying you intend to host Antipas's friends. People say you have compassion for the people in the 'Household of Faith.' Their previous leader was eliminated recently for dishonoring the emperor. The task for you is to commence expropriation of Antipas's village, not to be kind to those people."

Marcos looked up at the men with whom he had worked for four years. He knew each one personally. Through many encounters, he had become known for his good-natured humor. However, as a native of Bithynia, the Roman province to the north, he knew that he would always be considered an outsider in Pergamum.

"I am delighted to report my recommendations to you," he began. "Pergamum is a city of heroes, a city that has known many struggles. In battles against warring tribes, this city had no chance of success, yet people here still boast about those military victories. We owe a huge debt to the founders of Pergamum!"

Influential citizens sat on rows of stone benches. Scowls

darkened their faces, and a man at the back hissed.

He continued, "The principal of the gymnasium, Diodorus Pasparos, approached me yesterday asking, 'Will the Household of Faith continue to meet? When does the expropriation begin?'"

Marcos enjoyed the art of rhetoric, but that alone would not help him appease these suspicious citizens. It would be impossible to win them over totally. However, he might make them pause after what they had done to Antipas.

"Before I answer Diodorus's questions, I want to speak about Pergamum's enduring values. Its lasting history as a kingdom is known to all. Our city was later given to Rome as a bequest. Who is not aware of the generous donations of past kings to the entire region? Who does not value this inheritance? Remember Pergamum's golden age. Consider its riches in literature, art, sculpture, history, medicine, and religion. The most famous authors and philosophers, coming from both east and west, left us an incredible legacy.

"Close by, the great Library of Pergamum is treasured for its scrolls. People of great intellectual ability came together, but did they always agree with each other during debates?"

He stopped speaking, strolled across the front of the narrow platform, and then walked back to the center again. They followed every step.

"No! The Kingdom of Pergamum was at its best when it permitted differing intellectual viewpoints. This was true during the reign of each of its five kings. Each writer, mathematician, or specialist was encouraged to express his own perspective. Pergamum has always been like Rome or Athens, a center of learning. That's what continued to draw wise men here."

He started down a different track. "Last week on Thursday, Antipas Ben Shelah faced a trial in the Roman Theater. He was tried a second time on Sunday night, five nights ago, in the amphitheater. He was convicted and then offered as a sacrifice to the gods. He had paid his taxes as required, but he refused to say the solemn oath, 'Caesar is lord and god.'"

Now he spoke slowly. Everyone needed to capture the drift of his argument. In taking leadership of the Household of Faith, he was in danger of suffering a fate like Antipas's.[3]

"Pergamum still keeps its sense of competition alive. Listen to the comparisons people constantly make with Ephesus! People demand victory in the Games, but glory through athletic prowess alone will not recapture your Golden Age. Every day you hear the same phrase: 'We must surpass Ephesus again. Soon!'

"You have shown your zeal by dealing with Antipas, the leader of Yeshua Messiah's followers. You pronounced a more severe verdict than the judgment recently passed in Ephesus. There, the authorities asked the emperor to banish John the Elder. He has been sent to the island of Patmos. Where Ephesus gave a sentence of banishment, a lesser punishment, you condemned Antipas to death, something much worse."

He shuddered, remembering the dreadful scene. "Rest assured, with the death of Antipas, Pergamum will be known for its strict application of Roman law. Ephesus only banished John, whereas Antipas died in boiling oil. I take it, therefore, that Antipas's penalty was accepted as sufficient by the Imperial Priests. They demanded the most severe consequence. At the next Meeting of the Asiarchs, to be held in Sardis this year, everyone will exclaim, 'Pergamum submits to the Emperor with greater zeal than Ephesus!'"[4]

He looked at the mayor. "So now comes the question: What should be done with the village of these people who some call 'atheists'? Most are calling for expropriation. I suggest another approach that results in the most revenue for our city.

"I bring your attention to the recent commitment made by this august body. The space at the top of the acropolis is not big enough for a large crowd. It is far too small. Last year, Marcus Fulvius Gillo, the provincial governor, expressed his desire for a larger area for a larger and more glorious Imperial Temple.

"Compare the tiny space we have for our present Imperial Temple with what is happening in Ephesus! There, Rome is spending outrageous sums for their new Imperial Temple to honor Domitian. Considering the emperor's quest for imperial glory, Pergamum's

---

[3] The story of Antipas's trials and death at the hands of the authorities is told in *Through the Fire: A Chronicle of Pergamum.*

[4] The Annual Meeting of the Asiarchs brought leaders and athletes together each September. The meeting was held in turn in the seven major cities of Asia Minor.

splendor will be further diminished. Ephesus will be the province's primary center for daily prayers made in favor of the emperor.

"But let us think ahead! Our governor's wish for more space was an omen to a brighter future for Pergamum! If someday the construction of a large Imperial Temple were awarded to Pergamum, then might not some of the powers of the provincial government be moved back from Ephesus?"

The expressions on the faces of a few men began to change. He was raising their vision to a possible return to lost glory. Noticing some of the city's influential citizens were being persuaded, he spoke more rapidly. "Let us be clear and financially practical. Pergamum will not receive money from the Propraetor, our governor, in Ephesus. He has no desire to contribute to such a task. Even if he had the funds, do you think he would make such a massive donation to Pergamum?"

Laughter met his question. It was unthinkable that Ephesus would encourage the redevelopment of its ancient rival city.

"You've heard our governor's words: 'Find more revenues for Domitian!' Why? Thousands of soldiers in the vast Imperial Army must be paid. The emperor's huge villa in Rome is being completed. But we must look to our own future. Let us look to ourselves."

By saying "we" and "our," he had included himself in their future.

"Our nobility wants major changes, and they have made great sacrifices to help Pergamum to be universally recognized again."

Cheers sounded for the families of Manes Tmolus, Atys Tantalus, and Atydos Lydus. At Marcos's instigation and financing, these three family heads had been surreptitiously provided with incentives to give up their privileged mansion locations at the edge of the nearby cliff. Soon they would be moving into new houses on more advantageous and less dangerous parts of the acropolis.

Marcos had begun the effort two years earlier by selling properties owned by his four deceased brothers. Money raised in this way supplied the funds to convince these three noble families to move away from the cliff overlooking the ancient theater. Removal of their existing mansions would provide the larger platform area needed for a magnificent Imperial Temple in the future. Three modern houses were being built now.

A brash voice sounded above the din. "Marcos, tell us about Antipas's village!" The speaker was Potitus Vinicius, seven years his junior. Since Marcos had been chosen as the new Chief Counsel for the city, defeating Potitus, the young lawyer took every opportunity to harass him. Most present knew the question was motivated by jealousy. Potitus was the youngest son of one of Pergamum's noble families.

Potitus spoke for all to hear: "My father's uncle was governor of this province in the second and third years of Emperor Gaius Caligula. I know what we need to talk about. Leave things in Ephesus aside for right now. We are here to talk about Marcos, not the future of our city! Marcos, do you support the atheists?"

Marcos ignored the interruption. He carried on, speaking about taxes and the financing of a new Imperial Temple. "Let us think about the tax situation in Pergamum. Where will we find sufficient money to create the huge platform needed for a small building replacement? The task is immense!"

Marcos looked at the men in the front row. A nodding of heads in agreement with his concerns began to spread across the packed room. Taxes, money, and projects—these were daily topics in the city council. Their dream was to regain fame, and he was working with them to ensure the future magnificence of Pergamum.

"Now," Marcos said, "let me deal specifically with Diodorus Pasparos's questions. About the expropriation: I have been working on the legal complications regarding that issue. Eliab Ben Shelah, Antipas's father, bought the land twenty years ago. Eliab died two years ago, leaving his will, and all of that is in order. He has six heirs in this province and three in Egypt. To carry out Eliab's will, legal agreements must be reached with two courts. I must consult the Imperial judges in Egypt and Senatorial judges in Ephesus.

"At this meeting, I am recommending that this council not pursue expropriation of the Ben Shelah property. Having to interact with two widely separated courts will take time, consuming several years, and the legal fees to navigate the various jurisdictions will not be cost effective to the city. We will highly likely spend much more than we will get in return."

Most of those present understood the problems involved in inheritance laws but not how to solve them. Marcos had a reputation for handling those cases, and it further elevated their confidence in his recommendation regarding the expropriation.

The young lawyer, Potitus Vinicius, remained standing. He

started to question Marcos's motives and returned to his central topic. He called out, "Marcos, will the followers of Yeshua of Nazareth be meeting at your home?"

Before Potitus was able to finish his question, Manes Tmolus stood up and faced the assembly. A hush came over the room as everyone wondered at the intent of this esteemed businessman's interruption. Manes had been much impressed with Marcos a year and a half before.

Marcos remembered the evening meal during which he had proposed that each of the three aristocratic families give up their prized location. They lived at the edge of a cliff overlooking the valley, but by moving away, they would each be better off! At that meeting, held at his home, Marcos proposed an exchange for new homes on the less steep side of the acropolis.

Potitus opened his mouth, calling for more discussion, but Manes Tmolus spoke in a loud voice, drowning out the objections of the younger lawyer. "I propose we accept Marcos's report and recommendations. I clearly understand that Pergamum needs revenue now and not additional costs.

"The Ben Shelah village must continue as is. The payment of taxes will bring a more constant revenue to the city than dissolving each workshop and supervising the land's outright sale. I urge that we avoid wasting time and losing that revenue. I agree with Marcos. If we attempt to force expropriation of the property, we will create complicated legal tangles. That will cost the city both money and time. The ongoing revenue from allowing that village to operate will help us pay for new foundations of a greater Pergamum!"

Cheers sounded from most of the men. The stonemasons' representatives were especially delighted to know that the massive project was going to go ahead. A vote was taken, and the majority voted for the proposal.

However, as the meeting broke up, a small group, many of them religious leaders, shared grave concerns. They were led by two men, the high priests of the Imperial Temple and the Altar of Zeus. "We don't know how much damage this lawyer will do to Pergamum with this wretched teaching of a Messiah who was crucified," one stated.

Potitus cupped his hand to limit who heard his comment. "Marcos is much too smart, and he seems to have the aristocrats supporting him. I suspect there may be some business connection between them. Did you notice that Marcos did not directly answer any of the concerns we have about the atheists? This will not be the last time dealing with this in a public meeting."

MARCOS AND MARCELLA'S HOME, PERGAMUM

Marcos rushed home before his noon meal and was met by his wife. His sandals were yet to be removed before he broke out, "Marcella, our prayers have been answered! The city fathers accepted my report regarding expropriation of 'The Village.' They agreed it would be financially counterproductive for the city to petition the courts in Ephesus and Alexandria. They had to rule on an expropriation request. With unexpected support from Manes Tmolus, it was decided that the village will continue as before, which means that Antipas's shops will remain. All the workers have their jobs and their homes.

"I've already spread the word that we will no longer be using the cave at Antipas's village. When the people arrive tonight for the first service in our new house next door, I will announce that the meeting is not going to be called the 'Household of Faith' anymore. When the group gathers, it will now be called 'The House of Prayer.'"

"My dear, are you worried about anything?" Marcella asked.

"Yes. The high priestess of the Altar of Zeus, Lydia Naq, is the key person who brought Antipas to his death. She does not like me one bit. I fear she is planning to take some action against me now."

A few hours later, Marcella and Marcos greeted the people entering their new house for Friday evening prayers. They knew most of the visitors' names. Some had a Greek background, and others were Romans. Scythian slaves from north of the Black Sea had also become followers of the Messiah. Almost all had been filled with fear since the night Antipas was killed.

"Grace and "peace!" Marcos said, opening his arms and welcoming them for his first meeting. A murmur of approval went around, and the chatter slowly subsided.

"Welcome to our new meeting place! Several days ago, Antipas faced his first trial. Last Sunday, after his second appearance before the authorities, he was killed. We are in mourning for what happened to him. Some of us are afraid, others angry. Each one has a different story to tell. How can we begin to express the gratitude we owe him for his care, love, attention, and teaching?

"During the coming days and weeks, we will," his voice broke for a moment, "grieve his passing. I want to tell you what his last words were so that while we are grieving, we can continue to learn from the character of this remarkable man. His last words were 'From everlasting to everlasting the Lord's love is with those who fear him, and his righteousness with their children's children, with those who keep his covenant and remember to obey his precepts.'[5] We must not let bitterness or a need for retaliation dominate us. Remember, Antipas formed a new community, one based on Yeshua's teaching."

The people seated before him on woven rugs or standing around the room avoided contact with people in the city out of fear and were uncertain of their fate. Several people were sobbing unashamedly. The grief was palpable.

He asked, "Were any of you at the trial and execution on Sunday night?"

No hands went up. A robust and passionate energy flooded over him as he remembered Antipas's final words.

He blinked several times. *I was the only one there. These people are shocked following Antipas's death. They are fearful, but tonight they need to express their love for him. They are afraid, wondering what will happen, wondering if they will be the next to die.*

"My position in the city council meant I had to be present at his death. On Sunday night, as he was being lowered toward the hot oil, he had words of blessing for his enemies!"

His stomach churned as he spoke. Marcos noted the expressions on each face. *I care for these people as if they were my own children.*

"This is your first time at this place, and I hope it won't be the last. Some are asking, 'Why meet in this house and not in the cave?' I concluded that we should not meet at the village for two reasons. First, the cave has a purpose: to dry pottery before going to the kiln. Second, the city has determined that the village should continue as a business providing tax revenues. It would be unwise to continue holding services at the cave because it may renew their concerns about our religious activities."

People nodded. "The Cave" was the name Antipas's father had given to the long shed where meetings had been held for years. It

---

[5] Psalm 103:17–18

would only be used now for its original purpose, for drying pottery.

Everyone enjoyed Marcos's relaxed style of speaking. Although he was a prominent man in the Bouleuterion, he did not take on airs. He spoke to them as friends, and it gave them a sense of confidence after the shock of Antipas's death.

"My wife, Marcella, and I live next door, on the east side. This house will be our meeting place. Here is the story of how I bought it: My four brothers died in an earthquake in Nicomedia. This property was paid for from the sale of part of my brothers' estates. I sold a summer villa in Kisthene and bought this place, modifying it a bit. We took a wall out here," he pointed to a line on the floor, "without changing the roofline. Normally this would be the common area, large enough for a big family. Remember, Antipas helped us become a family. We are too many to fit in the original space!"

People laughed and relaxed a little bit. He stopped, remembering the myriad of details involved in selling houses, villas, and orchards during the past year.

"Just as Antipas welcomed people, I want you to feel comfortable in this house. Marcella and I welcome you. I invite each person to now tell what Antipas meant to you. Remember something he did, or what he said, or what he taught. We are taking this evening to express grief after his loss and to thank God for such a man as a model to imitate.

"I will give the first tribute. Many of you will follow a few minutes later." He took a deep breath. "Antipas Ben Shelah brought us together from many backgrounds. My personality and his were different. He was a businessman from Alexandria, a Jew. I am a Roman lawyer from Nicomedia, the capital city of the province of Bithynia and Pontus. He could have treated me as a pagan, but he was unusual. He accepted me and others from everywhere, from any province in the empire. He formed us into a new community."

As he spoke of his relationship with Antipas, the mood began to change. The intense fear in their eyes faded. "Antipas trained me to understand his beliefs. He never indicated who should take his place, so please know that I was not appointed to be a leader. However, he would want us to continue worshiping together.

"I want us to be known from now on by a new name: the 'House of Prayer.' This is a house, not a temple. This is not a place where Greek and Roman gods are worshiped. We do not offer animal sacrifices as was done in Jerusalem until twenty years ago. What brings us together is the worship of Adonai, the God of Abraham, Isaac, and Jacob. We pray in the name of Yeshua Messiah. In his name, we live as a people of faith. We will not be dominated by fear. The faith Antipas showed in his last moments came from the Messiah. Yeshua has anointed us with his Spirit. I give thanks for the life of Antipas. Now, who else wants to provide a tribute to his life?"

Over the next hour, many people stood up to express what Antipas meant to them. The stories showed how much the old man had been loved and appreciated.

At the end of the evening, before everyone left for home, Marcos invited them to come again the next day. "Tomorrow evening I will have some significant words for you."

Chapter 5
Lydia-Naq

THE ALTAR OF ZEUS, THE ACROPOLIS, PERGAMUM

Lydia-Naq Milon, the high priestess of the Altar of Zeus in Pergamum, gazed at herself in the silver mirror. Her eyelids, tinted with a bluish color, enhanced the glow of her long black hair. A slave, her favorite, commented, "High priestess, I've combed your hair and brushed it. You're radiant when the morning light shines on you like this." Sprigs of fresh green leaves woven into her tresses added a scent of spring.

Her son, Diotrephes, arrived at the door, and she met him. The constant scowl on her face had appeared the day before. "Come in, my son."

"Mother, I can see you are agitated. You look beautiful this morning, but is something bothering you?"

"Yes, I'm not in a good mood. I know Antipas is no longer a threat, and I hoped that his silly doctrines would die with him. But I am now concerned about Marcos, the lawyer. Yesterday, Zoticos thought Marcos would also be implicated in Antipas's crimes. But using clever words, he manipulated the city council. He is our new enemy. If Marcos continues Antipas's teaching, we will have to deal with him too."

"Mother, your wise words to the city council were accepted."

"Yes." A softer light shone in her eyes. "At both trials, Antipas refused to admit the existence or power of the gods. An excellent punishment, being killed like that. Closing my eyes, I can still see the Jewish merchant. I behold him being lowered by the crane. He's above a bronze effigy of a bull filled with boiling oil." Her voice took on a harsh tone. "No, things did not go entirely as we wanted them to. It was unfortunate that the fire spread, injuring several people."

She turned to her son. "Now, Diotrephes, what's on your mind?"

The young man sat up on the couch where he had been reclining. He lifted his head from the purple pillow. "I have a spy working for me. His name is Yorick. He was a slave years ago, six if I'm not mistaken. He did not get along well with Antipas Ben Shelah. The young man isn't a good worker. He's too fond of gambling at sports events apparently. I learned about his addiction when I was going to Antipas's house for his training sessions. Here's what has happened, from what Yorick tells me. Several days ago, Miriam and Anthony fled from Pergamum. They were in one of several wagons going to Thyatira.

"Mother, remember how we learned that Uncle Zoticos is the father of the baby they took with them? That scrap of parchment Yorick found in Antipas's house told it all. We know the name of Uncle Zoticos's baby girl. Her mother gave her the name Chrysa. The only thing we don't know is whether or not the baby was legally adopted or not."

Lydia-Naq nodded. As she did every time they talked, she admired her son's athletic body, his broad shoulders and narrow waist. "I'm happy to know this much. It will lead us to where the child is. I will instruct the city's guards to search for the baby in Thyatira. And my brother Zoticos must talk with the mayor, asking whether or not Anthony and Miriam legally adopted our precious child."

Diotrephes brought the conversation around to the topic he wished to discuss. "Mother, I've been thinking of the opportunity you shared about me teaching in Sardis. I like the idea, and I am going to Sardis this week to present myself to the elders. I like the ring of 'Director of the Department of History.' I will request an interview for the position."

"My, that was a quick decision!"

"Well, yes and no. It has been on my mind since you first mentioned it. I want to get there quickly to obtain a date for an interview and be back before classes start here again at the gymnasium."

"Zeus will be with you," said Lydia-Naq, crossing her long, shapely legs. "He will open the future for you to close down the Household of Faith of the atheists in Sardis, just as we will do here. Zeus will help you restore the Lydian language in Sardis. May you be the one to learn where our baby Chrysa has been hidden."

Half an hour later, she arrived at the Altar of Zeus for her Friday morning rituals. She stood on the top step of the wide staircase and turned to look at the valley below. From this vantage point on the edge of the western cliff on the acropolis, she could look down at

Antipas's village.

The high priestess was attired in an expensive red stola embellished with yellow at the neckline. A matching yellow border was added to her tunic, a separate piece of fabric with many folds. It demonstrated the wealth and status that she so enjoyed.

Keeping her mind on her devotions at the altar, her eyes glanced down at a cluster of buildings. The high priestess knew her prayers by heart, and in a moment, prayers and rites would begin. Still, she also kept a thread of personal conversation going through her mind concerning the recent events.

Since Sunday night, when Antipas was punished with death, Lydia-Naq had rehearsed a speech for her brother. "Diotrephes brought the news. Imagine you, Zoticos, fathering a baby! And you didn't even know about her! So I am an aunt, finally, after all these years. But how did the soldier Anthony and Miriam, his wife, come to adopt my brother's baby? We must quickly get the child back."

Lydia-Naq swayed gently at the top of the stairs. Softly chanting a song in praise of Zeus, she carried out the first part of her obligatory prayers.

THE ACROPOLIS, PERGAMUM

Later that morning, Zoticos-Naq Milon was going down the acropolis hill from the library to the city. He had a gift to buy as a surprise for his sister, Lydia-Naq. Less than an hour before, she had requested him to inquire whether-Anthony and Miriam had legally adopted the baby.

The mayor of Pergamum was on his way to the acropolis, and Zoticos greeted him. "Honored Quintus Rufus, how are you enjoying the festival? A lot has happened during the past week. I saw you in meetings, including the council meeting yesterday, when Marcos spoke about Antipas's village. Personally, I am disappointed that the expropriation was dropped.

"Oh, I can see you are in a hurry, but I want to ask you about an adoption that occurred. I believe it took place at Lawyer Marcos's home just before the festival began. As required, when an adoption takes place, an authority must be present for it to be legal. Were you the authority present at the adoption? Do you remember that happening?"

Quintus thought for a moment. "Yes," he said, "I do remember that. A soldier adopted a baby girl, two months old. A Jewish woman, younger than the soldier, was married to him the day before."

"Do you remember their names?"

"I can't remember right now," said the mayor. "It was over and done so quickly. I had to leave to join the festival procession leading up to the acropolis."

"Could the man be Anthony Suros? Was the woman's name Miriam?" Zoticos felt his heart racing.

"Yes, that's right! I must hurry on now." Mayor Quintus Rufus turned and kept going up the hill.

Zoticos turned around and rapidly made his way back up the steep steps, two at a time. Everything was becoming apparent. Several days before, after Miriam and Anthony fled from Pergamum, he and his sister had evidence suggesting Miriam had somehow adopted his previously unknown child. He knew now, beyond any doubt, that the Roman soldier and the Jewish woman had somehow stolen his baby daughter.

Lydia-Naq had to have this news immediately.

LYDIA-NAQ'S HOME, THE ACROPOLIS, PERGAMUM

Lydia-Naq stayed awake for a long time thinking about what Zoticos had been told by Mayor Quintus Rufus.

How did my niece fall into their hands? What kind of magic do they use? No matter! My spells are more potent than theirs! My brother Zoticos must have his baby back! Zoticos is her father. That will happen when we get the adoption document annulled.

Rising from her bed, she walked to her altar of Hera by the light from an oil lamp. In the *lararium,*_the private space in her house, were seven small brass figures. She gently fingered the goddesses, the *lares.* Several blown-glass bottles arranged on either side held tufts of wool from sheep that had been sacrificed at the Altar of Zeus. When she felt threatened like this, she sacrificed a lamb, took a tuft from the sacrifice, and dipped it in the blood. Wool covered with blood was sealed inside a glass bottle. Combined with incantations, each bottle was a talisman with power to control the enemy.

One year ago, she began to pray for Antipas's removal.

And now her enemy was gone.

Tomorrow she would make another offering, again using the ancient language of Lydia. A powerful spell had brought one leader down. This one, the second, would work against Miriam. And a third would have to be used against Marcos, the lawyer.

She held onto the brass figure and closed her eyes before slowly putting it back on the narrow shelf. *Thank you, Yorick. You have been extremely helpful to our family.*

GREEN VALLEY INN, BETWEEN THYATIRA AND SARDIS

The sun was setting the next day when Diotrephes arrived at Green Valley Inn. He had been traveling all day from Pergamum to Sardis, and he led his mount to the stable where a slave began to brush it. Sweat showed it had been ridden hard on the long ride.

"I'm interested in finding a friend of mine," explained Diotrephes to Tycho, the inn's master. "I need to give him a message, but he left Pergamum before I had a chance to speak with him. However, I don't know if he has been here or not. He might have stopped in Thyatira."

"What does he look like? What's his name?"

"He's a soldier traveling with his wife and a little baby."

"Does he have a long red scar on the right side of his face?" Tycho tried to recall his recent visitors.

"Yes, he does," said Diotrephes, hardly able to contain his excitement.

"Well, you missed him. He stayed here on Tuesday night and left for Sardis early the next morning. A woman with a baby, two cripples, and another baby came on Wednesday. They were not traveling together, but the woman asked if her husband had stayed here and already left for Sardis."

"He will be happy to see me." Diotrephes's smile reached his ears, and a light shone in his eyes. "I'll catch up to them in Sardis tomorrow."

Chapter 6
Tangled Hospitality

THE GARRISON OF SARDIS, THE ACROPOLIS, SARDIS

Saturday morning, Anthony stood up, stretched, and walked to the window on the second floor of the sparsely furnished garrison barracks. He had stayed in the dormitory for two days, hardly exchanging a word with any of the other soldiers. He did not know if Miriam had arrived at Simon's house. One thing pleased him though. He had been assured that his horse, borrowed from Olive Grove Farm, was being cared for at the garrison's stable.

Shortly after having breakfast, a guard came to take him to the commander. As they left the barracks, Anthony studied the thick, high wall protecting the upper reaches of the acropolis of Sardis, the highest point in the city. The acropolis in Sardis was better organized and easier to navigate than in Pergamum. In contrast, the acropolis in Pergamum had too many buildings crowded against one another.

Commander Felicior wore his long, unfriendly face. "You say you are an instructor. Explain the glory of victory."

Anthony stood tall. "As scouts, we often talked about this, sir. Incomplete or erroneous information in a battlefield leads to faulty leadership, to failure instead of victory. No one wants to be the cause of losing a battle. Accurate information brings about victory. That is what I taught new recruits in Pergamum. I hesitate to say this, but Commander Cassius, my superior in Pergamum, does not understand how enemies threaten us when hiding in forests. We are preparing scouts for Germanica, not Mesopotamia. Recruits must be adequately trained for reconnaissance and fighting in Dacia."

A thin line showed on Felicior's brow. Anthony knew he had taken a risk. A soldier should never mention the possibility of inadequate military leadership in his officer.

The line was now a deep furrow, and his words came one word at a time. "Why doesn't Commander Cassius accept your teaching?"

"Sir, Commander Cassius began his military service in the east, in Zeugma. Unproductive land along the Euphrates River barely supports trees. Forests are unknown there. His methods train recruits for battles against Persians, but fighting is not like that in dark forests. I was worried that our soldiers would not be ready for Dacia. I had a falling out with Cassius over strategies for training scouts."

Anthony took Felicior's puckered lips as permission to continue. "How do barbarians fight? They take cover in steep ravines, along riverbanks, and behind trees in forests. Crafty warriors fall back, drawing our soldiers into unknown territory. They don't use a full-scale attack. Wiping out one cohort at a time—that's their method. Twenty dead over here. Another fifty soldiers there."

Felicior's voice now carried an angrier tone. "You are overly confident of yourself, soldier! You have ignored the chain of command. You arrived here with no orders but your own, so you are guilty of a serious charge of insubordination. There can be only one punishment for this violation. You cannot present yourself at a new garrison without approved transfer documents. What other problems are there between you and Commander Cassius?"

"I am a follower of Yeshua Messiah, sir. Commander Cassius limited my contact with recruits, only permitting me to teach archery. Later, he sent me to the gymnasium to train boys for the Games. However, as you saw, my orders from our superiors in Philippi directed me to instruct scouts. The situation came to a head when Commander Cassius and the Director of the Gymnasium of Pergamum, Diodorus Pasparos, prevented me from taking the solemn oath of loyalty to the emperor on January 1 this year. Diodorus scheduled special lectures on Roman writers that day. Commander Cassius, knowing what Director Diodorus had done, said that I intentionally missed this annual event."

The commander glowered. "May a soldier ever abandon his assigned commanding officer? A severe punishment awaits you."

"Sir, I am fully loyal. Everything I have fought for came from my unswerving allegiance and obedience to the empire."

"You are disloyal to the emperor!"

"I am loyal to Emperor Domitian, as my father was to Emperor Vespasian, sir."

"Explain yourself, soldier!"

"Nero claimed he was divine, but he did not require people to declare, 'Caesar is lord and god.' I entered the legion in the time of Emperor Vespasian, and the words were 'Caesar is Lord.'

"However, Emperor Domitian has added to his powers. Only the Senate may declare an emperor to be a 'god.' That is the first order of business in the Senate after an emperor dies. Sir, the Senate will declare our emperor to have been, or not to have been, a 'god.' That will only happen after Domitian's death."

Felicior sucked in his breath; his voice was harsh and cynical. "You are bold, soldier! Far too bold! You should be tried for treason. You abandoned your garrison. Even worse is what you just said about Emperor Domitian."

Anthony raised himself to his full height. "I have eight years until I will be retired, sir. I am thirty-six-years old. If you accept me as an instructor, I would be honored to serve you, the legion, and the empire. I want to serve according to the political balance that Caesar Augustus agreed to with the Senate. Augustus delivered Rome from civil wars and brought us *Pax Romana*."

Anthony knew that his next statement would be the most difficult to deliver. "Sir, if I may be so bold, two weeks ago I married into a Jewish family. My wife and our adopted baby girl are both here at her uncle's house in Sardis. His name is Simon Ben Shelah. My wife is safer here than in Pergamum, where her grandfather was killed. I am ready to serve you, but if you want me to return to the Pergamum Garrison, I will do so without question. I stand ready for whatever decision you make."

Felicior nodded. "I wrote Commander Cassius on Thursday for information about you but no response yet. This is my decision. You will stay at the house where you said your wife is living. You may only leave there under my orders. I will keep two guards posted night and day at the house. I know where this businessman lives. Return here when I send for you. You will not discuss the reason you are in Sardis with anyone."

"That is very clear, sir."

THE GARRISON OFFICE, THE ACROPOLIS, SARDIS

Commander Felicior Priscus watched the guard lead Anthony to the stable. Two guards would descend with the prisoner on horses, passing through the center of the city to Simon's property.

Deep emotions showed on the officer's face. He thought, *By Jove, this soldier is close to the truth. I'll have to be careful. If someone submits charges against him, I don't want to be accused of harboring a rebel.*

Words from a quiet conversation the previous summer sounded again in his ears. A lawyer from the Senate had arrived unexpectedly in Sardis. After requesting a private talk, he went back to Rome, having delivered his message.

That lawyer had explained the purpose of his visit: "I came from the Senate to tell you that your cousin, Helvetius Priscus, was killed a month ago. He was condemned for publicly criticizing Emperor Domitian. Helvetius stood up in the Senate chamber and boldly declared, 'The emperor may not change the laws as he wishes and accuse a senator of disagreeing with him. We senators may dissent without breaking the law.'

"What is more, remember this! Your cousin's father, also named Helvetius Priscus, was killed by Domitian's father, Emperor Vespasian. That death took place twelve years ago. Both died for the same crime. The Law of Treason was brought against both your uncle and your cousin.[6]

"Felicior, my friend, both of your relatives were senators. Each one was executed for publicly declaring the same argument. Please take note. The family name Priscus does not receive favor in the empire's capital. I would suggest that you in no way anger the emperor."

Felicior turned his head, snapping back to the present. He watched two guards mount their horses; Anthony rode between them. The officer took hold of a pen and gripped it tightly.

He wanted his lawyer friend from Rome to hear his words. If he could write to him, he would say, "For their courage, my family suffered two executions. A few moments ago, I listened to a soldier utter the same case that brought about their death. However, I will not send Anthony Suros back to Pergamum. I must know more about him. I will keep him close by for his own protection, if for no other

---

[6] The Law of Treason, or *lex maiestatis,* dealt with crimes against the emperor, the state, or the citizens of the empire. Traitors were regarded as having the same legal status as public enemies. Punishment might include either banishment or death.

reason. Both of my cousins were philosophers, but Anthony is different. He is not a philosopher, just an able legionary.

"I will keep this wandering stray soldier under house detention to make sure he doesn't leave the city. "Recently married,' so he will remain with his wife. I have already sent that carefully worded note to his commander in Pergamum. If Cassius demands his return, he goes back, but I think it would be to my advantage to avoid that."

SIMON AND JUDITH'S HOME, SARDIS

Most of Simon's family members were at home, still talking after breakfast. Three couches in the large room were used at mealtime, and the crumbs had not been cleared off the tables. Only Tamir, the fourteen-year-old, was not there. He had left early to meet a friend.

When someone knocked loudly outside, they all stopped talking and turned to the front door. The interruption came from the entrance gate in the wall surrounding the house. They were not expecting visitors this early on the Sabbath.

Ravid said, "I'll see who's there." He walked to the gate and called, "Who are you?"

The answer was not what Ravid wanted to hear.

Three soldiers were standing beside their horses. One spoke to him, and the other two appeared to be ready to stay outside the gate.

"Who are you?" he asked. "What do you want?"

"We are here to guard your house."

"On whose orders?"

"Commander Felicior Priscus has determined that both of us will guard your house while the prisoner receives hospitality here."

"Who is the prisoner?" Ravid forced himself to speak, fearing an answer he did not want to hear.

"I am Anthony Suros, husband of Miriam. May I enter?"

Without saying a word, Ravid walked to the gate, unlatched it, and stepped back while it swung open.

Ravid pointed to the house. *The arrival of this soldier dressed_in armor is an insult to every ideal we believe in.*

Anthony tied his horse to the post outside the gate and passed through. Inside the door, he laid his armor against the wall and took off his red cape, his helmet, and his sword. Dressed in his brown soldier's tunic, he entered the house.

Ravid followed Anthony without saying a word. He lived in a

home where pagan influences such as floor mosaics of the Greek myths had been removed. New patterns depicting eternity had been installed. Thousands of tiny black, yellow, and white stones formed lines progressing over and under each other in endless loops.

Ravid stood in a corner, as far away as possible from the stranger. His breath came in short spurts, and his jaw was tight.

A word of welcome from a woman broke the silence. "Anthony, I am Chenya, Simon's daughter-in-law. Miriam is upstairs with Ateas and Arpoxa. All of us have been wondering where you were."

"I have been detained in the barracks since Wednesday. The garrison commander wants me to stay in Sardis. He has confined me to your house until information about me comes from Pergamum. I'm sorry, but I may have to remain a few days."

The aroma of fresh bread still filled the room, but a scent of fear had overtaken the family. Ravid swallowed hard with scorn ready to pour out, but he kept his mouth shut.

Judith rolled her eyes upward, turned on her heel, and marched to the kitchen.

Simon's mouth had dropped open, and he stood speechless.

Ravid's voice sounded throughout the house. "My niece, Amath, enjoys playing with two Gentile babies! This family repeatedly welcomes a fourteen-year-old pagan boy, no longer just a visitor but a friend! Two lame Gentiles take a place at our table! Tamir, my nephew, asks to study at the gymnasium, where non-Jewish boys run naked."

He stopped to emphasize his words, wanting them to cut deeply like a sword. "My father-in-law cannot stop the commander of the garrison from forcing 'hospitality' on us! And on our Sabbath day! Non-Jews, nude athletes, and enemies! How long will we tolerate them? I thought this was a Jewish family!"

He frowned and went to the front door. "Look, everybody! Two soldiers remain outside the gate! I thought they were joking when they said they were here to guard our house. But they are going to stay here! What is next? Nissa, I want you to come with me." He stormed out the back door with his wife.

Miriam stood unable to move for a few moments. She struggled to arrange all that she had just heard. *Anthony, you are under house confinement! How wonderful! You will be safe here. The commander hasn't sent you back to Pergamum!* Running down the steps, she jumped into Anthony's arms, almost knocking him over.

The situation was clear. Miriam's family did not want Anthony to stay, but soldiers posted out front allowed no other option. An unexpected arrival any day of the week was unwelcome. Far worse was Anthony coming like this on a Sabbath morning.

Miriam led him upstairs. No one had said a word to him, apart from Chenya's first greeting and Ravid's denunciation. She gave Anthony a warm kiss. "I'm so happy about how this has turned out! You'll stay right here, but it's going to cause a few problems for the family."

"I have a horse outside. Someone needs to care for it."

"Not a problem. Uncle Simon will take your horse to the stables behind the house. When Nikias brought me here, he indicated he would return the horse to Olive Grove when he brings the next cart of goods for the store."

She left him after a few minutes to go downstairs for a family conference.

Simon, Judith, Chenya, and Miriam talked together, the children having been sent upstairs. She felt obligated to explain things. "Uncle Simon and Aunt Judith, I want to talk about this awkward situation. Let me start with how I met Anthony. Is that all right?"

"Yes, explain everything!" Simon growled. "Who is he? Yesterday your husband was going to be my guest for only a few nights. Today Rome has imposed him here indefinitely. You've already noticed that Ravid objects to Gentiles in our home."

Miriam replied, "About these Gentiles...Ateas and Arpoxa were sold at the slave market in Pergamum. Two years ago Grandpa bought them at the auction and freed them. They came to Grandpa's village, learned Greek, and attended the Household of Faith meetings. They now believe in Yeshua Messiah and are followers of God's teachings. Both are exceptionally talented and good friends."

Judith demanded, "How did you meet your husband?"

"I sold goods in Grandpa's shop: perfumes, soap, clothes, necklaces, bracelets, and rings. One day Anthony came by. He had been attending the meetings at the cave for a year and was learning about our beliefs. Anthony had served in Upper Germanica. He was wounded on a scouting mission and sent to the retirement camp at Philippi to recover.

"The army sent him to the Garrison of Pergamum to teach

scouting, and he started coming to the Household of Faith with Marcos, our family lawyer. Both are followers of Yeshua Messiah. Anthony is respectful of our family and traditions and hasn't tried to change any of our customs."

Judith's voice trembled. "But, my child, he is a Roman soldier!"

"Yes," replied Miriam, smiling, "that was almost too much for Grandpa! When he learned that Anthony and I wanted to be married, it took months to speak about it. Grandpa made it hard for Anthony to become my husband. Last September, starting at Yom Kippur, Grandpa began to study the Scriptures. He made notes, asking himself a question: 'Does God accept a person whom we consider to be a non-Jewish enemy, such as a Roman soldier, if they have come to faith in Yeshua Messiah?'

"This question brought much agony. He stayed up late at night, but finally, through the Scriptures, he came to this conclusion: God does accept non-Jews if their hearts are sincere toward him. Grandpa concluded that no person is beyond God's grace. He told us this just before learning that the city authorities in Pergamum were placing him on trial. In the end, Grandfather encouraged our marriage. He insisted that we become a family, so we were married much more quickly than would have been normal in a Jewish home! He agreed on March 24, and we were married on April 14."

Simon looked confused. "I am puzzled. It seems strange that my brother would agree to this marriage. I would like to know all the reasoning that let him accept a soldier into our family."

Judith grunted. "God's acceptance of a sinner and marriage into a family are like different kinds of food; one is kosher, and the other is..." Her eyes were wide. "Miriam! Roman soldiers destroyed Herod's Temple! They caused the deaths of countless members of our family. How could you?"

Miriam noticed a shudder shake her uncle's shoulders. He asked, "How long will Anthony stay?"

"For now, the garrison commander decides. I'm sure it won't be for long, Uncle. If he stays in our room upstairs and only goes out to the back of the property..."

"Let's think!" replied Simon. "Judith, we must talk this over."

"Look at it this way, Father," interjected Chenya, who had been listening. She was used to finding the middle ground when her children argued. "Having guards outside is good for us. Robbers will not be trying to steal anything from your workshop! What's to complain about?"

She tried a smile, but only Miriam returned the favor after her gentle humor.

Just then, Tamir came running into the house with another boy. "Hail!" shouted Tamir, interrupting the conversation. "Guess what! Soldiers are outside! They have two horses!"

Tamir introduced his friend. "Hector, this is my cousin Miriam. She's here from Pergamum. Miriam, this is my friend Hector. Grandfather, why have soldiers been posted at our gate?"

Simon answered Tamir simply. "I'll explain later."

Hector stepped forward, kissing Simon's hand as Sardian custom demanded when greeting an older person. Then he approached Judith and did the same thing.

He moved toward Miriam and said, "I am happy to meet you, Cousin Miriam." Older schoolboys greeted others with their common designation until they were invited to drop words like "cousin."

Chenya turned to Miriam. "Hector's father, Jace, was descended from an old Greek family that moved to Sardis shortly after Alexander the Great expelled the Persian rulers. Tamir and Hector are best friends. They go everywhere together. Never mind the noise they make, Miriam."

Tamir ran up the stairs two at a time. He had his own room because he was the only boy in the Ben Shelah family. Hector followed, calling, "Wait for me!"

The rooms upstairs were built in a "U" shape in the middle of the back of the house. Under a high ceiling, a balcony led to eight bedrooms. In the winter, shutters on the outside kept cold winds out, but today they were all open.[7]

Three generations lived in the house. Elaine had the front corner room. It had two windows, one overlooking the valley and the Royal Cemetery to the north and the other facing west. Sometimes she counted horses or wagons on the Royal Road as they came into or left the city.

---

[7] This description is based on a house discovered during archeological research in Laodicea where ruins confirm the outline of the lower floor. Many homes possessed a second floor with bedrooms, or *cenaculae.*

Next to hers, in the middle bedroom, the younger sister, Amath, passed hours inventing stories and making simple dolls come alive with imaginary adventures. Her dolls, dressed in tiny clothing, were her prized possessions. Each one had a name, mostly those of the queens of ancient Israel.

The girls' parents, Ezar and Chenya, occupied the corner room facing west, beside the two younger girls. It also had two windows, one facing west and the other overlooking Chenya's favorite view, the high mountain to the south. She enjoyed the view of endless trees.

The fourth room, just to the left of the stairs, belonged to Simon and Judith. They found the stairs increasingly difficult to manage, and Judith often stopped halfway up to rest, relaxing her sore knees.

Heber had his own room to the right of the stairs. His window opened to the south, and he often stood at his window to pray, watching animals graze on the fields behind the house. His eyes lifted from the small farm to the foothills nearby, and beyond was the long mountain range. He could not see where the mountains ended, and often his prayers were like that—beginning with a clear focus and not ending but drifting off into a distant haze.

Tamir's room beside Heber's was where the two boys were now playing a noisy game.

All eight bedrooms were now occupied. Miriam and Anthony were in the next room and Ateas and Arpoxa in the front, opposite Elaine. Arpoxa nursed Grace in the night. However, when Grace awoke in the morning, her crying roused Saulius. Two babies crying woke everyone much sooner than they were used to.

MARCOS AND MARCELLA'S HOUSE OF PRAYER, PERGAMUM

Once again, Antipas's friends in Pergamum gathered. Marcos had opened the newly renovated room, and it was even more crowded than during their first meeting. People sat close together on carpets or stood next to each other along the walls. The scent of handwoven rugs soon mixed with various odors of sweat and olive soap. Many of the poorer people could not afford soap very often.

When the last of the stragglers arrived, Marcos started the service.–"I have several announcements tonight before we begin worship. As I said, I am changing our name from 'Household of

Faith' to 'The House of Prayer.' Prayer was influential in the recovery of my daughter, Florbella, and I have learned that God answers prayer.

"When people ask what you do when you gather together, you can explain, 'We pray.' For a longer explanation, tell them that we pray for each other. Explain that we intercede for the authorities in the city and for the emperor too. We pray for those who are sick in body and mind, widows, old people, and orphans.

"Tonight is Saturday. From now on, Onias—he's the man over here, the one who just now raised his hands and waved to you—will lead Jews in Sabbath worship on Friday evenings and Saturday mornings as a Jew knows how to pray, read, and explain the Scriptures!"

A ripple of laughter spread around the room. How would Marcos, a non-Jew, ever lead a Jewish service?

"Our meetings on Sunday mornings at sunrise will continue with the Holy Meal. That was Antipas's custom, and we want to continue it. Everyone is welcome."

Answering a question, he said, "Yes, of course slaves are welcome." Another round of laughter arose, this time a little louder. Slaves had to get up early and work late. Marcos's slaves were fortunate, not having far to walk, especially in inclement weather.

"Normal occupations in Antipas's village will continue. The city leaders have agreed that there will be no expropriation. No one is going to lose their job. Work at the village will not be affected. Antipas's shops, one in the Upper Agora and the other in the Lower Agora, are still open, and goods between the Ben Shelah brothers continue to be traded and sold."

A man asked a question about the house he was living in at Antipas's village. Marcos replied, "No one is going to be put out of their home. All who live in Antipas's community will stay. Onias is still the steward of the Ben Shelah village, supervising everything: the glassblowing; the making of bricks and pottery, linen, and woolen clothing; and the two shops. I don't expect anyone will lose their work.

At the back, Yorick looked on with mild interest. He had not heard anything tonight to make him suspicious. The man who paid him a silver coin for information had said, "Listen for anything that he says against the Roman or city government."

Yorick felt annoyed because he did not have anything negative to report about Marcos to Diotrephes.

The young spy did not like Onias or all the special holidays Jews loved so much, so he would not keep going to the Friday meetings. Also, he was far too interested in extra sleep, so he would not be getting up for the early morning meetings at Marcos's house. Besides, he could not understand why people called their gathering the "Holy Meal." Their service was just a simple set of prayers mixed with unleavened bread and a sip of wine. It was not a "meal" at all.

None of this made sense. Never mind...he would listen to gossip in the village. That way, he would still collect a few denarii each month. He would have something to tell Diotrephes each time they met. He left the meeting before Marcos could start the service and before the young people started singing.

Chapter 7
On the Royal Road

JAKOB'S SHOP ON THE ROYAL ROAD, SARDIS

Jakob, the chief elder of the Synagogue of Sardis, opened the shutters of his shop to greet a new day. Jakob's shop, located at the center of the city, overflowed with carpenter's tools. It was the feel of working with wood that he most enjoyed. Over the years, he had learned how to smooth out even the most resistant knot on a fully dried plank.

He called himself a simple carpenter, but his clientele enjoyed showing off the high quality of the tables, chairs, and beds in their homes. After he made rough wood feel smooth, he went home at the end of a day with a light heart and a broad smile.

Reaching over to a special nook at the back of the shop, Jakob unrolled a scroll. He had kept it hidden for almost a year.

May 21, in the Ninth Year of Domitian
From the Council of Elders, Synagogue of Pergamum
From Jaron Ben Pashhur

To: Synagogues in Asia and Mysia

Be it known that yesterday Antipas Ben Shelah, a resident of Pergamum, was separated from those who love the Covenant. He came from Alexandria, Egypt, many years ago, and is a successful businessman. Until recently, he was integrated into our fellowship, worshiping in the Synagogue of Pergamum.

We mourn his decision to ignore repeated warnings. He persists in false teaching, having departed from our ways. He places learning about "The Way" and its founder, Yeshua of Nazareth, before the elders' traditions. He teaches that this man was the Jewish Messiah.

His name has been officially removed from the registry of Jews. Will the Romans treat him as a non-Jew? We have concluded that he must not be accepted in any other Jewish community. This information is being circulated to all other congregations in Asia Minor.

Jakob carefully rerolled the scroll. His brow arched amid conflicting thoughts, for a Greek member of the city council of Sardis had recently approached him. As usual, the topic was money.

"Friend Jakob," began the counselor, looking him in the eye, "Domitian needs more revenue. Everyone knows it. He must pay the army as well as undertake large building projects, so the emperor is increasing taxes. Since the province of Asia Minor can no longer fund the restoration of buildings in Sardis, new sources of financing are required. Your Jewish community is more conservative in its spending habits than most of the Gentile population. Because of this, we are asking for donations."

Jakob asked, "And are you going to offer something in return?"

"Contributions by every Jew will be lauded publicly. Your names will be written in Greek for all to read. More importantly, the Jewish community will receive published guarantees that there will be protection against religious persecution."

Jakob met this initial attempt at obtaining funds with disinterest. The Jewish carpenter, who was skilled in bargaining, responded, "That is a very thought-provoking offer, but it is not sufficient."

The city counselor made a second, more tempting offer. "Well, since you demand more, the city fathers might just consider giving Jewish leaders a voice in the forming of the city's policies. A voice, of course, but unfortunately not a vote at the meetings."

"Then I'm not sure we would even consider your offer." Jakob turned away as if his answer was no.

The city council might agree to more, and he gave each concession grudgingly, but obviously he had come well prepared. "It depends on the contributions of your synagogue. We could examine the needs of the city, and in turn, your community might benefit in six ways. For those who donate more to the city, more time will be given to them to explain what they require. Second, such conversations might involve being able to acquire better lands for houses, businesses, or farms in the surrounding area. A better place might also be found as a Jewish cemetery. Fourth, we understand some of your families might want better security at night, especially if gold and jewelry are kept in their homes. We will commit ourselves as city officials to speak well of Jewish families and your history as well. Lastly, office space will be coming available soon in the Western Agora, and..."

He left his sentence unfinished, and Jakob wondered if the term "donate" suggested some underhanded political and economic advantages.

The encounter ended with the counselor's authorization for Jakob to present this offer to the synagogue's elders. Jakob went home with a broad smile. That conversation had taken place three weeks ago. Jakob knew it was tempting because it provided status, recognition, and a welcome hedge of safety from unjustified persecution. But it was complicated, too.

Jakob called it, "a contribution in return for future security."

After explaining that conversation to some of the elders, an unanswered question was repeated in several homes. Once the city became accustomed to that flow, what would happen if the stream of donations were disrupted by some unforeseen event?

However, Jakob mulled over another issue. His name, like that of the ancient patriarch and every other Jewish name, could only be written in Hebrew. The congregation might accept the benefits that were being offered, but would this lead to a diminishment of all they held dear—the deep significance of their names? Would their names have to be written in Greek when signing the agreement with the city?

Another matter brought a frown to all the leaders in the congregation. Simon Ben Shelah and his family were known to be sympathetic to the beliefs of Antipas, Simon's brother.

Jakob closed his eyes in thought. *The congregation of the God-fearers was formed with the hope of introducing our Jewish faith to Gentiles. I entrusted Gaius with the leadership of that group. But he has become a source of false teaching, just like Antipas. I must find an appropriate way to smooth out the situation, just as I do with wood in my carpentry shop. All must be satisfied.*

THE GYMNASIUM – ELEMENTARY AND HIGH SCHOOL, SARDIS

Diotrephes had recently arrived in Sardis, and he walked along the main road stretching from east to west across the city. For two days, he talked with strangers, always bragging about Pergamum. In the afternoons, he spent time at the hot baths and then ate scrumptious meals under white sheets erected as small tents outside various thermopolia. He enjoyed the entertainment each evening at the theater.

Staying at an inn attached to the Western Agora marketplace, he was up at dawn. The sounds of a bustling city excited him. His spirit was jubilant as he dreamed of future possibilities. On the last day of April, he would have his first opportunity to talk with the Director of the Gymnasium of Sardis.

He stopped at the reputable shops on the Royal Road, entering them one by one. The first was a hardware shop specializing in tools. A blacksmith worked in the back of the shop, forging hammers.

The next shop brought dried fruits and spices from Phrygia, the nearby province. Large sacks held pungent spices with powders sparkling in every shade of yellow, brown, and red. He inhaled deeply and told the shop owner that the aromas were enchanting.

At the next block, he found what he was looking for. The shop had a sign over the door: "The Ben Shelah Brothers." He entered the spacious shop and introduced himself to the store clerk. "My name is Diotrephes Milon. I'm from Pergamum."

They shook hands. "Welcome! My name is Cleon. Our store closes in less than an hour, but in that time, I am sure I can relieve you of lots of spare coins!"

Diotrephes looked around the shop, impressed by the quality of the goods. Clothing hung on the back wall, tunics of all sizes and colors. Some were cotton, others made of linen. Togas were folded neatly on the tables in the middle area. Beside them, a whole wall was covered with jewelry and pottery. Jewelry included everything a woman might want, rings for her fingers, ears, toes, and nose. There were bracelets, necklaces, and armbands made of bronze and silver. Headbands in different colors hung on hooks.

"Cleon, what kinds of jewels are these?"

"We have many jewels set in gold and silver. Look, these are sapphires and amethysts. These other ones are set with topaz and beryl gems. A brother of my master sends precious gems from Egypt. My master can also make special settings to order."

Diotrephes saw rows of small glass bottles. He sniffed the bottles one by one. "I like the perfume," he said, wondering how to ask if Cleon had met Anthony or Miriam.

"Those perfumes come from Egypt, but the bottles are from Pergamum. These cosmetic oils have saffron and aloes. They are mixed with calamus, which comes from Arabia. These are special oils for anointing the dead for burial. Other oils are good for curing skin problems. We start with an olive oil base and mix in myrrh and sometimes balm. Many of the perfumes come from Antipas's workshop in Pergamum. And you come from that city! Did you ever go to Antipas's shop? They say he's a kind man, getting his people to make every beautiful thing you can think of."

Diotrephes's eyebrows raised, and he smiled inwardly. *Cleon brought up the workshop. I did not need to. What does he know about the death of Antipas?*

On another wall, Diotrephes noticed beautiful bronze pieces. Bronze candle holders, decanters, and cups were the most prominent. He took a finely polished bronze mirror to examine his face. "That is produced by another brother, Jonathan, in Thyatira."

Looking more carefully, Diotrephes found dark wool coats for the winter months. They were folded neatly underneath the fine linen togas.

"These wool items come from another Ben Shelah brother, in Laodicea. His name is Daniel."

"How many brothers are there in the family?" Diotrephes asked.

"There were twelve. Three daughters died in Egypt. One daughter and two brothers still live there. Antipas died in Pergamum. There are five more brothers, all businessmen."

"You work in a good shop, Cleon. If I wanted to find the Ben Shelah family here, where would I go? Some of them are my friends, you know. I had a good friend in Pergamum. He was married to Miriam, Antipas's granddaughter."

"That's incredible! Earlier today, Heber, my master's son, told me that soldiers are keeping watch over her husband. Anthony, the soldier, is under house confinement. Imagine!"

"Oh, what a shame! Soldiers and confinements! Why are they there? How long does Heber expect the soldiers to be there?"

"I don't know. Anyway, welcome! If you want to visit the family, they live that way, just outside the city gates. You'll find the large property on your left as you go toward Smyrna. Or if you want to find them in the city, the best place is the synagogue. They walk by here on their way to worship every Friday evening. They also attend a meeting called the Assembly of God-fearers on Saturday evenings."

"Thank you for your help, Cleon. Here, I'm going to give you a denarius. You are most helpful. Spend it well! I may have more questions for you later."

THE SYNAGOGUE OF SARDIS ON THE ROYAL ROAD, SARDIS

After the earthquake in Sardis over seventy-five years earlier, the synagogue had been rebuilt and expanded. Jewish worshipers now met in a splendid hall accommodating about 800 persons. It was built at a high cost. The floor and the walls shone with inlaid stones in designs symbolizing eternity. Openings at the base of the roof drew warm air, forming a slight breeze inside and making it more comfortable, even on hot days. The location on Royal Road, between the shops and the gymnasium, gave the synagogue a visibility of unique significance.[8]

Jakob's most precious possession was an ancient letter describing the arrival of Jews in Sardis. It explained how the property was given to the Jewish congregation. The large block of land off Royal Road, a gift to Jewish families, was marked off by Zeuxis, the Persian satrap, commissioned in Antioch. As a new governor in ancient Sardis, Zeuxis had been instructed by King Antiochus to establish a Jewish colony in the region.

Zeuxis was told to deal kindly with the several thousand men, women, and children coming to Sardis. Since that time, many descendants of those families lived in Sardis and Laodicea. Jakob kept the letter in a secure niche next to his business accounts.[9]

---

[8] Historical ruins in Sardis include this synagogue, located between the gymnasium to the north and the shops just described to the south. The walls are well preserved and partially restored. The entrance area, known as the portico, is carefully repaired. A list of the persons who funded the restoration is found on the back wall. Excavations on the outside reveal foundations of buildings previously constructed on the same site. These foundations are likely those built by the earliest Jewish congregation shortly after they arrived in 212 BC. The evidence for this is based on the letter written from Antioch to Sardis, where Satrap Zeuxis governed.

[9] *"Letter from King Antiochus to Zeuxis, his Father, sendeth Greeting: If you are in health, it is well. I also am in health. Have been informed that a sedition is arisen in Lydia and Phrygia, I thought that matter required great care; and upon advising with my friends what was fit to be done, it hath been thought proper to remove 2,000 families of Jews, with their effects, out of Mesopotamia and Babylon, unto the castles and places that lie most convenient, for I am persuaded that they will be well disposed guardians of our possessions, because*

Jews met for their worship on Friday evenings and during the morning on Saturdays. Then, on Saturday evenings, God-fearing Gentiles occupied the portico, the large, covered entrance that opened onto Royal Road. A few families attended all three services, among them Simon and Judith.

The Saturday evening service originated when a few Gentiles told Jakob that they wanted to study Jewish beliefs. Sardian citizens were curious about Jews. Chief Elder Jakob, who was still young at the time, suggested that the portico of the building be used as their meeting place. He agreed to have a teacher lead this group. The man leading the God-fearing Gentiles was quiet spoken and well-qualified. Jakob's mother was born in Jerusalem, and his father was from Athens.

The city's residents enjoyed the presence of Jews. For their part, Jews were encouraged to know that a few non-Jews wanted to learn about their faith. Consequently, for fifteen years, the reputation of the Jews had grown enormously. Jakob secretly hoped that eventually some non-Jews would convert to Judaism.

For the city authorities, the comingling of Jews and Gentiles was a manifestation of their open-mindedness. After all, Sardian ideals included social harmony, a highly prized goal.

"We'll learn to get along," one Sardian said to Jakob.

However, two bankers had been overheard speaking. One said, "The synagogue of Sardis has a good reputation in our city." The reply came, "Yes, they can discuss religion with us. As a result, they will come to know why we worship Artemis."

---

of their piety towards God, and because I know that my predecessors have borne witness to them in that they are faithful, and with alacrity do what they are desired to do. I will, therefore, though it be laborious work, that thou remove these Jews; under a promise, that they shall be permitted to use their own laws and when thou shalt give every one of their families a place for building their houses, and a portion of land for their husbandry and for the plantation of their vines; and thou shalt discharge them from paying taxes of the fruits of the earth for ten years; and let them have a proper quantity of wheat for the maintenance of their servants, until they receive bread-corn out of the earth; also let a sufficient share be given to such as minister to them in the necessaries of life, that by enjoying the effects of our humanity, they may show themselves the more willing and ready about our affairs. Take care likewise of that nation, as far as thou art able, that they may not have any disturbance given them by anyone."
King Antiochus' letter, quoted in Josephus 12.3.3.148-153

That comment was increasingly bothering Jakob.

THE INSULAE, LAODICEA

Little Lion arrived home, tired but excited. Ever since he had heard two citizens speculating about the battle to be fought against King Decebalus, he had trouble sleeping.

"Mother," he said as they began their simple meal, "what would you think if I left this work of carrying firewood to the hot baths? I want to do something that has potential, something for the future! Working for Meres, the manager of the hot baths, I'm getting paid so little!"

All Laodiceans knew the Meres family paid low wages.

Charmaine answered, "What do you want to do instead?"

"Our home is little more than a room. We have to climb up rickety steps to our tiny apartment. On this second floor, the smell from the open sewer is terrible. And now I've got an answer. I want to join the army, Mother! I will earn more, I'll send you money, and you will be able to live in a better place, close to the big theater of Laodicea. Also, you will have better food on the table."

Little Lion knew his mother's deepest fears. Yesterday at supper, she had asked, "How could I afford to pay for this tiny apartment if I lost you? Please don't talk to me again about war!"

Her eyes opened wide, and her lips quivered. "My son, you are all I have! Your father and your three sisters died of that terrible cough. For four years, you've kept me alive by your work, by your generosity. You are a good son. What would I ever do if I lost you?"

"Mother, you don't have to worry; I can take care of myself! I can't stand the way people treat me around the hot baths. I'm small, and people pick on me, beating me up. They call me names."

"My son, I will not have you going to war. That's not for you!"

Charmaine Memmius shuddered because she could not afford to lose her son. She had to keep him home.

THE STADIUM, PERGAMUM

Final awards had just been given to the champion athletes at the annual Games of Pergamum. Commander Cassius, Anthony's officer, sat with Director Diodorus, headmaster of the Gymnasium. They chose a quiet section of the stadium for their conversation.

The crowd had started to break up and leave. Cassius looked

around and saw that no one would eavesdrop on them. "What are your thoughts? The letter from the Commander of the Sardis Garrison says Anthony is there under confinement."

The letter had been a surprise to both men. Cassius pulled out the letter and read it for a second time. "Why would Anthony go to Priscus in Sardis? And why is he under house custody there? Why not send him back here to us immediately? Anthony Suros came with clear orders from Philippi to instruct scouts. But wait, hmm, did his commission originate in Philippi? Could his orders have come from someone higher up, in Rome perhaps? I sent a letter to Philippi, and I'm waiting for an answer."

"I don't like the sound of this," said Diodorus, his forehead lined with tiny grooves.

Cassius heaved a huge sigh. "Neither do I, and now I'm concerned that we changed the army's orders when we put Anthony in the gymnasium. I did not notify Philippi. What bothers me is that I didn't take enough time to learn more about him earlier."

"At least we know where Anthony Suros is." Diodorus sighed.

"We'll have to be very cautious about what we say and do concerning this until we know more about the situation," agreed Cassius.

The two men made plans for the next day and then left the stadium. Both were feeling uneasy.

LYDIA-NAQ'S HOME, THE ACROPOLIS, PERGAMUM

The same evening, tired but satisfied, Diotrephes trudged up the steps to his mother's house in Pergamum.

"My son, you're back! Tell me about Sardis!"

"Mother, Zeus favored me. In the middle of June, I will have a second, longer interview."

"Excellent!"

"And better yet, I know where Chrysa is!"

"Oh, that's good news! When will you bring her back to Pergamum?"

"I don't know if that's possible just now. Our baby girl is in the home of Antipas's brother, Simon Ben Shelah. I couldn't get in since army guards are keeping watch. The garrison commander put Anthony under confinement, so I did not ask questions. Hopefully, I'll be able to learn more on my next trip."

THE SYNAGOGUE PORTICO, SARDIS

The next day, on Saturday evening, Heber was at the Synagogue of Sardis. The meeting of the God-fearers was over. His friend Gaius was standing at the entrance, his hand resting against the door. Apparently, Gaius was exhausted from the day's work. He looked up at the portico roof, which was supported by four slender, gracefully carved stone pillars. The roof, composed of red ceramic tiles, rested on wooden beams inserted into the outer walls.

Gaius loved this place. In the center of the small open space, a large stone basin held water for Jewish ceremonial washings. Unlike every other building in Sardis, no carved god or goddess could be seen.

"Hail, my friend!" said Heber, approaching Gaius. "How are you feeling tonight?"

Gaius, a slight man with an ashen face, shifted his stance and leaned against the large portico doorway. Heber had learned that Gaius's mother had been a Jewish trader in woolen carpets in Ephesus. His Gentile father, now advanced in years, managed the shop at the foot of Harbor Street, at Ephesus's famous port.[10] Two generations before, his grandparents had left Rome when the emperor expelled Jewish families. When he was a young man, Gaius worked with his father in the carpet business.

Heber appreciated his friend; together with other families from Rome, Gaius had become active in the group of followers of the Jewish Messiah. In Ephesus, the church leader, Elder John, had been Gaius's mentor. But after his parents died, Gaius came to Sardis. Since the Ben Shelah family needed help in the shop, Heber invited Gaius to work as a helper.

Two years before, Heber asked, "Gaius, would you accept teaching the Jewish faith to the Gentiles? Our previous leader is ill and unable to carry on. We need a teacher to help us every Saturday evening."

"I've been attending at the portico and I would like to do the teaching, but I don't know if I'm well enough prepared to start that,"

---

[10] The ancient harbor of Ephesus has gradually filled in as silting occurred faster than the city's ability to remove the sediment. The entire Bay of Ephesus occupied a space five miles from east to west and three miles from north to south. It is presently used for agricultural purposes.

Gaius answered.

"Why?" Heber asked.

"Lots of controversy! The synagogue elders are concerned about the God-fearers. They don't like the talk of a messiah. Some want to totally ban us from the premises. Still, I don't know if that will happen, because of a possible backlash from the Sardis community. Many are attracted to Judaism. Also, the synagogue leaders fear that initial discussions with the city elders could be scrapped. No one wants a controversy to erupt. You know Sardis...everyone wants to get along together."

Despite the social situation, Gaius eventually agreed and accepted Heber's invitation to teach. Gaius now worked mornings at the family shop, and in the afternoon, he ministered to poor people in the insulae section of the city. The rest of the time, he was teaching Gentiles in the portico about the Jewish Messiah.

Today, however, there was a reason for Heber to be concerned. Gaius's dull facial complexion and yellow eyes worried Heber. Gaius kept complaining of being worn out and short of breath. His lungs hurt continuously.

"How are you feeling tonight?" Heber asked for a second time.

"To be honest, Heber, I'm not well. I can hardly do the work in your shop. I'm trying herbs—every combination of dried seeds—but nothing works. In my earlier days in Ephesus, our family worked from sunup to sundown. Back then, I was a young man. Now those days are past!"

"Is that all?"

"Well, I'll be honest with you, Heber. I am exhausted. Jakob came to talk with me today. He's worried that Jewish families will be pressured to accept the social standards of this city. What if the congregation takes the city's offer to grant different kinds of privileges in exchange for donations to civic projects? I think he likes the idea of the Jews having more rights, and I understand that Jakob has increased his demand for privileges. Specifically, he's asking for more than a voice in city affairs. But something else is bothering me. He's begun to pressure me. He instructed me to limit my teaching to God-fearers. He said, 'From now on, you will not teach from any document except the Torah.'"

SIMON AND JUDITH'S HOME, SARDIS

Ravid was satisfied that Anthony mostly stayed confined in his room. The soldier conversed only with Miriam, Ateas, and Arpoxa. He could be heard singing to his baby daughter. Sometimes, in the early evenings, he took a walk around the back of the property.

Raising his voice loud enough to be heard upstairs, Ravid continually made sure to comment loudly on how upsetting Anthony's arrival had been to the family.

"Heber and Ezar follow their father's example. They don't say a word to Anthony, but I've overheard them talking freely with Miriam," Ravid said to Nissa one evening.

Ravid and Nissa no longer came into the house, even for meals. All day long, he and Simon worked side by side in the workshop making jewelry. But Ravid cautioned his wife, "Nissa, don't eat at your father's table until all those foreigners leave!"

The sun shone brightly on Monday. Ravid and Nissa, with Simon, Judith, and Miriam, rested on the roof of the house. The noon meal was over, and people were walking by, going back to Smyrna.

Ravid said, "I'm glad the annual festival of Artemis is almost over," he said. "This city goes wild, forgetting the good morals it had before this final week of the April festival."

He walked to the front of the house on the flat roof. Seeing people leaving Sardis for home, his lips were drawn tight. "I won't watch this display of paganism anymore. Nissa, come downstairs."

Simon smiled, glad to be left alone with Judith and Miriam. This was the moment he had been waiting for, a chance to talk personally with his niece. "Miriam," he said, chuckling, "I almost forgot! Here is a little present for you, a belated gift for your marriage."

Simon handed Miriam a little bag.

"Oh, how beautiful, Uncle Simon!" exclaimed Miriam, placing the intricate gold pendant around her neck and giving the old man a kiss on his cheek.

Simon, a man of unbridled enthusiasm in business, was also generous. "It's nothing, just a little gift, from both of us." He was smiling at Judith.

Grace let out a cry, and Judith and Miriam left to attend to the baby. The baby had just woken up from a nap. Simon sat alone, enjoying the shadow under the grape arbor. Even though he tried to dismiss the nagging thoughts, they kept returning. They were related to the ever-present contradiction in his everyday life.

Eliab's words of blessing from his deathbed still rang in Simon's ears. He wondered how his father had been able to summarize the inner conflict so accurately. Two years had passed, but he remembered every word uttered by his dying father, and during that time had never opened up about his hidden tension to anyone.

Simon, you desire truth and wealth, reaching out to experience what you honestly know is right while being held too tightly by that which you fear. That struggle has left you tired. I bless your home and your table, for around it, you will find real joy. Even if your guests are impoverished, you will grasp their hands, finding friendship and wealth. You will know the difference between false security and a lasting community. When you are an overcomer, your open door will bless others with riches beyond your understanding.

The memory of his father's death renewed the acute grief of separation. He bowed his head, melancholy washing over him again. Last night, Simon had gone to sleep thinking of his workshop, where he produced rings and necklaces, but he quickly drifted back to his own conflicts and his father's blessing.

Father knew me better than I know myself! Others don't understand how tired I get. They can't see the tensions that pull me in so many different directions. What should I do with this soldier in my home? Antipas asked me to welcome him! And now I have the possibility of being a partner at the Bank of Hermus. Is that really what I want, to have greater wealth and increased social status?

Chapter 8
Simon's Home

SIMON AND JUDITH'S HOME, SARDIS

Heber beamed with delight as his mother made an announcement at the breakfast table. It was Wednesday when Judith announced, "Tomorrow is Heber's birthday! He'll be thirty-seven—a good reason for another festivity! Don't we love events in our home?"

Heber, Simon's second son and a widower, still hoped to have a family of his own. Someday. His memory took him over a painful path, what he secretly called "my might-have-been years."

Sheerah, his wife, had died after childbirth. That happened five years ago. Reclining at the breakfast table, every detail of that painful event returned. She had delivered a breach baby. Her smiles expressed both the tears of joy and pain as she held her newborn son. But both mother and son died. Only a few days afterward, the whole household was in mourning.

Heber still mourned that loss. *What might have been...*

A suitable bride, part of Judith's clan, was found for Heber. Letters went back and forth for two years before she embarked on a ship from Alexandria, Egypt, to Miletus, in Asia Minor. Tragically, the vessel sank in a sudden storm off the coast of Rhodes, and for the last three years, he had been carrying another burden.

What might have been! What will be? were his recuring thoughts. But no one ever talked with him about them. He only spoke under his breath, his mind busy in a never-ending silent conversation.

To cover up his sense of loss, Heber had developed a way to make people laugh. Not letting anyone in on quiet suffering became his way of dealing with stressful situations.

Responding to his mother's reminder of his birthday, Heber said, "Tomorrow evening, our Sabbath begins. One day it's my birthday, and the following day, I'll be blessed with Pentecost!"

This morning, Simon would begin work early and continue until late in the afternoon, stopping before the Sabbath began at sundown. But with Thursday marking the evening before Pentecost, a service known as Erev Shavuot would bring them together with other Jews.

When the breakfast table was ready, the family gathered at the three couches set on three sides of the square table in the middle. Miriam reclined on one couch, and Ateas and Arpoxa reclined on either side.

As before, Ravid refused to join them. Nissa was absent as well.

Simon heard Grace crying. Anthony was in his room upstairs, caring for the baby.

Beginning the meal, Simon covered his head with his prayer mantle. "Hear, O Israel, the Lord your God is one God."

He said words of thanks for his brother Antipas, killed twenty days before. They said, "Amen," together as a way of agreeing with the prayer. Sweet aromas made them conscious of their hunger.

Lyris, the widow, brought hot bread and warm milk from the kitchen, and Simon broke the flatbread into pieces. Using a wooden spoon, he spread soft cheese and honey on the hot bread. The servant woman went back and forth between the kitchen and the dining area several times. Lyris kept piling on more dried fruits, nuts, warm bread, and sliced cucumbers.

Heber's birthday had put everyone in a good mood.

"Having soldiers guarding our house has made this a secure place to work with gold!" Simon began. "I was never so safe until Anthony came!" It was his first positive comment about their unwelcome situation.

"And I'm happy too," said Miriam, smiling. "What would I do if the guards weren't keeping my husband here with me? How would I feel if he had to stay in the barracks all day?"

Simon watched Ateas and Arpoxa, who were looking at each other, grinning and holding hands. In their homeland, north of the Black Sea, they were never able to enjoy sitting like this with a warm-hearted family. Ateas, the tallest man present, had laid his crutches beside the couch, and he smiled lovingly at Arpoxa.

Yesterday, Arpoxa had whispered in her language, rubbing his blond beard, saying that she was going to sew a set of Scythian clothes for the little girl, Amath.

SIMON'S WORKSHOP

Breakfast was over, and Simon's work apron was tied around his waist. He bent over his small forge, bringing the dull coals back to life.

"May I see the working shop?" asked Ateas, who stood outside the doorway, interrupting Simon's reverie. The long room smelled of fire and smoke, leather protective clothing, and sweat-covered tools. While the young man's ability to speak in Greek was still limited, he longed to use his skills in workmanship.

The young man's head was half in the doorway, and Simon was pumping the bellows to blow air through the glowing charcoal.

"Come in," Simon invited, but his voice indicated irritation at being interrupted. He heated a thick strip of gold, wrapped it onto a round iron cylinder, and tapped the ends to weld them together. He held the ring close to the window, examining it. With the gold soft enough to shape, the goldsmith pushed the band farther down the cylinder. This enlarged the diameter, and he used tools to develop the design on the surface.

Ateas watched, taking in every detail. "What are you making?"

"This is a man's ring, I sell many of them in my shop."

Ateas walked over on his crutches, bent down, looked carefully, and hesitated. "If you are making this...longer and spreading that one out more...like an eagle flying. I am riding a horse...traveling to east...mountains of white snows...men with slanting eyes. Horses are stopping for resting and eating...always watching eagles floating in the sky."

It was a long explanation for Ateas, and Simon waited for each phrase as the story continued. "I am coming home...two long trips. After that, my leg useless. Wall of the well collapsed...unfinished well. Not riding horses anymore...broken leg. Now I am making pots...birds floating...Grandpa Antipas is taking ideas, and I am painting pottery."

Ateas spoke without bragging about his trips or his outstanding work as a guard on the Silk Highway.

The lame man was better as an artist working with his hands than speaking Greek. "I can be making delicate rings...showing eagles," he said.

Simon, realizing that Ateas had a new idea, stepped away from the workbench. Intrigued by the story of the young man's travels, he pulled up a bench and sat down. He motioned for Ateas to use his tools.

Ateas heated the gold and added a bit more, forming the wing of a bird. He added another bit, but it didn't look right, so he decided to melt the ring and start again. By noon, working together, Simon and Ateas had created a golden eagle soaring silently on a man's ring.

Uncle Simon called Anthony before the family left for the Sabbath service. "You are confined and can't come with us to the synagogue, so you will care for Grace tonight, Anthony. Ateas and Arpoxa are also staying. For once, you will have quiet without my grandchildren singing, running, and making so much noise. When we get back, we'll enjoy Heber's birthday party. I am inviting you to join us for the celebration. Lyris will also be here in the kitchen, preparing the meal while we are gone."

Since Anthony had arrived at their house, these were Simon's kindest words to the prisoner.

THE SYNAGOGUE OF SARDIS ON THE ROYAL ROAD

This evening the gossip being whispered around the synagogue was about the Simon Ben Shelah family. One man asked, "Why is the family bringing disgrace to the Jewish community?"

His question was met with another. "What could be the cause of soldiers taking turns to guard their home?"

The Jews in Sardis were of two minds. Some wished they, too, had guards. That would keep their property safe. Others made cruel jests, reminding Simon how Romans had destroyed their holy city two decades before.

Jakob went to his home and reclined at his table with his wife. "I'm in the middle of negotiating with the city to get us special privileges. Is the Ben Shelah family going to make this difficult for me? I'm afraid that the city council will see us as being an unruly, complicated bunch. One of our people has to be guarded by the military!"

SIMON AND JUDITH'S HOME

Simon talked with Judith as they were walking home from the synagogue. "I invited Anthony to the meal."

Judith frowned and whispered, "What made you change your mind? I thought Anthony was to eat every meal upstairs as long as he stays in our home! And now you want him with us at a family birthday party?"

At home, everyone was cheerful. Simon watched Anthony come downstairs to join Miriam, while Grace stayed upstairs with Arpoxa and Saulius. Lyris, the servant, was serving lamb cut up into bite-sized pieces. Steam rose from lentils cooked with spices placed inside flatbread. Lyris brought more trays of food from the kitchen.

Simon was in a happy mood. He laughed at anything Lyris said. A large part of his happiness came from the successful new ring design, and he had a new appreciation for Ateas, the lame ex-slave. The time spent with the crippled man provided him with an item that would sell well. Ateas had said there were also other ring designs that they could try.

He raised a cup of wine, saying, "I'm going to ask Miriam to tell us about her marriage to Anthony. It's not often that we have a prisoner who is forced to stay in our home. I think we need to know more about this unfortunate man. But he's married to Miriam, so we must say he's fortunate." Laughter sounded from around the table. "But first we have a meal to eat."

Lyris had been with the Ben Shelah family for many years. Long white hairs showed against dark black ones beneath her scarf. All loved Lyris, and she reciprocated with hard work born of love.

The name Lyris meant "one who plays the harp." The widow did not play the harp, but she did play the flute and appreciated music. Lyris broke into song one day, and Miriam asked her if she wanted to learn some new tunes. So while working together in the kitchen, Lyris was learning many of Miriam's songs.

She learned both the tunes and the words. By nature, she was outgoing, often completing something being said by others. Her quick, spontaneous comments made people laugh. Sometimes her references were about how much Uncle Simon was eating or how slowly Aunt Judith was walking.

She placed a cheese dish on the table and asked everyone to eat her olive paste. If someone fell ill, she could heal them quickly, "If only you would eat more of my food!"

"Lyris, before Miriam talks, would you explain to her how you became a widow?" Simon asked.

"Certainly! My husband was a good man. We had only been married for six months, and I was expecting, but I was beaten by boys who yelled and screamed at me. I lost both the baby and my husband during the anti-Jewish riots. That was when Nero was emperor."

When the meal was over and the plates were back in the kitchen, Miriam began, "Our wedding was very dull. No other word will do. It was basic if you compare it to a Jewish wedding."

She smiled. "But if you are a Roman, you would say it was a decent wedding!"

"Better explain all that since your husband is right beside you," Judith said with a sour expression. That brought giggles from Elaine, Tamir, and Amath.

"Well, since it's a long story and it's also getting late, I promise that Anthony and I will describe further details later. We'll tell all about our wedding and the ceremony for adopting Grace."

As they lay down to sleep, Judith opened herself up to her husband. Deep lines marked her face. "How I wish our son-in-law Ravid was in better spirits! Simon, his words are cutting, more severe. He's increasingly distant and says his father is pure, more dedicated to the Lord."

Long after Simon had gone to sleep, she continued her thoughts in silence. *Oh, my daughter Nissa! You still do not have a child! If Ravid was a Gentile, he might have left you for another woman.*

But Ravid is not like that! My little grandchildren have no idea how complicated life gets—how emotions, bitterness, and selfishness get the better of us!

THE ACROPOLIS, PERGAMUM

The morning sun shone brightly on the acropolis in Pergamum, where an important meeting was in session. Lydia-Naq had suggested that Diotrephes hold a conference with the three leading priests of the temples on the acropolis. She sent an invitation to Damon, Nestor, and Mehu. The time had come to inform them that her son had a spy watching Marcos, the lawyer, and the House of Prayer.

Damon, the high priest of the Imperial Temple, responded, "So, Diotrephes, are you paying someone for information about Marcos and the new meetings at his house?"

"Yes, he has been bringing me details of what has been going on there.""

Nestor, the high priest of the Altar of Zeus, beamed. "That's just what we need—someone to give us inside information!"

Diotrephes puckered his brow. "My spy's name is Yorick. He still has his job at the village, but I would not be surprised if he were fired by Onias, Antipas's village supervisor. Yorick is not a good worker."

"Is he trustworthy for our needs?" Damon asked.

"As long as he is paid, yes, but he goes through money faster than water running down a mountain into a stream. Before being ransomed by Antipas, Yorick was a slave, but he never fit in well in the village. He wants higher pay for his job of mixing perfumes."

Mehu, the high priest of the New Temple being constructed by Egyptians in the lower part of the city, added, "These atheists know strong magic. After their leader was killed, Marcos, one of the most important men in the city council, has taken a leadership role. I want Yorick to bring us the names of everyone attending the meetings. If Marcos starts teaching beliefs against our gods, he will be treated the same way Antipas was."

THE INSULAE, LAODICEA

When Little Lion tried again to explain his hopes of being a soldier to his mother, he was not surprised by her harsh reply.

"My son, you cannot leave me here alone to go join the army! If anything happened to you, I would starve in the streets. You have a regular job with the Meres family, bringing wood to the hot baths, and your job does provide for our needs. Why would you want to leave and join the army? I need you here to survive!"

""Mother, I don't want to carry wood all my life. I am young and strong!"

"I won't hear about it again! I'm a widow and frail. How would I get food? Where would I live?"

"Don't worry! The army pays regularly, and I will send money to you."

Little Lion decided not to tell her he had already asked men at the baths how to enlist in the Roman army.

Chapter 9
Eliab's Will

SIMON AND JUDITH'S HOME

On Friday, about midafternoon, a postal courier dismounted, bringing another letter from Pergamum. Simon paid the delivery fee and quickly skimmed over the contents. He decided to wait until their meal after the Pentecost service tonight to tell Miriam the details.

Marcos, the family lawyer, had written the letter to share his grief with her and to let her know he was working to fulfill the requirements laid out in two wills.

May 8 in the 10th year of Domitian
From: Marcos Aelius Pompeius, in Pergamum

To: Simon Ben Shelah and Miriam Bat Johanan in Sardis

Grace and peace through the kindness of God our Father and Yeshua.

I am writing because I learned from Jonathan in Thyatira that Miriam has safely arrived at your home. Please give her this letter to read.

Antipas was like a father to many, a dear friend. He was called to testify at two trials. The first took place in the Roman theater on April 19, and he gave a good witness. Confronted by priests, he told the crowd about the Messiah: Yeshua's life, service, death, and resurrection. He captivated the crowd of over 15,000.

On Sunday, three days later, he was led to the great amphitheater. An even more massive crowd watched. Antipas gave a powerful testimony when questioned by the high priest of the Imperial Temple. Although he paid his taxes for the year, he refused to declare, "Caesar is lord and god." Rebellion against the authorities was the accusation leveled against him. They took that as a political act and led him inside the area prepared for the New Temple. A large kettle shaped like an ox, originally used in the old Temple of Artemis, was filled with oil, and brought to a boil. As Antipas was being lowered toward the oil, a timber fell in, and the fire spread. Antipas died almost instantly. Only his bones remained to be removed once the fire had died down.

Most of the people who attended the Household of Faith continue in their commitment to the covenant. Miriam and Anthony stayed in the house next to mine, and that house has now become our new meeting place. We will no longer gather at the cave in Antipas's village. We have a new name too, the House of Prayer.

Differences between Jews and Gentiles compelled me to form two worship groups. Also, the house does not comfortably accommodate everyone in our assembly. I am not a teacher, and we really need someone here to instruct in the ways of the covenant and ministry of the Messiah. Onias needs a helper. Pray for a teacher to come and help us.

Marcella and I send our sympathies. Everyone is praying for you.

Miriam, this letter is also about your grandfather's will. I owe much to Antipas for the recovery of health to Florbella, my daughter, and building up my faith in the covenant. So I will not be charging the Ben Shelah family for my legal services.

Simon, the following section of this letter, about the two wills, has been copied to Joshua in Smyrna, Daniel in Laodicea, Amos in Philadelphia, and Jonathan in Thyatira. I am also sending similar letters to your two brothers and sister in Alexandria, Egypt.

To summarize, here in Asia Minor, there are six heirs: five brothers and Miriam. Three more are in Egypt: two brothers and one sister.

The city council of Pergamum wanted to expropriate the village. I have managed to prevent that by showing that it would cost the city too much money for legal fees. Antipas's property will continue to operate as before.

The two wills appear to be contradictory. First, Eliab Ben Shelah's will: He wanted his entire estate divided into ten shares and given to the nine living children of the Ben Shelah family. Amos, as the oldest son, is to receive two of the ten shares. Each of the other eight will receive one share. There is no mention in Eliab's will about improvements to the property, such as the workshops and houses.

All those are to be awarded through the second will.

Antipas wrote the second document. In his will, he left his entire estate to Miriam. If my recommendations below are accepted, Miriam will be a wealthy woman.

I presented the two wills in court. The court determined that a conflict exists between the two documents.

The judge stated, "According to Eliab's will, the property is to be divided between eight brothers and one sister. I must point out that these two questions remain: First, does Eliab's will include the buildings and workshops since it was written many years ago? That will was written before Antipas made all the improvements. Secondly, can Pergamum legally expropriate the village?"

The answer I gave the first question was no. Eliab, the old man, bought the land. However, all improvements made in the village were paid for by Antipas. No one ever suggested that Eliab lived in rebellion against Rome, as they did against Antipas, so there is no reason for a penalty, an expropriation, against Eliab's estate. Therefore, the first will cannot be challenged.

However, about the second question, the possible expropriation of the village, Antipas's will may undoubtedly be challenged later.

Specifically, what does "Antipas's' estate" include? The shed, which he called the Cave; a huge warehouse for supplies like sand and clay; the kiln; the pottery workshop and the glass blowing studio; a storage area for olives and workshop for making olive soap; the carpentry shop; the shed for wagons; a large shed for the horses; the thirty-eight houses in the village; two shops at the acropolis; and two shops in cities along the Aegean Coast.

The court asked me for a solution, so here are the recommendations. I am considering two jurisdictions, in Egypt and in Asia Minor.

Asia Minor is a senatorial province governed by the Senate. Egypt is an imperial province under the authority of the emperor. So in dealing with two different courts, a Senatorial Court decision made in Ephesus must also be accepted by the Imperial Court in Alexandria, Egypt.

As soon as I have word from the office of Claudius Varro Zosimus, the procurator for Asia, I will inform you of the options for settling the estate with the heirs. As mentioned before, I am sending a copy of this letter to each of the families in Alexandria.

I pray for peace and comfort for each of you.

ON THE ROYAL ROAD, SARDIS

For the second time in two evenings, the Ben Shelah family walked to the center of the city. Judith took Simon's arm, and they talked together. The Pentecost service had brought back some of her best childhood memories.

Simon bent close to her ear and said, "Isn't life a constant surprise? Just think! We are forced to 'give hospitality' to a Roman soldier. My niece, recently married, is in mourning, as are we, since my brother was killed three weeks ago. A former slave who uses crutches teaches me new skills in my workshop. And a lame woman cares for Miriam's baby. But Miriam is not the real mother!"

Moving slowly because of her aches and pains, Judith chuckled. "Imagine us feeding a legionary in our house after Roman soldiers starved our family in Jerusalem! Still, we don't have to pay for the protection that the guards are giving us night and day!" For the first time, she was willing to see a touch of humor in the situation.

Her husband replied, "Antipas had to pay taxes the same as non-Jews, but he did not declare, 'Caesar is lord and god.' He kept his integrity though it cost him his life. I received a letter from Marcos today explaining all that. I'll read it to everyone after we get home tonight."

They passed their shop, already locked, and bolted, unlike the other shops, which were still open. Suddenly Simon whispered, "Miriam and Anthony didn't even have a betrothal! A wedding without a proper betrothal! For a betrothal, we would have been invited to go to Pergamum. Join in with their family, you know?"

Judith murmured a tart comment, for that thought had been with her for days. "Well, it was Roman! Typically unmemorable and substandard. They weren't sleeping together before they were married. I trust Miriam when she says the baby came from another woman. Look at Grace's eyes. Completely different from Miriam's and Anthony's! Anyone can see Grace is not Miriam's and Anthony's baby!"

"Hush! Now don't you go asking around saying, 'Was this their baby or not?' I know the questions you women ask!"

"Well, I'm worried about Nissa," Judith said, changing the topic. "She desperately wants a baby."

"Ravid's gone on, far ahead of us, and look how Nissa has to walk quickly to keep up with him. In my workshop, he hardly says a word these days. If he says more than 'I need that tool,' it's always to point out a flaw. I never met anyone better at noticing tiny details. These days, he comes to work, makes his jewelry, and goes back to their quarters. Why, he hardly says a word to me! He's stopped Nissa from coming to meals with us. I don't think he will ever accept Anthony."

"And you, my husband, are you starting to willingly accept a soldier staying in our home?"

"Maybe. I invited Anthony to eat with us again. The grandchildren asked for him to come."

"Yes, and for that reason, neither Ravid nor Nissa are coming to eat at our table."

SIMON AND JUDITH'S HOME

The family returned from worship at the synagogue and gathered in the great room for the evening meal. Judith had them all sit around the table, and soon the conversation turned to questions about Miriam's wedding.

Lyris appeared from the kitchen. "What kind of dress did you wear for your wedding, Miriam? Did you weave flowers into your hair? Or wear a special belt made of soft lamb's leather, like the people of Sardis do?"

Heber leaned across the table and made everyone laugh again. "Miriam, did Anthony have to work that day, or were you the only one in his thoughts?"

Simon raised his hand, wanting to make a statement. "Why don't we hear about this from Anthony? Miriam, fill in all the details. Shall we see if Anthony remembers anything about it all?"

Judith did not appreciate the smile that came over Anthony's face. Her turned-down lips hid the sudden anger springing up in her heart. Right now, she would not tell her husband how irritated she was. But when they went to bed that evening, sharp words were sure to come out. She clenched her fists as she listened.

"The first thing we had to solve was my being Roman and Miriam being Jewish," Anthony began. "Miriam's grandpa, Antipas, was not happy with me since I am a reservist. Before I arrived in Pergamum, he had built a long shed along the side of a cliff. It was near the bottom of his property. He called it 'The Cave' and held the Household of Faith meetings there. He was happy enough to have me come to learn of the Messiah but was against me becoming part of his family!"

Soft giggles were stifled from the children.

"Miriam wanted to marry me, and I wanted to marry her. After I asked him for permission, Antipas thought about it for many months. Finally, he called me in one day and asked me if I ever worshiped idols. I said, 'No, I have never worshiped a man-made image.' Somehow that satisfied him. The next thing we knew, we were in the cave, and he was telling everyone we were betrothed."

"How exciting," Elaine exclaimed. "Miriam, you must have been so happy. How long were you betrothed, a year like Father talks about?"

Miriam wanted Anthony to keep speaking, so he kept on. "No! We did not have a proper Jewish betrothal! Instead, Grandpa Antipas decided we should be married quickly. I know now that he was aware that he might face death soon. I did give Miriam a ring, but I can't remember much else."

Everyone laughed because their suspicions were confirmed. Men could not remember much about essential details.

"Miriam's turn," pronounced Judith. "Tell us more about Grace coming to your home." She looked forward to learning more about the story of the unknown mother.

Miriam looked around at her family. She held Grace up for all the family to see. "Chrysa Grace is a gift from heaven. I don't even know who gave her birth! But I pray that someday I will meet her mother. Grace came to me in February, just three months ago. I had been told that an unknown man would bring her in a wagon to the edge of the city refuse dump."

Everyone gasped. Who would leave a baby to die out in the open, all alone?

"A woman who was not the mother, someone I had never seen before, climbed down from a wagon. She placed the baby carefully at the edge of the dump! She waved to me. I was standing a little way away and wanted to talk to her. I would have asked who the mother was and why she was giving away a baby. But I was so moved that I burst into tears. The wagon drove off.

"As you know, many baby girls are abandoned, but I loved her the moment I picked her up. My heart was pounding. One moment I was a woman without a child, and the next I walked into the city just like a thousand other young women who come and go. I knew that this little one was special. After I took her home, Grandpa said, 'Keep the baby until we find a home for her.'

"Anthony told you just a little bit about our engagement. Do you mind if I tell you more?"

Judith nodded. Everyone else wanted to know the full story.

"Grandpa definitely didn't want Anthony to be part of the Ben Shelah family. His army uniform made him an enemy. However, Grandpa had been teaching, 'Our Messiah changes everything. We can no longer look down on others because of appearances, traditions, language, or customs.' I could tell from his moodiness that Grandpa was caught in a tug-of-war. We've never had a non-Jew in our family. However, Grandpa was teaching people about Yeshua's acceptance of all people.

"One day Grandpa called us together. He was so jolly and wanted us married. The wedding was planned to be in Marcos's house. Marcos is our lawyer in Pergamum, and he, too, became a Messiah follower because of Grandpa."

She laughed. "How simple a Roman wedding is! There is nothing to it! You simply stand in front of the magistrate with a few witnesses. Marcos even had to tell the witnesses where to stand! The magistrate asked Anthony three questions about the adoption documents: Is this your name? Were these your parents? Is this where you live?

"He asked me the same questions. We said yes to each question. Then, 'Are you committed to each other for life?' Anthony said yes, and I said, yes! The judge said, 'Then you are married.' That is all! Nothing more! Oh, Romans have no imagination! They require no ceremony. No beautiful canopy of blue over your head and no words of blessing!"

Judith exploded, "This is not how a Jewish girl should get married!" Sitting up, she used her hands to emphasize her thoughts. She looked to both sides and spoke with gusto. "When Simon and I were married in Alexandria, we enjoyed a week of festivities. A full week! A proper marriage should take a year to plan. Everyone has to give their own ideas of what should happen!"

Memories returned, and Judith described events in Alexandria forty-one years before. "We had no end of jubilation, fun, laughter, and festivities! The best man put on a party for Simon one night. Another evening, my best friends, the girls, put on a party. I can still remember it. They made fun of me and thanked me for my friendship. One woman recited poetry, and the evening ended with my favorite songs.

"It took us a week, not two minutes, to get married. Anthony, if it takes only two minutes for the wedding, you might get 'unmarried' after a short fight. But if the ceremony takes a week, all the relatives get involved. A marriage becomes everyone's business! Simon and I will always have each other. In a Jewish family, it costs a lot. And when you are married, you are really married!" Her lips were tight together, and she spat out the words, "Not like a Roman wedding!"

Simon gave Judith a soft poke in her ribs as he interrupted her. "Anthony, Romans build bridges and theaters, aqueducts and water systems, so I think you should do better for a really complex thing—like a wedding!"

His comment made Anthony burst into laughter, and everyone laughed. Anthony could take a good teasing.

But Judith was not finished asking questions. "Antipas didn't want you together, so how...?"

Miriam interrupted, "Anthony was an army instructor, but he had one afternoon off every week. On Tuesdays, he came to the shop where I was working. Slowly, he built up trust with me, and I saw his good character."

Arpoxa listened, happy to be at the table. She was feeding her infant son, Saulius. Ateas leaned over and spoke to her in a quiet voice. He spoke in Scythian so none of the others could understand.

"I never knew we would find a love like this. Uncle Antipas paid an expensive ransom to get us out of slavery. He built our house and made us part of his Household of Faith, but who could imagine us living in this beautiful home in Sardis?"

She answered him in Scythian, "And we've stayed together! Remember that terrible day when the slave master put us up for sale? They took all our clothes off, walked us onto the slaver's platform, and auctioned us off. I was so afraid that you and I would be sold to different slave masters!"

"Yes, I feared that ever since we were married in Chalcedon by that temple priest, remember? Listen, I have been making gold eagles on rings for Simon. He is pleased but hasn't said anything to the family about it. And Miriam is going to ask him to have you start doing embroidery work on linen tunics. You will help their business just like you used to do for Antipas. I will help Simon create some new jewelry designs too. We aren't much good in the legs, but we can both use our hands!"

Arpoxa leaned against him. "I love being in a family. They are so fortunate here. In Scythia, every family lives with troubles. I told you that I was sold by my brother to pay off his horse-racing debts. And you had to dig the well. When the wall fell in, it broke your leg and pinned you all day at the bottom. I'm happy to live here in Sardis, where everything is peaceful."

Lying in bed late at night, Elaine kept trying to place herself into Miriam's story. Isidoros, about whom she dreamed so often, was her age.

She had not told anyone yet about the new feelings she felt stirring in her heart, only Star, her favorite horse.

If only Grandfather would invite Hector's parents to come to the Ben Shelah home. If only I could meet them here! Then Isidoros might be able to come here more often.

Chapter 10
The Games

THE STADIUM OF SARDIS, THE ACROPOLIS

Over the years, an agreement had been reached between the five most important cities in Asia Minor. The Games were crucial to each region, and sports programs took into account the weather, the harvest, and travel time between cities.

Each year, sports games began in Ephesus about April 15, concluding five days later. Then they rotated through Smyrna, Pergamum, Sardis, and Laodicea. In this way, competitions in the most populated centers included all the provinces' best athletes. By the time hot weather arrived in the middle of June and the early harvest began, athletes were back in their homes.

More than 15,000 spectators, mostly men, were screaming and urging on their favorite athletes at this year's games. The stadium in Sardis ran from east to west. It filled a flat area along the lower slope of the acropolis. At the east end was the Greek Theater. Most spectators sat on stone seats built around the stadium. When there was no more room around the track, others moved up the hill and crowded onto a grass-filled area overlooking the stadium.

The stadium running track was a long oval. A pair of parallel running tracks rounded with a sharp bend at each end. This forced runners to slow down for a moment. Just like the Great Stadium in Athens, the track length was one *stadia.* Winners in Sardis competed in Ephesus the following year. Then, if an athlete was an overcomer in Ephesus, the victory brought an invitation to Athens. Every four years, champions from many provinces competed at the most prestigious Games in the empire.

Hector was competing today, and he looked up to the viewing stands around the running track. Three men in his family were together near the starting line: Jace, his father; Isidoros, his older brother; and Eugene, his grandfather.

And there, beside Isidoros, was his best friend, Tamir Ben

Shelah.

The midmorning air was perfect for this race. The runners had just completed the first lap. Five and a half more lengths would require every ounce of energy. The race promised much excitement before the winner crossed the finish line. At the end of the seventh stretch, one athlete would be crowned the champion.

Hector felt alive, aware that he should not use all his energy too early. Another runner might win by overtaking him at the end of the race. He wanted to catch up to Athan, who was ahead of him, but when Hector sped up, he became uncoordinated. His shoulders felt off balance, so he slowed a bit to regain his equilibrium.

As the runners rounded the second bend, he took a quick look at the viewing stand. Tamir, his fourteen-year-old friend, was screaming. The veins on his neck stuck out, and his face was red.

Hector heard screams from men as he passed close by them.

One shouted, "Athan will win. He's ahead but only by a little!"

Another yelled, "I love watching the Under-Sixteens race!"

Hector was on Athan's heels now, and as they entered the third stretch, they were running neck and neck.

The stands around the stadium overflowed with fathers, friends, and spectators. Loud voices filled the air as the boys raced naked.

In the middle of the third lap, Hector felt a strain in his right side and let up slightly. He had caught up to Athan but could not take the lead. Straining every muscle and looking ahead, he thought, *If I come in first, I'll run in Ephesus, maybe even in Athens! But first I must pass Athan!*

At the next abrupt turn, Hector glanced back to see the competition. Behind him were the other twenty runners.

He faced the stretch and took his eye off the track for a second. Once again, he took in his three family members and Tamir.

Running down the fourth stretch, he remembered a conversation the day before. He and Tamir were walking out of the gymnasium, ready for the public holiday. Various sporting events would take place throughout the day.

"I'm hoping to win, Tamir," Hector said. "I have a plan for victory tomorrow. Here's what I'm going to do in the race: I'll stay close to Athan and rush past him at the end!"

"I would love to be there to watch you race, Hector, but my mother will disapprove. She doesn't want me watching Gentiles competing in sports activities."

So Tamir came! He must have gotten approval from his parents.

Spectators were screaming as athletes rounded the bend. Hector felt sweat pouring down his face. He looked back as the screams died down for just an instant. One boy had bumped into another, and both had fallen. Back on their feet now, they resumed the race, but they were several steps behind.

Yelling from the spectators grew louder as the young athletes rounded the fifth curve and all were closer to the end of the race. Hector grinned at his father, Jace, who was waving his arms over his head. Jace's students from the gymnasium were there too, all grouped in the same area. All were jumping up and down, cheering on their classmate.

Isidoros, like his father, was standing on the stone bench. Hector's brother's voice rang out above the others. "Faster, Hector! Watch out for that boy beside you, coming up on your left! He's going to overtake you! Keep him behind you! Go! Go! Go faster! Oh no! Don't let Athan get so far out in front!"

Hector also saw his grandfather, Eugene, shouting louder than he had for decades.

But his breath was running out! His arms were swinging wildly, and his feet felt out of alignment. Hector dodged a runner who was entering into the sixth length, but the maneuver caused him to lose his concentration.

He gasped for air as Athan gained slightly. Two boys passed Hector, and suddenly he was in fourth place. Finding hidden strength, the young runner sprinted by one of them and found himself in third place. He stayed there around the sixth and final bend.

They had completed the long track six times. On the last stretch, only a short distance separated the four runners. As they approached the finish line, Hector was gasping. Pain jolted every bone in his body.

Hector turned back and saw a runner gaining on him. With a final spurt of energy, he put more distance between him and his new challenger.

But now Athan was raising his arms in triumph!

Disappointment covered Hector's face. An instant earlier, Athan had been the first runner over the finish line. And here he was, celebrating his win with his father and friends!

Hector's rival in his father's classroom was the new champion of the "Under-Sixteens."

Hector fell to the ground on his hands and knees, gasping for air as if he were drowning. He wanted better training and coordination. *I might have finished second, but I slipped back close to the finish line. I ended in fifth place.*

He stood up slowly and waved to his grandfather, father, and brother. What else could he do but grin? He walked back and hugged Jace. Standing beside Isidoros was his best friend, Tamir.

Hector vowed that he would be the winner next year. Somehow, he would become a better runner.

THE INSULAE OF SARDIS

Gaius felt a bit stronger today. He lived on the top floor of an apartment building at the edge of the city's impoverished section. For the hundredth time, he shook his head in frustration.

How can anyone get a good night's rest around here? Too many people, too much noise, and too many husbands yelling. So much anger at their wives and children!

The people in the next apartment seemed to be continuously crying, fighting, or singing. Life in the insulae was a constant commotion. Bringing water and food up to his small apartment wearied him too. He took the chamber pot down to the open sewer each morning. Unfortunately, the steps were not safe because they were slippery, so they demanded extra care during the rainy season, from November to April.

In this part of Sardis, many were sick and wounded. People lived in poverty. Accidents had affected several of Gaius's neighbors. One man was injured while cutting down a tree, and now he was lame. He made a meager living by carrying wood. He loaded it on his back and hobbled along with a crutch under his armpit.

Another worker was partially blind. He had been shaping a marble block into a round pillar for the new buildings at the Western Agora when a chip of stone punctured his eye.

Gaius worked in the Ben Shelah shop until noon. Usually he made afternoon visits to people interested in learning more about the Way. Today he decided to visit the home of a woman he had met when she was shopping for clothes in Simon's shop. Soon she started attending the meetings at the portico. At the last meeting, she began asking questions. Before leaving, she asked, "Why did Jerusalem suffer so much destruction?"

She met Gaius at the door and invited him in. Their conversation revealed her deep fears. Tomorrow, Gaius decided, he would return to this home. He would tell her how the Messiah had overcome the worst fear of all, the fear of death.

THE STADIUM OF SARDIS

On the last day of the Games, crowds gathered at the stadium to wait for the victors' parade. Several athletes were champions in various races and raised their hands in thanksgiving to Nike, the goddess of victory.

Athan drew himself up to his full height, ready to be crowned in a long line of young athletes. His family and friends would always remember this day.

The victors lined up inside the gymnasium to begin the parade to the stadium. Athan waited for the mayor, who would lead the procession. Mayor Tymon Tmolus was wearing a white linen toga lined with a purple hem, the Roman mark of honor and dignity. In his right hand, he carried the symbol of Sardis, a golden incense burner.

Behind him came forty-eight athletes lined up in pairs, the winners of various sports: the discus throw, javelin, wrestling, running, and jumping.

The youngest champion, Athan, walked beside Mayor Tymon Tmolus during the parade. The procession left the broad central court of the gymnasium and then turned east onto the Royal Road.

The Royal Road was lined with thousands of excited spectators cheering as the Parade of Champions passed by. The procession, accompanied by musicians, climbed the lowest section of the acropolis, and entered the stadium at its western end.

Still walking beside the mayor around the stadium's running track, Athan was followed by the other victors. People in the stands screamed with joy as the victors passed by. Arriving at the place of honor, they stood proudly. These seats were reserved for the most prominent citizens. Tymon Tmolus stopped at a polished white marble throne and turned to face the spectators.

Standing on a step below the mayor, Athan waved in victory. The young man wore a new white linen tunic, symbolizing victory. His father rejoiced at being able to give him this expensive gift.

As Athan bowed low, voices fell quiet. A crown of green laurel leaves was placed on his head, and then thousands broke out in shouts, chanting his name. "Athan! Athan!"

Next Tymon Tmolus gave the young champion the most coveted trophy, a headband made of gold. With the laurel wreath on his head, Athan raised the golden band high over his head and in a loud voice shouted, "Never enough gold!"

The crowds filling the stadium yelled back, shouting with all their strength, "Never enough gold!"

While Mayor Tymon Tmolus awarded the prizes to the remaining victors, a passionate feeling stirred in Hector's heart.

I shall win the race against Athan next year!

SIMON AND JUDITH'S HOME

It was a special day in the Ben Shelah home. The month of mourning for Antipas had come to an end. Black prayer shawls were removed, and the black cloths covering the couches in the large living area had been put away. Judith raised her hands to the heavens one more time, thankful for a faithful brother-in-law who had stayed committed until death. She was the keeper of important family events, and she wrote in her diary. "May 22: The end of our outward mourning for Antipas. His memory will always remain with us."

THE INSULAE OF LAODICEA

Little Lion's heart jumped as he read the letter he had just received from the Garrison of Sardis. He was to be present there on September 1 for an acceptance interview. He counted off the days and calculated how long he had to bring his mother around to his thinking.

I don't want to go without her consent, but I must join the army. All the stories I've ever heard about the military make me want to be a hero, to stand at the front, serving in the Roman army against our enemies.

SIMON AND JUDITH'S HOME

On Sunday evening, a few days before the longest day of the year,

Jace brought his family on a visit to Simon's house. Chenya had wanted to know more about Jace and had asked Simon to send an invitation to the family to come for supper.

Lyris brought clean towels for the five visitors. A bowl of water was ready to wash their feet.

Jace smiled as Tamir introduced his family to the household. "Mother, this is Jace, my teacher at the gymnasium. You already know Isidoros and Hector, the two brothers. This is Jace's wife, Kalonice. And the older man here, Kalonice's father, is Eugene.

"Now Jace, Kalonice, and Eugene, these are my family members. Oh, and this is Miriam, my cousin. And Anthony is a soldier. He's staying in our home for a few days."

Standing slightly off toward the dining area, Jace noticed Elaine blushing. He saw her red cheeks and wondered what that meant.

Eugene excused himself, saying, "I don't mind working in the kitchen. I think I'll help there rather than be at the table. It's what I do every day...always preparing meals for our family." Jace knew about his father-in-law's aches and pains. The old man was still physically strong, but his slower movements gave away his age.

Before the evening meal was served, Simon hushed the jabber and stopped the games being played by the youngsters in the room.

A sheep had been butchered, and small squares of cooked meat were served. Family members filled pieces of flatbread with lentils, beans, onions, and spices. The first fruits of the year were tasty. Lyris mixed berries and a few nuts with last season's dried apricots before serving a dessert.

Once they were around the table, Simon said to Jace, "So your son aspires to be a champion?"

"Yes, his heart is set on it. He got it into his head six months ago that he wants to be an athlete." Jace was reclining close to Simon. "Hector wants to run faster next year. The only way that can happen is if he has someone to help him run better. Hector earns higher marks in rhetoric and history classes, yet with all his heart, my son wants to be the youngest 'overcomer' in the Games. However, I would prefer to see him study history and government. Those subjects would lead to law. Athletes don't make much money."

Chenya nodded to her father. The reason she had urged her father to invite Gentiles into their home lay in the questions they had been asking about what Tamir was learning in class.

Simon's words were tinged with reluctance. "Jace, I invited you to our home to learn what kind of an influence you are in the classroom. Before anything else, I must tell you that Tamir was disciplined for going to the stadium to watch the races. I'm sorry your son lost. I heard that he came in fifth.

"We are all here except for my son-in-law, Ravid, and Nissa, my daughter. Ravid isn't happy because Tamir is studying in a place filled with mostly non-Jews. In my home, my children are divided on this topic.

"It was Chenya, my daughter-in-law, who asked for you to come. She said, 'Before we judge Jace, the teacher, we should get to know if he is a bad influence.' She wants to know how and what you understand about discipline in your home. Also, you are a teacher of history, so we all have a question for you. As a family, we want to know this. Do you teach anything about our Jewish history?"

"Well, this is an excellent topic, and I'm happy to talk about it with you." Jace laughed. "I can see that I am going to enjoy today, not only the meal but also talking about ideas."

Throughout the meal, Jace noticed that Judith's smile seemed forced. He got the impression that she had a hidden animosity toward him.

Chenya began to shower Jace with questions. "What do you tell students about Sardis? Do you ever tell them how Jews came to live here? Do you only talk about all the kings and generals, or do you talk about the common people too?"

Jace's face brightened up further. At times, several people were talking at the same time. Chenya's questions led Jace to carefully explain his teaching methods and the content of his classes.

After a while, Heber, who had been watching, said, "I can see that you are only going to talk about Jace's work. Once you start talking about the olden times, my eyes glaze over. Father, I relish the chance to talk with the younger ones, so please let me give up my space at the table. I want to sit with my nieces. So much of my day is taken up with practical details—running the household farm, maintaining the sales shop, and keeping your business records."

The children had been sitting at tables in the great room. Heber joined Isidoros and Hector. Elaine, Tamir, and Amath completed the table with six persons.

Lyris served a meal with several courses. Arpoxa was feeding the babies, and Ateas stayed in the kitchen with Eugene.

Toward the end of the meal, Jace commented, "Anthony, Miriam said you coached athletes in Pergamum. Would you consider being a coach for Hector? My son desperately wants to be a runner and to win a race."

Anthony sat back and looked at Jace. "Why not?" he said with a matter-of-fact look. "I'm restricted to the house by the garrison, so training Hector would be the perfect thing to keep me active. We can use the sloped field out back as a practice area. It is rough ground and will help build stamina."

Jace did not tell them what he had done earlier that Sunday morning. He knew this Jewish family would not be happy with his having made an offering to the gods. The history teacher had gone to the Temple of Artemis to offer a sacrifice and to ask the goddess Nike to give Hector victory next year.

And now, this same day, in the Ben Shelah home, a Roman soldier was offering to train his son! Was this a sign that Artemis and Nike were blessing him? Would Nike answer his plea this quickly?

Kalonice, for her part, exclaimed loudly. She had learned that Miriam had married a Roman. Jace had learned a lot more about the Ben Shelah family. The conversation during mealtime focused on Jewish families. They talked about customs in their home and how were they different from non-Jews.

Jace overheard Kalonice's whisper. "Miriam, how is it that you, a Jewish girl, can be married to a Roman? I thought a Jewish girl could never be allowed to marry a Gentile!"

Suddenly, Kalonice became more animated. She commented on every plate, the fruit, and a cup of wine. Learning Miriam's story was bringing out something new, a different side of Kalonice's personality.

Even Jace, who was used to her spontaneity, was amazed at the sudden change. Then Jace glanced across the room at Hector.

The boy said, "I cannot not believe my good fortune. A soldier is going to help me become a better runner!"

Before Jace left for the evening, he stood next to Anthony, who was talking with Hector to establish the ground rules for the training. "We cannot train at the stadium because soldiers are taking care of me here, so this is where you will have to come. I will make you work awfully hard because you need more strength and better stamina. You will have to train on fields and run up and down the hills behind this property. Do you agree to train this way?"

During supper, Kalonice glanced across the room to the table where her boys sat with Elaine and Tamir. Kalonice noticed that Elaine seemed to be fond of her son, Isidoros. And she thought Isidoros was attracted to the Jewish girl who was about his age.

Kalonice found a moment to whisper, "Miriam, I think we have many things in common, and I want us to become friends. Would you let me introduce you to my acquaintances, Mayor Tymon Tmolus, and his wife, Panthea? You must also meet my friend Delbin and the other wealthy women in the city. I want you to meet the important people in this city, and I want to get to know you too."

Afterward, in the warm mid-June evening, Kalonice had much to think about as they walked home.

For the first time, I've found someone who is Jewish and married to a Gentile. Miriam will understand me better than anyone else. What will Jace say when I finally tell him I am half-Jewish? Until now, I never thought I could tell the full story of my mother, Jerusha.

Chapter 11
Answers

COMMANDER FELICIOR'S OFFICE, THE ACROPOLIS, SARDIS

A message arrived for Commander Felicior from Pergamum. The letter was written two days before, and the army courier system delivered it to him just before dusk. Two lamps were burning in his office. He left the scroll open with small weights on each corner as he thought through the implications of the message.

June 16, in the 10th year of Domitian:

From: Commander Cassius Flamininus Maro, Garrison of Pergamum

To: Commander Felicior Priscus, Garrison of Sardis

Further to your request for information about Anthony Suros. His orders originated in the army's offices of Rome. Due to wounds received during service in Upper Germanica, he was retired and awarded a small farm in Philippi.

He recovered and two years ago was sent from Philippi to Pergamum as a reservist trainer for scouts.

Continue to keep him under your care. House arrest is satisfactory for the present time. I will have his monthly salary transferred from Pergamum to Sardis.

There was no further explanation and no accusation. It seemed evident that Commander Cassius did not want Anthony to return. The transfer of his pay to Sardis would be necessary if Felicior accepted him as an instructor. Also, one letter would be sent to Ephesus informing them of the transfer, and another would be filed at the army headquarters in Smyrna. Felicior found nothing to prevent Anthony from being assigned as an instructor if he was under the garrison's watchful care.

There was only one accusation Felicior could formulate. Anthony's own mouth condemned him. The legionary had voiced opinions about the emperor that came close to being treasonous.

Felicior called a guard. "Tell Anthony Suros to come tomorrow at midmorning fully dressed and ready for inspection."

THE INSULAE, LAODICEA

Charmaine reached out for Little Lion, opening her arms wide as tears poured down her cheeks. She knew she could not hold him back because he was eighteen years old and wanted to leave Laodicea. He did not back away from a fight, even with tougher boys, and now he wanted to join the army.

"I am so afraid for you," she said, holding him close to her thin body. "I watched you grow up. You were always small and wiry. You are not afraid to confront boys who bully you."

"I'll be all right, Mother," he said quickly. "You don't have to worry. Look how many soldiers serve for twenty-five years and then retire. That's what I am going to do! I'll come back to you someday. I will have a little farm and care for you until you die."

She continued to weep, and tears splattered the floor. "You are agile but really do not know what fear is, my son. You know how to use your tongue, making all the others laugh, even when they bully you. You can imitate cruel boys. Your sharp wit is a strong defense. But Little Lion, you are not going to be facing bullies. There are barbarian enemies in Dacia! And enemies kill!"

"Mother, I am going to Sardis to become a legionary. I will send my wages to you. But first, I must be accepted. If I am accepted, my salary from the army will let you continue to live here. And I will still be here at home for six more weeks!"

Charmaine sobbed because of the determination she saw on his face and his desire to join the other recruits in Sardis.

SIMON AND JUDITH'S HOME

A soldier came to the main gate of the house and told Anthony that Felicior wanted him to report for inspection the next day.

Miriam said, "My dear, I am hoping for the best but fearing the worst." Her worries overwhelmed her, keeping her awake at night.

Miriam and Anthony talked long into the night, and she tried to reassure him, despite her own worries. "Who knows why you've been summoned to the garrison? You should not fear; that's what Grandpa said. He lived by the words of the Messiah. Remember what he said when we asked him what he was going to say in the Roman theater before his first trial? He said, 'Don't worry about what you are going to say when they call you before governors and kings because the words will be given to you.' When the time comes for you to talk with Commander Felicior, you'll have the right answers."

However, long after Anthony had gone to sleep, questions continued to keep Miriam awake. Snuggling up to him, she rested her head on his chest.

What will become of you, my love? Will you be sent back to Pergamum? I fear for your future. If you are sent back, what will happen to us, to Grace and me? God of our fathers, protect Anthony tomorrow, giving him wisdom in every word he says.

She did not know how else to pray.

THE GARRISON OF SARDIS, THE ACROPOLIS, SARDIS

Anthony woke up as the roosters announced the dawn. His uniform included a clean *chlamys,* the short, brown woolen mantle worn by soldiers. Around his waist, he strapped the military belt with his short sword. After greeting his house guards at the front gate, they escorted him to the garrison offices.

Commander Felicior waved him in, and the door was shut. "Soldier, a message arrived from Pergamum. Commander Cassius asked officers in Philippi to clarify your orders."

"I understand, sir," said Anthony. He was unable to determine from the abrupt introduction whether the interview was going to be favorable or not.

"In our first conversations, I learned this: You value honesty. Otherwise, you would not have risked your life by talking about the emperor. I want to know more about you."

"What would you like to know, sir?"

"You have unusual ideas. You are outspoken, and I am not sure I like it. You are a scout who supposedly knows more than his assigned commander in Pergamum. Your statements of support for the Senate and comments on Rome's present political situation are dangerous. Further, you did not declare full loyalty to Caesar. Just one of these concerns could be a cause for discipline. Taken together, they probably are sufficient for a court-martial."

Anthony tried to keep from blinking.

Obviously Felicior had been thinking a lot about what he had said. If the officer wanted to court-martial him, he would not have called him for an "inspection." Believing that he could be safe with the commander, he decided to speak openly. Miriam was right about what she had said last night: "Don't worry about what you will say. The right words will be given to you."

He drew himself to his full height. "May I speak openly with you, sir?"

"Permission granted."

"I joined the legion and was placed at the front, in the most dangerous areas. As a scout, I fought many battles. Do you want to know about those battles?"

Felicior dismissed the question with a wave of his hand. "No, I want to know about the course of events leading up to the rebellion in Upper Germanica."

Anthony realized Felicior was asking about Vettulenus Ceriales and the rebellion of the legions. "Flavius Vettulenus Civica Ceriales was my general until three years before the uprising, when he was promoted to be governor of Moesia.[11] Later he was assigned to Asia Minor as governor. Two years ago, he was publicly executed for rebellion.

"I had nothing to do with inciting any rebellion. I was affected directly by those circumstances. The leaders of two legions in Upper Germanica intended to keep their soldiers fighting together, but that meant disobeying orders from Rome.

"One day I overheard a conversation between two tribunes and a third person. I think he was an officer because he met with them in the officers' tent. Over the weeks, I found excuses to be in their tent again. They became used to my being there, I suppose. Their conversation included strategies to overcome villagers, but they began making political comments that only their general would be allowed to make. They wanted to be free of Domitian's commands. Moreover, they mentioned Nero favorably. Those two tribunes were expecting Nero to return from the dead to reclaim his position as emperor. Our general had no idea what was going on behind his

[11] Until AD 86, Moesia was a large province in southeastern Europe, presently including portions of Romania, Northern Bulgaria, Northern Macedonia, Kosovo, and Central Serbia. During his wars against Dacia, Emperor Domitian divided the province into Upper Moesia and Lower Moesia, using the Danube River as the boundary.

back."

After this stunning announcement, Felicior blinked several times. He leaned forward to catch every word.

"I reported what I had heard to our general. I risked everything by communicating to him instead of going to my immediate superior, my tribune. Two weeks later, I was assigned to a scouting patrol with a group along the Neckar River. The army had recently built a large wooden bridge crossing to the eastern side. A report came saying some Germanic tribesmen had been spotted close to the bridge supports. A new squad was formed immediately. All eight members of that squad were unknown soldiers to me. Once on the eastern side of the river, we talked to the guards there. They had not seen anyone. We walked under the bridge. The worry was that an intruder, or more than one barbarian, was preparing to damage or destroy the bridge.

"Under the bridge, the space was dark. As the light and shadows suddenly changed, I looked behind me toward the brighter light of outside. I ducked just as a sword came down on my head, but I went down, lunging around with my sword aimed at someone's leg. I can't remember what happened after that.

"I was unconscious and never saw any of those men again. I was found right away by another squad of scouts, but I almost died from loss of blood. That was May 19, four years ago. I spent a lot of time in a hospital, but then I was taken to Rome for questioning. What happened on that day was officially reported as 'very irregular.'

"Months later, after I dictated an incident report to the army chiefs, I was removed from active duty and not expected to live. Or if I did, the doctors thought that I would be an invalid, so they sent me to Philippi, and I was given a farm. But I did recover. I requested duty as an instructor and asked to be a reservist."

Felicior frowned. "Let me understand this: You suspected subversion, you reported it, and later you were ambushed and wounded. An investigation was held, but no one was found to have been responsible?"

"Yes. During the investigation, I was asked many questions. What the army learned was that some leaders in the legions resisted Domitian's authority. Those two legions were separated. Mine, the Predators, was sent to Pannonia and is now preparing to attack Dacia. Nothing of importance ever came out about the attack on me."

Felicior drew in his breath sharply. "But you were sent to Philippi?"

"The authorities in Philippi gave me a small farm because I had helped to calm barbarians, been wounded, and ended my active duty with sixteen years on the front. After recovering my strength, I told the commander of the Garrison of Philippi that I wanted to train scouts in Asia Minor."

Felicior came directly to the point. "Nothing you said has explained your difficulty with the commander of the garrison in Pergamum." It was a statement, not an accusation.

The threat of a military trial still stood over him, and Anthony knew he was in danger. "I will explain how and why I came into conflict with Commander Cassius Flaminius Maro in Pergamum.

"I was brought up in a home where the honor of the legions was legendary. All my friends wanted to be soldiers. My family home was not a happy place. My father took another woman while in Syria. My mother moved me from Damascus to Rome, and she became a follower of the Jewish Messiah there."

Anthony looked at the commander's long, lean face. *No reaction to what I've said, either negative or positive.*

"When I came to Pergamum, sir, I met many people. One of them was a Jew, a businessman from Alexandria, Egypt. He taught me many things about the Messiah."

Felicior interrupted, "That is interesting, but what does a man from Alexandria have to do with not getting along with your commanding officer?" His eyebrows raised slightly. "Ah-ha! I see. Was this man named Antipas? The man recently executed in boiling oil?"

Anthony sucked in his breath, unable to respond.

The officer stiffened, giving a direct order. "Soldier, I ask you to take your oath of allegiance to Caesar. You must declare, 'Caesar is lord and god.'"

Anthony could not escape the consequences. All he had to do was make the simple declaration: "Caesar is lord and god!" If he said those words, then his life would be saved. His future, and Miriam's and Grace's, depended on what he said next.

He stood at attention, the way he had to do on January 1 each year, saluting with his right hand. "I, Anthony Suros, a scout in Legion XXI, the Predators, Cohort Number Four, swear my allegiance to the Supreme Commander. I declare, 'Caesar is lord.'"

He stopped for a second and then continued. He had worried about what he might say beforehand, but now words he had never strung together before poured out without a pause.

"Caesar is lord, installed by the Senate of Rome, worthy of my commitment and loyalty. For that, I discipline myself to be the best I can be. I will die for Rome and for my fellow soldiers. There is no community stronger than Legion XXI. I will faithfully carry out every assignment. I respect and obey the orders of my general and officers. I am in compliance with the highest values of the Roman Empire and will remain so...sir!"

Anthony had no idea where the words came from. They flowed like a stream of bubbling water, overflowing from his heart. He was an army man, trained as a soldier, disciplined, and resilient.

However, Anthony would also be faithful to God. Yes, he had told his commander about the collusion between two officers and another soldier. He could say, "Caesar is lord" of the Roman Empire, but he would not declare that the emperor was "god."

'You have made an extraordinary oath to demonstrate your allegiance, soldier. All you had to do was declare, 'Caesar is lord and god.'

"Here is my decision. You will remain under house detention with guards at the gate. I will let you walk to the city, but you must stay in sight of your guards. Get my permission first. You must not leave Sardis. You cannot speak about your religious beliefs to anyone in the army. You are dismissed!"

Felicior walked to the window. He never tired of the magnificent view of the city and the valley beyond. He thought about what had just taken place between him and Anthony. He spoke to himself, deciding what to do.

"This soldier is calm in battle, a natural leader. He doesn't shy away from conflict. If no accusation comes against him during the summer, I will have him train the next recruits, beginning in October. I need to finalize Commander Cassius's approval to officially transfer Anthony to my command, not just the transfer of his salary. After that, I will inform the army's office in Smyrna and confirm it with a letter to the governor's superintendent in Ephesus.

"But Anthony will have to agree to keep his ideas to himself! He caused trouble for Commander Cassius, and I can see why. I want this soldier as an instructor, but I'll forbid him to speak about beliefs that can undermine the authority of the army's chain of command."

Felicior called in the guard who stood outside his office.

"Follow the soldier who just left. He is leaving with two soldiers, one on each side. Instead of returning him to house detention, take him to the mountain combat exercise area. I want to know what kind of an archer he is. Bring me a report tomorrow morning, first thing. Make his test for archery exceedingly difficult. After that, he is to return to his home."

Chapter 12
The Great Agony

LYDIA-NAQ'S HOME, THE ACROPOLIS, PERGAMUM

On the last Sunday in June, having arrived from Sardis late the previous night, Diotrephes sat with his mother. Lydia-Naq had her wish of hosting him for a late breakfast. She had returned from her early morning prayers at the Altar of Zeus. As usual, she looked stunning. Her hair was braided with colorful ribbons, and her summer tunic, made of fine linen, shimmered in the light.

"Welcome back from Sardis, my son!" she said, throwing her head back as she ate a black olive. "What good news do you bring us?"

"Mother, the gods have been generous," he replied. His voice overflowed with enthusiasm. "I'll tell you all about the interview and the opportunities that have opened up for me."

"What about Chrysa? Are we any closer to welcoming our little baby girl?"

"Well, that's a bit of a mystery! The day after my interview with the directors of the gymnasium of Sardis, I walked past the Ben Shelah house. That day, no soldiers guarded the house! It's a nice property; I wouldn't mind owning it. I could not think of a good way to go in and just take the child without complications. The next morning, the day before returning to Pergamum, I intended to write an order in the name of the mayor of Pergamum. Not completely legitimate of course. I wanted to demand that the child be given over. However, if anyone had questioned the legitimacy of the document, I could have been in big trouble for fraud."

"You went to the house on a day when no soldiers were guarding it?"

"Yes, and then I talked to Cleon, my informer in Sardis. He reported a strange comment by Heber, one of the sons. He said, 'Anthony had an interview with the commander of the garrison yesterday.' Now listen! By the end of the day, the soldiers were back as guards."

"What does that mean, 'an interview with the commander of the garrison'? Surely it does not mean that Anthony is going to work for the army there, does it?"

"I don't know, Mother."

"So Anthony went away from the house. He could not have stopped you from taking the baby, but others could have! I must make a sacrifice at the Altar of Zeus later today for a favorable result after your interview. And I must whisper special words of protection over our child, Chrysa."

It was the first time in many days that Lydia-Naq could not find the right words to express her deep, troubled anxieties.

SIMON AND JUDITH'S HOME

The days leading up to the ninth day of Av, the Jewish month, brought a somber mood to the Ben Shelah home. Simon was quiet at mealtime while Judith spoke sharply to the girls. "Keep quiet! These are days when we remember the terrible destruction of the temple."

Of all the people in the Ben Shelah home in Sardis, only Miriam had lived through the tragic events when Jerusalem was overrun by the Roman legions.

Simon called everyone in the family together. "Three days from now, on the Sabbath starting Friday night, we will spend one whole day in fasting and mourning. We begin at sundown and go until the next sunset, remembering the fall of Jerusalem. This year, I want Miriam to tell her story on the Sabbath day. She will be our witness this year for Tish'a B'Av. We will also have visitors from the God-fearers group with us.

"Then, next week," he continued, "the annual observance day of Tish'a B'Av begins on Wednesday evening. That will be a holy night of remembrance of the destruction of the temple, when we fast and wear sackcloth for the time of quiet meditation."

Seven-year-old Amath whined, "Can't we have one meal, please, Grandpa? Can't Lyris make at least one good meal for us? They will be such long days without proper food!"

Anthony's eyes shifted from one person to another, considering the possibility that his presence would be an obstacle. He suggested that he should stay upstairs with Ateas and Arpoxa during the gathering.

However, Simon disagreed. "No. You, as a soldier, will learn what the Roman army did to my people."

Anthony nodded and said, "I will mourn with you. Antipas taught us about the destruction, and I also grieve the loss of your family members."

Simon later explained to Nissa why Anthony was included in the Tish'a B'Av gathering. She ran out to speak with Ravid and rushed back to tell her father what Ravid thought about it.

She burst out, "Ravid says, 'Tell my father-in-law that I'm deciding to join the family. I want to enjoy this opportunity. Anthony must learn how the siege of Jerusalem harmed our family. This Gentile soldier will learn what it was to suffer at the hands of the military. I consider Miriam's marriage a mistake! How I hate the visitor who stays in our home. He does nothing but bring shame to the good name of Ben Shelah.'"

On Friday night, July 6, hardly a word was spoken. Instead of a table full of delicious foods and wines, Miriam watched Simon take a small cup of water and pour salt into it. He tasted it and said, "That's all. Everything is bitter."

A supper without food was over. Everyone went to bed early.

Miriam wondered what to say when describing her memories. Tears came as she thought about the fall of Jerusalem. She got up in the dark, unable to sleep. She worried about how best to tell about the siege of Jerusalem. However the words came out, she would include a song about her mother.

She composed her song in the dark of the night, and a strange thing happened. Panic did not push her down. Instead, she imagined her mother somewhere up above. And she was smiling. The story of the destruction of Jerusalem would end with words of love.

Love in her heart was replacing the panic she had felt for so long.

Saturday morning, July 7, was quiet and subdued. The atmosphere in the home was one of silence. They wanted to dwell on the destruction of the city they loved. They only had one sip of water to last them until the noon meal.

Even Tamir was wise enough not to complain about the absence of his friend Hector.

At Simon's invitation, Miriam took the central place on the large couch. She sat up straight. The horrors of what she was about to explain still shook her. She looked around the large room and counted the visitors and her family. Twenty people were gathered including Lyris and the two babies.

"I'm going to tell you my story," Miriam said, placing her hair entirely under her white and blue shawl. "It is a story about what I am a witness to. I don't remember all the details, but because Grandpa Antipas told me about it each year, I can explain it.

"Before I was born in Alexandria, Egypt, we Jews lived in two of the five districts of Alexandria. Oh, what a great city! My great-grandfather, Eliab, married Ahava Bat Caleb, and they had twelve children. Eight are still alive. Uncle Simon is one of those eight.

"Our family did well financially, and Grandfather Eliab employed many Egyptians. He bought ships and purchased expensive spices, carpets, silks, and blue porcelains imported from the East. Once they were loaded on the docks by his workers, he sold them far and wide, to Jerusalem, Antioch, Ephesus, Athens, and as far away as Rome.

"Anna, the oldest daughter, was about to get married when an anti-Jewish riot broke out in the city. Anna was eighteen and getting ready for her betrothal party. Her younger sisters were Deborah, who was sixteen, and Zibiah, eleven. That terrible day, and in the days following, many homes were burned, including the one Eliab owned. The fire consumed all three girls. Thousands of Jews died that day."

Miriam watched Elaine, who began to stand as she watched, unblinking, her eyes wide open. Miriam remembered that Elaine was almost the age of Deborah, the sister who had been burned in her own house.

"Life in Alexandria had become dangerous! All the Jews were now forced to move into just one district. Overcrowding was terrible! People had lost homes. Clothes. Possessions. Jobs. Everything!

"My grandfather, Antipas, married Ruth in the fourth year of Emperor Claudius.[12] They had only one daughter, Tamara, who was my mother. After that fire on their street, they began to think of

---

[12] Antipas and Ruth were married in AD 45 in Alexandria, Egypt.

moving to Jerusalem. There had to be a safer place than Alexandria!

"My mother, Tamara, married Johanan Ben Elam, my father. He was determined to move to Jerusalem, but Uncle Simon, who had married Aunt Judith, wanted to stay in Alexandria. That is how our family started living in different cities.

"Only Amos, the eldest, and Antipas, the next eldest, and their families decided to move to Jerusalem. They wanted to live near the temple. In the ninth year of Nero, Herod's Temple was almost finished.[13]

"When they were planning to leave, my mother was pregnant with me, and I was born before they left Egypt."

Elaine and Tamir sat with their parents throughout the story. They had heard it before, but Elaine was gripping her mother's hand hard. Miriam overheard her say, "Hearing the story like this makes my skin tingle. It's so real."

Miriam continued, "I was born just before we left Egypt. I didn't know it, but in that same year, restlessness began in Judea. Zealots were protesting against the Romans. Our family arrived in Jerusalem and it was already crowded, so we moved to a village close to Bethlehem. That is where my first memories came from. Later, I will sing you a lament from my childhood memories.

"Mama and Papa and I lived with the others on a farm with many olive trees. There was a swing, and Papa would push me. I would turn my face up to the sky to watch branches brushing against fluffy white clouds. Uncle Amos and Aunt Abigail and their children lived there too. Their house was crowded with five boys and two girls: Annias, Ater, Azetas, Leah, Arah, Agia, and Arom. I was younger than all my cousins. Life was peaceful and calm."

Miriam described the growing hostilities between the Zealots and the Roman army stationed in Caesarea, the coastal city. She told how paying taxes to Rome upset many. The eagle standard, the symbol of Roman authority, was set up in Jerusalem. That incensed the Zealots. She explained how the harsh controls of Governor Gessius Florus led to increased riots and uprisings against Roman rule.[14]

"Grandpa Antipas and Uncle Amos became alarmed at what was

---

[13] Herod's Temple in Jerusalem was completed about AD 63.

[14] Governor Gessius Florus killed 3,000 Jews because they would not bow to Caesar.

happening, so they talked with their parents. 'We think it wise to sell a ship in Alexandria. Let's use the money to buy a house inside Jerusalem. Once inside the walls, we will be much safer.'

"Well, they bought two houses within the city, right beside each other. Some Jewish families were moving out. We lived on the west side, in an area known as the Upper City, close to the Upper Marketplace and Herod's Palace. The walls of Jerusalem were strong, and our farm near Bethlehem supplied us with food, so we were ready for anything: peace or war. I was young, but I remember a couple times when men talked with their heads close together. They said, 'Triple walls will keep the Romans out!'

"The Roman army marched down from Galilee. Gradually, bit by bit, every town surrendered. Jews poured into Jerusalem, and the city closed all its gates. The siege had started. We were eighteen people living in two small houses. Uncle Amos and Aunt Abigail had their parents living with them plus their seven children. In our house, where I was a small girl, we spanned four generations. When scared, I crawled up on Mama's lap for safety."

For almost half an hour, Miriam stopped speaking while Heber, Ezar, and Ravid argued, trying to get the chronology of the events exactly right. Heber and Ezar generally agreed, but Ravid always insisted on calculating the number of Jewish deaths at each stage of the Roman attack. He would say, "See how many more Jews they slaughtered at this point of the siege!" Then he added caustically, "Never was there such a cruel army!"

Miriam saw Ravid scowl repeatedly at Anthony. *Is he implying that my husband was personally part of the siege?*

She drew a breath and continued. "Much earlier, more than a year before, we had begun to stock up on food. Grandpa feared things might get worse. The men dug a secret storage depot under our home to hide several kinds of grain. If a siege came, we could hold out for a long time! The Ben Shelah family, as we all know, is always ready for anything, right?"

Laughter momentarily broke the tension of her awful story.

"Next came the Feast of Passover and Unleavened Bread. Pilgrims for the festival flooded into the city just before the Roman troops began their final siege. But something terrible happened. Two fanatical Jewish generals, Simon Ben Giora and John of Gischala, each controlling an army numbering in the thousands, had forced their way into the city. All were Jewish soldiers, but each army wanted to control the whole city and the temple.

"They started a civil war inside the Holy City over one issue: Who would manage the temple grounds? Simon came from the south. John, his rival, was from the north. Besides these two hotheads, other zealots led smaller Jewish factions. The priests did not take sides, because they did not want the temple to be harmed.

"So inside the city, there was a battle between the two Jewish armies. Outside, we were fighting against the Romans. In the many internal skirmishes, our defense force killed the high priest."

Miriam hid her face in her hands. "Oh, Lord, how could we have been fighting two wars at once?" She paused and wiped her cheeks.

"Everyone knew how Babylonians had attacked our city centuries before. Annually, the Jewish people mourned the destruction of Solomon's Temple. They lamented the events of that devastating day. All of that happened so long ago. But no one knew that a similar devastation was about to happen.

"Of Uncle Amos's and Aunt Abigail's seven children, only Arom escaped alive. He is our cousin and lives in Philadelphia with Amos and Abigail.

"Their oldest boy, Annias, was twenty-five years old, and he offered to take a lamb to the temple as a sacrifice. Just as he was giving the lamb to the high priest, an arrow hit him in the back. Shot by one of John's soldiers, he was severely wounded. He bled to death less than an hour later. Uncle Amos gasped with sorrow and anger as he dropped his son's body over the city wall because the gates were shut against the Romans. The stench of thousands of other bodies rotting there was overpowering. We cried for days in mourning for my cousin Annias."

Young Amath covered her eyes with her hands and leaned against Chenya for comfort. She whimpered, "Mommy, I don't like this story!"

"The soldiers loyal to Simon wanted to make sure no supplies got into the hands of John's warriors, so they began to search their part of the city for hidden food. One day they reached our house. A Jewish soldier yelled, 'Open up!' I heard them and ran to my mother for protection. She took me in her arms while Uncle Amos opened the door.

"Simon's men shouted, 'You're hiding food! We were told that you were seen bringing in a lot of food months ago. You must have a hidden storehouse! Give the food to us!'

"Four more Jewish men forced their way in. The six soldiers went from one room to the other. Finally one man noticed a grain of wheat on the floor. We hadn't been careful enough to clean up the grain when it dropped. They pulled back the carpet and exclaimed, 'Here it is! Under the carpet, just as their neighbor said. They do have a secret hiding place!'

"They ripped the carpet off the floor, but one of Amos's sons, Azetas, stood up to the intruders. 'You can't do this to our family!' he screamed. In a flash, he was knocked down and slashed with a sword. Azetas was my second cousin to die. Those soldiers, our Jewish 'friends,' stole our food.

"Annias and Azetas had been killed by Jews but by different Jewish armies! Oh, how we wept! We had no food! 'How could our own people do this to us?' my papa wailed. Uncle Amos refused to be comforted after the death of Azetas. He took the body to the top of the wall and mournfully dropped his second son on top of the rotting corpses outside the wall."

Miriam watched Ravid. His eyes darted back and forth between her and Anthony.

She took a deep breath, feeling her mouth becoming very dry. "Ater was the third of their children to die. Some Jews dug a tunnel under the wall, coming up outside the city. To their surprise, they came out of the ground right beside one of the Roman war engines. They burned it, but Ater, who was twenty-four years old, was captured. He was slaughtered along with five hundred other young men. Aunt Abigail didn't sleep for days, and dark patches formed under her eyes. She still has them.

"Then Simon's crazy soldiers let a blacksmith's fire get out of control. It spread to the storehouses, and the food for the whole city was suddenly gone! The resulting famine was severe. If the soldiers had not burned all that grain, we might have withstood the Romans! Our walls were thick, durable, and reinforced. And we had sufficient water coming into the city.

"The Roman soldiers would not have had enough food to last them into the winter until the next harvest.

"More cousins died. Arah was my favorite male cousin, and he was eleven. Leah was thirteen. Agia, the other girl, was fifteen. They died from starvation and sickness. We cried and wailed when they died.

"Our bodies were fading away. Nothing could bring my cousins back. I remember one night when I was so frightened, I crawled on my father's lap and put my face into his chest. That was the day Arah died. Uncle Amos stopped speaking for days after that. We had traded all the furniture for food, so we simply sat on the floor as the temperature outside got hotter and hotter.

"Grandpa was walking around the city one day when he overheard a conversation. He stood in the shadows and listened. One of the priests' families had concluded that the only way to survive was to flee. Anything was better than the terrible civil war they were facing inside.

"Grandpa Antipas came home that evening and said, 'I've learned that there is a group secretly preparing to break out. We must leave this city with them! If we don't, we'll all be dead in a month from starvation.' That night, while I was sleeping, our family made the decision.

"Uncle Amos stood up and spoke for the first time in days: 'I agree with any plan to abandon the city. I believe that we must surrender to the Romans! They might not be merciful, but they cannot be worse than our two armies fighting inside our walls.'

"That day, Uncle Amos and Grandpa Antipas went out of the house with their father, Eliab. They quietly talked to one of the priests about when and where the escape attempt was to happen.

"We left in the early morning through one of the small service gates in the wall. It was barred but not guarded. I was too weak to walk, so my father was carrying me. As quickly as we could, we pulled open the door, and our family, with about 150 others, surged out. Almost immediately, the Jewish soldiers on the wall started shooting arrows at our group. We fled, and my father ran as fast as he could. Not too far from the walls, an arrow pierced his back. We both fell to the ground.

"Behind us were the walls of our city. In front of us stood the Roman soldiers. Grandpa shouted at Daddy, 'Johanan Ben Elam, don't die! Don't leave us!' But he was dead. He never moved again. We had to leave him where he fell outside the walls of Jerusalem.

"My mother scooped me up from the ground. The city's soldiers were still shooting arrows, and one hit my mother in the leg. She fell, no longer able to carry me. So Grandpa picked me up and helped my mother hobble along. The Romans were delighted to see us coming out and shouted, 'The Jews are giving up! They are surrendering!'

"Some soldiers took us to a small town nearby and gave us food. One of them said, 'Don't eat too fast, or you will die! Your stomachs can only take in a little food!' However, Abigail's mother and father both died two days later because they wouldn't listen. They were starving and overate. Eight people in Abigail's family, six children and two old people, died during those eight terrible months.

"I can't remember some things very well, but I know there were too many people crowded into that small town. Grandpa spoke to a centurion, saying, 'We are strong enough to move away now, and others in the city will need food. Please let us cross the Jordan.'

"Mama was crippled and could barely walk. She developed a fever. She kept complaining about the pain in her leg."

Miriam started to cry. All had tears in their eyes, and no one dared to speak a word.

After a bit, Miriam recovered. "We stayed with a family in Philadelphia, that big city to the east of the Jordan River.[15]

"A family took us in, and we wanted to stay there for a long time because the name was so good. Philadelphia means 'the city of brotherly love.' These people had moved from Judea to Pella, a small city close by, and words of a prophecy made by Yeshua the Carpenter had a profound impact: 'When you see armies approaching, go to the mountains, quickly!' This generous family gave us hospitality, and my mother had poultices placed on her leg. With their help, she started to get better, which gave us hope.

"That's how we left the land of our fathers, Abraham, Isaac, and Jacob. We went from Philadelphia to Gerasa, and from there, we walked to the coast. A small boat took us north to Tyre. I remember gulls flying around the ship, dancing around the masts, and fresh wind in our faces. We embarked on another ship and arrived in the port close to Antioch. I remember looking up from the harbor at the mansions on the mountainside. Inside the harbor wall, many fishing ships had docked in the port.

---

[15] Philadelphia was an earlier name for Amman, the modern capital city of Jordan. Pella was located about 15 miles (20 km) south of the Sea of Galilee. The prophecy of Jesus, recorded in Matthew 24:16, motivated many to flee across the Jordan River before the siege of Jerusalem.

"By the time we arrived in Antioch, Mama had to be carried. But because of all the walking, her leg was getting red, and an inflamed line ran up her leg. She was showing it to Aunt Abigail one day when I came into the room. She died three weeks later.

"I felt so lonely and afraid. Flutes played sad laments as we walked mournfully along the colonnaded street, over the bridge, and out past the homes of the wealthy to the Jewish cemetery. The tall mountains around Antioch made me feel so small. Grandpa held me in his arms. I cried and wouldn't lift my head from his shoulder.

"Before lowering Mama's body into the little grave, Grandpa Antipas put me down on the ground. He looked up at the mountains and said, 'My child, you will always remember this day and the evils of war. Your mother died, wounded by our own people, but don't let hatred grow in your heart. Those Jewish soldiers were protecting our city. And you must not hate Romans either. Soldiers took us in. They gave us food when we were starving.'

"I can still hear his words."

Her cheeks were wet again, and she wiped them dry. This time, she took longer to start her story again.

"Grandpa looked up at the sharp mountain crags surrounding Antioch. He held my little hands, and I saw tears pouring from his eyes. Several men lowered Mama's thin body into the black earth. Grandpa chanted a prayer. It was the same one he quoted when he first entered Jerusalem. 'I lift up my eyes to the hills; where does my help come from? My help comes from the Lord, the Maker of heaven and earth. He will not let your foot slip; he who watches over you will not slumber. The Lord will keep you from all harm; he will watch over your life; the Lord will watch over your coming and going, both now and forevermore.'"[16]

Miriam had been talking for a long time, and she stopped. She ran her tongue around her lips several times to wet them before she could keep on.

"Grandpa used to tell our story this way: We came to Jerusalem as a family of eighteen people. We left Jerusalem as twelve, including both families, but three more died before we got here. So of the eighteen in our family, nine recovered from hunger and lived.

"Six of us immediately came to Pergamum. That's where Great-

[16] Psalm 121:1–3, 7–8

grandfather Eliab put down roots. Two years later, three others—Uncle Amos, Aunt Abigail, and my cousin Arom—followed. They found a place to live in Philadelphia, where they still live.

"Then four more Ben Shelah families joined us. They settled in Smyrna, Thyatira, Sardis, and Laodicea. That's how six brothers and their families came to Asia Minor. And here I am, with you, in Sardis!"

Silence descended on the family. They mourned the loss of their beloved city, Jerusalem. After what seemed like a long time, Miriam wiped the tears from her cheeks. She had said she would sing, but it would be incredibly challenging after a story of such deep grief.

"About two years ago, I started writing songs that tell stories. Music takes away some of my fears. This song speaks of Mama's life and then her death. It is my lament. I will sing without an instrument, and later Lyris will play a funeral dirge on her flute. We want this song about my family to remind us of all the different sorrows we have faced.

"I was so young. For me, Mama was like the wife of noble character in Proverbs. We all want to be that woman, don't we?"

Miriam's lip quivered, and she struggled to carry on. "I can't even remember her face, and sometimes that makes me cry again. But I loved her, and this song is called 'Mama! What a Name!'" Then she sang softly.[17]

Mama! What a name; worth more than rubies!
Sustained us, brought health; kept us free from harm.
Prosperity grew. She helped Daddy farm,
Kept our home and relished all her duties.

Mama! She made a covering for my bed!
Held the distaff, weaving with the spindle,
Revived coals to make the fire rekindle,
Baked fresh bread, and made sure we all were fed.

Mama! Rising before the early dawn,
Gave lavish portions to our servant girls.
She held me on her lap and brushed my curls.
Working late, she tried to cover up a yawn.

---

[17] Miriam based her song on Proverbs 31:10–31

So patient even when I made her wait!
In Jerusalem, stayed beside my bed.
"We will survive this vile siege," she said.
But divisions grew. Conflicts nurtured hate.

Soldiers stood tall, ready for an attack.
"Daddy!" I cried when barely out the gate.
He lay lifeless, our escape made too late.
A Jewish soldier's arrow pierced his back.

And what remained after the shock of war?
Walls were breached! Hateful abomination!
The temple burned. Vile contamination!
Stunned and scared, we were wounded to our core.

Then surprise! From that unrelenting pain,
We found kindness, food, and peaceful comfort.
In Philadelphia, we found support.
One family helped, and Mama walked again.

But Mama! Antioch's sod was broken.
We prayed for recovery! But healing
Never came. Unwelcomed, death came stealing.
My love lives on through memories softly spoken.

Lyris played the funeral dirge. For a long time, no one spoke. The sacred moment blended an intimate story of childhood grief with the universal pain of loss. Miriam's song had invited them to recall their own stories. She told of love in the home, the destruction of their city, the sadness of the cemetery, and, finally, her mother's tender love.

Deep affection still lived on in Miriam's memory. Her story brought them back to the covenant and the other Jews who, like them, had suffered fire, siege, and death.

As Anthony listened to Miriam's song, new thoughts swirled like bees that would not leave. In Jerusalem, hundreds of thousands had perished, yet many had died at the hands of their own people.

Ravid had made sure that he knew how many people had died at the hands of the army. "Over one and a half million Jews perished. Did everyone understand that?" he asked in a loud voice. He had carefully counted the dead at each point in Miriam's story.

But Anthony was keeping track of the losses in the Ben Shelah family. Then it hit him. *The person who suffered the most in Miriam's story is Abigail. She lives close by, in Philadelphia, a day's journey from here! She lost six of her seven children during the siege.*

As he prayed, he felt a forceful desire to talk to Abigail. *Surely, she is the most wounded person in the family. Lord, give me the right words if I ever meet my wife's aunt.*

THE SYNAGOGUE OF SARDIS

Four days later, Jakob, the chief elder of the Synagogue of Sardis, took the well-worn scroll handed to him. Today all the congregation came in sackcloth, many with ashes covering their heads, because this was a fasting day. Tears flowed. This was the Night of Sadness.

Jakob opened the Book of Lamentations. Every so often, his voice quivered. The congregation knew every word by heart.

> How deserted lies the city, once so full of people! How like a widow is she, who once was great among the nations! She, who was queen among the provinces, has now become a slave. Bitterly she weeps at night, tears are upon her cheeks.
>
> Among all her lovers, there is none to comfort her. All her friends have betrayed her; they have become her enemies. After affliction and harsh labor, Judah has gone into exile. She dwells among the nations; she finds no resting place!
>
> Her foes have become her masters, her enemies are at ease. The Lord has brought her grief because of her many sins. Her children have gone into exile, captive before the foe. How deserted lies the city, once so full of people![18]

Grown men wept openly. Women folded their arms across their bosoms and rocked back and forth. Some raised their hands until they grew tired and could no longer hold them up. The words of the

[18] Lamentations 1:1–3, 5

prophet Jeremiah were written so many years ago. This passage was repeated everywhere that exiles lived, and it had become a part of the inner life of every Jew.

Psalm 79 described the Babylonian invasion of Jerusalem and the destruction of Solomon's Temple. This occupied everyone's hearts. Wedding songs of brides would never be sung on this day, and widows were silenced in their laments of loss and desolation. Those ancient words seemed as alive and real in the ninth year of Domitian as when Jeremiah wrote the poem. The prophet's lamentation brought forth expressions of repentance for the sins of Israel.

Jakob could only whisper. His throat was dry. "Tish'a B'Av is the saddest day of the year."

Sitting in a back corner at the synagogue, Ravid sat transfixed. During Miriam's story, he had watched the expressions on Anthony's face. Her narration of the events made for a scathing denunciation of military cruelty. Why had Anthony had tears in his eyes several times?

Miriam's words captured what Ravid wanted to say: "An awful abomination!" She even described the actions of malicious Roman legions! She described their family's gloom, humiliation, hunger, and unspeakable shame. Six cousins died. Then Miriam's father and two elderly ones perished, even after escaping through the small gate. His wife's precious family! They could not bury any of the children. Surely Miriam had to realize that she was wrong to marry Anthony!

Yet she had said nothing against Anthony. She told her story and came to an end without condemning the Romans. There was no criticism at all!

Ravid shook his head in disbelief and frustration.

LYDIA-NAQ'S HOME, THE ACROPOLIS, PERGAMUM

Diotrephes ran up the steps to his mother's house and burst through the door. "Mother, a message arrived from Sardis! I've been accepted as Director of the Department of History!"

"That's wonderful news, my son! A blessing from Zeus, for he has given you strength, according to the meaning of your name—'nourished by Zeus.' A new opportunity is opening for you. Come! Let's go and tell your Uncle Zoticos this good news!"

RAVID AND NISSA'S HOME

Once again, Nissa could not sleep. Ravid was snoring softly. Standing beside the window with the shutters open, she listened to the summer stillness. Frogs croaked, calling to each other, and crickets serenaded, but rest would not come for her.

Nissa hurt for reasons other than Jerusalem's destruction.

I want Ravid in the social life of my family. Why does he forbid me to be a part of my own family? Oh, God, hear my cry!

Ravid, my dear husband, show me compassion!

I am still barren! I want a baby. Eight years and two months now. And I still am not pregnant! Look at those two, Saulius and Grace! Two Gentile babies growing up in a Jewish home!

Chapter 13
Secrets of the Heart

ON THE ROAD TO SARDIS

Little Lion had reached the point where the road from Laodicea to Philadelphia sloped downhill. From the top of the hill, they could see all the way to the Hermus Valley below. Below them, lush green vineyards spread out from a small town. Farther on, as far as he could see, vines formed a vast sea of luxurious green.

Little Lion was accompanied on his trip by two friends. The three young men had walked for two days, and he would soon be in Sardis. As poor young men, they had to travel on foot. They planned to stay in Philadelphia for two days, then walk one day to Sardis, and spend several days there. They talked about seeing gold and riches but wondered if precious objects would be easy to find.

Then, after a few days in Sardis, his friends would return to Laodicea, leaving Little Lion at the Garrison of Sardis. His face brightened as he pictured his mother, Charmaine, receiving the first silver coin he had promised.

My mother will laugh and cry at the same time. She won't believe that I am already sending her money. I sold my wood cart for five silver coins. My friends will give her one each month for four months, and by that time, I'll find a way to get my payment to her. Hurray! I'm going to be part of the famous Legion XXI, the Predators. We will march against Dacia! When I come back, we will have won a great victory for the glory of Rome!

"I'll race you to the change station!" yelled Little Lion as they approached the station and horse farm beside the postal road. Fresh horses were only for the use of couriers and soldiers. He carried only a change of clothing, little more, and he washed his clothes at night. His food and staying in inns would cost him the one remaining coin of the original five silver coins.

His friends rose to the challenge. They yelled and shrieked with joy as they ran down the long hill, galloping down a long, straight stretch with a steep hill on one side. Then came three sharp corners, and they sped on with their arms out, imitating birds. When they set foot on the flat plain, the vines were almost as tall as they were. They could no longer they see the horizon. Ahead lay the joy of staying in Philadelphia, a city they had never visited.

LYDIA-NAQ'S HOME, THE ACROPOLIS, PERGAMUM

Lydia-Naq was talking with Diotrephes at the end of the day. She wanted to hear his plans for moving to Sardis. She was ecstatic that he had been appointed to head the history department there. Striding across the room, she glanced out a west-facing window. "Look at that sunset!"

From her home high on the Acropolis at the end of August, Lydia-Naq had a broad view of the distant Aegean Sea. The sky was covered with two layers of cloud. The higher clouds reflected the darker colors of yellow and orange. She never tired of the delicate tones at the end of the day.

"I wrote to Alala, the high priestess of the Temple of Artemis in Sardis. She replied, saying that she had found a house where you can stay. What are your plans?"

"I'm packing my documents, but I'll have to leave some things here."

"Are you studying those Jewish customs? You will need them when you get there."

"I'm having trouble with their calendar, rituals, and sayings."

She chuckled. "Never mind. Deep magic will give you the right words when you need them."

"Mother, has the city council expropriated Antipas's village?"

"No, we are learning further details. Marcos, the lawyer, explained to the District Court that the city must satisfy imperial laws for Egypt and senatorial laws in Asia Minor. Eliab's final testament has precedence over the will written by Antipas. Marcos said that the expropriation process would be difficult and expensive for the city.

"That old fool, Manes Tmolus, agreed with Marcos! He is letting the village businesses continue operation so the city will get tax money from them."

"Never mind, Mother. You will find a way around Marcos. I know it."

COMMANDER FELICIOR'S OFFICE, THE ACROPOLIS, SARDIS

A week later, Felicior paced the office slowly and then exhaled, his breath escaping through tightly drawn lips. Today he had examined ninety-nine of the one hundred candidates, but he only had training facilities for forty recruits. He needed the strongest and most intelligent to serve in Legion XXI, the Predators.

He sat down behind his desk and told the last candidate to come forward. A small young man with engaging eyes stood up and proudly posed before him.

"What is your name?" asked Commander Felicior.

"My friends call me 'Little Lion,' sir."

"Why do they call you Little Lion?"

"I'm not afraid of anything" came the cheerful answer.

"What are your abilities, Little Lion? You appear to be too small for the army."

"I can control others without the use of arms. I use other skills."

"What skills?"

Little Lion was the last candidate being interviewed. He stepped away, turned his back, and then faced the commander using one of Felicior's fierce expressions. The officer realized what had happened. While waiting for his interview, the young man had studied his posture, the movement of his arms, and his speech.

Little Lion was much smaller than Felicior, but the tone of voice, the way he stood, and the squint of the commander's eye were identical.

Felicior frowned, wondering what the recruit was up to.

The young man crossed over to the other side of the office, imitating the first candidate and several other young men. All had been interviewed by Felicior earlier in the day.

Here was Felicior talking to the strapping young man whose bent shoulders and curved back showed he simply wanted to get off his father's farm. Little Lion then changed places and imitated the commander's speech. "You've never fought anything larger than a chicken, and even then, you couldn't catch the wretched thing!"

Felicior chuckled to himself. He sat back, folding his arms across his chest.

Little Lion acted out another scene. "And you, young man from Sastora village! What else have you done besides harvest grapes and drink old wine?"

The answer came back just as that young man had answered. Little Lion perfectly imitated the slow Sastora village drawl. "My father...told me to come here. He doesn't like the way I act...at home...and he said...the army could straighten me out."

Felicior did his best not to smile. Inwardly, he prepared to tell his colleagues about this episode at the upcoming Meeting of the Asiarchs. Every commander of a garrison in Asia would hear of Little Lion's ability to copy another person's speech. This little fellow had an inherent intelligence he had not seen in the other candidates.

"Fair enough, Little Lion," said Felicior. "I have no idea how you will use what you can do, but I see your ability to observe and imitate. This could be particularly useful if you are selected to join the army. I must warn you. It will not be easy for you. You will have to use a sword and spear, just like any other soldier."

SIMON AND JUDITH'S HOME

On Sunday, Tamir burst into the big front room. "It is a hot day! Please let me climb the hill behind our house, Mother."

"Too dangerous!" replied Chenya. After his last hike, he had twisted an ankle and limped for two days.

"Well, Hector is coming, and we want to do something! Can Isidoros come too? Please, Mother!" He had already committed to a climb to the top of the hill.

Elaine, listening to the conversation, rubbed her hands together. Isidoros might be at their house, even for a short time. She offered her opinion: "Mother, I'm sure Tamir will be more careful this time."

"Well, Tamir, if you climb with Isidoros and Hector, then the three of you may go together. Oh, please invite Kalonice, their mother, to join me while the boys are here. Tell them to come this afternoon. And, yes, their grandfather can come too if he wants. You'll have to be careful! Steep cliffs and loose stones are not good friends!"

When the weather was at its hottest during the day, people took time to rest. Even slaves were given time to eat and sleep. In the afternoon, about the tenth hour of the day, active life started again.

Now the weather had cooled slightly. Their guests arrived as the sun's rays began to cool. Judith and Chenya invited Kalonice to the flat roof, and they sat on chairs in the shade. Green vines spread out over most of the roof, crawling along the strings that formed an overhead network.

Kalonice wore a cream-colored stola with an orange sash around her waist. Her long black hair was done up in a bun because of the heat. Like all women, she wore a small nose ring. She placed her chair under a shady spot and watched Lyris and Elaine come up the stairs to join them. They brought a jug of lemon juice, and Lyris served the drink.

"This is delicious!" said Kalonice.

"Yes, Lyris is a wonderful cook," agreed Judith.

Kalonice asked, "Lyris, where did you live before coming to Sardis? Do you mind if I ask you questions like this?"

"Ask me anything you like! I came to Sardis with this family. Before that, our family lived in Alexandria for generations," Lyris answered. "I don't know how long my ancestors were there, perhaps for a hundred years or more. I came to Sardis because Judith wanted me with her, to work as a servant in her home."

"Did you come alone? Were you ever married?" Kalonice was interested in this good-natured servant woman. Moreover, she enjoyed learning about others.

"My husband died. He burned to death...."

A gasp came from Miriam "I'm so sorry! I didn't know anything about your loss. How terrible!"

Elaine placed her arm around Chenya's shoulders. "Mother, I don't want to hear about more people dying like that!"

Kalonice leaned forward and blurted out, "Oh, he must have died in the pogrom in Alexandria when Nero was emperor."

"Kalonice, what do you know of the pogroms of Alexandria?" asked Chenya with a surprised look on her face.

Kalonice looked at each one in the circle, took her cup, and drank a sip. *I will reveal my secret to them. Today they will know.* She cleared her throat and looked at each of her new friends.

"Let me tell you about my mother. Her name was Jerusha, a Jew. She was two years old when the first pogrom took place in Alexandria. Her family left as refugees and landed in Miletus harbor. In that city, my mother met my father, Eugene. They were married there, and I was their only daughter. My father got a job making wine, so we came to Sardis and he worked in a winery. I met Jace here but decided not to tell him the details about our family's history."

Judith's smile reached up to her eyes. "You are Jewish," she breathed quietly. She reached across the small table and took her visitor's hands.

"Listen, the deepest secret of my life is coming out," Kalonice explained. "May I ask you to keep it a secret for a while longer? I must tell my own family before they hear it from somewhere else."

Chenya asked, "What happened to your mother?"

"She died when I was fifteen. My father, Eugene, is a widower." She turned to Miriam. "Please come to my house. Tell me what it is like to have two identities in one home, Jewish and Gentile. I want to talk more with you because you, too, have a Gentile husband."

Elaine jumped in, "Could I go too, Mother? May I visit your house, Kalonice?"

Kalonice warmed to the growing friendship. "Certainly! You must come to our house. Look, here come the boys! They're back from their hike. One week from today...could you come then?"

Isidoros, Hector, and Tamir raced up the stairs, puffing from the exertion. "Someday can we climb to the top of Tmolus Mountain?" Isidoros asked. "Please, Mother! There's a road over the mountain. We'll take it, and I'm certain we'll be safe. Please!"

"Let me think about it," said Kalonice. She did not want her sons to take a long, risky hike.

Kalonice and her sons left for home. She smiled because her secret was out and because she could trust Judith's family.

I belong.... I'm a friend in a new way.

Looking out over the city from Simon's house, Ravid felt restless. August had passed and September was upon them. The relentless summer heat had faded, but tensions with his father-in-law had increased.

Every time Ravid talked to Simon about sending the Gentiles away, the old man agreed. Simon was easy to talk to, but the old man simply would not follow through on anything he promised!

Two days ago, Ravid had requested that Anthony, Ateas and Arpoxa, and their son Saulius move out of the home. Simon had replied, "I should ask Judith. You know, she keeps the house. I run the business, this property, and my shop. That, and keeping everything straight with my brothers, takes all my energy."

Ravid did not want to be disloyal, but he insisted on getting the strangers out. Last night he had tried talking Ezar and Chenya into helping to change Simon's mind. "Look, Ezar, you're his son! What kind of an influence are Miriam and Anthony having on your children? Your daughter, Amath, cannot get enough of handling the two Gentile babies! Non-Jews will lead them astray.

"I'm pleading with you. Look at the failures of our ancestors. Captivity in Babylon. Punishment for having served other gods. You should examine the Torah. Learn from our writings!"

Ezar had not seemed too concerned, and Ravid shook his head at the response. "You know how Father goes back and forth on things, Ravid! One moment he wants to make money. The next he would rather spend more time studying the Torah. He talks about the covenant but then spends time making more gold rings. He relishes his work. Those jewelry items bring in a lot of money."

Ravid shot back, "Tell him to stop making little flying eagles and start spending more time respecting the elders' tradition. Making images of eagles is an offense. An eagle is a Roman image."

Chenya laughed, butting into the conversation. "Ravid, Jakob says we have to be like Sardians, as long as we don't violate the covenant. Can you stop our father from making jewelry? We can't! He made so much money this summer selling those rings. Now he wants to branch out. I heard him talking to Mother about the purchase of a vineyard."

She pointed to the vineyards around the city. Grapes hung in bunches, indicating a joyful harvest would start in a few days.

The conversation had infuriated Ravid. How could Simon value money and property more than the tradition of the elders?

Ravid closed his eyes in deep thought as he considered his situation. This morning's conversation at the shop came back.

Heber was smiling. 'Eagles soaring on rings forged in our workshop—these are the most popular item now. I sent some back with Nikias to Thyatira. He also took back the horse that Anthony rode when he came from Olive Grove."

Those words infuriated Ravid, and for the first time, he thought of leaving Sardis and going back to live with his father in Smyrna. As he looked out over the city, his lips pressed together tightly.

This means Anthony is going to stay here for a long time. Nikias took more rings with flying eagles to Jonathan Ben Shelah in Thyatira.

No, I really don't want to take Nissa and go back to my father's house. If no one else is ready to uphold the Torah in this family, then it is up to me to confront this sinfulness. I must think of something to wake up this family to the dangers that face them.

JACE AND KALONICE'S HOME, SARDIS

With the extreme heat of the summer fading, Kalonice sent a message with an invitation to come and visit. Miriam accepted and took Grace. She spent a long time telling about Anthony, explaining how they fell in love.

Kalonice was a good listener, letting Miriam speak and then going back over the details. She was fascinated by the story of how Chrysa Grace had come into Miriam's home.

The baby started to cry, indicating that it was time for her to be fed. "I'll have to come to your house again," said Miriam, rising quickly from the couch. "Thanks to Arpoxa, Grace has all the nutrition she needs."

"Will you let me introduce you to some of the important people of Sardis?" asked Kalonice. "You must meet my friend Panthea, the wife of the mayor, Tymon Tmolus. I have been invited to a lady's meeting at Panthea's home while their husbands are at the Annual Meeting of the Asiarchs. Perhaps you can come with me."

"Let me think about that tonight, Kalonice." Miriam did not want to give a quick reply to this unusual request. "I really must get going; Grace's meal is waiting. Arpoxa loves to feed her; she's Grace's third best friend."

"Who is her best friend, then?" questioned Kalonice. She called out because Miriam was already walking toward the Royal Road.

"Her father is her best friend! I'm in second place, and Arpoxa comes in third," Miriam answered, looking over her shoulder.

She took a step back toward Kalonice's house. "I feel contented. Lately, I've felt buoyant, cheerful, and accepted. Anthony is safe. He's now grudgingly accepted by Heber and the children. Mostly though, Anthony keeps to himself, staying in our room and taking care of Grace."

Miriam turned and walked back home quickly. She could become a friend to the woman who, like her, had married a Gentile.

MARCOS AND MARCELLA'S HOME, PERGAMUM

The House of Prayer in Pergamum was full, and some were standing in the front portico. Marcella, Marcos's wife, looked around the assembly and saw a young, attractive woman with long black hair.

"Hail! Welcome, Trifane. I'm so very glad you could join us. How are you?" whispered Marcella, moving to sit beside the young lady.

"Hail! I was hoping to see you again. It's been a year since I met you in Kisthene. I was hoping to see you here," replied the young woman.

"Trifane! Such a lovely name! And we remember you so well," exclaimed Marcella.

Memories of the previous summer in Kisthene flooded back.

Trifane and her mother, Cratia, had stayed on at the family's summer residence at the beach to care for their properties. The young woman, twenty-five years old, was prettier than the first time they met.

Florbella, her daughter, saw Trifane and came running across the room to sit with her friend.

Just then, Onias stood to lead the Friday evening service. The special event was just beginning, and even non-Jews had been welcomed to celebrate the arrival of the Jewish New Year.

Never Enough Gold

Part 2

September AD 91

Acquaintances in Sardis

Chapter 14
Friday Afternoon

BANKER DIODOTUS AND DELBIN'S HOME, WEST HILL

Diotrephes arrived in Sardis on the day after Little Lion reached the barracks at the garrison. At the beginning of September, everything needed for teaching was piled in the rented wagon that brought Diotrephes from Pergamum. The driver would return to his home after unloading the baggage, clothing, and scrolls.

The next day, Friday, his first stop in the city was the Ben Shelah shop to see his informant. "Cleon, I am moving into Sardis permanently. I need to find Banker Diodotus and Lady Delbin's home. That's where I will be living. Mother said her house is on West Hill, overlooking the Mint. Can you tell me how to get there?"

For a month, Diotrephes would use his time to meet as many influential people as possible. Until October, he would publicize his upcoming course on the Lydian language.

He tasted something new, something delicious. He rolled his new title around on his tongue, savoring the sound: Director of the Department of History.

Also, he knew where the God-fearers met, and he had plans to arrive unannounced at their meeting. He could not decide which made him happier, his new status at the Gymnasium or his anticipation at meeting the Ben Shelah family.

COMMANDER FELICIOR'S OFFICE, THE ACROPOLIS, SARDIS

The potential recruits stood in ten rows, each with ten young men in the file. One by one, Felicior called out the names of those selected. When all forty had stepped forward, groans came from the sixty men not among the chosen. With disappointed expressions on their faces, they remained a short distance behind the ones designated to train as recruits. Those who failed entrance into the army could only watch the initiation, not participate.

Felicior led the new recruits to a small fire, where a tuft of hair was cut from their head and handed to them. Each recruit let it slip slowly through his fingers into the flame. The smell of the burning hair raised goosebumps on their arms and backs, just as Felicior had experienced more than twenty years before.

Little Lion was the last to act out the symbolic gesture of total obedience. When it was his turn to drop his tuft of hair between his thumb and index finger, he watched the flame consume it.

He repeated the words the others had said: "I am as ready to die for Caesar as I am to let this hair dissolve in the fire. My life is no longer my own." Then he spoke softly. Felicior saw the young man's lips moving and bent over behind Little Lion to hear what he was saying. Listening, he wondered about the young man's home in Laodicea.

"But, Mother, I will return from war, and when I come back, I will be rewarded with a small farm. You will smile at me, and I'll say, 'I thought of you every day when fighting barbarians in Dacia.' Mother, my two friends from Laodicea are now returning, and they carry four silver coins to give to you—one for each month until the New Year comes."

With the last of the newly chosen young men now standing in formation, Felicior stood between them and the others, who would start returning home this afternoon.

"Recruits," Felicior bellowed, "this is Prosperus, your instructor. He will train you to serve in Legion XXI, the Predators. As the name of your legion implies, you will devour your enemies!"

He waited. The thrill of the moment washed over them; their former lives were being left behind. Never would a single recruit forget the pungent aroma of their hair going up in smoke.

Concluding the initiation, Felicior repeated the phrase that had been declared at the beginning. He bellowed, "Caesar is lord and god!" The recruits shouted with one voice, "Caesar is lord and god!"

THE SYNAGOGUE OF SARDIS

Friday night at the Synagogue of Sardis at sundown was the beginning of the first day of the Jewish New Year. Rosh Hashanah always saw a full congregation. More than eight hundred had gathered in the long sanctuary with its elevated roof. Three services were in store for them: Friday night and Saturday morning services to welcome in the New Year and Saturday night was set aside to include the Gentile God-fearers as an occasion to teach them about this beautiful Jewish religious feast.

Tonight the shofar was blown to call the congregation to repentance. It was the Jewish New Year.

Strangely, many of the elders had difficulty concentrating on the service. They had been chatting all week about an emerging situation. Jakob had gathered them in groups of two or three to consider a decision, asking, "When should I tell the whole congregation about the proposal from the city council? Will our people accept a change in the relationship between the Jewish community and the city?" Jakob had posed the questions in a way that indicated the acceptance would greatly benefit the whole Jewish community.

At one home after the service, three men bent their heads close together. An elder, the owner of this home, argued favorably in a low voice, hoping his wife would not hear the discussion. "To bolster what we desire, the city council has proposed a formal legal agreement. If our community agrees to make donations to the city to help complete building projects, we will enjoy certain privileges." He smiled and closed his eyes, thinking of future profits from a new store in the western marketplace.

Another man was also supportive of Jakob's work. "At first, these additional rights were going to only involve greater participation in financial institutions and written guarantees of religious freedom. But at Jakob's insistence, other benefits will be forthcoming. He has smoothed the way for many of our families to profit from the city. We will be allowed to give input into policies to be enforced by the city." He shook hands with both his friends.

The first man interrupted, "Also, the authorities have recently added the inducement of enabling us to open new shops in the Western Agora marketplace—shops with walls and strong doors!"

Their friend disagreed, speaking through tight jaws. "It all sounds very enticing, but we must be wary of potential problems. Will not the removal of social barriers with the Gentiles lead to contamination of our Jewish moral standards? Can we even imagine the conflicts that will arise concerning the elders' tradition? No, and I, for one, will not accept these favorable conditions with the city!"

Jakob knew more tongues were wagging as others became

aware of the city's proposal. A few men suggested that the process should be implemented gradually. That way, their leaders would have time to assess the effect on the Jewish congregation and the requirements of the covenant.

He decided, *I will call a meeting on Sunday afternoon. The thirty families that most stand to profit will express their opinions, and then I'll decide what to say to the city council.*

SIMON AND JUDITH'S HOME, SARDIS

Simon walked home with Judith from Friday night's Jewish New Year celebration.

He was content to let his wife walk slowly. Judith complained about the pains in her legs more than ever, and she kept talking, sometimes opposing Ravid, their son-in-law.

"Ravid won't walk with us or even join us in our home," she said, irritated. "And I'm more than a little bit upset! You must be less compassionate, Simon! You asked Anthony to come with us to the meeting tomorrow night. Even if some non-Jews accept him as a 'God-fearer,' to most Jews, he will still be an outsider, an 'enemy.'"

Simon responded, "I asked for Jakob's permission to bring Anthony to the God-fearers' meeting. He consulted with the elders. They said, 'A soldier must never come to the service where only we Jews attend, but everyone may learn to worship the Almighty. They can come into the portico. Anthony must stay out of sight, cause no trouble, and not wear his soldier's uniform. That's what Jakob said, and I agree with him."

Chapter 15
The God-Fearers

THE SYNAGOGUE PORTICO

Late Saturday afternoon, the sun was setting as the Ben Shelah family headed to the portico for the God-fearers' service.

Simon was convinced that Anthony should attend because he was learning about the covenant and studying the Torah and the Scriptures. Anthony had explained that he was permitted to go into the city, but the guards were required to follow him.

Simon and Judith came along slowly. Ahead of them, their grandchildren walked with Miriam and Anthony.

Judith strained as she walked, puffing with the effort. "Really, Simon," she said crossly, "Anthony being at our home is going to cause trouble. Those two soldiers following us keep a distance, but people are going to notice and comment. They want to know what's happening when things look different."

Simon disagreed with his wife but refused to be drawn into an argument. "I so enjoy this day of remembrance. I want to examine my life, what I've done, and who I've been this year. I am going to make resolutions, Judith. I feel I have not been firm enough about many things this past year. I need to be more loving and kinder."

"By allowing Anthony to come, you are too open to Gentiles! You are already too kind! What do you mean by 'kinder'?"

"But didn't you enjoy last night? The shofar was blown one hundred times. And the grandchildren! Elaine, Tamir, and Amath couldn't get enough of the apples dipped in honey!"

Anthony was not wearing the soldier's chlamys. To be more inconspicuous, he wore a light brown linen *chiton.* The basic tunic of all people came to the knees. He wore a well-crafted *zane* around his waist, the money belt having been a gift from Arpoxa and Ateas to him two weeks before. It was a Scythian custom to give a gift to parents when a baby reached six months.

Because it was Jewish New Year, a time to begin anew, Simon longed for resolutions to unresolved questions. His mind went back to his favorite psalm: "May your unfailing love come to me, O Lord, your salvation according to your promise; then I will answer the one who taunts me, for I trust in your word."[19]

For Simon, worship was like a bridge bringing together the world of his forefathers and the more complex, immediate world governed by Rome. Above everything, the Eternal One reigned supreme. Prayer displaced his concerns about profits in the marketplace, even if it was only for a few hours.

Gaius was about to begin the service for God-fearers. He called upon Simon to recite the Shema.

Just then, he saw Diotrephes walk in. The stranger was wearing a bright yellow toga contrasting with his expensive, pure white linen tunic. A white linen turban covered his head. He turned to make sure that people noticed the gold bracelets on his right arm. The young man swaggered in, refused to sit on the carpet, and waited until someone found him a small stool. Like most men, his black beard was short and had been carefully trimmed that afternoon at the hot baths.

"Hear, O Israel, the Lord our God, the Lord is one," began Simon. He glanced at Miriam and Anthony. They were sitting in the corner of the portico. Simon noticed Miriam's face turn pale. She held the baby tightly in her arms.

At the end of the service, Diotrephes was acknowledged as a visitor.

"Hail!"" he said, standing up. He greeted the assembly with a grand sweep of his arm. "My name is Diotrephes Milon, descended from an ancient Lydian family. I come from Pergamum. Have you heard of the Jew who was killed in Pergamum by a mob several months ago? Antipas Ben Shelah and his followers, known as the Household of Faith, are scattered far and wide. They no longer gather together."

His dramatic arrival and pronouncement took Simon's breath away. Did this stranger have inside information? *What other things does this stranger know?*

"There is another congregation in Ephesus. It's like this one, I think. There, people are struggling because of a lack of love and respect. Strong objections are being made against their leader, John

---

[19] Psalm 119:41–42

the Elder." He smiled and waited for the impact to sink in.

"Perhaps you don't know this, but I was trained by Antipas. Before he died, he gave me a task, saying, 'Go to the assemblies. Encourage them and make them strong!'"

Simon looked at Miriam. She put her arm through Anthony's, and the two looked at each other. Miriam whispered, "How can Diotrephes utter these lies? He was with Grandpa for six months. One night, he explained his beliefs, and Grandpa excluded him on the spot! Grandpa would never have given him such a task. What a scoundrel!"

Simon shifted his gaze to Anthony and could make out beads of perspiration on the soldier's brow. He heard the soldier whisper, "Yes, a year and a half ago…I was there. Why has Diotrephes come to Sardis?"

Within minutes, everything had changed.

Simon wanted to call out. *Don't listen to him! Diotrephes is steering us away from the bubbling joy of the Jewish New Year. We are anticipating wonderful upcoming feasts, but he is trying to steer you away from them. In his words, I hear stiff opposition toward God-fearers in Pergamum and Ephesus. Everything he says raises questions. Will God-fearers here in Sardis face danger as well?* Instead, he kept quiet.

To conclude his dramatic entry, Diotrephes approached Gaius, saying in a loud voice, "Look, here is a manuscript Antipas was working on when he was killed. Onias, his steward, wanted me to give this to you. I will share more information about the difficulties Antipas faced but at another time. Thank you for welcoming me."

Diotrephes sat down, throwing the edge of his toga back expansively and clearing ample space around himself.

SIMON AND JUDITH'S HOME

The outburst began before the family even entered the house. Miriam's lower lip was quivering, "What a liar! Grandpa was not killed by a mob! He was pressured by the powers of the city and by the imperial priest. In his first trial, a priest from each temple brought accusations.

"I know that man! Diotrephes is the son of the high priestess of the Altar of Zeus. I am positive she was the one who organized the persecution against Grandpa. I think Diotrephes has come here to make trouble! He said the group isn't meeting anymore—a total lie but given as a small bit of misleading information! Our friends are meeting in Marcos's home. That's what we read in his letter. Diotrephes used the change in their name to imply that they don't exist as a congregation."

Lines had appeared on Anthony's face. "A powerful young man from Pergamum has come and upset the God-fearers' meeting. He stated unverifiable lies and half-truths."

Miriam looked at the family. All leaned forward, wanting more information. "Demetrius comes around every year, visiting each important city. I believe Diotrephes has twisted some information that came from Demetrius last year about those in Ephesus."

The three grandchildren sat on couches, their eyes wide open.

Anthony stood up to emphasize his point. "The whole speech is a lie! Diotrephes is up to something. I know him. He's a bit too clever. Antipas did not give Diotrephes such a commission.

"I was there. Here's what happened: Antipas trained us by meeting with us two evenings a week. After a while, he wanted to see what we had learned, so we had to give a declaration of what we believed.

"One evening it was Diotrephes's turn. His beliefs showed that he had accepted the teachings of the Nicolaitans. For example, he does not accept that we should put away sin after receiving forgiveness from God. He disagreed with Antipas's teaching, saying, 'No! We should sin even *more*! Because God forgives more, sin increases the flow of God's grace.' For Diotrephes, God's grace is the doorway to a house full of sin. The Scriptures do not teach that!"

Miriam had her head in her hands, and Anthony addressed her. "Diotrephes came prepared to make that dramatic entry. He appears knowledgeable. Look at how he appeared! He relies on his ability to make a good impression on people. And that business about Onias and a scroll! I looked at it after the meeting, and it was apparently a business contract Onias was working on. The document had something to do with Antipas's shop, nothing more! It was not from Antipas. Onias would never have sent it to Gaius."

Miriam moaned, "Our Jewish New Year started so well! It took only a few sentences from a deceiver to turn our lives upside-down."

She refused to be comforted, even after Lyris served an excellent supper. It had been cooked with care and she simply bubbled with joy, but no one seemed happy tonight.

Simon opened his heart to them. "Miriam, I want you to know we are not the first to face hard situations. Liars have imposed their will throughout history. Isaiah the prophet said, 'The fool speaks folly. His mind is busy with evil; he practices ungodliness and spreads error concerning the Lord; the hungry he leaves empty, and he withholds water from the thirsty. The scoundrel's methods are wicked; he makes up evil schemes to destroy the poor with lies, even when the plea of the needy is just. But the noble man makes noble plans, and by noble deeds, he stands.'"[20]

He sat down and beckoned for Amath to sit on his knee.

"My dear family, every generation faces difficulties. King Nebuchadnezzar brought great evil upon us. Think of all our fasts and why we remember them. The Fast of the Tenth Month reminds us of the day Babylonian troops began their final siege.[21] The Fast of the Fourth Month reminds us of the day Nebuchadnezzar's army breached Jerusalem's walls.[22] The Fast of the Fifth Month is the saddest, when the Temple was destroyed, buildings were burned, and the articles used in worship were taken away to Babylon.[23]

"Why do we fast? We recall our history. We will not submit to those like Haman, who used cowardly means to gain power.[24] These fasts not only remind us of who we are today; they tell us of Adonai, our God who will not change, who will not abandon us.

"Men such as Diotrephes will not flourish, although they may prosper for a while. He has not come with good intentions. By placing our faith in Adonai, we choose not to be afraid.

"The covenant means more to us now than ever. Our Messiah has come. He has called us from darkness to light. This is a holy month for us. Yom Kippur, the Day of Atonement, is only a week away, on September 10. I want us all to prepare our hearts and our spirits for this coming celebration."

JAKOB'S SHOP AND THE SYNAGOGUE IN SARDIS

Jakob added his profits at his desk in the back of his shop. He

---

[20] Isaiah 32:6–8

[21] 2 Kings 25:3–4, Jeremiah 39:2, Zechariah 8:18

[22] 2 Kings 25:3–4, Jeremiah 39:2, Zechariah 8:18

[23] 2 Kings 25:8–10, Zechariah 7:5

[24] Esther 3:1–15

took a deep breath, relishing the aroma given off by the pinewood shavings spread across the floor. Pinewood planks had been made into a bed. Wood chips, like the lines in his accounts, brought him success. He sighed, stood up, and went to open the door, ready now for customers. Jakob made a silent prayer, asking for similar achievements for his close friends.

When the sun was halfway up the morning sky, Jakob walked a short distance along the Royal Road. The thirty men he had asked to come to the portico were already gathered.

He looked around at his friends, the heads of many families. "May the King of the Universe be blessed! A New Year has dawned! Welcome, as we have an important decision to consider together.

"I want to summarize the situation, and then each one can speak. The city council in Sardis debated long and hard how to reestablish their former status in Asia Minor. Six centuries ago, this place was known as the 'City of Gold.' Now the council wants to regain its former high ranking among the other cities. However, political maneuvers beyond their control are squeezing Sardis.

"For one thing, Caesar Augustus awarded the first Imperial Temple in Asia in Pergamum. That happened 105 years ago. Thirty-five years later, Smyrna, the great port city on the Aegean Sea, was awarded its Imperial Temple by Caesar Tiberius.

"Finally, just five years ago, Ephesus was given the same privilege. Domitian has authorized a fortune to be spent on an Imperial Temple. At the same time, the emperor is determined to conquer Dacia. For that, he recently increased pay to the army's soldiers by thirty percent. Consequently, he is enlarging the number of soldiers in several legions.

"However, building a costly third Imperial Temple in one province has eliminated any possibility of Sardis getting additional income. Rome must approve any major civic project. Like Sardis, other cities of Asia Minor need to complete renovations because many buildings were damaged by earthquakes. Are you all with me to this point?"

"Yes, we are," came a loud voice. "Keep going."

He continued confidently. "Sardian leaders are becoming alarmed. Harmony in the social life is based upon maintaining trust in the city's government. Facilities must be kept in order, but too many buildings still require renovations. The city fathers fear increasing crime and rowdy crowds. Mainly, they are concerned that unemployed young men would create unrest.

"It is in this spirit that the Sardis city council approached me. In January, they proposed a few concessions in exchange for significant donations to their building projects. We would be able to speak at a council meeting but would have to leave the council chamber when it came to a vote. I repeatedly pressed them for more concessions. They suggested a few of our families could be given an outdoor section of the new stoa in the Western Agora. I pushed them further and demanded that a whole part of the stoa in the marketplace be given us for a minimum rent. It had to be under a roof and secure, not out in the open.

"You have all heard the plan presented to us. First, our families will receive advantageous legal recognition by the city government. Second, the most valuable shop and office space in the Western Agora will be ours. We will donate some of our added profits to support the city's building programs.

"Now, not every family will benefit directly. However, I made sure that those families that see growth in their business will be able to hire other Jews to work for them. Thus, almost all our people will profit. There is a catch though. The city wants us to support their social activities, and..."

Several voices erupted, all speaking out against the idea of being present at social events.

To smooth over the objections, Jakob had to raise his voice. "...specifically, the mayor told me, 'We believe that it's important for you Jews to be part of the activities. However, you may arrive late. The law permits you to avoid the oath to Caesar. But the city's citizens must see you becoming involved! Arriving late and just being there will help the city council to justify your new status and privileges. You know Sardis; we want to live together. We never want people to sense they are being excluded.'"

Two men had been debating this topic for years. One of them commented, "We have been over this a hundred times! The central question is, 'How can I be a faithful Jew and be present in Sardian society'?"

"What does the elders' tradition say?" asked another.

Voices began to drown out Jakob's explanations, but he calmed them down. "Divisions about matters of faith are always of concern.

I appreciate your worries about our community. However, earning our livelihood is also essential. It is not easy for us to live under Roman law. Some of our most valued families trace their lineage from the colony sent to Phrygia more than 250 years ago. Descendants of those families want to maintain the purity of our food laws. As your rabbi, I have to balance all your opinions. We will listen to each one until we reach an agreement.

"Now, before we get back to the topic of discussion..."

Jakob looked at his circle of friends. He thought of the accounts sheet rolled up in his office and the wood chips on the floor. Some of those shavings were scraped off from rough knots. Smoothing out differences between his friends was like that. He knew he had the tools to smooth things out this morning.

The moment had come for him to launch his new idea. If his plan were adopted, he would make sure Gentiles would never influence his congregation or how it made decisions.

"Listen," he said, encouraging them to pay attention, "elders govern our congregation. However, it's not simple to decide on some issues. We interact within three social groups: the old Jews, the newly exiled Jews, and now some Gentile God-fearers. Our council must somehow reconcile the various points of view.

"How can we make allowances for our diversity and yet maintain unity in our community? I would like to suggest something new. We should have *representatives* from each of those three groups. They will petition the elders. They should not be men already on the council.

"The oldest families would be represented by *three persons* chosen from their group. Those are members descended from the time of the Persian and Seleucid kings. Those families are the most numerous, and they provided the funds for this magnificent building.

"Second, Jewish families like mine, those more recently arrived, would also be represented. When issues come up that affect these families, then their *two representatives* can address the elders.

"What to do about the third group? Their *single representative* would report to our elder's council. He will share opinions and concerns from the Gentiles. It is a concession we must make. The Sardis city council wants our traditions to become known by its citizens. In turn, they want us to value their customs."

Jakob's proposal unleashed a torrent of discussion. For the rest of the morning and all afternoon, voices called out. Some wanted seven representatives; others suggested eight. One man thought the Gentile God-fearers, who were growing in number, should have two representatives, not one.

Simon left for home. He had been one of the thirty men invited, and before the meeting was over, he suggested two representatives for the Gentiles. Strolling homeward, Simon examined a new question. *Who can explain Anthony's hunger for God? I'm surprised that a Roman would want to learn about the Jewish Messiah and Jewish customs.*

In his room upstairs in the Ben Shelah house, the soldier had been studying the Scriptures, especially the first book of the Law but also the psalms and Isaiah. Right now, he was reading a Greek translation from Simon's library of the original Hebrew writings. Two days before, Anthony had asked for Nikias to bring Antipas's scrolls from Olive Grove on his next trip.[25]

An imaginary conversation played itself out. Simon wished he had been bold enough to challenge Jakob in front of all those other men. He went over his imaginary dialogue.

"Jakob, do you intend to completely dominate the congregation? Is that why you formed this plan? I think you want to avoid a split in our congregation. Not everyone agrees over the issue of closer ties to the Sardian city government. Knowing that, you intend to make lesser minds think the real issue is how to 'represent' potentially different factions. As people debate the number of representatives, six, seven, or eight, they will lose sight of the principle change you are bringing in, our relationship to the city's government.

"In the end, Jakob, we will have closer ties with the city. The representatives can debate all they want, but you will find ways to implement what you want done. You will even obtain more concessions from the city, and we will learn the consequences later.

"Through your plan, you are reducing the influence of the one group that is growing, the God-fearers. You know how to keep each group loyal to you. Your scheme is to maintain control through both

[25] At the end of *Through the Fire,* Anthony and Miriam had left Antipas's scrolls at Olive Grove near Thyatira, and they were to stay on the farm until asked for.

the council and the new group of representatives. After these discussions, only a few will reject your plan."

Simon was late getting to sleep after he shared his frustrations with Judith. Usually she grew sleepy more quickly, but tonight she was wide awake. He added, "Jakob has already decided to say yes to demands from Sardis, but he can only do that after keeping the strictest followers of our Jewish traditions happy. Jakob will not allow a civil war in the synagogue, and he's too smart to allow divisions to grow."

MARCOS AND MARCELLA'S HOME, PERGAMUM

Marcos wrote a short letter and had it sent to Simon's home. He was going to be in Sardis for the Asiarchs' meeting, so this was a perfect opportunity to see Miriam and Anthony. He planned to explain the latest legal status of Eliab's will in the courts of Alexandria and Ephesus.

September 9, in the 10th year of Domitian
From: Marcos, friend of Antipas
To: Simon Ben Shelah

Grace, peace, and mercy from God our Father.

I will visit your home after the Meeting of the Asiarchs and see you on Thursday, September 13. I have news and information for you and Miriam.

Chapter 16
The Asiarchs

THE CITY OF SARDIS

Bright banners lined the streets for the Meeting of the Asiarchs. This was the most important annual event in the Province of Asia Minor. Young men were already gambling on possible champions in various sports events. At the same time, their fathers prepared to welcome civil authorities arriving on Tuesday from the eighteen most significant cities.

The whole city was on edge, impatient for the sight of Governor Lucius Ocrea. Normally the governor of Asia Minor would come to Sardis only once every seven years, and he would give the opening speech this year. One young man standing in the crowd lining the highway explained to his little brother, "Next year this governor will not be here. Gossip has it that he wants to be a senator since his assignment in Asia Minor is for two years."

"Look, here comes the governor!" someone called out as horses appeared over the shallow hill to the west. Crowds were waiting for a look at the governor's wavy silver-white hair. Everyone wanted to watch the famous orator go by. He had outwitted Emperor Nero and then supported Emperor Vespasian. Their governor had lived through the Year of the Four Emperors. He even gave speeches in Rome! Few other governors in the empire were as popular.

Trumpets blew, and people cheered every time another mayor arrived. Each of the eighteen asiarchs arrived accompanied by majestic horsemen. A forerunner rode in front carrying the bright-colored banner of the official's city. Women commented on every detail of the mayors' clothing, and horse lovers admired the stately creatures that were so well groomed.

By sundown on Tuesday night, the city buzzed with comments, a lot of it gossip. People stood for hours along the Royal Road to catch a single glimpse of the province's ruling class. As evening came, thousands marched in a procession with candles to the nearby Temple of Artemis.

All the dignitaries arrived at the ancient site of the Phrygian gods, and priests trained in divination examined the liver of an ox for any evil omens. After impassioned prayers to Artemis, the high priest, Ankara, lowered his arms.

All heard him cry out, "The gods have favored Sardis. This will be a successful meeting for the province's administrators. Many athletes will become famous!"

Earlier in the year, Wednesday, September 5 had been chosen by the goddess of fortune as the most auspicious date for the opening procession. The officers agreed to meet for six days, until Monday evening.

Six Roman knights rode black horses in front as the governor's honor guard this morning. Each had a red cape and wore shining armor. Governor Ocrea wore a toga with a purple border that caught every eye. His military chariot was pulled by two matching white horses.

Born into a wealthy family, Lucius Ocrea lived in the governor's mansion near the Acropolis of Ephesus. Facing the beautiful harbor, the palace was the most splendid building in Asia Minor. Ocrea relished the end of each day, when majestic sunsets reflected on rippling waters in the Bay of Ephesus. Coming to Sardis, he was curious to examine the famed acropolis, and he brought an expensive offering for the Temple of Artemis.

In the long procession behind him, each mayor rode a white horse. Horses tossed their heads in the fresh morning air. They, like the thousands lining the Royal Road, sensed the excitement.

The mayors of the three cities of Miletus, Tralles, and Sardis rode abreast in the first file. The mayors of Aphrodisias, Ephesus, and Smyrna followed behind them. Pergamum, Magnesia-on-the-Menderes, and Thyatira came third. In the fourth file rode the mayors from Nysa, Laodicea, and Hierapolis. Priene, Adramyttion, and Alexandria Troas were next.

And the last group was formed by the administrators of

Hypaepe,[26] Colossae, and Halicarnassus.[27]

Following the province's eighteen mayors came high priests, high priestesses, and attendants from each temple in Sardis. Bright colors decorated their clothing. Highly decorated turbans gave them an appearance of being taller than they really were.

Athletes could hardly wait for the procession to begin, and many young men were jumping up and down, limbering up their muscles. Sounds of shouting, laughing, and bragging carried across the crowds lining the Royal Road.

Word came that the procession was ready to begin. Governor Lucius Ocrea gave a sign to the trumpeters, calling out, "Let the young champion proclaim our arrival!"

This was the word Athan, the young champion athlete, was waiting for. As the newest hero of Sardis, he rode ahead on a brown mare, calling out, "The procession is coming! Clear the road! Prepare the way for the governor! If you listen, you may hear him speak. Make way for the most famous orator of our times!"

Athan's horse tossed her head several times. In his hand, he held the city's standard: a tall, narrow red flag. On it, a black eagle with golden feathers on its wings was flying above a mountain. Flashing golden trim around the banner set it off from the others.

Sardis was the host city, and Sardian masses cheered Athan as he passed by. The procession proceeded along the Royal Road, went over the bridge, then turned right toward the Temple of Artemis. The visitors went past the Mint, where gold coins were first fabricated and followed the little river that had yielded its precious secrets, making Sardis a place of such renown.

Black and gold newly made banners hung from trees lining the path to the temple. Spectators lining the road yelled and waved their arms.

All work had stopped. The procession was passing by!
Governor Lucius Ocrea's drew in his breath sharply as he took in the

---

[26] Hypaepe was a major city within the kingdom of Lydia. Located on the road between Sardis and Ephesus, today it is known as Odemish. D. H. French spent a lifetime analyzing the system of Roman roads within the province of Asia Minor. My descriptions are based on much of his work.

[27] Halicarnassus is known today as Bodrum. Most of the cities mentioned here are still undergoing archaeological excavation. The best museums in the region are those in Ephesus, Pergamum, Miletus, and Aphrodisias.

scene. There it was! Artemis lived here! For him, this was the pivotal moment of the entire event. He remembered the moment he had left Ephesus two days before when he had explained his enthusiasm to his wife.

"My dear, for years I've longed to visit Sardis. Everyone who describes the magnificent Temple of Artemis uses superlatives. It's immense. Dazzling in beauty. The temple speaks of incredible dedication of Sardians to Artemis. Incredibly, five people with their arms stretching wide barely circle a single outer column. The roof is supported by three rows of twenty pillars along its length and two rows of nine pillars across its width at the altar. It takes seventy-eight columns to support the massive roof. Resting on the pillars are enormous marble capital stones. The supporting roof timbers are covered with red brick tiles."

"But isn't their temple just like Artemis's temple here in Ephesus?" His wife's hesitation to accept his admiration came from jealousy. Usually she would go with him to such an event, but she had sprained her ankle.

"No, Sardis was the first place for such worship. More than three thousand years earlier, Phrygians in Sardis began worshiping the mother of the gods, Cybele. Then the Greeks arrived. They brought the worship of Artemis as part of their culture. Believing that she granted special favors to Sardis, the city began to build a massive temple. That's why Sardians added the worship of Artemis to the adoration of Cybele."

"I thought the Temple of Artemis here in Ephesus was older than the temple in Sardis," she insisted, favoring her right foot. She did not want to travel from Ephesus to Sardis.

"I'm taking a gift with me. Artemis is their protector goddess. She is their highest power, unseen of course. The goddess cares for her people, never letting them be injured. Befitting such popularity and worth, constructing her colossal temple has taken several hundred years, and the building is yet to be completed. I am asking a favor of her. But please don't breathe a word of this to anyone. I'm confident that if the Temple of Artemis is completed, there will be no further earthquakes in that city. And for myself, I am praying to be appointed to the Senate in Rome. That's my prayer."

His wife embraced him tenderly. "I won't say a word to anyone, my dear husband." She touched his nose with her index finger. "And if the gods answer your prayers, then I'll be back with my family members in Rome. Oh, how I miss them all!"

Arriving at the Temple of Artemis, Governor Lucius Ocrea descended from his chariot to meet with Ankara, the high priest. Ankara, a short man, walked beside the tall governor to the entrance of the temple. "Sir, is this your first time in Sardis?"

"Yes, and I was waiting anxiously to meet you. What do you teach your people about Artemis?" Ocrea stood still to listen.

"Your honor, I've been the high priest for five years. I'm forty-seven years old, and I'm thrilled to be the leader here. Artemis speaks to our hearts. She blesses us with fertile fields. One of her best gifts is a mystic juice. It's what we get from poppies. Priests, especially, worship Artemis for her mysterious powers. The sap that comes from the flower is mixed with juices. When I drink it, Artemis gives me prophetic visions.

"Our goddess is powerful. We credit her with providing success in hunting. She offers protection from wild animals and helps women in childbirth. She also guards the virginity of young women. Relieving diseases among women of all ages, Artemis gives her devotees health. She brings them to old age."

Ocrea took in the aroma of incense coming from the temple. Close by were trees, their branches weighed down with fruit almost ready to be picked. Sheep, led by a shepherd, walked along the riverbank. "For years I have desired to be here, at the entrance to this magnificent temple."

"Many others come here as well. For seven decades, Artemis's popularity has been growing. People always crowd around her temple. You see them around you, imploring for her protection."

Governor Lucius Ocrea stopped in front of an ornately carved pillar at the steps leading into the temple. Names written in stone were dedicated to those who had died seventy-four years earlier. Hundreds had perished in the earthquake.

Trumpets sounded and temple workers, more than two thousand men dressed in yellow robes, waited outside. A bull was being led to the altar. The crowd fell silent, respecting the beast that was about to give its life as a sacrifice. During the ceremony, virgin priestesses danced and sang slowly. Their songs had originated hundreds of years before.

The governor leaned close to his secretary, "While Rome

governs the world, the songs of Artemis rule the hearts of these people. These tunes were composed during the time of the Lydian Kingdom."

Lucius Ocrea stayed there while the sacrifice was made. Then he bowed his head, made his intercession, and gave a leather bag containing an offering to the high priest. Once this event was over, the procession moved to the Greek Theater.

Trees along the Hermus River shimmered with vibrant harvest colors, and crowds lining the streets of Sardis cheered as the procession went by. Today was the opening day of the Meeting of the Asiarchs. Visitors from the most important cities in Asia Minor were experiencing the morning splendor of Sardis.

Visitors from surrounding villages shouted at the sounds of horses' hooves. Most people would never again be able to reach out and almost touch provincial dignitaries.

Two hours before, the pageantry moved toward the temple. Now they witnessed splendor again as the powerful men went past them for the second time, the procession moving toward the Greek Theater.

The theater was full to overflowing. Wealthy men occupied the seats behind distinguished guests. Those with places of privilege only. Poorer spectators crowded in as a faceless blur in the upper sections and on the grassy hill beside the theater.

Tymon Tmolus, the mayor of Sardis, took center stage to declare the ceremony open. "Caesar is lord and god!" More than twelve thousand Sardians shouted, "Caesar is lord and god!" He stepped back and motioned for the governor to come to the center of the stage. People clapped and cheered.

Governor Lucius Ocrea gave a short opening speech. "I declare this meeting of the Asiarchs to be in session in the tenth year of Domitian!"

His gestures were large and expansive. "Mayors and magistrates, ladies and gentlemen, I bring you greetings from all regions of our province. We joyfully accept your kind hospitality in Sardis, the golden jewel of this province. May Pax Romana continue!"

The governor's outspread arms included everyone and everything around him._"Today the sun shines in your favor! Emperor Domitian is pleased with the loyalty shown by the people of this province. He is grateful for prayers offered every day at the Temple of the Imperial Cult. Events such as this annual event bring out the best that citizens have, and they share with one another.

"Moreover, Domitian notes with pride the ongoing efforts to rebuild Sardis. The Great Earthquake..." He left the sentence unfinished because the damage caused by earthquakes touched on the sensitivities of Sardians. He was proud of their building skills but secretly dismayed that so much rebuilding still had to be carried out. Ocrea had not expected to see the large southwest section of the Temple of Artemis still damaged.

"The Temple of Artemis is almost completely restored. Only the renovations to a small section needs to be completed. An hour ago, I stood beside the pillar that lists the names of those who died more than seven decades ago. Your public buildings, the gymnasium, the stadium, the baths, and the city's gates are in good condition. Even the Western Agora marketplace will soon be fully restored!

"We know that many original Lydian monuments were destroyed in that disaster. Thankfully, we acknowledge Zeus, Artemis, Demeter, Hera, Apollo, and all the other gods for their continued protection. Thank you, Mayor Tymon Tmolus, and all Sardian citizens who made our arrival so pleasant. We especially enjoy the luxury of sweet waters in the hot baths."

The Sardian people had done their best to make a good impression on the guests.

However, Ankara had not fully opened his heart when talking with the governor. While Artemis was said to be a kind deity, other gods were cruel. And the high priest knew those gods were both powerful and harsh.

For seventy-four years, Sardis had been slowly rebuilding from the Great Earthquake. On that day, many years before, incredible destruction had darkened the city. The collapse of the acropolis caused people to live in fear of another landslide.

Every day, Ankara and Alala, the high priestess, let it be known that Artemis blessed them. They comforted people, saying, "Our goddess brings us health. She will preserve us from further destruction."

But the high priest with the intense look in his eyes kept secret words of the Lydian language alive. Those oracles, meant to satisfy the dark spirits, were only uttered late at night.

Chapter 17
The Women's Gathering

THE MAYOR'S HOME, SOUTH HILL, SARDIS

A courier came to Simon's house with an invitation for Miriam. Her name had been given to the mayor's wife by Kalonice.

Miriam asked Judith and Simon, "Should I go with Kalonice to meet the wives of the elite families? The wife of Mayor Tymon Tmolus is opening her house on Sunday, and she's invited some people in Sardis to meet women from other cities."

Simon answered, "Well, I think it would do you good to meet these women. You need to know what it's really like to live in a city dominated by greed, conceit, and aspirations for status. I've had years to learn about it. You'll see it all in one day."

Judith disagreed. "Simon! You should be ashamed of yourself! How can you encourage her like this? Those people aren't like us!"

After more discussion, Miriam decided to go with Kalonice. She desired a better understanding of the society but would not open the door to friendship. Uncle Simon had his driver take them in a wagon to South Hill, where luxurious homes overlooked the Hermus Valley.

As the wagon passed the lower slopes of the acropolis, the driver pointed out a dozen massive storehouses. Supplies of wheat, wine, olive oil, building materials, and other products were kept there. Administrators supplied the city in the winter months. Nearby, the Temple of Apollo overlooked the Eastern Quarter.

Their driver pointed toward the poor section farther down the road. "In the *insulae*," he said, looking at a dilapidated apartment building, "a single small apartment can hold a family of eight or ten. I'm happy you're going to spend the day at a luxurious home."

The wagon came to the bottom of a hill where the road branched to the left and right. Homes of the rich were built along both branches of the way. Gardens blossomed with oleander bushes and other colorful flowering shrubs. Songbirds, attracted to pools of water, splashed, flapping their tiny wings. Water abounded along the "Pearls of the Necklace," the popular name for this road. Three aqueducts bringing water to the city from springs high upon Mount Tmolus joined at this point.

The driver stopped in front of an enormous mansion, the home of Panthea Tmolus. Many carriages were already parked along the road. Horses twitched their ears while using their tails to swat at flies. Some guests were still arriving, ambling, laughing, and talking happily.

At the front entrance, slaves bowed low, removing sandals as guests arrived. They washed the women's feet with warm water. A few guests brought babies in their arms. Infants would be taken care of in the half-basement built into the side of the hill.

Kalonice and Miriam were escorted through the entrance and into the great room. The older woman introduced Miriam to her hostess.

"Hail! Panthea, this is Miriam, Simon Ben Shelah's niece. You will remember that Diodotus recently approached Simon to be a partner in the Bank of Hermus. Miriam is a newcomer to our city. Miriam, this is Panthea Tmolus, the wife of Mayor Tymon Tmolus. Cynthia, this is Miriam. Cynthia is the mayor's lovely daughter."

"Hail! Pleased to meet you, Miriam!"

"Hail! Pleased to meet you, too, Respected Panthea, and Cynthia."

"Where was your home before coming here, Miriam?" asked Panthea.

"I lived in Pergamum until April."

"Come, let me introduce you to some other women." Panthea introduced Miriam to her circle of friends and the wives of some of the visiting officials. The women of Asia Minor were being treated with a special honor at the open house.

The mayor's property dated back hundreds of years. Miriam looked around the spacious home, which had initially been owned by a succession of Persian satraps assigned to govern the region around Sardis. Consecutive improvements added to its size and beauty.

A colorful hall led from the large room to the latrine. There, running water flowed quietly down the wall, where an idyllic mountain scene was painted, and then it splashed into a pool in which water plants grew. Painted on the white marble was an underwater scene showing fish, frogs, and turtles swimming among plants. The room was spacious, with windows high up on the wall.

Water ran continuously along a small channel in the floor, which supplied the water for cleansing after using the latrine.

Miriam returned to the gathering. A small statue of Hera in the lararium stood at the center of the front wall between two open windows. In the portico was a small courtyard with four pillars holding up a roof covered with red tiles. A square, slightly sunken marble space was filled with water. Sunlight came through the open roof and was reflected in shallow, shimmering ripples.

Coming back to the enormous central room, Miriam counted the women. Most were reclining on couches. Some sat on plush Persian carpets. She got confused after reaching eighty-nine people, and she moved about the room to see if there were others she had not seen.

Miriam looked around the great room once more and took better notice of the guests' clothing. Never had she seen such a display, even on the most memorable days of public processions in Pergamum. Many ladies also wore a *stola,* a draped garment. It was attached at the shoulder with a brooch and a pin called a *fibula.* These were made from silver or bronze and cast in the shape of animals or other symbols. Most of them were quite elaborate.

Women had their hair done up, with their long black braids intertwined with red, golden, or blue strips of cloth. Some wore colorful headbands too. Their garments were made from expensive materials. White tunics with colored patterns matched olive skin, brown eyes, and black hair.

All wore jewelry. Miriam's eyes went from hammered gold necklaces, earrings, and bracelets to nose rings. Gold lunates hung down from their ears with a half crescent representing the moon. Hands were decorated reddish-brown with drawings made by using henna. All the women were scented with expensive Egyptian perfumes.

The guests fell silent as Panthea went to the household statue of Hera. To begin the meeting, she placed fresh flowers beside the image of the goddess. A spoonful of incense was sprinkled into a small bed of hot coals. Then she bowed, raised her open hands above her head, and placed her hands over her heart.

"Caesar is lord and god," she said and added, "Hera, hear my prayers and bless our gathering."

Turning to the women who had come from many places, she said, "Welcome to my home. While the men ponder politics and soldiers, armies, and taxes, we will talk about the issues of the heart. You have heard it simply said that Sardis is built upon several civilizations. I would like you to take a correct, fuller impression of our city back to your homes, so we will tell you some interesting stories."

Some called out or clapped, enthused by such a purpose.

"We will hear two speeches," said Panthea once it was quiet again. "Lady Delbin, the wife of Diodotus, Chief Manager of the Bank of Hermus, and I will introduce you to Sardis. After that, we have a luncheon prepared by the best slaves in Asia."

The mayor's wife introduced Delbin, the banker's wife. She wore a tunic of fine linen, gleaming with intricate embroidery around the neck. A gold band held her hair back, and tiny gems on her headband sparkled as she bowed. Her stola shone with threads of gold woven through the white linen. All spoke of extravagant luxury.

She smiled pleasantly at everyone and started her speech by explaining the Sardian phrase, "Never enough gold." Delbin held the women in rapt attention as she recounted the association between wealth and power. She told many tales of wealthy families, stories of intrigue, discovery, war, and conquest.

For more than an hour, she held her audience in total awe. Finishing with a challenge to seek yet more wealth, she said, "The story of gold is stamped deeply in every Sardian family's soul. The faces of kings remain on our coins. In ancient days, Greeks remarked, 'Sardis is the most splendid city in the world!'

"Those days brought the best sculptors and artists, and our influence spread far beyond the shores of Asia Minor. Today Sardis plays host to the most important families in our province, and you, most honorable ladies, represent those homes! Please enjoy every moment while you are here, and take home our best Sardian phrase, 'Never enough gold!'"

A noisy round of applause greeted these words. With the morning half over, slaves brought fresh grape juice. After enjoying the morning treats, they sat down again to hear their hostess, Panthea.

"Welcome, everyone! I'm proud to have you in my home and speak to you about my family. The mayor asked me to marry him twenty-four years ago. Both of us are descended from ancestors from the Hittite culture. They ruled this area long ago. Those fierce warriors came to this valley and established my ancestors as a powerful clan. The Lydian Empire grew out of that culture.

"I am one of eleven children. Artemis protected my family and gave us this lovely home. My husband is the mayor, the asiarch of Sardis, and he is now meeting with your husbands in the ancient Palace of the Kings.

"All Sardians share our heritage. Our tradition is built on three great values. The first is strength of character. The second is wealth: owning lands, jewelry, and the honor of a name. Third, we are known for our wisdom. Was anyone ever wiser than Aesop, the writer of fables who lived here before moving away? His stories captured the wisdom of the land."[28]

Like the first speaker, the mayor's wife urged her audience to covet the great treasures of life. "Some say Antioch is where East meets West, but that is not true. Sardis is *the real* meeting place, the crossing point of the world. Antioch is not an accurate conveyor of Roman values as there are too many influences from Persia and other eastern lands. No, Sardis is where the peoples of the world meet, blend, and value their interaction. No idea is opposed here; all concepts are examined.

"We tolerate every religion and encourage dialogue between all. No one here is excluded because of an individual's beliefs; Artemis holds all her children close to her bosom. She is a willing mother who adopts and loves all. For more than 1,300 years, Hittites, Lydians, Persians, Phrygians, and Greeks brought her gifts. And more recently, Romans, Egyptians, and even Scythians have come. All brought peace and commerce to our people and our city. Opinions and disagreements do not divide us. Here in Sardis, the East has met the West. What could be of greater value than the elements of true wealth: character, glamour, fame, and honor?"

A round of applause began, and then all the women rose to their feet, clapping with joy. The rest of the day was dedicated to leisure. Wine flowed in abundance. Trays of fruit were replenished continually, and laughter floated above every table.

Even before lunch was over, quiet whispers began. Some spoke of the rising number of thefts that were causing consternation in the homes of several women present. Women spoke louder, and some

[28] Historians understand that Aesop lived in Sardis for part of his life.

made cutting comments about people in their home cities. Complaints about slaves, neighbors, and merchants began to circulate.

Miriam knew that to be accepted by these wealthy women, she would have to spend much time learning their ways. They drank from cups overflowing with self-congratulation. However, having tasted these two explanations of Sardian life, she had had enough. In a few hours, she would be with her family for the most holy day of the year. Judith was right. This world was not for her.

Miriam rode home with Kalonice. She could hardly wait to describe the afternoon event for Anthony. "These people are different from our way of thinking. What a contrast! Prayers of repentance and forgiveness with my people are my real source of wealth and peace. How can I share my kind of wealth with Kalonice? She is so enamored with Sardis's traditions!"

Going to sleep, two lines of a new poem came to her.

Hair done up in braids, locks with fancy curls,
Eyes enhanced with black; necklace hung with pearls...

DIODOTUS AND DELBIN'S HOME, WEST HILL

September 9, in the 10th year of Domitian
From: Diotrephes
To: My dear mother, Lydia-Naq

Greetings and peace, and I trust this letter finds you well.

I have been here for one week. Zeus blessed my journey in several ways. It is Sunday night, and I am glad to be in Sardis. The Annual Meeting of the Asiarchs concludes soon, and then the Sardis games will start. I am staying with your friends, Banker Diodotus and Delbin. Diodotus is the chief manager of the Bank of Hermus, the largest bank. They have a splendid view from West Hill across the Pactolus Valley, from which gold has been extracted since ancient times. From their great room, I can gaze at the temple of Artemis.

I am happy about the arrangements you planned for me. I went to the gymnasium on Tuesday. I am getting familiar with the Department of History. Still, I have not yet met all the teachers in my department.

I asked about Anthony and Miriam. From Cleon, I learned that Miriam changed the name of our baby from Chrysa, "The Golden One," to Grace. Fortunately, no one here knows that Zoticos is her father. I am working on a plan to bring Chrysa to you.

I now know that Simon Ben Shelah is much respected for his wealth in the Sardian community. He is being sought as a partner in the Bank of Hermus. Remember, Antipas and Simon were brothers. One has already died.

I send you my devotion and respect and hope you are enjoying good health.

Diotrephes sealed the letter and pressed his ring into the hot red wax. He watched it harden as he blew on it to cool the wax and preserve the imprint, and then he leaned back, proud of his personal inscription.

It was normal to place himself at the beginning of every sentence. Diotrephes had already sealed the letter when he remembered something. He had forced himself into the parade when the civil servants from Pergamum were lining up for the procession. Suddenly he saw Marcos, the lawyer. Viewing him as a visitor in Sardis caused dismay, but he decided against including this unease in the letter to his mother.

While projecting a sense of well-being in the letter, Diotrephes was not entirely at peace. He reasoned, *Marcos brought the Pergamum atheists under the protection of his roof. He is their leader but not for long. My mother will put a stop to that!*

THE GARRISON OF SARDIS, THE ACROPOLIS, SARDIS

Garrison commanders had gathered for their own meeting. The top eighteen military officers exchanged information and carried out a status review regarding the previous year.

Today they sat together for a meal at the acropolis. Commander Felicior hoped to use this time for some subtle fact-finding, and he called Cassius aside. "Did you receive news from Philippi about Anthony Suros, the legionary I've had under observation for four months?"

"Yes, a short letter arrived recently. About two years ago, the commander in Philippi received orders from Rome. Suros was sent to the Pergamum garrison as an instructor. But gossip has it that Anthony discovered political discontent in his legion. He may have reported something to his general. A military inquiry followed, but no one knows what came out of it. Some wonder if he was assigned to be a spy by Domitian."

Cassius continued, "Mark my words! There's more to this story than has been revealed. Aside from that, he became a follower of that Jewish messiah. He even took a dozen recruits to a meeting where false teaching was given. In that way, he is a harmful influence. However, as an instructor, he's competent."

Felicior put his finger against his lips. He thought for a moment before saying, "Well, since you have had his pay sent to us, I should try having him teach scouting to my recruits."

"Fine. Keep Suros in Sardis but stop him from influencing recruits! He loves forests, so let him stay outside the city. That way, he cannot invite recruits to go to the atheists' meetings!"

Felicior nodded, looked around the room, and said, "Enough about Anthony! Let's get back to our regular business. Thank you for your information, and if more arrives from Philippi, I'd like to receive a copy."

On the way back to the garrison office, Felicior decided, *Next week, I will take him off house arrest and see how he handles a bit more freedom. I'll also start planning how to use him as an instructor.*

THE STADIUM OF SARDIS

On Tuesday, September 11, athletic competitions began, the activities taking place at the stadium and the gymnasium. Athletic competitions caused considerably more stir among ordinary people than all the grand assemblies and speeches from mayors.

By Friday afternoon, the sound of noisy celebrations rose from the taverns. Revelers, fueled by too much beer, overflowed onto the streets singing old childhood songs with modified lyrics. Arbitrators and elders, judges and nobles, butchers, rope makers, and government officials stood together, basking in the glory of overcomers.

Young men marched from the Eastern Agora market area to the Western Agora and back again, their voices hoarse from yelling. Only a few could be present at the awards program in the evening, but all were delighted with the newfound sense of importance for their city.

As evening came on, the stadium filled for the victors' awards ceremonies. For light, long poles with rags wrapped around the tops were placed into holes bored into the marble seats. The cloths were oiled and set afire to burn as torches during the ceremony. Slaves circulated around the stadium. They reoiled the rags whenever a flame stopped burning brightly.

Before Athan came to the stadium, he had taken off the old tunic he wore every day. Now, as a Hero of the Games, he had been presented with a dazzling white linen tunic, one sewn especially for this occasion. It was made of expensive Egyptian fabric with gold crowns embroidered into the neck and the sleeves. He had won local races in Sardis and Laodicea. Now the Asia Minor-wide games had shown everyone his amazing abilities.

Athan and the other competitors lined up outside the stadium entrance, where they would receive their prizes. They slowly paraded into the stadium and around the track, stopping as a group before the main area where the governor and other dignitaries waited to start the award ceremonies.

Names were called out. As the youngest champion, Athan was the first one to receive recognition. He had won first place in three different races, so he was considered a hero. Spectators at the ceremony exploded with joy. He received a crown of laurel leaves placed on his head, first by Governor Lucius Ocrea and then by Mayor Tymon Tmolus.

Then the governor took Athan's right arm and held it high as he and Athan walked around the running track in front of the spectators in the stadium.

In the future, athletes entering through the ramp into the Stadium of Sardis could read the engraved name of this young overcomer in the Games of the tenth year of Domitian. For years to come, young men competing in the games would repeat, "Let me tell you about Athan, the young man who walked with the governor!"

Here was an honor! His name, carved in white marble at the base of the Eastern Gate along with the names of previous overcomers, would be there forever for others to read.

After the governor returned to the presentation stand, the other winners in the competitions were announced. When the name of a city was called out, further cheering sounded out. Winners walked forward, bowed down, and received their victor's laurel crown.

On Saturday, thousands would start the trip back to their cities with trophies, souvenirs, and memories. By the end of the following week, even the ones who lived farthest away would be home, telling and retelling the glories of the sports and the honors of fame.

Chapter 18
Genuine Riches

SIMON'S SHOP ON THE ROYAL ROAD

Cleon had learned how easy it was to earn money. Giving information was not "real work," yet it paid more.

"Well, Cleon, your name means 'The Famous One.'" Diotrephes grinned, sticking his head through the open door. Today no one else was in the shop. Heber was away with the bankers, answering their questions.

"All this information you supply me is significant. Maybe you will become famous, like my Uncle Zoticos, the Director of the Pergamum Library." Diotrephes pulled a silver coin out of his leather purse. He made sure the store clerk heard other coins while he was thinking and planning.

Continue giving me such useful information, Cleon.

"Well, let me tell you something more," Cleon responded, gradually standing to his full height. "Tomorrow the Jews are going to keep a special fast. No one will eat or drink until the sun goes down. I've learned that there is an argument at the Ben Shelah house, but I don't know what it's about. Sometimes Heber has a far-away look in his eyes."

"Thank you, Cleon. I have known the Ben Shelah family in Pergamum for years. This gift may help you with any 'extra expenses.' Now I want you to learn what the quarrel is about. Perhaps it's about a child. Or..."

The store clerk did not hear Diotrephes finish his thought. The denarius Diotrephes had given to him was equivalent to a full day's wages.

SIMON AND JUDITH'S HOME, SARDIS

Simon wanted the entire family present for the beginning of Yom Kippur, the Day of Atonement. Miriam was invited and told Simon that Anthony would stay upstairs, caring for Grace in their room.

On Wednesday evening, Ravid explained to his mother that he and Nissa would join the family for the evening gathering to start the fast. He said, "I still believe that Gentiles staying in our home will be a source of trouble. However, I want to improve my attitude. I've been thinking about the sin of anger. I shouldn't get so irritated at Miriam for being here. I want her to know that I accept her, but that doesn't mean I am in favor of Anthony living here. Do you think the army can be persuaded to move him to another city?"

That evening, their fasting began. Simon led his family in the declaration of their faith. "Hear, O Israel, the Lord our God is One." He poured water on Judith's open hands and dried them.

Then Judith poured a little water on Heber's hands from the jug of water. In turn, he poured water on Ezar's hands. The pitcher went around the table, symbolizing the washing away of sin, guilt, and judgment. Their Holy Day, the Day of Atonement, had begun. This was a fasting day; the water would cleanse their hands, but not a drop would pass their lips.

COMMANDER FELICIOR'S OFFICE, THE ACROPOLIS, SARDIS

On Thursday morning, a soldier arrived at Simon's door. "Commander Felicior wants Anthony to report to his office this morning."

Shortly afterward, Anthony stood before the commander again. "You called me, sir?"

"You did well in the archery test on the mountain," stated Felicior flatly.

"Thank you, sir."

"I am going to assign you as a scout instructor for our recruits. We will be sending forty soldiers to Legion XXI in a few months. Explain to me how you would train new recruits as scouts."

Anthony had guessed that this meeting was either to send him back to Pergamum or to assign him as an instructor.

Simon and his household will be fasting today, repenting of their sins. Here I am, in Commander Felicior's office, seeing whether I am considered fit to train recruits. What will Ravid think of me now? Will it make things more complicated than ever?

With these thoughts, he turned to the task at hand. "When we trained recruits in Upper Germanica, sir, we often divided them into two groups. One took a defensive pose; the other had to go on the offensive. I would lead the group that had to attack, and another instructor worked to keep the camp safe. The groups would occasionally switch the offensive and defensive roles."

What seemed like a grin passed over Felicior's lips, but the moment passed so quickly Anthony could not be sure.

"I am giving you a chance to prove yourself, soldier. As you suggest, you will lead twenty of our new recruits as one squadron against another detachment of rookies led by Instructor Prosperus.

"In a few days, I want you ready to start the training, but first I want these forty young men to be toughened up a bit with their initial training. You will show me if your kind of training can bring victory when the army invades Dacia. The garrison training camp is halfway up the mountain. A horse will be provided when we are ready for you. Now return to the house. Wait for my instructions."

SIMON AND JUDITH'S HOME

Marcos's official responsibilities at the Meeting of the Asiarchs were over. Now, on Friday morning, he had some tasks to fulfill. At the gate opening to the property, two soldiers stood on guard.

"Hail! Is Simon Ben Shelah at home?" he asked.

"Yes, he is at home. Who are you?"

"Well, I am a stranger but not dangerous. I'm a lawyer from Pergamum."

Marcos had written to Simon about coming to Sardis. He knew the family would want to know what had happened when Antipas gave his final witness. A knot tightened in his stomach as he prepared to go over how his friend had died. Simon and Judith would want to know the truth. He thumped loudly on the wooden gate and waited until a servant opened it and escorted him to Simon.

They gathered in the main room around the table. Judith and Simon sat on one side, and Marcos was in the middle. Miriam and Anthony played with Grace on the third couch. The baby smiled and put her fist in her mouth, screaming with delight when Anthony lifted her high over his head.

Simon called Lyris. "Please go to the shop and call Heber to come." She left quickly.

Simon asked the children to go outside and brush down the horses. He did not want them to hear details about the death of his brother.

When the adults had all gathered, Marcos told them the sad news. "Antipas's last days still make me sad. I knew he was going to be tried. I explained that many people wanted him dead. Execution was always a possible outcome. Before the trial, Antipas and I planned for Anthony and Miriam to be married right away. Then the next day we celebrated Chrysa's adoption. I made arrangements for them to get out of the city undetected."

A small chuckle went around. Simon and Judith had heard that story from Miriam.

"There were two trials, and the first hearing took place in the Roman Theater. High priests from each temple were there, but there was such a contrast! Antipas was dressed in a simple white robe, while his accusers wore colorful attire. They brought many charges, and he answered each one courteously. They tried to trap him with his own words, but he responded by telling stories about the Master. All 15,000 people fell silent. Publicly accused, without a hope of going free, he withstood their denunciations. That's my summary of the first trial."

Simon rested his head in his hands and sighed loudly.

"Three nights later, Antipas was taken to the Roman Amphitheater. It's half as big again as the Roman Theater. It was full to overflowing, with maybe 25,000 people present. Some arrived hearing the words 'a possible death,' so those men imagined a gladiator contest. Some were ignorant and said Antipas was a professional gladiator.

"Instead, it was a trial about taxes. Your brother had to declare loyalty to the emperor. Once again, he faced their accusations, and at the end, he gladly paid his taxes. These included his business levies as well as his personal taxes. The extra payments were added since he was no longer a Jew. A year before, the Synagogue of Pergamum had revoked his Jewish status, so he was no longer exempt from taking the oath. He would not honor the emperor by declaring, 'Caesar is lord and god,' and for this, he was condemned. Men were anxious for blood; many cried out for his death.

"Within the hour, the imperial and religious authorities led him to the New Temple. It's an enormous building being built in the lower section, in the center of the city. It will join the worship of ancient gods from Pergamum, Lydia, Syria, and Egypt.

"A huge metal pot in the shape of a bull, previously used in the former Temple of Artemis, was placed in the center. It had been filled with oil, and a blazing fire brought it to a boil. I stood and watched as they lifted him up over the oil using a crane, one used to move huge stone blocks. An accident at the last minute caused the oil under Antipas to catch fire, making him die almost instantly—far quicker than the priests had intended."

Simon gasped, gripped by the horror, trying not to imagine his brother being lowered toward bubbling oil.

Miriam pushed her head against Anthony's shoulder. Her eyes were shut, and her chest heaved. She stifled a scream.

Heber entered the house at this point, and Marcos went back over the story. Tears welled up in the lawyer's eyes. For many moments, Marcos could not speak. His voice wavered. "I took over the fellowship that Antipas formed. That congregation now meets in one of the two houses that I bought last summer."

Hearing of Marcos's family, Miriam said, "I want to know how Florbella is."

"My daughter, Florbella, continues to improve since she was healed by Antipas. We had come to Pergamum to get away from horrible memories. How could we ever get over the loss to our family after that earthquake in Nicomedia?[29]

"Florbella feared the dark and even the thought of earthquakes. You also helped her, and now she is chatting all the time and free from fear.

"Now, here is Antipas's last gift to you, Miriam. When I had informed him of the coming danger, the possibility that the authorities might arrest, banish, or even kill him, he entrusted this to me. It's a considerable amount of money."

Tears of joy and sadness filled her eyes. Miriam was speechless as she looked into the money pouch. "Thank you. What can I say?" After she regained control, she asked for more information about the

---

[29] Marcos's loss of his family members took place on August 18, AD 85. I based this story on two massive earthquakes along the Marmara Sea fault line. On August 17, 1999, the quake had a magnitude of 7.5. It hit the NE Marmara Sea region, the densely populated industrial region of Turkey. It killed about 20,000 people. About 250,000 buildings were damaged. More than 600,000 people were left homeless after a second quake in November 1999. These two events left social and economic wounds that took years to heal.

congregation meeting in the village.

Marcos answered, "We don't meet in the cave anymore, but most all your friends are still with us. A few left to retain membership in the synagogue." He paused to gather his thoughts. "Of course, the big issue Antipas faced, of having to declare, 'Caesar is lord and god,' has not disappeared. However, I think I am safe from accusation for the next several years.

"I own three houses side by side. We live in one with our slaves. The second one has been turned into the 'House of Prayer,' the new name for our congregation. The third has become a home for widows.

"Now, for my concerns. The Jewish group is causing me a few problems. On Friday nights, Jewish families meet as a congregation with Onias. In our fellowship, Jews also gather on the Sabbath. We thought questions of Jewish worship in our congregation were over. However, Jaron, the leader of the Synagogue of Pergamum, not only dismissed Antipas but he also asked three other families to leave that congregation. They decided to join our Jewish fellowship and have become interested in learning about the Messiah. But they spend hours on genealogies, family histories, births, and deaths. Strange ideas also spill out because some brought notions from Persia.

"The Gentiles attend on Saturday nights and Sunday mornings. Here is my dilemma. Marcella and I can host the two groups and help the widows, but I do not have sufficient knowledge to teach them! Onias, Antipas's servant, is busy keeping the business side of things going, and he needs an assistant. Therefore I need help. Antipas's house in the village is empty, so if we can find a teacher, he could live there. If you have any ideas, I would like to hear them.

"Now let me hold this beautiful little girl!" Marcos took Chrysa Grace in his arms. Her dark brown eyes focused on him, and she smiled up at him. Her black hair, clean and washed, gave off the fresh smell of olive orchards. Grace reached out to touch his face and giggled happily. She made funny noises and responded to his comical faces. The time passed all too quickly.

COMMANDER FELICIOR'S OFFICE, THE ACROPOLIS, SARDIS

At the garrison, Felicior could hardly hide his pleasure. Anthony's proposal would not diminish the authority of the present instructor. Felicior had some doubts about Prosperus, who needed additional self-confidence. Prosperus came from one of the best military families in Italia, but he was an ineffective instructor in certain areas. He did not have all the skills that Felicior needed.

The other instructor working with the Garrison of Sardis had been called to Moesia in preparation for war in Dacia. So Felicior determined that Anthony, with the weakest twenty of the forty recruits, would go up against a stronger squad. Prosperus would be given the twenty most reliable recruits.

The training method used in Upper Germanica would test Anthony's leadership abilities against biased odds. If he were successful, the garrison would gain an excellent instructor. If he failed, he would be sent back to Pergamum for being inept. Either way, Felicior stood to gain.

SIMON AND JUDITH'S HOME

Marcos, having explained about Antipas's death, went with Simon's family to the roof and sat comfortably in the shade under the grapevines. Wanting to explain the status of the two wills, Marcos took a deep breath and sighed again before beginning the family conference. "I will now tell you about my work and what is happening in the courts.

"Eliab Ben Shelah left a will when he died more than two years ago. It was written shortly after he arrived in Pergamum, and he never updated it. He divided his estate among his nine children: six brothers in Asia and the three in Alexandria—Judah, Samuel, and their sister, Azubah.

"Antipas's death was unexpected. His part of his father's estate will pass on to Miriam. That means nine heirs will receive Eliab's estate. Amos, the oldest, will receive twenty percent. The other eight heirs will each receive ten percent.

"Eliab's estate in Pergamum refers only to the property and not the buildings on the land, which has caused a real problem for the courts.

"Here is the conundrum. To honor your Eliab's will, I would have to sell the property and divide the proceeds into ten parts. However, doing that would make it impossible to execute Antipas's will. Why? Because Antipas also left a will. His estate includes all improvements made to the property.

"Antipas formed an exceptional village. His workshops represent a significant investment of funds: one for glassblowing, one for pottery, one for spices and perfumes, and another for making wool and linen clothing. He also built a kiln, a carpentry shop, a smith's shop, and a warehouse. He left sheds for wagons, the shed for drying the pottery, and shelters for animals.

"Then there are the houses! The village includes thirty-eight homes. Further, the estate includes two sales shops in Pergamum: one in the Upper Agora and one in the Lower Agora. Finally, he had built a shop in Assos and another in Adramyttion, both on the Aegean coast. A third, the Assos shop, was closed a year before his death. The animals, the pastureland, and the wagons and horses are also part of your grandfather's estate."

Marcos leaned back and laughed. "Strangely, there are no slaves! Usually the division of the property of wealthy families is most sensitive around one issue: dividing up the slaves. All of Antipas's estate goes to Miriam."

Everyone glanced at Miriam. Chenya gave her a hug, and the others congratulated her warmly.

"But it's not going to be simple. City officials in Pergamum demanded the expropriation of Antipas's estate. I presented them with the many legal problems, which convinced them that the costs of expropriating the land were not worth the return. They agreed to let the village remain in business, paying taxes over the years to exceed what the city would receive from selling it after the legal fees were paid. Aside from that, Antipas paid his taxes before his death, so they lost that as a significant legal point. The trials the city held may not have held legally in the first place. I haven't brought that up yet and will keep it available if needed later.

"I have been to court five times since then: twice in the District Court in Pergamum, in both the Provincial Court and Senatorial Court in Ephesus, and once to see the local representative of the Egyptian Imperial Court. All these courts agree that Eliab's document must be executed first. Only then may your grandfather's will be completed. So I am requesting that the land, buildings, and business remain intact.

"In my first major audience, I presented my proposal to the provincial judges in Ephesus. The second time, I made a presentation personally to senatorial judges and Claudius Varro Zosimus, the provincial administrator. The document I presented stated, 'I propose that the profits from Eliab's businesses be divided into ten portions for five years. This is to satisfy the intent of Eliab's will.' I showed them business records. Hopefully, after five years, the sum of profits will be about the equivalent of the value of the property without Antipas's added improvements.

"So stipulated amounts will be sent to Eliab's heirs with payments to be made in April and October for five years. If the banks are timely in releasing the money, you can pick it up in early May and at the beginning of November. After ten payments have been made over five years, Eliab's last testament will be executed. During this time, Antipas's village will remain intact. If things turn out the way I hope, Miriam will eventually own the whole estate."

Once again, smiles were directed toward Miriam. "Congratulations, Miriam," said Simon. "You are the youngest adult here and perhaps are going to have the largest estate!"

Marcos continued, "I think the province's financial administrator will accept my plan. He specializes in complicated situations, and he has tentatively agreed with everything. We should have word back from Egypt by late March or early April next year. Copies of the agreement will then be sent to each of Eliab's children."

Miriam and Marcos talked over the details while the others listened. Over 130 people lived in Antipas's village. Miriam spoke of the many business details regarding the village workers: the shepherds, carpenters, horsemen, and workers who fetched the sand and clay.

She explained what she knew about stocks of wine, olives, perfumes, necklaces, and matching bracelets. However, she had little working knowledge about the shop in Adramyttion because Antipas had rarely mentioned it to her.

Marcos saw Miriam in a new light. Faced with business matters, her ability to make wise decisions was evident, and he was delighted. "My, you know almost all about your grandfather's business!"

"I sat at Grandpa's table for years hearing the directions he gave to Onias and other discussions about daily work at the village. As long as I can remember, I have been absorbing information about his business. But so far, I have never had to use it to make business decisions."

After discussing the activities in Pergamum, Marcos was

interested in how Miriam was enjoying her stay in Sardis. That immediately led to the disastrous God-fearers meeting. Simon explained what had happened: how Diotrephes had barged into the meeting, demanding that everyone pay attention to him, and the loud arguments that resulted.

Marcos listened intently, recalling the evening when Diotrephes had severely criticized Antipas. "I know from being with Diotrephes during the training classes with Antipas that he is an accomplished debater. For him, stretching the truth to win an argument is acceptable. With the knowledge that he picked up during Antipas's classes, he can craft a hard case against anyone unfamiliar with the facts.

"And now I have saved the best for last," he said. "You will never have guessed this. I have met Chrysa's mother!"

Miriam had been holding Grace, who was sleeping now. She sat bolt upright. "Tell us! Who is she?"

"She's a bit younger than you, Miriam, and strikingly beautiful. She started coming to our meetings around April but was always completely silent. I recognized her right away since she and her mother took care of my beach properties up north last winter.

"Her family stayed in one of our beach houses over the summer. She played with Florbella and even helped her learn how to speak again. She and her mother stayed on for the winter as caretakers of our property. In January, I went to check on the two villas we had sold. I saw then that she was expecting a baby. We talked, and I told her about the people in the village who show real love. I explained that agape love gives, and it demands nothing in return. She says she knew right away that those were the people that she wanted to have her baby. She wanted that kind of love for her baby girl."

Miriam jumped from her chair. "I knew Grace's mother lived outside Pergamum! Oh, I'm so happy to know all of this!"

Marcos hid a smile, aware that he could not correct Miriam's conjectures. *Grace's mother, Trifane, lives close to me, only five minutes away.* He decided to give Miriam only one clue about the mother's identity.

"A couple of weeks after the baby was born, your daughter's mother arranged to tell you when the baby would be left near the trash dump. She did, and now Chrysa is yours!"

"Yes, Marcos, I love my daughter so much!"

"After several months, her feelings of guilt became overwhelming. She started coming to our meetings because of the reality of forgiveness and love that she found there.

"At the end of August, she came to talk with Marcella and me: 'You are the only people I trust. I continue to carry a lot of guilt after having to give my baby away! In my mind, I sometimes feel that I will never be clean again.' She poured her heart out to my wife, sharing that she was not ready to bring up a baby, but she still wants to get married someday. I have told her what has become of Chrysa, but she does not know who or where you are."

"Oh, if she is coming to your meetings," Miriam exclaimed, "then she's not in Kisthene. Does she live in Pergamum? Do I know her?"

Simon and Judith stared at each other, and then Simon said, "Here is the proof that Miriam is telling the truth and that Diotrephes is lying. Of course we always believed you, Miriam!"

Marcos had more to tell. "She told me the story of how she gave Chrysa her name: 'I had my baby during a storm, or rather, as the storm died down. A golden dawn was breaking, so I named her Chrysa, meaning Golden. The storm had come and gone.'

"I asked her if she wanted anything. She said, 'If you ever see the woman who has my baby, please tell her how much I love my little girl. I love the woman who has her now, even though I do not know her. I want to talk to her someday face to face.' Grace's mother started to cry at that point. My wife tried to comfort her, but she is still crushed by feelings of guilt and shame. She continues to attend our meetings."

Miriam lifted Grace, who was sleeping, and passed her to the lawyer. After a short silence, Miriam asked to know the mother's name, but he had said enough. "Someday you may learn more about her but not now."

The sun had moved, and the shadow from the grapevine no longer protected them, so they got up to change their positions.

Miriam looked at her daughter. "And I have a message for Grace's mother. Tell her that her daughter's name is Chrysa Grace, Golden Grace. Since she is meeting in your congregation, she will understand what that means. Let her know that her child is safe. Tell her that she has a wonderful, caring father too. Tell her thank you for giving her to us, for her trust in us to bring up her little girl. Tell her that Grace has the sweetest disposition."

Chapter 19
Wilderness Days

THE SYNAGOGUE PORTICO

Two days had passed, and at sundown on Saturday, the second day's service for the Feast of Tabernacles was beginning. The portico of the Synagogue of Sardis was full because this was a special evening.

Gaius glanced around the portico and spotted Miriam in the back row. She was sitting with several people on the far right. Anthony was there too, hidden by the shadows in that corner of the portico. Gaius nodded to Simon Ben Shelah, who was sitting beside Judith. The others with Simon were his children and grandchildren.

When Gaius came into the portico area, someone told him, "The whites of your eyes are really yellow!" He still felt weak as the service was beginning, and he did not know if he had enough stamina to make it through the evening.

He had carried out too many visits recently. Having invited people who only occasionally joined the congregation, he was worn out. Sitting down, he rested then leaned over and spoke to Simon, struggling to catch his breath. "I am asking you to declare the Shema, the call to worship. Others will carry out the opening prayers and today's reading from the Torah."

This evening's service had been planned with God-fearers in mind. Gaius would explain how the covenant had been given through Moses. The Lord had provided food and water during those seemingly endless years in the desert.

After the welcome was made, Simon rose and stood before the congregation. "Good evening to everyone. I see a few new faces with us, and I welcome you, newcomers. I, too, am a 'newcomer' to Sardis. I arrived only sixteen years ago!" Everyone laughed. To be a real "Sardian" meant having been born in the city.

Gaius wondered if he could continue leading the meeting. His knees were weak, and he walked over to a stonecutter seated in the front row and whispered to him for several seconds.

Immediately the man stood up. "Gaius is not feeling well tonight, so I will speak for a moment, as he requested. Since Yom Kippur was observed last week, Gaius asked me to explain what the Day of Atonement means to me. Two years ago, I had a disagreement with a friend. We were doing business together, and I understood things one way. Of course, he had other ideas. Angry words were said, and then we didn't speak to one another for a long time. Family members also became involved.

"Recently, he came to my house. He wanted to be forgiven. He said God had spoken to him. 'Well,' I said, 'I forgive you,' and then I added, 'I ask your forgiveness. I'm sorry that I said bad things about you to others.' On this day, the second day of the Feast of Tabernacles, we are friends again. This is what forgiveness means to me."

Gaius felt a surge of energy. He knew others would also be encouraged. "As we begin this service, we are grateful for the eight-day-long feast known as the Festival of Tabernacles," he said. "Tonight, I am going to explain..."

Just then, he heard a noise. Gaius turned toward the door. Diotrephes's arrival caused a disturbance. He was dressed in a resplendent green toga, and he made his way to a bench on the front left, where he had a good view of all the attendees.

Gaius waited while Diotrephes sat down, realizing the stranger would probably be looking for possible advantages to exploit. "For those of you who are not Jewish," Gaius said, picking up from his previous statement, "I need to tell you a story. You have seen a few families preparing to live in little makeshift shelters. These are usually built on the flat roof of the house using sticks and string. They take blankets inside to sleep for eight days. The reason they do this is to celebrate the Feast of Tabernacles.

"Now, why would anyone sleep in a temporary refuge? Jewish families remember the painful experiences endured by their ancestors. Long ago, their forefathers left Egypt to follow Moses. They had a long walk through the desert, where they fought against desert winds, heat in the day, and cold at night. They always lacked sufficient food and water.

"Let me make an application for all of us, Jews and non-Jews. Families spending eight days in temporary shelters remember that our lives here are passing. We will live on in eternity but not here on the earth. While in the wilderness, God provided manna for food, and he performed many miracles. So why spend eight nights out in the open? To remind us that whatever trials come our way, Adonai will help to deliver us. He will always care for us.

"Those Jewish ancestors suffered in the wilderness for many years. It reminds us that our lives are short. Think of how grass grows in the fields. It soon disappears and dies."

Diotrephes stood up, interrupting, "Perhaps I can tell you something about an unexpected death. Let me..."

Gaius mustered his most persuasive tone. "Please do not interrupt me!"

But Diotrephes had started and would not stop. "Antipas Ben Shelah died recently! How sad! For months he taught me the importance of having a strong leader in the place of worship. He was such a good leader."

One man, highly irritated, spoke. "Stranger, sit down! Let Gaius finish what he was saying!"

Diotrephes ignored him. "I came to Sardis two weeks ago, so I am probably the last one in Sardis to speak with Antipas. Did anyone here see him after I did?"

Gaius's knees threatened to buckle under him. He tried to stay standing, and he took a step toward the young man dressed in such stylish clothing.

"Antipas was a hero when he died. You probably heard that he came to Asia with nothing. Eliab, his father, bought a good property. He became a rich man and taught me much of what I know today. I want to share it with you."

Simon commanded, "Listen, young man, you can have a turn speaking after Gaius has finished!"

Diotrephes looked in Simon's direction and continued as if he had not heard. "I learned many good lessons from Antipas. He was strong, showed good leadership, and kept his followers together."

Anthony, leaning over to Miriam, spoke a little too loudly. "I don't like this. Diotrephes is greedy for power."

Diotrephes continued, "This is my second time here, and I see that your leader seems to be ill. Have others noticed this too? Yes? So I ask you, what is being done for the health of such a beloved leader?"

Several voices were heard. "The visitor is right. Gaius isn't getting better."

"Yes, what have we done to help him? He needs a rest."

Diotrephes cut them off. "You must be asking, 'Who is this stranger?' I speak as a son of this land concerned for the best traditions. But at this moment, I fear for Gaius. His health is failing. I am not Jewish, and I don't know the Torah, but I was trained by Antipas. If he were here, he would have an answer for Gaius's situation."

Gaius leaned against one of the four columns. "This is a meeting, and we are in a worship service! Stranger, please sit down! I can carry on with this meeting, just as I have for years!"

Anthony walked from the shadows into the light. "I was with you in Pergamum, Diotrephes Milon! Two years ago, we began studies together, training with Antipas. Six months later, he asked you to explain your beliefs. As a result of what you said that night, Antipas asked you to leave, isn't that true? He looked at you and said, 'You teach false doctrine!'"

Muttering broke out from all sides. Gaius looked around, trying to control the outburst.

Remaining calm, Diotrephes drew himself up to his full height. "No, you are the one not to be trusted! You are Anthony Suros, a Roman legionary. You were not at Antipas's house for all his training events. Commander Cassius of the Pergamum Garrison demanded that you stop going to those meetings. Obviously, then, there are many things about Antipas that you do not know.

"There are things that this congregation should know. Antipas asked me to come here. He was about to write a letter of commendation recommending me, but the citizens of Pergamum killed him."

Miriam jumped to her feet. "Diotrephes! How can you tell such lies?"

The man who had spoken about a restored relationship exclaimed, "A quarrel at a meeting between men is bad enough. Now a woman is speaking!"

Diotrephes searched the shadows. "I know this woman's voice! Antipas told me that he had a special plan for me. But you were not there for that meeting with your grandfather, were you, Miriam?"

Gaius looked around, perplexed and disheartened. *I've*

completely lost control of this meeting, Lord. help me!

Anthony silenced the intruder, bursting out, "Listen, everyone! Diotrephes does not speak the truth. Gaius, you need to know what happened. Antipas called us together twice a week for training sessions. He did this for years as he was training leaders. After three months, he wanted to know our individual beliefs. One day, after hearing Diotrephes speak, Antipas said, 'You are full of wrong ideas about Yeshua the Messiah.' He turned to us and said, 'Beware of this young man's false teaching!'"

Diotrephes waited, apparently preparing his reply. "I am happy to speak about false accusations. However, Anthony, have you or have you not spent your life as a legionary? Was your father active or not active in the battle against Jerusalem, causing the city to go up in flames?"

Gaius sucked in his breath. Here was a much more dramatic story! *The association linking Anthony and his father to the siege of Jerusalem twenty-one years before has caught me off guard. How did the story of Anthony's father enter this conversation? I don't want to hear about General Titus, who besieged Jerusalem and destroyed the Temple.*

Diotrephes made a second, more severe accusation. "Anthony, were you married to Miriam just before the death of Antipas?"

Gaius gasped. *Two strangers are arguing on a holy day!*

Anthony sat down, refusing to give an answer.

The man who had earlier given an example of forgiveness pleaded again. "Friends, let's leave this argument to be worked out after the meeting."

He remained standing, waiting for the stranger to sit down. However, Diotrephes's eyes were now inflamed, and his voice had taken on a harsh tone. "So is it true! You married Miriam about four and a half months ago. And now you have a baby girl! You call her Grace, do you not? You tell people she is *your little girl*. Now, is your baby about seven months old?"

Gaius waved his hand to end the argument. *Diotrephes is deliberately trying to damage Miriam's honor!*

Diotrephes kept attacking. "So if she is your daughter, how is it that she was conceived outside of marriage? It's true, isn't it, that she was born before the day of your marriage?"

The question hung in the air, worse than the stench in the

Southeast Quarter on a hot summer evening. "I take your silence as an affirmation. Did Miriam give birth to this baby before you were married? Or did a prostitute have your baby, Anthony? Is that why you adopted her? Friends, what could this couple be covering up?"

Diotrephes had everyone's complete attention.

"Look! A soldier with a bad reputation! Yes, Miriam, you are an honorable daughter of the Ben Shelah family. You come from a well-known clan in the tribe of Judah. Onias, Antipas's steward, long-time family friend, told me your family history. He said your ancestry goes back almost 1,800 years. You trace your history further back than most Jewish families, isn't that so?

"If so, that raises questions for Jews. Since you belong to such a devoted Jewish family, how did Antipas permit you to marry a soldier with a tainted reputation? Did Antipas really permit you to mix your family's bloodline with that of your enemies? And why did he permit you to marry only half a man, unable to fight anymore?"

He turned to face the congregation. "I have shown you why there are reasons to doubt Anthony's integrity. He will tell you wonderful stories, saying, 'Antipas helped the poor.' He will work on your emotions and will tell how Antipas bought slaves, setting them free. I will show you that this man is your enemy because the way he lived generated conflict with the authorities!

"How do you know I am telling you the truth? Because I am a witness! Perhaps this evening will make you think more clearly. I have asked you many questions. Why doesn't anyone give me an answer?"

Diotrephes paused to let this sink in. Again, no one could give an answer. "Think about these things during the week. Think about Gaius. What can be done for him? It would be hard for him to teach if he is no longer strong enough to be your leader."

Gaius stood up to speak but did not know what to say. He tried to understand what had happened in the last ten minutes.

Diotrephes has turned everything upside-down. He brought my failing health out into the open. Next, he attacked a Roman soldier, cutting Anthony's reputation to shreds. Then he called a woman's virtue into account. Diotrephes is a master of exaggeration, misleading questions, and dreadful lies.

Gaius's lips were pursed, and he paused before speaking. The message he had prepared to give on the meaning of the journey through the wilderness would not be delivered this evening. He laid those lessons aside and brought the meeting to a quick conclusion.

Afterward, individuals hurried out, whispering troubling questions about the things they had heard.

Chapter 20
Responses to an Interruption

SIMON AND JUDITH'S HOME

Not everyone left downcast. Strangely, Simon felt his spirit coming alive in a way that had not happened before. For years he had been struggling, wandering back and forth between contrasting ideas and longings. Sometimes Simon wanted to bask in the glory of wealth, to be a respected citizen of Sardis. At other times, he longed to devote more time to studying and praying.

He talked with Judith on his way home. "I remember, as a young boy, unloading a ship in Alexandria. A strong wave almost knocked me off my feet, and at that moment, I reached out my hand to steady myself against the vessel. With strength I never knew I had, I stayed on my feet, protecting the crate of precious spices. I needed both hands that day. I saved that container of spices from falling into the waves. In the same way, I intend to keep my family from a coming wave of destruction."

"So what are you going to do?"

"I feel both anger and anguish. I'm furious at this young stranger, and I will stand up against Diotrephes and his evil lies. Miriam and Anthony have been brutally attacked, and my heart aches for them.

"The references he made about Antipas made me focus on my brother's courage, his care for the poor, and his strength of conviction. Diotrephes, on the other hand, brings doubts to the minds of people. His denunciations have had the opposite effect on me."

Judith reached for his hand and squeezed tightly. "I like that," she said quietly.

They arrived back at Simon's home and gathered in the great room. Anthony lowered his head, unable to look anyone in the eye. "I should not have gone. All this happened because I was there."

"Absolutely not!" burst out Simon. "I clearly see Diotrephes as hungry for power. He's clever, and I think he has come to do harm to the God-fearers. He seeks total control. He has his own purposes, but I can't see what he wants to do if he gains power. You and Miriam were simply a convenient way for him to make his lies sound like the truth."

Judith had her arm around Elaine's waist. Her oldest granddaughter looked up at her. "Will this bring us problems, Grandma?" she whispered.

Miriam exploded, "I have explained how this baby came to us. Marcos confirmed it. The mother couldn't keep her. Grandpa's response was 'We take in slaves and give jobs to poor people, so we can certainly care for a homeless baby.' He suggested that we adopt Grace the day after our marriage. But Diotrephes intends to ruin our reputations!"

Tamir suddenly grew wiser than his years. "I am only fourteen, but I understand what that man is doing! He's made everyone hate Cousin Miriam. I'll tell you my opinion. Deep down, he doesn't believe a single story about Yeshua Messiah, Moses, or any of our prophets. Did you see the gold rings on his fingers? That huge turban...and that flowing toga. He imagines himself as a king!"

It was the only humorous moment in an otherwise gloomy evening.

Simon's new determination swept him along like a swift current entering a slow-moving river. A transformation within had begun, one he did not yet fully understand. He remembered how his father, Eliab Ben Shelah, had given him a final blessing. Some of those words came back:

I bless your home and your table, for you will find real joy. Even if your guests are poor, you will grasp their hands and find friendship and wealth. You will know the difference between false security and a lasting community. When you are an overcomer, your open door will bless others with riches beyond your understanding.

Simon resolved to encourage his family. He felt love welling up within him as a spring as he comforted his family.

"We will have nothing to do with Diotrephes. I will not say, 'Simply put all this out of your mind.' Instead, I tell you, 'Let's transform ugly lies into words of blessing.' His words were intended to sow seeds of doubt. Our natural tendency is to curse the person who curses us. However, Yeshua Messiah taught us to love those who do anything evil against us."

The room was hushed, and the children's eyes opened wide with anxiety.

"Anthony, you blessed us by staying calm when your honor was being attacked. I bless you with knowing what to do the next time you see Diotrephes. We are thankful for your caring for Chrysa Grace. She was a castaway, but now she is your child. Her life will be blessed because you kept her honor intact. If you had fought back with harsh words, you would have brought harm to all of us.

"Miriam, I bless you as a true daughter of the Ben Shelah family. Remember what your grandfather used to say: 'What is spoken in secret will be shouted from the housetops.'[30] I bless you with patience and strength when evil is spoken against you. Godly patience is your shield of protection. You are walking in the steps of your grandfather. You are raising a healthy little girl.

"Ateas and Arpoxa, you, too, are blessed of the Lord. Antipas saw you in the slave market, ransomed you, and brought true riches to your lives. Neither of you will ever walk normally, but I bless you with walking in God's ways. You may yet master the language of the Greeks and speak it correctly, but more important is that you utter the words of God.

"Heber, Ezar, and Nissa, my three precious adult children, I bless you with courage whenever you see evil lurking nearby. This evening you witnessed deceit, but you know the truth and remain free by living in the light. You will not be taken in or shaken by falsehood. Instead, songs will fill your hearts!"

Simon reached out his hands as he had done when his grandchildren were toddlers. Elaine, at age fifteen, was drawn into his embrace, as were Tamir and Amath.

"My precious grandchildren, on this Saturday, the second day of the Feast of Tabernacles, I bless you with songs of joy and salvation. You know so little about redemption, renewal, and restoration. You live in a city where few understand who you really are. In the name of the Almighty, the One our ancestors served before the days of Moses, I bless you with understanding beyond your years. I bless you with hearing God's voice saying, 'This is the way, walk in it!'"

---

[30] Paraphrase from Luke 12:3

He stood up, asking the family to do the same. "Ravid, my dear son-in-law, let me hug you this evening! Come to me! You are quiet, and deep thoughts dwell in your mind. You are zealous for the Law, and your heart is directed toward the Most High. I bless you with clarity, purpose, and an open spirit. You can discover such fine points in the Law! I bless you with understanding the width and breadth of the Lord's loving-kindness. May you love the One who sent Jonah to preach to those who did not know their right hand from their left."

They stood in a small circle, a small family facing a threat to their peace. Simon did not need a scroll of the Law; he chanted the words by heart.

"Your commands make me wiser than my enemies, for your word is ever with me. I have more insight than all my teachers, for I meditate on your statutes. I have more understanding than the elders, for I obey your precepts. I have kept my feet from every evil path so that I might obey your word."[31]

It was time for bed. As the children laid down to sleep on the flat roof in little houses woven from tree branches and twine, Ezar explained to them, "Moses and the children of Israel went from place to place, living in tents and never knowing where they would go next but knowing that God showed them the way. At the service, we learned a lesson: Uncertainty and danger are part of living."

Ravid left with Nissa to return to their house behind Simon's. Opening the door of his little house, he realized that he sometimes thought his father-in-law was an unorthodox man. At other times, he loved Simon for his spiritual insight. Tonight, the old man's blessings uplifted his heart.

SIMON AND JUDITH'S HOME

Early Thursday, Gaius arrived at the Ben Shelah home for breakfast. Five days had passed since the Tabernacles service, and he was going to spend time with the family discussing those events.

Judith and Simon talked with him for a long time, and after they had finished, Simon recommended, "Gaius, we want you to stay here

---

[31] Psalm 119:98101

today. Stop everything for several days. No more work, not at the shop nor to visit anyone! You must rest and regain your strength. Let us pray with you. We do not want any more trouble with Diotrephes!"

That afternoon, Miriam met with a small group of Jewish women from the synagogue. Immediately, all were talking about the disturbance caused by Diotrephes at the last meeting. They had not been sleeping well since then. Two women wondered if Miriam was guilty of hiding the ugly secret Diotrephes had implied.

"Please keep this story to yourselves," she said, realizing she needed to tell them her story. "When Grace was a newborn, she was given to me by a woman who could not keep her. I have never met the mother. After Anthony and I were married, Grandpa Antipas wanted us to adopt the baby, so Grace is our daughter by legal adoption. Diotrephes's attack against us is a lie, but it still stings."

Their conversation turned to needy babies and children in Sardis. One woman said, "I am genuinely concerned for an old couple. They live in a building that has wide cracks on the walls. It may crumble at any time. And their neighbors have hardly any food."

Miriam felt the same sensation flood over her as when she had seen Grace left alone on the ground beside the trash heap.

Lord, provide for that old man and his wife.

While Miriam was meeting with her Jewish friends, Simon talked with two men from the God-fearers congregation. They sat on a smooth white stone bench outside the front entrance of the synagogue. The topics of Gaius's weakened health and Diotrephes's aggressive intrusion were discussed.

Simon gave his opinion. "Gaius's health has weakened further. This is unfortunate because it allowed Diotrephes to accuse him of being an ineffective leader. I have asked Gaius to take a few days off to rest."

All three men went home shaking their heads, not able to help Gaius any other way. They also feared further interference by Diotrephes.

Arriving home, Simon called Judith aside. "I'm facing several problems. First, currently, Gaius isn't healthy enough to either work in our shop or lead the congregation.

"Second, I can't stop thinking about Jakob. He wants to change our relationship with the city. Our friend likes to ask for opinions from everyone, but why does he pay so much attention to the old, established families? Is Jakob trying to get more control? Families believe that by following him, they will gain wealth and social acceptance from the city.

"Lastly, another intrusion by Diotrephes could have serious consequences. The stranger arrived at a crucial moment. I know that Jakob will not want news of an internal disagreement with the God-fearers reaching the mayor's ears."

Chapter 21
Victory

THE SYNAGOGUE PORTICO

A week had passed since Diotrephes had made his hurtful accusations. Simon arrived at the portico for the Friday evening meeting, the first person there. Gaius came soon after and said he was feeling a little bit stronger. He was prepared to teach, but his eyes still had a shadowy, yellow look.

Men and women came early, all taking their regular places. They were there to worship the God of Abraham, Isaac, and Jacob. The few Jewish men wore a skullcap and pulled a prayer shawl over their heads, and women also covered their hair with a prayer covering. Jewish women sat in an area designated for females. Gentile families sat together, with men, women, and children.

Simon and Judith moved over a little to give space to Miriam and Anthony. Ezar and his family filled up a row. Heber sat behind them.

Simon's voice rang out clearly as a chant; it was halfway between ordinary speech and a song. "Hear, O Israel, the Lord Your God is one! Love the Lord with all your heart and with all your soul and with all your strength."

Diotrephes walked in, late again. This evening he wore gold bracelets on his arms. A long gold chain hung around his neck. A stool had been placed in the central portion of the portico on the south side. Somehow everyone knew the stranger would be back.

Gaius read the passage before explaining it. "All men are like grass, and all their glory is like the flowers of the field; the grass withers and the flowers fall, but the word of the Lord stands forever. And this is the word that was preached to you."[32]

He finished his short talk and sat down as one of the elders read a psalm, the long *maskil* of Ethan the Ezrahite.[33]

---

[32] 1 Peter 1:24–25

[33] Psalm 89

Simon, sitting between the two doors that opened onto the Royal Road, could not concentrate. He watched Diotrephes, who had a smug look on his face. Simon was concerned about the probable outcome of this evening because Gaius's failing health had become an issue. Something he heard as people walked in bothered him. One phrase kept going round and round: "Do you think Diotrephes would be a better leader instead of Gaius?"

As the congregation came to their feet for a psalm, Diotrephes also stood. His hands were on his hips, and his elbows stuck out to the side. When people sat down, he flung his right hand out, the gesture taking in the entire congregation.

"Of course you've been thinking about last week. I know what you have wondered: 'What kind of a leader do we need?'"

Anthony whispered to Simon, "Diotrephes identifies with ambitious people, fame, and riches."

Several men shot to their feet. They wanted to speak. "We appreciate the years of service you have given to us, Gaius," said one man. "During this past week, we talked this over in my house. We need someone who can help our people. I'm looking for a person who understands how things work in this city. Personally, Gaius—and I don't want to hurt your feelings—but I don't see how visiting poor people in the Southeast Quarter helps our congregation."

An old man stood and asked, "Why not ask John the Elder for advice? Won't he be able to help us find a new leader?"

Diotrephes snapped, "From what I have heard, Emperor Domitian now has him in exile. He's on the island of Patmos."

A young man asked, "Can we choose our own leader?"

Gaius answered, "Rabbi Paul of Tarsus appointed leaders to go to one assembly or another. He sent Titus to Crete and Timothy to Ephesus. That's how others were trained. I studied with Timothy and John in Ephesus. That gives me the authority to indicate a successor."

Simon moved to the front, standing close to Diotrephes. "Listen, everybody. Demetrius comes in October each year. He's always given good advice. We don't need to solve this situation right now. Let's wait five weeks. He'll be here soon and will help us know what to do."

A cloud fell over Diotrephes's face. "Why should anyone outside Sardis have authority over this group?"

Simon's voice rang out, "Demetrius has authority because he knows the truth."

"Truth?" replied Diotrephes, standing tall. His lip curled up. "Do you believe you can know the truth? Can one single person possess all the truth in the world? No! This congregation needs someone who understands all points of view. Those who don't believe in Yeshua should be welcomed as much as those who do. We have to listen to someone who is very well versed in all kinds of truth."

Several heads nodded in agreement.

Simon heard many suck in their breath as Anthony stood up. "No, Diotrephes. Antipas taught us that there is a higher authority. When you read the scrolls of the covenant..."

Diotrephes quickly cut Anthony off. "What falsehood! Can a defeated nation follow its laws and still obey Roman law? I'll give one example to show how out of date you are. The Jewish covenant says sacrifices must be made daily. Tell me, where may Jews offer sacrifices today? There is no longer a homeland. No temple, no place for sacrifices—thanks to your army, Anthony!"

With eyes narrowed, Diotrephes looked around. "Does anyone want to listen to a soldier who talks as if he was born in Jerusalem?"

A ripple of amusement spread across the crowd.

"Anthony loves to quote Antipas. But remember what happened to that old man? He was killed in boiling oil—killed for what he believed. What he thought was the truth got him killed."

Silence hung over the congregation as Diotrephes tightened his arguments. "Antipas's teaching was 'show love toward the poor.' Tell me, what would that mean in Sardis? Who here wants to welcome beggars, the lame, the weak, and the sick into your home? Many people haven't had a bath for days, and will you give them a towel? Many don't even have money for rent. Who wants a wealthy congregation? Who votes to have a poorer one?"

Anthony interrupted. "Diotrephes, I told this group what Antipas said about you. He said you were a 'false teacher,' but you did not answer. How do you reply now?"

Diotrephes avoided the question as quickly as Anthony might deflect a double-edged sword in battle. "Last Saturday evening, I said to this congregation, 'Anthony is the father of an illegitimate baby.' Did he deny it? Who received a satisfactory answer?"

They were at a standoff, calling each other a liar.

Diotrephes addressed the congregation. "The major topic is what to do now that Gaius is sick. I gather he has been a great help in the past, visiting people and faithfully passing on the teaching of Rabbi Paul of Tarsus. To live well and prosper, you also must learn different kinds of truth. That's where my specialized knowledge comes in.

"You do not know me very well, so let me tell you a little about myself. I am the new Director of the Department of History at the gymnasium located here, next to the synagogue, only a few steps away. Also, I will soon be a featured speaker at the Lecture Hall of Karpos, and few ever get that level of recognition.

"Pliny the Younger, the son of Pliny the Elder, is already a famous writer. He is an up-and-coming lawyer and magistrate in Rome. He is one of the few to not only survive under Domitian but rise in rank and stature during these difficult times in the empire. Well, I, too, was a student of Nicetes Sacerdos, the philosopher in Smyrna, just as Pliny the Younger was. Each student received special knowledge through Nicetes Sacerdos. He desires safety and prosperity as well as respect for the old ways."

Diotrephes's hands opened in large circles as he said the words "safety and prosperity."

"Your leader Gaius is beloved by all, but pardon the word, he is a little lethargic. Perhaps he needs an assistant—like me. How many of you would like that?"

Simon looked at Judith. In a soft voice he asked, "When did you ever see this kind of arrogance? He's so aggressive!"

A few hands went up. Diotrephes waited in silence as a way of forcing the issue. Many more hands rose, slowly at first. "I see that most people want me as an assistant, and if the rest agree, then I would be happy to do my best here."

DIOTREPHES'S ROOM

Arriving home long after everyone had left the portico, Diotrephes had a lighter step. He could hardly believe his good luck. He tried to imagine a conversation with his mother and Zoticos, his uncle.

"I won! No one can say I forced Gaius out because everyone knows he has become weak. Now I will guide these families to enter the city's social life and not stand aloof. Just as Athan wore the crown and had his name engraved in stone, so I, too, will be remembered forever. People will say that I brought them recognition and glory, pride, and honor.

"And Uncle Zoticos, I will soon have your daughter in your arms. I will get information about the family through Cleon at the Ben Shelah shop and through Diodotus, the banker, at the home where I'm staying." He settled down to write his weekly letter to Lydia-Naq in Pergamum. He knew his mother would do a little dance after reading it.

Chapter 22
New Challenges

THE SYNAGOGUE PORTICO

Jakob called for ten elders to come together on Sunday evening. His home was close to the base of the acropolis, and it took only a few minutes to walk from his house across Royal Road to the synagogue portico. As he walked in the fresh twilight air, he prayed silently.

Oil lamps in the portico were burning when he entered, and he was joined by the other men he had called together. "Today I received news about an important meeting, and I have made a decision. I must leave for Antioch. I will leave in three days. With the winds favoring us, a ship will get me to Seleucia port in two weeks, and then it is a one-day walk up the road to Antioch."

"What takes you to Antioch? Why the hurry?" asked one of the elders, shocked to think Jakob might leave them with so little warning.

"I will be meeting with rabbis from several provinces: Asia Minor, Galatia, Bithynia, Pontus, Cilicia, Cappadocia, and Pamphylia. We must organize ourselves afresh. We must achieve unity for all our congregations in our beliefs, rituals, and authority.

"Rabbi Zacharias is there already, and our other fellow rabbis are coming to study our concerns and worship. I may be away for a long time, perhaps a year or more.

"Many issues face us! What must we do about the Gnostics, who believe spiritual growth depends upon learning special secret knowledge? Some want to combine dreams and 'revelations' with our tradition of the elders. What should be done about extraneous writings appearing concerning the carpenter from Nazareth?"

He looked around the circle at the men who were like a family. "While I am gone, I want you, Achim, to stand in my place as the Ruler of the Synagogue. Your name suits you well, 'established by God.'

This thought, and your name, will strengthen you."

He was going to leave after having settled several concerns.

"I have completed an agreement with the city's leaders. They agreed to give us privileged locations for shops in the Western Agora. In turn, we will not speak out against things that we disagree with in the Sardian society. Our people will be encouraged to contribute to the city's building program. Some of us will have to attend civic and social functions, but we will not have to declare, 'Caesar is...and...'"

He bowed his head in place of saying the holy title.

"I negotiated other privileges that may take a while to use to our best advantage. I wish events would always be pleasant, but something unusual happened last evening. Gaius is weak, too sick to continue as a leader. At the same time, a newcomer to our city, a young man from Pergamum, has won the people over. His name is Diotrephes Milon. His family name indicates that he is related to all the ancient families in Sardis. People say he has a golden tongue."

The men nodded. The news had spread quickly.

"Diotrephes met with me this morning, saying he would be happy to serve in whatever way he could to form a bridge between the God-fearers and the society of Sardis. He only asked for one thing: that the Ben Shelah family and the soldier should be excluded from the God-fearers meeting. He is willing to return to the gathering if they accept Gaius as leader and him, Diotrephes, as his assistant.

"I have only met the man once, but he seems like a fine, strong young leader. He's just what the God-fearers need because he told me, 'I do not believe that the carpenter is the Jewish Messiah.' That makes it more important that he be accepted by the attendees."

Jakob struggled to conceal a smile, knowing he had triumphed in his attempt to rid the God-fearers' group of influences. He disagreed with the direction being taken at those meetings, and he had already challenged Simon Ben Shelah about the way Gaius was leading the group. Moreover, with Diotrephes as a leader, he hoped there would soon be little, or nothing, left of twisted teaching.

It would be better if the group of God-fearers disbanded. They are like a stubborn piece of wood. I shape it and use it as I wish.

"I have just returned from Simon's house. I stipulated that he must not speak against Diotrephes, as he did after the meeting. I told him he had to accept the group's decision, or he and his family would be barred from attending the God-fearers' meetings. He is still welcome at our regular Jewish-only Sabbath meetings, but he told me that under no circumstance will he accept Diotrephes as an assistant to Gaius. I hope that he accepts my offer to continue attending the Sabbath meetings because I do not want this to create a financial loss to the congregation.

"The sailing season will end soon, so tomorrow I will finish getting my business in order. In three days, I leave for Smyrna, and I will go on a ship to Antioch."

The men committed Jakob's path to Adonai, and soon all were openly weeping. They loved their leader because he had guided them well. All the families were willing to adapt to the demands of the city while still maintaining their historic faith. Social recognition and favorable locations for doing business were now theirs.

MILITARY TRAINING AREA, TMOLUS MOUNTAIN, SARDIS

Commander Felicior's day for starting Anthony's trial had arrived. A soldier came to the Ben Shelah house, and Miriam answered the door.

"Anthony!" she called. "The soldier you expected is here. He has two horses, his own and one for you. The messenger said, 'The commander wants you at the Tmolus Mountain training area. Bring everything you need for living in the forested area. You'll be away for two weeks.'"

"Ask him to wait a few minutes," replied Anthony. "Miriam, I will send you a message if possible. Do you understand what this means? I'm not being punished! I'm not being sent back to Pergamum. I am actually back working for the army."

Anthony put on his soldier's uniform and armor. He wrapped his belt around his waist and attached a short dagger then grabbed his red cape, sword, shield, tent cloth, and bedroll and tied them to the back of the saddle. Provisions and food would be supplied at camp.

"I will miss you so much! Be careful!" said Miriam.

Anthony and the soldier rode through the city, passing the stadium and the city's food storage area. They turned to the south, going parallel to the main aqueduct that brought water to the Southeastern Quarter. After the insulae and the numerous children playing in the open spaces, the road went in front of the homes of the wealthy and snaked up Mount Tmolus.

Below them, the city of Sardis spread out within its high, protective walls. In many places, the walls were still broken, ruins left by the earthquake. Thirty minutes later, they were looking down on the acropolis itself. Anthony could make out the palace, the treasury, and the Odeon, where the city fathers made their decisions. He had slept inside the garrison. From up here on the mountain, everything seemed so small.

They climbed still farther and arrived at a clearing. It was the military training area where several tents were set up in straight lines. The recruits were training with wooden swords, practicing thrusts against an imaginary enemy. Until they possessed improved skills, they would not be given real swords. But within a month, they would be training with heavier swords, double the weight of those used in battle. When they eventually charged against enemy troops in Dacia, their swords would seem lighter.

Arriving at the officer's tent, Anthony dismounted. He took off his helmet and saluted his commander. The recruits were called to attention, and they quickly lined up in ten lines each four deep.

"I have formed you into two squads of twenty men each," Felicior instructed. "One squad will be given the eagle standard. You must keep it away from your adversaries."

He took the standard from where it stood beside his field tent. At the top, an eagle's wings spread out in flight. This was their symbol of pride and honor. No greater shame existed than that of losing the eagle to an enemy.

Felicior handed it to Prosperus, a tall, heavy-set man. "Instructor Prosperus, protect the standard as if you were in a real battle! Form your camp in the forest with those twenty recruits. Assume you are invading Dacia. You do not know when you will be attacked. The other twenty recruits are your enemy. They are barbarians coming to take the standard from you."

Felicior turned to Anthony's unit. "Instructor Suros, you and your twenty recruits are the enemy, the barbarians. Young men, see the scar on your leader's face? It was a gift to tell you that real barbarians attacked your instructor in Upper Germanica. It's what will happen to you in Dacia if you're not careful."

Anthony was their leader, three weeks after training began.

"Soldier," barked Felicior to Anthony, his long face as stern as could be, "you must capture the standard from the team led by

Instructor Prosperus.

"Each squad has sufficient supplies for ten days. Set up your own camps at the place of your choosing. Prosperus, you have five tents.

"Suros, you will take only four. For ten days, you will lead your detachment. Seeking help from other soldiers is not permitted. You must deliver the eagle standard to me in ten days. I will be here again at noon on October 4. If you fail, you will be returned to Pergamum as quickly as it can be arranged.

"One cohort will overcome. The other will fail."

"Sir, do you have any other instructions?" Anthony asked.

"No. Instructor Prosperus, protect the standard! Suros, you must seize it! Have I made myself clear?"

There were no questions.

Anthony studied the recruits he was given—the smaller, younger, and weaker men.

I'm starting from an impossible disadvantage. Is Commander Felicior trying to make me fail? Every advantage sides with Instructor Prosperus.

Anthony lifted his right hand to his face, running his finger along his long red scar. He sometimes caught himself touching his face like this when he was in a moment of weakness. He had been so confident that he could train recruits, but this assignment seemed impossible.

All Prosperus has to do is dig in for ten days and protect his camp well. If I cannot capture the eagle standard, then I will be sent back to Pergamum.

Lessons in the army's history came back._Anthony had studied the loss of the Syrian Legion's eagle standard in the twelfth year of Nero. Jewish zealots had overcome a legion in a hilly location. That was the reason for Rome's invasion of Judea. The entire military action, which took years, eventually led to the besieging and destruction of Jerusalem.

Anthony recalled the first lesson every recruit learned: how significant the eagle standard was to a legion. His first-lesson memories came back. He, too, was a recruit. "Face your enemy without fear!" his instructor had yelled.

Anthony recalled joining the army and training on hills to the west of Rome. He was seventeen years old, and his instructor made them feel victorious on their first day.

With that long-forgotten lesson in mind, Anthony approached Prosperus and saluted as he greeted his new opponent. "Hail!" he said loudly enough to be heard by all. "Be aware! You will lose the eagle standard. It will be taken from you when no one is looking!"

Slow-moving Prosperus did not expect this. A scowl crossed his face, leading to a puzzled look, and his mouth was slightly open as he watched the new instructor confidently walked back to his recruits.

Looking up at the majestic mountain, whose peak was lost in a cloud, Anthony repeated a prayer learned from Antipas: *I lift up my eyes to the hills. Where does my help come from? My help comes from the Maker of heaven and earth.* [34]

Looking intently, he noticed a flat, rocky ledge higher up the mountain. Slightly to the right of where they stood, a black rock protruded. It offered the advantage of a high point above the site Prosperus would likely choose. From higher up, Anthony could look down for fire or smoke from the detachment led by Prosperus.

Anthony's helmet made him look taller than he was. With the red cape flowing behind, wafting a little in the breeze, he walked silently back and forth before his detachment. He eyed each recruit before uttering a word. Then he spoke boldly. "We have been named 'The Cohort of the Overcomers.' I have good news. Each of you is an 'overcomer'! Now repeat after me, 'We are the Cohort of the Overcomers.' Good! Again! Louder!

"Welcome! In the future, you will join Legion XXI, the Predators. Today your march to victory has begun."

The recruits standing with Prosperus snickered.

Anthony heard quiet glee mixed with mockery in some comments, and he doubled down on his instruction. He was using his first exercise to prepare them for war.

"When this exercise is over, you, as new recruits, will have the eagle standard. Look carefully at your fellow recruits. Now remember this: They are not your enemies. You are being trained as warriors to face King Decebalus. That barbarian king is our common foe. But this exercise is for real, and I demand the best each can give. I am here to train you to fight and survive."

---

[34] Psalm 121:1

"Commander Felicior has done you a great service. He has given you an opportunity to learn how to overcome your foe. He stacked the odds against you in the same way as when you go into battle. Cohort of the Overcomers, you will succeed!"

Anthony marched his squad out of the camp and onto the road. They turned left to go up the mountain. Horses carried supplies: tents, bedrolls, and cooking equipment. The animals would be brought back down before the evening. Anthony didn't want recruits under Prosperus locating his camp by hearing horses neighing.

One recruit was assigned to carry live coals in a ceramic pot to start a campfire. Anthony had them take a brief rest and pointed out the different trees at higher altitudes. He pointed to the moss growing on the trunks on some trees and showed them how they could always find their way on a cloudy day when the sun did not shed a shadow.

Judging that they had gone far enough, he found a way through the trees to the right. The rock ledge he had seen from the camp had an area behind it that was both wide and deep. It offered a secluded area for training and was invisible from below.

Close by, a stream flowed down the mountain with clear, cold water. Recruits found dry branches and broke them into shorter pieces to make a small fire. Then they formed a stone pit to keep the embers hot and to use for cooking.

Others set up the four tents. Anthony judged that neither the smoke nor the glow from the flames would be seen at night by the other cohort. The mountain ledge protected them well.

Each tent offered space for eight soldiers. He divided them into ten teams so that each person had a companion. Four teams were assigned to each tent, while in Anthony's tent, there were only two teams. The fourth tent held equipment and food.

Four recruits were assigned to take their horses back to the city while several others prepared the evening meal. Their shared meal of lentils and dry bread gave them a sense of camaraderie.

"Where do you think Prosperus set up his camp?" Anthony asked. The consensus was that their opponents' camp would be close to a tall clump of trees they had previously seen. Prosperus had shown them that area in their first week of training, before Anthony had arrived.

One recruit kept Anthony and the rest laughing. Little Lion

imitated Prosperus instructing his recruits to clear the bush and cut down trees. Another rookie, Cohn, asked him, "Little Lion, you've got his gestures perfectly! How did you learn to imitate so well?"

Anthony needed to plan for the coming days, so he asked, "Who is good with a bow and arrow? I need to know your best skills." Several hands went up.

"Who's an expert in hunting, at following animal tracks?" Two said their fathers were excellent trackers, and they had spent time in a forest learning to hunt.

"Does anyone have a relative in their camp?" Divided loyalties were a potential Achilles heel; used well, filial relations could be advantageous.

Cohn had often been beaten up by his older brother, Dares. He put up his hand and answered, "My older brother is in the other camp. Dares is one of their strongest recruits."

Anthony asked about any other family connections, but there were none. "Work in pairs. Never let the other fellow out of your sight."

"Each night I will teach you by telling a story," Anthony began. "You must learn about defeats in our army. We'll learn from what they suffered in failures. Learn why a scout's post is dangerous and celebrated too. During the day, we will exercise, practice, and explore. Tomorrow morning, we'll start with archery. You must learn to protect one another in the forest. We have much to learn before we get into our opponent's camp.

"Tonight, in our first instruction, I will tell you about my own life as a soldier." They approved of their new instructor and looked forward to hearing his stories.

SIMON AND JUDITH'S HOME

Miriam held her baby close and walked out of the back door of the Ben Shelah house. She stood on the marble patio as the sun dipped behind the mountain. A slight breeze brought a shudder. Nearby, a horse neighed. All around was the aroma of farm animals. The place seemed peaceful with cows, sheep, and horses ready for sleep.

I knew this day would come, his having to go! I've felt alone like this before. Oh, I won't sleep tonight for worrying about him! And I thought I would be expecting a baby by now! Uncle Simon says, "God will give us quietness and confidence," but why can't I relax?

Miriam grieved the troublesome events of recent days. Worse, she dreaded the coming weeks. Her anger against Diotrephes rubbed like a sharp stone lodged in her sandal. The pain was impossible to ignore. She could remove her sandal and the annoying stone, but Diotrephes had come to stay.

Panic rose as a bitter taste, and memories returned. One moment her father was carrying her to safety. The next, he was spread out on the ground, face down and lifeless.

She looked down at her little girl. Grace's little hands reached up to touch Miriam's face, and she buried her face in the little baby's chest, blowing softly. Grace squealed with delight and tried to push her mother's face away. Miriam's scarf slipped down, and Grace tugged on her mother's black wavy hair. She felt overwhelmed and full of joy for the baby, but she was far from her husband.

Little one, soon you will be walking and no longer crawling. Then you will be learning words. Your daddy is a soldier.... Will he be here to see you learn to walk?

MILITARY TRAINING AREA, TMOLUS MOUNTAIN, SARDIS

"No high flames at night, only what we need for cooking," Anthony instructed. "Learn to live in the open. In Dacia, it gets very cold. The winters are terrible. One night a couple years ago, our troops suffered a major defeat. Many enemy soldiers walked across the frozen Danube River, coming into the camp. Thick ice supported grown men, but our watchmen had fallen asleep."

One of the recruits commented that an early winter storm might come and deposit snow on Mount Tmolus. They chatted and chuckled. The stars above shone brightly, and the splendor of the heavens silenced them. All around was wordless beauty adding to an endless mystery of hidden blackness.

"Look! I see a fire!" It was Little Lion. He had crawled in the dark to the edge of the cliff, and his excitement was contagious. They crawled over to look. Darkness hid almost everything under a dark blanket, but two points of light in the forest below intrigued them.

Anthony cautioned them against pushing any rocks over the edge. They lay on their stomachs, looking down into a black void. As they looked down from the cliff's side, they saw one fire off to their right. Little Lion whispered, "Of course, that must be where our opponents set up camp. The eagle standard must be there."

Then Little Lion pointed to a second fire. "Is Prosperus playing a trick on us?"

Almost directly below them and slightly to the left another flame flickered in the darkness. A burst of sparks leaped upward, climbing an invisible ladder of warm air.

They watched for a long time in silence as the cold from the black rock penetrated their cloaks. Discovering two campfires brought great excitement.

"What is Prosperus up to?" asked Cohn.

Anthony strained his eyes in the dark. *Prosperus is clever dividing his unit into two camps. Which one has the eagle standard?*

During the night, Anthony dreamed that he was beginning his military training. Each time he tried to talk to his instructor, a fire glowed. In his dream, he approached the campfire, looking around. He saw a man swinging a double-edged sword. Then that sword was coming down on him, but he managed to turn away from the deadly weapon at the last moment. It was his recurring, hated dream. He woke up in a sweat and stayed awake for a long time.

SIMON AND JUDITH'S HOME

Grace woke up in the night, and Miriam sang quietly to get her back to sleep. Her worst fears always came alive in the dark. Remembering how often she had been overtaken by dread at night, she hummed a tune. She remembered one of her grandfather's favorite psalms and put her mind to writing a song of hope.

She shut her eyes. *What if Anthony is hurt and never comes back? Uncle Simon said he would invite some of the people from the God-fearers to meet here, those who do not like Diotrephes. If Diotrephes replaces Gaius, then we might have to have services at this house instead.*

In the meantime, she began to sing a new song.

Chapter 23
Instructors

SIMON AND JUDITH'S HOME

Simon woke at dawn. Going to his workshop, he lifted the iron bars off the windows to open the shutters. The fresh morning air announced the coming of pleasant fall weather. He stared out the window after he examined the fifteen gold rings ready to send to Joshua in Smyrna.

The last days had been tumultuous. One day he was safe with his family, recognized by all in the congregation. Then, after Diotrephes publicly argued with Anthony, Jakob came to say that he must accept Diotrephes in the God-fearers assembly.

Simon tested the rings in his hand as though weighing a decision about his future. He knew that Jakob was naïve in allowing this deceptive man to help Gaius. Diotrephes would not stop at being an assistant. This stranger intended to take over. Further, he was sure that if Gaius were replaced, any teaching about Yeshua would be replaced with Diotrephes's false beliefs.

A passage he knew by heart came to him as he squeezed the bellows to get the furnace heated.

> "Mourn for all the houses of merriment and the city of revelry. The fortress will be abandoned until the Spirit is poured upon us from on high; justice will dwell in the desert, and righteousness live in the fertile field. The fruit of righteousness will be peace; the effect of righteousness will be quietness and confidence forever. My people will live in peaceful dwelling places, in secure homes, in undisturbed places of rest."[35]

The morning meal was ready. Ravid and Nissa joined in, having been informed that Simon would announce a decision of some kind.

Simon explained, "As I stated before, Jakob gave me an

---

[35] Isaiah 32:13–18

ultimatum. He said that unless we accept Diotrephes in the group, we will be barred from attendance at the God-fearers assembly. This is to punish me for that loud argument during that time of worship. None of us are permitted back until I agree with Diotrephes being an assistant to Gaius.

"This morning I want to tell you about my decision. Until Diotrephes leaves, I will not be going back to the God-fearers nor will I worship with the Jewish congregation. Don't be distressed. God will instruct us what to do in Sardis, just as in the past. Now, as then, we will walk by faith."

Breakfast turned into a discussion of the influence that Diotrephes's presence would have on the Synagogue of Sardis. A division in the path ahead was clear.

Simon and Judith would stay away from all services.

However, Ravid still intended to attend regular worship on Friday evenings and Saturday mornings as he had been taught to do since his youth.

At his work, Ravid smiled, relishing the turn of events. *I was right all along. Anthony has brought shame to the Ben Shelah family. Nissa and I have no problem being part of the synagogue and fellowshipping with the congregation. And now, with Anthony out of the house, I must concentrate on getting these lame people out.*

Meanwhile, Nissa went to their room. As she made the bed and tidied up, the lines on her face hinted at buried feelings. The shame of barrenness washed over her once more. She heaved a big sigh for she was the daughter of a wealthy man who was willingly removing his family from the Synagogue of Sardis.

MILITARY TRAINING AREA, TMOLUS MOUNTAIN, SARDIS

Anthony woke his cohort early. At the mountain stream, the cold water sucked the air out of their lungs, and for an instant, they could hardly breathe. They laughed quietly, made jokes about purple lips, and shivered as they dried themselves off. Each pair shared a cutting tool for shaving, sharpening it with a small honing stone. As they huddled around the firepit, warm water was poured into shallow bronze cups, and dry bread, dipped into the water, provided them with a frugal breakfast.

"Recruits, you are fortunate that Commander Felicior has developed this exercise for us. It's like a real event in a war," Anthony explained. "Let's take advantage of it and use the time to learn why the work of a scout is important. Fifteen of Rome's twenty-six legions face barbarians at great cost to Domitian."

Anthony took a deep breath and rubbed his hands close to the fire for warmth. "I was transferred from Pergamum, where I taught recruits like you preparing to face our foes in Dacia. Here is your first lesson: Your troop commander should never make a move until his scouts understand the position and strength of the enemy."

An hour of energetic exercise was followed by archery. Anthony set up a target to test them, most of whom had inferior skills. As a group, he showed them the fundamentals and then the details of archery with the Roman bow. Then they had more practice.

After the noon meal, he taught them another skill: how to cover one another as they crept through the forest. In battle, an enemy could hide behind trees. Anthony took the young man whose father had taught him to track animals and had him explain the subtle signs to be aware of when looking for the enemy. Then they spent several hours in the forest practicing how to protect each other while moving in small teams.

Cohn was clearly not an excellent archer, although he said his older brother could hit the target every time. However, he loved the title "The Cook," and he preferred staying near the warm fire, preparing, and sampling, the food to be served. This young man would never be a scout. Instead, he would be an auxiliary, one of the thousands that supported a legion when combating the enemy.

After supper, the orientation continued. "You are being trained to fight in forested regions. Starting tomorrow, I will teach you how dangerous a forest can be. You'll learn of actual battles won or lost because of scouts.

"Tonight we'll go to bed early. I want you to be alerted, to learn about a scout's duties. Remember, orders in battle depend on what a commander's scouts provide as information. He has to juggle what he knows about the locations, strengths, and weaknesses of the enemy. You are an important contributor to a commander's decisions. Tomorrow night I will tell you a story about the horrible end of three legions."

Suddenly being a scout was a serious business.

JACE AND KALONICE'S HOME, SARDIS

Jace, the history teacher, left his home early on Wednesday morning. He welcomed the early fall weather after the scorching heat of the summer. Isidoros and Hector, his two sons, were on their way to the gymnasium for the first day of classes. Jace was looking forward to meeting with the new director of his department, and he keenly anticipated sharing ideas with his new leader.

Hector kept badgering his father. He wanted everything possible to be done so he could be victorious at the Games next year. On their way to the gymnasium, Jace stopped near the Temple of Zeus.

A small sacrifice table dedicated to the goddess of fortune stood outside the temple. Jace knew his wife would despise him for offering a sacrifice to the goddess of fortune, but he deliberately risked her wrath. On the other hand, he felt resentful that she had kept her Jewish family history from him for so long.

Why didn't Kalonice tell me that her mother was Jewish? Why did she have to wait until she met Miriam? Could she not have mentioned it earlier? Her father doesn't mind that Kalonice finally told me, but it's been a shock to me!

Jace purchased a pricy vial of consecrated olive oil for one dupondius.[36] He poured the oil on red oleander flowers at the altar and prayed for Hector to the goddess of fortune.

Oh, goddess Fortuna! Hector wants victory! Oh, Fortuna, bring success to my son! Make him an overcomer!

The plump woman selling the oil made her living from sacrifices offered to this goddess. Jace and his sons stood shoulder to shoulder before the small statue on the altar. The lady held a small pouch of brown powder, the drug that she could not live without, the mysterious powder made from the poppy pod. Just now, it granted her a prophecy to give to them.

A phrase came to the obese woman's mind as she drifted back and forth between the spirit world of her dreams and her present foggy thoughts.

"The gods predict a victory. Your destiny and success are one and the same."

Jace wondered how anyone could pronounce such a mysterious

---

[36] The dupondius was a brass coin worth one-fifth of a denarius. A denarius was the usual workman's pay for a day's labor.

prophecy. His sons complained, not understanding what her message meant. Hector and Isidoros looked back over their shoulders at the woman as they walked to the first day of lectures.

THE GYMNASIUM, SARDIS

Diotrephes, satisfied with his first day of classes, left his office at the gymnasium corner and walked down the colonnaded hall of the massive building.[37] On the western side, the high wall rose to the height of a five-story building. Pillars with fluted, concave ridges snaked their way upward in a long, graceful counterclockwise swirl. The stunning beauty of the four main reddish-pink marble columns mirrored the Greek values of excellence, grace, beauty, and knowledge. These values had inspired the builders a century earlier.

At the front, the central hall could be open to the sky or covered with a tightly woven goat-hair cloth during the rainy winter months. This space had served as a meeting place, first for the asiarchs and then for the adjudicators at the recent Games.

Extensive quotations were chiseled in Greek on dark brown highly polished marble capstones. These pulled Diotrephes's eyes upward. Each time he read another inscription, his face brightened. The school surrounded him with the best wisdom that Greek philosophy and literature had produced. The beauty of words had been translated into swirling bands of sculpted marble.

The exquisitely engraved letters were painted in red. This was the way Sardis memorialized the sayings of the wise, the legendary heroes of old. From days of old, educators wanted this wisdom to be engraved in the lives and minds of their students.

He turned and looked around the extensive courtyard.

This gymnasium occupies twice the space provided for the gymnasium in Pergamum. What a history! And what tradition! This is the perfect place to bring back the Lydian way of life! I will spend time in the classroom with each teacher. They will relish my support. Thankfully, my first interview with each teacher went well.

MILITARY TRAINING AREA, TMOLUS MOUNTAIN, SARDIS

The following day, Anthony gave his recruits time to practice

---

[37] The Sardis gymnasium is the most extensive restoration project completed in this historic city.

their new skills. He made sure they did not overdo the bow's use since the skin on their fingers could be damaged by pulling on the bowstring too much.

Moving about the forest, he divided them into groups of three. Taking turns, one of the three in each group was to cover his eyes and point to one of the others when hearing them make the slightest noise. In the late afternoon, the recruits were given time to rest and prepare their evening meal.

Anthony remained curious about the second fire below their lookout point. Possibly Prosperus did have a second camp, and if so, it would be necessary to view it. He decided to take Little Lion, the young man who had first spotted the fire, to investigate the source. They walked down the mountain a short distance and turned left toward a rocky area beneath their cliff. The cliff rose above them, a black jagged crag jutting out of the mountain. Boulders and large stones lay at the base of the cliff. The little mountain stream made a fifty-foot-high waterfall nearby, splashing noisily against a jumble of rocks.

They looked up at the rock ledge above, calculating. *This location should be close to the area where we saw the second fire during the first night on the cliff.*

They advanced toward another precipice and heard men's voices coming toward them, so Anthony and Little Lion quickly moved back into the shadows. Three men walked out on a path coming from a pile of boulders.

The men were dressed in woolen tunics as common laborers. They looked slightly disheveled with uncombed hair and bushy beards.

One man said, "Hurry up! I want to get to the tavern earlier, so we don't have to stumble our way back here. The idea for us to work putting mosaics on floors of luxurious houses was genius! What a plan! Easy access to the loot, and no one can trace us. This road over the mountain to Ephesus will remain open for only a few more weeks. Snows fall after the middle of October.

"Until then, a few more treasures, and then we're done for the year! In the spring, Taba can take everything to Craga, and we will get our share! I plan to take it easy all winter this year. I have a list of everything that was taken. I'll give that to Taba at the tavern."

The men passed within a few paces of where Anthony and Little

Lion were hidden.

"I'm going to ask Taba to have the General tell us where we'll be working next year. If it's a nicer city than Sardis, we can move there over the winter."

The three men walked toward the main road while Anthony and Little Lion watched them disappear down the trail through the trees.

Sensing that they had stumbled upon bandits, Anthony and Little Lion walked forward. After several minutes, they crept past a boulder to the entrance of a cave. At first, the darkness was almost complete, but as their eyes became used to the faint light, they saw an inner and outer chamber. The outer portion, which was partially open to the sky, was the location of the fire they had seen the first evening. Warm ashes lay on the ground between three stones. The men cooked their meals here, and the flames could only be seen from above the camp. Anthony showed Little Lion how to brush the ground with a pine branch to remove the footprints that would reveal they had been there, and they left the cave.

Anthony and Little Lion walked back to camp, where, at the end of their third day, everyone was in high spirits. As they ate, Anthony said, "After dark, we'll see if we can spot both those fires again. I have so much to teach you yet so little time. I want to tell you more about our most significant defeat, how three legions were annihilated. Listen carefully.

"Remember, when scouts fail to do their job, it leads to defeat. My story this evening is about the most significant military defeat in our history.

"Three legions had gathered under General Tiberius, who had to conquer the kingdom of Maroboduus. That man was the leader of the German Marcomanni tribe. Unfortunately, a rebellion broke out at that time in nearby Pannonia.[38] It took Tiberius three years to put that revolt down.

"Enemy troops had been reassembled during Tiberius's absence, and now they were a worse threat than before. Unknown to Varus, an ingenious trick—one that his scouts should have perceived—had been planned.

[38] Pannonia was a Roman province in Southeastern Europe, taking in Western Hungary, Eastern Austria, Northern Croatia, Northwestern Slovakia, and Northern Bosnia and Herzegovina. Pannonia was known in Roman literature for large oak trees and dark forests.

"Our forces were gaining momentum and preparing to transform that region into a province. Roads had been built between cities. They went straight over hills and mountains, through bogs, and across deep ravines. Rome demanded taxes from the barbarians, but resistance came from one area of small villages. This forced Varus to divide his soldiers among the settlements.

"After his forces were widely dispersed, news came of a new rebellion to the west. It was a trick of course. There was no rebellion. But the method succeeded. Varus quickly gathered his troops, not taking time to investigate or plan, a sign of faulty leadership. Wagons and supplies, soldiers and armor, machines of war, and women and children all marched out at once, hopelessly mixed up. There was complete disorder.

"The enemy had planned with skill under the Germanic General Arminius. Troops were dug in on a hillside, well hidden behind a protective wall close to the Roman forces' path. On the army's right, across a narrow field, perhaps three hundred paces away, was an extensive swampy forest.

"To the left, there was a steep hill. Behind a wall far up the hill, barbarian soldiers were waiting behind the long stone wall. Not a single Roman scout investigated the area where our army was going to march. Faulty decision making and the failure to collect sufficient information caused the coming momentous defeat."

Anthony acted out the scene. "First the legion passed through this narrow area. On one side of the clearing was the forest and the bog. On the other side, the hill gradually narrowed, crowding in on their marching space. Soon our troops would no longer be able to maintain their normal marching formation. Everyone became disoriented. The army marched on, unaware of impending danger. The enemy let one legion march through, numbering five thousand soldiers and the same number of auxiliaries. The terrain seemed peaceful. I am going to stop now and will tell you the rest tomorrow."

Anthony's new recruits held their breath, knowing that the disaster was going to unfold. One recruit asked, "Did you know that so many different parts of the army have to work together to win a war?"

Night was upon them, and Anthony asked Little Lion to tell about their find of the three men and the cave. Exclamations of surprise and delight met his words upon describing their encounter.

"So the second fire doesn't belong to Prosperus and his group," concluded Little Lion. "From what we overheard, it sounded like they are robbers."

Wanting to look over the rock ledge again, they crawled forward on their stomachs. Once again, two fires were burning below them, one to the left and the other to the right. The robbers had returned.

"That is the camp we have to get into. Prosperus is there."

They all agreed, pointing to the right side of the main road.

"And down there is where the robbers are, closer to us and not so high up the mountain."

When the camp was secured for the night, Anthony lay down. He prayed for Miriam and Grace, thanking God for each blessing. His thoughts kept racing, and after some time, finding that sleep would not come, he started to plan. The three men he had seen walking out of the forest were apparently organized thieves, bandits of the worst kind.

Who is Taba? Who is Craga? And who is this "General" they talk about?

Anthony jumped between the memory of the men who apparently lived in a cave and his task: the eagle standard he had to take away from the careful watch of Instructor Prosperus.

On the fourth day of training and practice, after the evening meal was over, Anthony gathered his recruits around the fire again.

"Scouts work as teams, but they must also think individually. They gather tiny bits of information. Although every piece cannot be found, they should provide enough of the total picture to enable a general to decide on his coming plan of action. This is not easy! Your general will have his offensive plans against the enemy, but your opponent also has his offensive plans against your troops. And that's not all! You must keep your adversary's possible defensive strategies in mind while entrusting your life to your own army.

"Above all, stay alive! Be ready to fight one more day! A small noise in a forest, the bark of a dog, the flight of a bird from a tree—tiny signs like these can be clues that indicate people are moving about, or they may just be ordinary sounds.

"You are not yet ready to invade the other camp. One false move from us can bring about a disaster that destroys any further opportunities. We must cause him to make a wrong move that will give us victory. What will it be?"

His recruits had to learn to trust one another with their lives. Anthony's second part of the story illustrated how vital discipline was to the survival of an army legion.

"Yesterday I described how one legion passed through the narrows between the hill and the forest in Germanica. Varus's other two armies were waiting farther back on the trail and ready to pass through that gap.

"Suddenly, when they least expected it, Arminius's troops attacked. At that moment, Commander Varus followed the first legion. He was at the narrowest point. About 250 knights were protecting him when the attack began. Arrows suddenly poured down from behind the extensive earthworks built along the upper part of the hill. Horsemen, panic-stricken, went in all directions. The army was in total disarray. In all that confusion and noise, the commander's voice could not be heard.

"A few legionaries rushed up toward the earthworks but were instantly slaughtered. Others scattered backward and were killed on their comrades' lances. Varus could not decide where safety lay, in going forward or going back. An orderly reorganization was impossible. The outcome was defined in a moment of indecision.

"Next, the formation split up. A few soldiers went on, spreading false news, saying, 'Our commander died.' One regiment ran off around the hill, expecting to reach a port on the river. Others raced into the forest, confronted the bog, and were picked off, five or ten at a time, by enemies who knew the terrain. Soldiers fled into other traps. No one could regroup.

"The enemy pursued Commander Varus. Fresh soldiers were unable to come to the place of battle. Squeezed between the bog and the hill, disorder abounded. Varus had no contingency plan. Worst of all, wagons lay on their sides, making passage impossible.

"Four days later, General Varus took his own life. Swords and daggers, javelins, spears, arrowheads, sling stones, helmets, and sandals lay everywhere. Belts, chainmail, and armor plate fragments fell beside personal items: locks, keys, razors, scales, weights, chisels, hammers, pickaxes, buckets, and finger rings. The possessions of the army doctors and styluses of scribes lay about in chaos. Cooks abandoned everything: cauldrons, utensils, spoons, and amphorae. Women's things, such as jewelry, hairpins, and brooches, showed just how confused the scene must have been.

"We lost fifteen thousand soldiers and the same number of auxiliaries. Only a few escaped alive. Let's learn from this. Never had our army suffered such a defeat! What did the enemy do right, and our army do wrong? The enemy knew where to attack and how to confuse us. They invented a rouse and made us march into an ambush. What a great demonstration of discipline on the enemy's part! They waited for long hours while an entire legion passed by."

Anthony took his new recruits beyond their present task, which was limited to a ten-day training exercise. He continued to inspire them with tales of both the honors of victory and the horrors of defeat. Disgrace was a silent enemy, never visible yet always feared. Service demanded complete obedience, and constant attention was not enough. They needed each other for survival.

After a while, one young man stood at attention. "Sir, I am ready to be a scout. I realize that I must be the eyes and the ears of the regiment to which I am posted. I thought this was going to be easy, but it's not. I want to learn everything you have to teach me."

Others murmured their agreement.

Anthony asked for thoughts from the recruits. "Now, if you could change one thing, what would you have done to prevent the worst defeat in our army's history? Thinking of that will help us in our assault on the camp below. We should learn from the story I have just finished telling you. Think of today's lesson this way: There is only one thing more dangerous than acting on incomplete information. It's having no information about the dangers ahead."

Their discussion around the campfire continued long into the night.

SIMON AND JUDITH'S HOME

Simon tried to be cheerful, and he called the family together before the Friday night meal. He had learned that several other families had also been barred from attending the meeting at the portico. They, too, complained to the elders and were refusing to accept Diotrephes as a coleader of the God-fearers. Most told Simon that they would also stay away while Diotrephes was part of the leadership.

Now that Jakob was gone to Antioch, Achim would be faithful to enforce his requirements on the God-fearers. Simon was sure that

Achim, a forceful young man, feared any unrest might upset the new relationship between the Jewish community and the Sardis city council.

Earlier, Simon had sent out short letters to the others who had been barred, and Judith had agreed to host a meeting like the God-fearers' at their home. The invitation included coming to a small gathering and participating in a meal. Gaius would be teaching, and they would be discussing Judaism, its history, its traditions, and Yeshua's fulfillment of ancient prophecies.

Just a week ago, they had been with Jews gathered at the Sabbath meeting in the synagogue. Much had changed. In the quiet of their home, they would be friends ready to worship and learn from one another. As the sun was setting, fifteen people arrived at Simon's house.

Leaving the house, Ravid made a sarcastic comment: "All of this happened, Father Simon, because you permitted Gentiles in our home. Look at the damage! Well, I'm not part of it, and I refuse to join you in avoiding the synagogue. I will have nothing to do with any gatherings here with the Gentile God-fearers or with Diotrephes." With that, Ravid left.

Simon began the meeting. "Shabbat shalom." They responded to each other with the ancient greeting of peace. "Shabbat shalom."

"Hear, O Israel! The Lord, your God, is One!" he said and then prayed an unspoken prayer.

O God, King of the Universe, am I wrong to withdraw like this? Is it a "sin" to stand up to that man's lies? Guide my steps, for I know less than a child. Thank you for a loyal family, my wife, and children, and those gathered here who share our convictions.

Simon knew why Ateas and Arpoxa were not present. Judith had explained that they felt uneasy about meeting so many people unknown to them.

He agreed it was wise for them to stay upstairs with their son and Grace while the group sat around the room in a circle, listening to a discussion about the proposed future of these gatherings.

Afterward, everyone was again invited to join the family for the Sabbath meal. As the kitchen doors opened and food began to be brought out, Miriam spoke. "As we are preparing for the meal together, we have a new song to end this meeting tonight. It is called 'Sing a New Song,' and it helps children to worship Adonai." She had agreed with her uncle before the worship time that the girls and Tamir would sing the song for the group.

The three children took their places in preparation to sing. Each one played an instrument, and they had practiced for hours. Elaine was learning to play the harp. Amath had been instructed on a child's hand drum recently purchased in the marketplace. Tamir played the tambourine, and he insisted that between the verses, he should blow on the shofar, the ram's horn used as a trumpet.

The notes of the ram's horn rang out across the property. Grace sat on Miriam's lap and clapped her hands completely out of rhythm but smiling, showing her two new teeth to everyone.

For centuries, Psalm 96 had been sung, chanted, memorized, and repeated in different ways.

Today these children in Sardis had their own version of the psalm.

Sing a new song and glory bring.
Praise is flowering.
Worship God, summer, winter, spring,
Even the trees sing!

Before him strength and majesty,
His reign prospering.
His praise will last eternally.
Hear the children sing!

For great salvation, praise his name,
Choirs are answering.
Yeshua cured both sick and lame.
Listen! Angels sing!

The splendor of his holiness
Leads to wondering,
Messiah came in righteousness!
Everyone should sing!

They sang her song several times. At first, the pace of the music was slow, but it sped up, faster and faster. Miriam's sacrifice of thanksgiving, her song of praise, was created during her time of feeling alone. She had composed the words, fit them to the music, and taught the children how to use the instruments.

Miriam's nieces would not be silenced tonight. "Come on, Miriam! Let's sing more. You know so many songs. Teach them all to us!"

While Anthony was away at camp, she could not hold him close for comfort, but she could hold on to the ageless promises of the Eternal One. Miriam's sacrifice of thanksgiving to God was real. She thanked Adonai for many things. Her husband was alive and working at what he liked doing best, and her precious daughter, Grace, had a birth mother who was on the way to faith.

And the Ben Shelah family children were singing with joy.

Chapter 24
Unexpected Treasures

MILITARY TRAINING AREA, TMOLUS MOUNTAIN, SARDIS

While Anthony trained his new recruits in archery and sword fighting, his mind was on the hideout. He took Little Lion and Cohn with him down the mountainside to the narrow path along which the three robbers had walked, leading to the caves. Cohn carried a small pot of embers. They listened at the cave entrance but heard no sounds.

As in their first encounter, Anthony concluded that the men were on a trip to the taverns in Sardis. Cohn made a small torch from a pine knot, and with its light, they ventured into the inner cave. Just as he suspected, at the back of the cave, the torchlight revealed precious treasures. They were the ones stolen from Sardian homes over the summer.

Anthony made a mental list of the stolen articles as he asked himself questions about what the thieves had said.

Who is Taba, and who is Craga? Who does he report to? Why hide stolen treasures here? They won't trust anyone, so how can we find out more about them?

Again they carefully erased the signs that they had been there and retreated to their camp.

Anthony assumed that Prosperus would continue his defensive mode, simply waiting for an attack and trusting in the greater strength of his recruits. Only once had his men seen any of Prosperus's scouts. Two from Prosperus's detachment had been roaming the forest, talking loudly and not concerned with any kind of security.

The stolen treasures would not leave his mind, but he did not want to have divided objectives. Even though he needed to keep his attention on his task, visions of the bronze utensils, jewels, and gold necklaces stored in that cave kept interfering.

I cannot win a battle against Prosperus using swords, and I don't want a single recruit in my squad to be injured. Therefore, I must capture the standard without injuries.

Realizing that Prosperus had no offensive strategy and was waiting for an attack, Anthony took Little Lion and two others to investigate the "enemy." They advanced as close as they dared to the camp and climbed a large oak tree to spy on them. Looking down at the campsite, they saw that branches stacked around the encampment formed a tight wall. The only way in was through a narrow gate, and guards had been posted there. Inside the camp were five large tents. Four tents encircled a central one.

Looking down through the branches, Anthony figured the standard was in the large tent at the center. It was almost certainly the tent that Prosperus used.

Back at the overhead camp, night fell as Anthony described the layout of the other position and what their opponents had done to protect the eagle standard. Their small campfire was burning low, giving just enough light to see one another. They felt bound together as a tight community.

"Who is ready for action?" Anthony asked. No one said a word.

"Good! Just because you know where Prosperus is staying, are you ready for the next step? No! Be disciplined. Tenacious and clever but not quick. Do not give away your presence. Never be responsible for losing a battle. Death on the battlefield is a terrible end."

He rubbed his hand down his scar, turning his face toward the men. No one dared ask how his face had been slashed from his eye to his jaw.

"Watch, listen, and learn! I want you to hear the story of the man who was responsible for losing Sardis to the Persians. It is the story of a successful scout. Which of you can tell the story?"

A volunteer stood up. It was Little Lion, and he knew the story from childhood. He looked around the circle while putting his whole body into his actions. His voice and facial expressions retold the historical event.

"In the days of old, the city of Sardis was an unconquered citadel, the Lydian Kingdom's pride. Legend has it that Midas, the richest king in the world, made his wealth through his magic touch."[39]

The young man illustrated the king's magic touch with greedy,

---

[39] Legends regarding King Midas date back to the 8th century BC.

gleaming eyes opening wide with joy as one gold item after another was placed in cabinets in his palace. His hand movements added to the story, placing one imaginary treasure beside another in a large cupboard. The others began to laugh.

"Cyrus, the Persian king, wanting to expand his empire to the west, faced one city standing in his way. Guess which one! Yes, Sardis, the Lydian capital! If Cyrus captured it, he might be able to cross into Europe and invade the strongest Greek cities! All of Egypt and then Babylon, the Eastern city of trade, would bow before him. The Persian king's eyes popped with joy at the thought of commanding the whole world's attention."

Little Lion's eyes popped open and shut repeatedly, and his audience softly cheered.

He bowed. "Great kings came from far and wide, using golden bowls for drinking wine, enjoying the Sardian palace, and desiring King Midas's golden treasures. Midas was renowned for being able to find gold, and he made articles for use in his palace. Kings of the Lydian Kingdom became exceedingly wealthy. Who could have dreamed that gold diggers would pan so much ore in the little river running through Sardis?

"Several hundred years after Midas, another famous ruler, King Croesus, ruled the city. A famous Athenian philosopher and poet, Solon the Wise, was amazed when he laid eyes on such wealth."

Little Lion's face mirrored each character in his story. "Solon, on his visit to Sardis, gave a great lecture on wealth. Croesus asked Solon, 'You have traveled much. Who is the happiest man?' Solon named Tellus of Athens as the happiest man in the world. 'Why would you choose Tellus?' asked the king. 'Because he lived well and happily and then died in battle. You, because you are so rich, may still become the unhappiest of men.'"

Little Lion's expressions, first of joy, then of misery, and finally of woe, brought more laughter.

"Pure gold and silver coins weighed down the pockets of the rich. Croesus became so rich that he paid soldiers to guard his wealth. He also brought mercenaries to keep King Cyrus, the Persian king,[40] from invading Lydia."

---

[40] Cyrus the Great, c. 600-530 BC, also known as Cyrus II, was the founder of the Persian Empire. His appearance in the Bible covers 576-530 BC.

Placing imaginary coins into the outstretched hands of each recruit, he beckoned with eyes, shoulders, and hands, creating an image of an army being formed, all responding with greed.

"Cyrus knew that if he could cross the Halys River, his kingdom would stretch to Sardis. But to capture Sardis, he had to do the impossible."[41]

"To capture the acropolis!" his audience breathed in one voice, repeating the proverb ordinary people in Sardis uttered every day, meaning "to do the impossible."

All the men knew the story by heart, but none could tell the tale as Little Lion was doing. "To draw Cyrus into a war, Croesus captured Peteria, an outpost of the Persians. Cyrus responded by bringing his troops forward, and he fought well. At the end of the day, the battle was almost a draw.

"Persian troops drew back, for the season for fighting was ending. In Sardis, foreign mercenaries prepared to return home, and Croesus bid them goodbye. 'Come back in five months! We will finish off the Persian king!'

"But Cyrus was determined even though the odds were against him. Winter was coming, but he didn't head back home. He knew the Lydians depended upon those mercenaries for protection and knew that Croesus had disbanded the troops at harvest time. So Cyrus plotted his attack. He crept in, facing significant obstacles.

"First he had to overcome the defenses around the lower part of the city and win what was sure to be a hard battle on the plain. Secondly, and more difficult, he had to take the citadel perched high above, on the acropolis. Unless Cyrus won both encounters, Croesus would live to fight again."

Next Little Lion imitated the Persian troops assembling and pushing their camels to the front. Then, placing their horse cavalry behind the camels, their battalions were lined up on foot. It was hilarious. The young man acted out the part of a frustrated commander demanding the camels go to the front. It was something never done before. Usually camels carried the baggage. Now they were supposed to lead and win a fight!

"King Croesus woke up to see his army below, trampling down

[41] Cyrus's invasion of the Lydian Kingdom and subsequent defeat of Sardis took place in 546 BC.

the vines and making room for a great battle. However, his horses had never smelled a camel! So when the Lydian cavalry attacked the Persian army, those horses sniffed long and hard. The smell of Persian camels made those Lydian horses turn around and run! No fight left in them!"

He imitated horses sniffing at camels. Tears ran down the cheeks of his small audience.

"All that stood between Persia and an invasion against the Greek shoreline was a tiny citadel, but it was impossible to capture. There it is, the Acropolis of Sardis, down there below us in the dark! Defeated Lydian soldiers retreated to the safety of the acropolis, secure behind the walls.

"The siege lasted fourteen days, during which Cyrus promised a huge reward to anyone who could capture the citadel. Hryoeades, a Persian soldier from Mardin, watched day and night from the South Hill. Get this—he was a...?"

The recruits happily completed the phrase. "Scout!"

Little Lion carried on. "A Lydian soldier accidentally dropped his helmet over the wall, crashing down the hill and getting bashed up on the ground! The soldier could not see anyone watching, so he climbed down, put his smashed-up helmet on, and climbed back up to his secure place on the wall. He didn't know that Hryoeades was watching."

Little Lion acted it all out.

"The next night, Hryoeades led a small troop up the wall by the same route he had seen the Lydian soldier use." Little Lion showed men climbing in the dark, almost falling, and dying of fright halfway up the cliff, practically breathless from the steep climb. "From crevice to crevice and ledge to ledge... What a soldier! No defenders were on guard when they got to the top, and that night Croesus was murdered in his palace."

Little Lion took a bow.

"Like a thief in the night!" said one of the recruits.

"Men, tomorrow we, too, will prepare our attack," said Anthony. "'Beware the thief who comes in the night.' That is how Prosperus is going to lose the eagle standard. It will have to be at night. The impossible happens, and then we also can succeed against his camp. You just need to be good..."

His unfinished sentence was met with the word "Scouts!"

"To capture the acropolis!" they murmured the second time.

"Men, this was your lesson today: Never, ever let down your guard. Don't be overconfident thinking you are safe and secure."

Before Anthony went to sleep, he tossed and turned. *What can I do to win this little war game without harming Prosperus? It seems impossible!*

Over half of Anthony's time to capture the standard had come and gone. Monday, Tuesday, Wednesday, and the last day, Thursday, would soon dawn. He drifted off to sleep, dreaming that a road wound up a hill. He was hiding at the side of the road when, suddenly, robbers came out from behind a rock and chased him. Now he was carrying the eagle standard, and three men were catching up. But now it was not the eagle standard he was holding. He was running with Uncle Simon's eagle rings, the ones Ateas had been crafting.

In his dream, Prosperus was close by, and he knew he had to hide the rings from the robbers. The tree he had climbed to observe the "enemy" camp was right in front of him, so he bent down to bury the rings at the base of the tree. He saw Little Lion trying to slow the robbers down, pulling them one way and another.

He woke up with a start, sweat pouring down his face. Why had the eagle standard changed into gold eagle rings in the dream? Gradually his heartbeat returned to normal. It was too dark to get up and start the day, but suddenly he sat straight up. His warm blanket fell around his lap. He had an idea. His mind had been working all night for a solution.

Thank you, Lord, that even a bad dream can show the way. And as for Prosperus, perhaps I can express agape love toward him in this situation.

He turned over, thinking through what Little Lion and each of the others would have to do.

DIODOTUS AND DELBIN'S HOME, WEST HILL

Diotrephes reread his letter, a wide grin filling his face.

September 29, 10th Year of Domitian
From: Diotrephes

To: Lydia-Naq, my dear mother

Peace and health. If you are well, then I am well.

I left Pergamum only a month ago, and I am happy because your wishes are being fulfilled. Your first assignment is almost complete for I have taken control of the assembly of atheists. The second, to take Chrysa back to Uncle Zoticos, will follow shortly. The third, teaching the ancient ways of Lydia, will take longer.

I found three groups in the Synagogue of Sardis: Jews who came here generations ago, Jews who recently arrived from Judea, and the God-fearers. The last group is a gathering of atheists like those in Antipas's village.

I confronted the leader of the God-fearers, named Gaius, who is infirm. I met with him two days ago after being assigned by the elders to be Gaius's new assistant. We had a long argument, but I was not able to change his philosophy. That will not be a problem for long.

The Ben Shelah family has been active in the synagogue, and Antipas's brother, Simon, follows the same beliefs. Following an argument contested in a God-fearers meeting, I quickly pushed Simon out.

I am well accepted in the gymnasium. Only one of the teachers in my department, a man named Jace, may cause problems. He is well educated, and I must keep my eye on him. He is Lydian by ancestry, and he speaks the language a little, which is good! However, he did not agree with my urging him to accept a new program, one that would include more of the Lydian way of life. I believe that he will not be agreeable to my proposed curriculum, so I expect conflicts with him.

May health and all precious gifts become yours!

MILITARY TRAINING AREA, TMOLUS MOUNTAIN, SARDIS

After days of training, the recruits were more confident in their abilities to win this war game. However, what Anthony now demanded of them seemed impossible. "I have a plan for catching the robbers. Little Lion, if you perform as well as you normally do, I believe we cannot fail!"

Anthony drew a map in the dust, showing the cliff, their campsite, and the robbers' cave on the left as they faced the valley. To the right, he drew the camp they had to invade to get the eagle standard and included the giant oak tree that he had climbed to spy on the "enemy" camp.

"I am not permitted to go to the city, but Commander Felicior did not prohibit you. Little Lion, this evening you will go down the mountain to my wife's Uncle Simon's house. Introduce yourself and explain what is happening. Tell him that by Tuesday, I need four of his gold eagle rings and two soft leather pouches. You will hide three rings at the base of this oak tree. I chose it because it's near the tent where they mostly likely are guarding the standard. Hide the fourth ring at the bottom of another tree, not far from the oak tree. I will explain that in a minute.

"You will stay at an inn each night until Thursday. Ask Uncle Simon for a small loan to pay your expenses and tell him I will pay back the loan and return the rings.

"Drift through the city, going in and out of the taverns. Be courageous. Pretend you're drunk. Say something like, 'I have heard that certain people have hidden treasure for safekeeping up in the forest.' I believe the robbers frequent the taverns in the Eastern Agora. You'll also have to go to the western marketplace taverns to make sure you find them. Talk fast, but don't say much. This is a dangerous assignment. If they hear of the rumor you're spreading, they will find you. They must not suspect you are a spy."

Little Lion swallowed hard. "I am up to anything, even a fight with the biggest man in our enemy camp."

Every ear and eye followed Anthony's instructions. "There may be a few problems. First, you will have to identify the robbers and make them believe that you know where gold jewelry has been hidden on this mountain. Second, you must lead them to the single ring on Wednesday. Then, having succeeded in that, you must convince them that you want to join their gang and that you have learned where another stash will be hidden sometime that day. You will then lead them early on Thursday morning to the big oak tree where you buried the other treasure, the three rings. This is where it gets more difficult."

He spoke to Cohn, the cook. "Cohn, your older brother Dares

must be already gloating in confidence within the other camp. You will have to sneak into their camp. You are going to have to be as clever an actor as Little Lion. You will find your brother at the right moment. You will tell him, 'Prosperus has made it impossible for our squad to get into your camp, so how can Anthony get the eagle standard? Now listen, while we were exploring the area, we learned there are highwaymen close by. Our squad is not strong enough to capture them. We need your help to round up the robbers. It will be glory for all of us recruits!'"

Anthony smiled broadly at his men and chuckled, "This is my plan. They will help us round up the crooks."

The men looked at Anthony, waiting, and Anthony looked back at them patiently. One recruit became indignant. "What? You are telling them our plans? They're going to win!"

"You will make them heroes without doing anything!" another recruit chimed in. "Why should we do this? Why should we give away information to the enemy camp?"

Anthony smiled and then chuckled. "We will certainly not tell them *all* our plans. But yes, both squads are going to be heroes. I hope that this is what they will believe. These next four days may be your most crucial preparation before going to war.

"Here's today's lesson: Battles are lost when scouts forget their primary objective. Think! Do not focus on secondary interests. Learn the difference between *primary* and *secondary* tasks. Getting the eagle standard is not the hardest thing."

"Not the hardest part? Then what is?" prodded Cohn.

"Where will we keep the eagle after getting it? They will come after us. They do not want to lose, so they might torture one of you until you tell them where to find it. We do not have a protected camp as they do. They will fight hard, causing real bodily harm. However, we hold the advantage. They do not know our plans. Our element of surprise outweighs their advantages."

"It's a crazy plan!" one of the recruits muttered. "It requires a lot of luck. And I still don't understand how we'll win."

"I don't look for luck to guide me," said Anthony. "I look to the God who made the heavens and the earth, mountains, and hills. He sends the rain, the lightning, and the thunder. Sometimes he sends us good ideas too."

"I've never heard of that god," the same man said. "To me, all those are different gods. One god sends the rain, another sends the lightning, and a third holds thunderbolts in his hands."

"My God answers prayers, sometimes using dreams. Now, Little Lion, run to Uncle Simon's home. Ask him for a common laborer's garb and change into that. Ask him for the four gold eagle rings and two leather pouches. I will write a short note for the introduction. When you have the rings, you will return and bury them by the trees we talked about.

"Later, go around gossiping in the taverns about gold hidden on the side of the mountain. Remember, lead the robbers to the pouch containing one ring at dawn on Wednesday. Then have them find three rings on Thursday, early in the morning. That is when we will capture the eagle standard."

One man scratched his head. "What do the robbers have to do with the eagle...?"

Another cut in, "I trust Anthony's plan. Remember, if he fails, he gets sent back to Pergamum. I heard him explaining that to Little Lion. It doesn't sound good for him if we fail."

Anthony continued training his cohort in the tactics needed to win their skirmish with the other twenty recruits. He gathered his cohort and waited on the rocky crag high above the city. The days were getting chilly at that altitude, and they all gathered around the little campfire, listening to Anthony.

"We must practice the plan several times. Each of you will be in a team at the designated places. You must know your own area of the forest well. If the plan holds together, the trap will snap shut on the robbers on Thursday at dawn."

SIMON AND JUDITH'S HOME

On Sunday evening, Simon stood in the doorway of the house watching Little Lion disappear up the road heading toward the agora. Judith stood beside him, and he placed his arm around her shoulders.

He closed his eyes, astonished at what he had just done. *I've just trusted a young military recruit whom I've never met before.*

"Judith, what is happening to me? Anthony is high on the mountain. He sent a strange request: the 'loan' of four gold eagle rings, a tunic worn by common laborers, and lodging expenses for a little man I've never laid eyes on before! He said that he would personally return everything within a week! Why does Anthony need gold rings? I almost rejected Little Lion's request, but Anthony asked, and I have come to trust the judgment of Miriam's husband.

"My dear, I feel something strange. Since last week, when I made the decision to stand up for Anthony and Miriam, I can think more clearly. But is it really 'thinking clearly' to lend gold rings to a man I never met before? A month ago, I would not have loaned gold rings to anyone!"

THE CITY OF SARDIS

Little Lion found that Simon had required a lot of convincing to accept Anthony's request. He finally agreed after reading the introduction letter.

Early on Monday morning, Little Lion hurried back up the side of the mountain. He buried the pouch with three rings under the oak tree Anthony had previously climbed. Another large tree grew about fifty paces south of the oak tree, and the bag with one ring was hidden in the ground. He wrapped both pouches in small pieces of parchment and put them in shallow holes covered with two large rocks. Satisfied that the locations looked like they had not been disturbed, he then returned to the city. His main task was to find the robbers and gain their trust.

Little Lion visited several taverns in the Eastern Agora with beer splashed on his face and muttered about "secret treasures" to anyone who looked even slightly disreputable. He got to know every tavern in the Eastern and then the Western Agora.

Late on Tuesday afternoon, as he returned to where he was staying, two rough-looking men stopped him as he entered the door to the inn.

The older man quietly demanded, "Were you telling the truth last night when you bragged about knowing about a hidden treasure on the mountain? Or were those simply the words of a tavern song? If you know something about a real hidden treasure, we can help you get some money from it!"

Hiding his fears and pulling at the few hairs on his chin, Little Lion answered, "Me and my big mouth! No, it's true. A Jewish family here was robbed many years ago in Jerusalem. They didn't want to be robbed again. I learned that they have buried gold valuables in several places halfway up the mountain."

"Ha! A Jewish family!" the scruffy man with the gruff voice growled. "They do seem to have a habit of hiding money. But how did you find this out?"

Little Lion told them a long tale, a partial story of the Ben Shelah family. Anthony had told him that nothing convinces like the truth.

Holding their attention, Little Lion bent his head close to the two men. He confided, "While eavesdropping, I learned about that family, who had left Alexandria, Egypt, seeking peace and security. The man dealt in gold, usually rings and necklaces. They lost everything in Jerusalem before they came here."

The story of Simon Ben Shelah carried such a strong sense of reality that the robbers accepted it. They asked a few questions, still distrustful.

Little Lion said, "Quite honestly, I wasn't able to learn everything, but trust me about the gold. I know I can find it. I would tell you, but you'd probably go get the treasure without me."

He spun out the story, and before he was finished, he had the two unshaven men dreaming of easily obtained gold. Little Lion had convinced them there was treasure buried on the mountain.

MILITARY TRAINING AREA, TMOLUS MOUNTAIN, SARDIS

Before the sun rose on Wednesday morning, Anthony's men were stationed and watching from their hideouts.

Little Lion led the two robbers to the area where he had buried the single ring. He acted very unsure of the location and fumbled around a while before looking under the two large stones.

"Ha! Look under these rocks! The dirt has been dug up here recently!"

He dug carefully into the soft earth and gently pulled out the leather pouch wrapped in parchment. When the robbers saw the gold ring that he pulled out of the bag, they were ecstatic. The ring was obviously costly. Little Lion replaced the two rocks to look like the ring would still be buried there if the owner returned to check on the site. The robbers were impressed that he showed such forethought.

As they returned to the city, Little Lion started to weave the second part of the trap. "Now that I'm sure that the man I was listening to at the tavern was not just telling a tale, I can tell you the rest. Listen! I overheard him describe where several rings are going to be hidden on Wednesday afternoon, today, near the place we were just at. It will be easy for me to find them, so let's go early tomorrow morning and dig them up before anyone returns to get them! I am going to keep the first ring for now, and after we dig up the other rings, we'll work out how to share the profits."

The robbers now trusted him. The trap had been set.

Chapter 25
The Reward

THE CITY OF SARDIS

Little Lion sat with five men at a dirty table in one of the taverns in the Eastern Agora on Wednesday evening. The two men who went with him to dig up the first gold ring had been joined by three others. They called one of the newcomers Taba.

Covering up his fears at this critical moment, Little Lion puckered his lips and concentrated on the next morning. "We must be up early! Get to bed. Don't drink any more of this horrible brew! I'm going to take you back to the area that we went to this morning. Since we did find that first ring, I know we will find more gold rings. I overheard where they would be buried."

A gleam shone in Taba's eyes, and he smelled of stale beer. "If we find these rings, then you qualify to become part of our gang!"

Clearly, he was the scoundrel who controlled this band. "You say you heard about these treasures by eavesdropping in a tavern. I think that's a pretty clever way to get information. You're the kind that we need as part of our group. We want new recruits. Leave this idle life of going from tavern to tavern, trying to earn a little bit of money. You told us how your dream is to buy a house for your mother in Laodicea. You want to care for your sickly mother. Well, if you get to join us, we can make your mother a rich woman!"

Taba put his beer mug down forcefully. "In our gang, we each provide opportunities for making money, and we share the results on equal terms. We need smart young men like you to help provide the treasures that we will share. You've been using the loose talk that happens in taverns to find out what's going on."

He leaned forward, his voice a whisper. "I will tell a secret too. If our little trip works out tomorrow morning, I will let you in on a huge secret. If you think it is only about Sardis, you're wrong. We are going to control entire provinces soon! And the money gained through selling slaves..." He stopped and blinked, realizing that he was saying too much—too many mugs of beer.

Before the break of dawn on Thursday, Little Lion led the robbers out of the city. They went into the forest using a lantern. Dogs barked as they passed the homes of the wealthy.

"We know those places well!" bragged one of the robbers.

They climbed the mountain and turned right, leaving the road near the army's training area. Little Lion led them up the same path as before, staying well clear of the camp where Prosperus was sleeping. The sky lit up in its first gleaming, promising another bright day, but down in the forest, it was still dark. They moved slowly and carefully, finding their way through the trees and underbrush.

Little Lion took them to the same tree they had gone to the previous day. The two stones were as they had been left. Little Lion took them slowly northward, counting off paces and acting as though looking for a particular tree. He stopped at the base of the large oak. The gang, composed of five men, was eager to pounce on the hidden treasure. Little Lion held the lantern high to light up the base of the tree.

"Look! There are two rocks, just like at the other tree. And I see fresh dirt under the edges! This is it!" Digging in the earth, Little Lion found an outer parchment wrapper and held it up, smiling broadly. Inside was a small bag sewn from expensive purple material, the kind used by the wealthiest families. A muted shout of glee came from the men.

Taba growled, "Pass the purse around. Everyone! Look at the gold rings. Then hand them to me! I'll hang onto those!"

Little Lion raised his hand to touch his right ear as a signal. He heard the rustling in the forest, gave a loud yelp, and jerked as though he had been hit by something. He dropped to the ground, his part in capturing the men now over. The three rings were still in his tight grip.

Yelling as loudly as they could, Anthony's men broke the quiet of the morning. "We've caught the robbers!"

Little Lion shouted, "Taba! Someone has betrayed us! Run for it.... I'm hit!"

The highwaymen jumped up from their hands and knees in the dirt, startled by the voices. Anthony's cohort closed in from every direction except toward the camp. The fifteen recruits assigned to this action had gone over this moment several times.

The bandits didn't know which way to run, never having been in this part of the forest. As Anthony had planned, in this moment of confusion, they could not see how many men were closing in.

"After them!" recruits' voices roared at the same time.

Prosperus had surrounded his camp with tree branches as a temporary wall of protection. His gate was a narrow opening. Two recruits stood on guard, peering into the gloom. Suddenly, shouts seemed to come from all around. Almost all Prosperus's recruits were now awake. They rushed out of their tents to stand at the gate of their enclosure.

"What's happening? Who's shouting?" Prosperus yelled from within his tent.

Voices sounded close by. "Come! Help to catch these bandits!"

"Help me! This one is getting away!"

"Get that one! Another one is running that way!"

"No, he's turned back, and I've caught him! There, I got him down on the ground!"

"Quick, everyone, we need your help! Come quickly!"

The second bandit lay struggling on the ground, his arms pinned behind his back.

Their leader, Taba, cursed loudly, searching for the young man who had brought him from the city to the forested side of the mountain.

In the confusion of the moment, while running away, he yelled, "Little Lion, remember my offer! If you escape, I want you with me."

At the center of the camp, the two men guarding Prosperus's tent were on their feet. They had been instructed that dawn today was the probable moment for a head-on attack by Anthony's group. However, there had been no hint of an incident, and they had relaxed a bit. Now, hearing loud shouts and voices bellowing in the forest, they stood nervously in the tent, protecting the eagle standard. They could not understand what was going on. Inside the tent, all was dark. Prosperus, who had left his tent, sent ten reliable recruits into the forest to respond to the calls for help. Ten were left at their posts inside the camp: two at the gate with Prosperus, six more at the inside walls, and two in the center tent guarding the eagle standard.

One of the guards keeping watch in the central tent was Dares,

Cohn's brother. "Stay at the gate! Don't leave your guard positions!" he shouted.

Where the encampment was enclosed with the thickest branches, a voice rang out. "Dares, come! It's Cohn! I need to tell you what's going on!" He kept calling, trying to get his brother's attention.

In the tent, Dares heard his brother calling and finally gave in to his curiosity. "Can you guard the eagle standard by yourself?" Dares asked.

The other guard answered, "Where's the danger? You'll be close by."

Dares went in search of his brother. If Cohn did not reveal willingly, he could always twist his brother's arm. *Perhaps Cohn would tell him what Anthony was up to.*

"I have something to tell you," begged Cohn. "Let me in."

Dares, craving information, moved the branches aside and snatched his brother by the neck. After pulling him into the campsite, Dares pushed Cohn down. "What's the noise all about? Where is Anthony? What do you know about his plans?"

Cohn did not struggle. He only pleaded, "Dares, don't hurt me! You don't understand! Prosperus has made it impossible for us to get into your camp, so how can Anthony get the eagle standard? Please listen! When we were exploring this area, we found a bunch of highwaymen camping close by. Our squad isn't strong enough to capture them all. We need your help to round up these criminals. We'll all get the glory for capturing them."

"Little brother, what are you talking about?"

"We discovered the gang of bandits that have been robbing homes in Sardis. Honest! I want you to be part of the group that gets the honor of capturing them!"

Dares was disgusted because he had been dragged away from his watch and wondered if it was a trick. He kept Cohn pinned to the ground, yelling, "Where is Anthony?"

Finally, when the pain was too much, Cohn said, "Anthony told us, 'I will come back to camp at noon, and Prosperus is going to be the hero.'"

"So what does that mean, little brother?"

"You and Prosperus are both going to be the heroes, probably for all Sardis!"

"Does that mean he is giving up? Is he admitting that he failed? I don't believe it!"

"Please, stop choking me! Yes, I'm telling you exactly what he told me."

Dares could not make heads or tails of his younger brother's strange statement. "Little brother," he said, "I think you are going to get hurt if you stay here, and I do not want to have to tell Mother that you came to us begging for mercy. Go back to the safety of the forest."" With that, Dares pushed Cohn back through the fence, replaced the branches, and returned to the tent.

The noise in the dim morning light kept rising in volume. By now, three robbers had been captured. Anthony's group knew how many men they were hunting, while Prosperus's men were utterly unprepared for such a tumult. In the early morning dimness, one could not tell the difference between "friends" and "enemies." One of Prosperus's men returned from the forest and requested more help. "One got away! They are bandits! We need more men to chase him!"

Prosperus sent six more into the darkness to determine what was happening. He stood at the gate for a few moments looking very indecisive, and then he also headed into the forest to where the most noise was coming from.

"Everyone! Come quickly! We've captured another one!" came two voices.

"Over here! We need more help! We cornered another robber!"

In front of Prosperus's camp, everything was in confusion. Meanwhile, Anthony and two others crawled silently through the brush. They quietly dragged branches away from the fence to make an opening at the back of the campsite. Speeding half bent over, they raced to Prosperus's tent. Two went to the front entrance, and one of them said in a loud whisper, "Is this where they keep the eagle standard?"

Hearing them, Dares and the other guard ran outside and lunged at the two intruders, who ran toward the entrance gate. They were captured and put up a brief but noisy struggle. They had successfully moved both guards away from Prosperus's tent. When the two intruders were flat on the ground, Dares kicked one and asked how they had been able to enter the camp. "We came in where no one was looking. Look, who's there?"

Dares assumed that meant they came in through the gate, and now alarmed, he screamed for help. "They're here! They're inside the camp! Two opponents are in the camp! I've got them on the ground. Hurry! Come and help!"

The two guards at the front gate looked back into the dark camp, bewildered, waiting for orders, but Prosperus had left the campsite.

The two opponents were apprehended *inside,* while *outside* Prosperus's men were shouting, elated. They had pinned the fourth bandit to the ground. All were convinced that this was not related to the eagle standard.

Noise now erupted everywhere. The gate sentries could not leave their spot for fear that others might come through the gate into camp. The two men who had come in with Anthony were adding to the din. They lay meekly on the ground but would not stop yelling, "Over here! Over here! We are Anthony's men! Please, we give up! Don't hurt us!"

Dares and the other soldier were the two guards assigned to keep their eyes on the eagle standard. They sneered at the two intruders and spit on the ground.

"You guys are pathetic. You are a disappointment to the army and could never take the eagle standard from us."

While the two guards were distracted by the intruders at the front of the tent, Anthony crept to the back of Prosperus's tent, cut the fabric close to the ground using his dagger, and slipped inside. Loud commotion continued around the camp. Anthony felt around in the dark and discovered what he was looking for. He lowered the eagle standard, pushed it through the small opening where he had entered, and ran quietly to the breach in the fence. Anthony went through the breach and replaced the branches.

Prosperus's voice came back through the dawn, gradually calming everyone down. "Hold the bandits there! Do not let them go! Stay where you are. We have captured four thugs, but one seems to have escaped!" He was cursing and terribly angry at the unexpected predawn activity.

But he was a little proud too. Prosperus was forming a story in his mind of how his soldiers had captured the whole gang.

Oh, the coming glory!

One of the watchmen at the gate left his post to discover that Anthony's two captured recruits made a lot of noise but gave little effort to resist Dares and the other guard.

He was puzzled. "Why do you need help with these two weaklings already on the ground? Why have they given up without a fight? Why do they keep shouting?"

Dawn was a dull yellow in the east as Anthony walked quickly through the forest, moving away from the noise. He worked his way up the steep incline around the eastern side of the mountain, quietly pushing through the underbrush.

By now, he was puffing, half running and half walking because the eagle standard was heavy and awkward to carry through the forest. When he was high enough up the mountain, he walked back toward the rock ledge, toward his camp.

Crossing the stream, he waited in the forest, panting. *Prosperus was too sure of himself. He didn't think the eagle could be taken. He will get the credit for rounding up the thieves. My opponents will still have until noon to recover the eagle standard, but they don't know where I am. Even my twenty recruits would not be able to find me here. Prosperus will twist their arms and my recruits will lead him to our camp, but they won't have a clue about what to do next.*

SIMON AND JUDITH'S HOME, SARDIS

Gaius's visit to Simon's home was planned for early Thursday morning. The air was crisp and clear, and a light fog hung low over Hermus Valley. Simon, Judith, and Gaius talked about their first worship meeting in the home. Almost a week before, they had met as a small group, but the sense of vitality, joy, and commitment made them all stand a little taller.

Nissa, Ezar, and Heber were present, but Ravid would not come. He told Nissa, "As long as non-Jews are at your table, count me out. I am no longer welcome even in my wife's home! When is my father-in-law going to start following our traditions?"

His strong opinions would not be changed, and Nissa once again longed to be with the rest of the family.

MILITARY TRAINING AREA, TMOLUS MOUNTAIN, SARDIS

Prosperus was shouting, waving his hands up high. He was victorious, having captured the gang of thugs that had been robbing homes in Sardis. The four robbers lay on their stomachs, being watched as captured criminals. The foot of a guard held each robber's neck to the ground. He could not believe his good fortune.

Outside his camp gate, which was now unguarded, he walked around the four scoundrels. Congratulating the guards came naturally.

Anthony's entire "enemy" detachment had been told to lay on their faces with their hands stretched out. Not one of Anthony's twenty recruits had put up a fight. No one was injured. Prosperus would present the eagle standard to Felicior, together with his "captives."

Roman honor was all about declaring victory over the enemy!

He walked around the group, standing over twenty sheepish-looking, smaller, weaker soldiers. Seeing that no one could run away, he told them to sit on the ground. All were then positioned with their hands tied behind their backs.

Suddenly a tremor of fear shot down Prosperus's spine. Not everyone was accounted for.

Where is Anthony? These recruits were too easily captured. They submitted without a fight. What do they know that I don't know?

He dashed to his tent, tripping over a tent peg on his way and hurting his ankle.

His eagle standard was gone!

Baffled and bewildered, he stared at the empty silver base where his treasure had stood for the past ten days. The sun was just above the horizon, and bending down, he noticed a faint light coming through the bottom of his tent.

A cold, clammy feeling came over him, chilling him more than the cold water they used each morning for washing. He visualized himself standing before Commander Felicior without the standard.

This cannot have happened! They were the weak ones and had no chance of taking it. But they did! How did Anthony do it? That was a rouse catching us unaware, but how did he plan such a thing, capturing criminals? Oh, he designed this! All were in on it!

With visions of his career crumbling, Prosperus ran outside, swearing and screaming at his "prisoners."

"I'll kill all of you! Where is Anthony? Where is the eagle standard? Tell me, or I'll carve each one of you to pieces!"

His words were threatening, but mostly it was a cry borne from an overwhelming fear of failure.

Each one gave the same story: "Anthony used the unexpected presence of bandits to enter your camp. He told us, 'I will take the eagle standard when Prosperus least expects it.'" Each of his enemies told the same story.

"Where is he? Where did he take it? He played a trick on us!" Prosperus drew his sword as a threat, but no one answered.

Only Cohn spoke up, following Anthony's instructions. ""I think Anthony might have gone toward the caves. That would be a good hiding spot!"

"What caves? What hiding spot?"

"We found caves after we set up our camp. I told Dares about the thieves. Here they are on the ground. I can take you to the items they stole."

"Where are they? Show me!"

"They're hidden in a cave. I'll show you, but we'll need a torch to see inside it."

Anthony's still tied-up squad was moved and placed in rows. Ten of Prosperus's recruits watched over Anthony's nineteen prisoner-recruits and the four bandits. A rope was tied around Cohn's neck, and he was ordered to lead the way to the cave. Using the coals they had brought with them to light a torch, they entered the cave. Prosperus saw treasure stolen by the robbers and started thinking about how he could use this discovery to save his job.

I lost the war game set up by Commander Felicior, but a new situation is unfolding. Four burglars who have plundered the city are captive in my camp, and here I am, gazing at the treasures stolen during the last months. I lost the eagle standard but am standing overwhelmed in a cave filled with stolen riches.

At noon, Commander Felicior rode into the camp, followed by a squad of foot soldiers from the garrison.

He looked at the strange scene before him. His face turned a dark red, and his eyes closed to mere slits. Both squads of recruits were lined up, waiting for inspection. They were in the open area in the forest used by their commanding officer.

Prosperus stood before his twenty men, but Anthony was missing as the leader of the second group. Close by, four very worried-looking robbers sat on the ground, ropes bound tightly around their hands and feet.

"What has happened here?" Felicior shouted. He looked over the soldiers and fumed. Even Prosperus did not seem to know how to answer the question. Felicior watched the deep shade of red growing on his instructor's face. Anthony's men started to laugh.

Mirth was rising from one detachment, bewilderment from the other.

More importantly for Felicior, the eagle standard, which should have been present, was nowhere to be seen.

How could Prosperus let the eagle out of his sight? He was given the most straightforward assignment possible!

Felicior turned as Anthony walked into the training camp. In his hands was the eagle standard. He carried it proudly, waving it slightly as if he were returning victorious from a skirmish against an enemy.

In a thunderous voice, he called, "All present, sir! All accounted for! Here it is! It is safe and being returned to you, sir!"

Little Lion spoke up. "Instructor Prosperus has something to show you, Commander Felicior. He discovered caves with treasure stolen by these robbers."

After asking a few questions about the morning's events, Felicior directed Prosperus to lead the way to the caves. Anthony and Little Lion were told to come also and to continue explaining the story behind the discovery. Gradually Felicior learned the story of the four men captured at dawn.

As the sun reached its highest point, Felicior entered the caves. He immediately understood the connection to the robberies.

"The robber who escaped is a bandit by the name of Taba," said Little Lion.

"What else do you know about him?" questioned Felicior, facing a new situation.

"Sir, I learned several important facts. Taba reports to his boss, a man named Craga, who reports to another man called the General. These five robbers are a small part of a bigger gang.

"Taba invited me to join their organization. He says it is a much bigger movement than anything yet seen in Asia Minor. I believe he was going to explain it to me later. I don't know any other details. How he got away, I really don't know. But he's not stupid like the four criminals we caught. These are locals, Sardians gone wrong, doing what the more prominent gang members told them to do. Unfortunately for them, death, the fate for thieves, is well defined by Roman law."

Felicior swore by the dogs of Rome as he gazed at the treasure in the cave. He ordered the items to be listed before taking them back to the city.

"All stolen property will be returned to their rightful owners," he instructed. "Tell the mayor immediately." He ordered two of his foot soldiers to be sent directly to the acropolis as messengers and assigned two others to remain to guard the cave.

Prosperus listened as Little Lion chattered about the events of the last ten days. The remaining recruits came to attention when the commander walked into the camp.

As they approached the assembled soldiers, Anthony spoke to the commander. "Sir, Instructor Prosperus and I need to talk to you in private about what has happened."

"Recruits, stand at ease!" The instructors walked with the commander out of view from the camp for a conference.

"Sir, if I may speak candidly," said Anthony, "this morning Prosperus captured a gang of robbers and found their loot. He captured my entire squad with no injuries to report. He is a capable instructor. Any decision regarding what has happened is totally yours to make, sir. Still, it is a shame to lose a good man in battle, much more so in training, where lessons learned are more important."

Felicior stared at Anthony for several moments. Then he looked up. The peaceful mountainside was far away from Dacia. These recruits would soon be legionaries facing war. The mountain peak rose high behind them, and the slight wind in the branches breathed a sense of peace.

Standing slightly apart, Prosperus's dark fear of demotion, so strong earlier in the day, now faded as light dims at the end of a day. He began to believe that he might not be demoted. He imagined a conversation with his best friend back home.

"Anthony fooled me completely! He cut his way through the back of my tent and stole the eagle standard. His squad struck down the bandits almost at our camp gate, which took our attention away from our assignment.

"Yet Anthony is rewarding me, telling Felicior that I captured the robbers. He had Cohn take me to the robber's cave, and I showed the cave to our commander as if it were my discovery. Yesterday I didn't even know it existed. Why is Anthony doing this?"

"Is there a reward for capturing the robbers, sir?" asked Anthony.

Commander Felicior did not know what to make of the events. He had made a clear statement at the beginning. The instructor with the eagle would be promoted, the other demoted. Now he was in a predicament. *Anthony doesn't want Prosperus shamed. Why?*

"Yes, high recognition is awarded for arresting bandits. Prosperus has kept his honor. It's intact. At the same time, Suros, you made yourself a hero. That was a difficult victory.

"Prosperus, you will be rewarded despite losing the eagle standard, not by me but by the mayor of Sardis. Families suffering theft will identify their stolen items and claim them. Your group will be invited to visit the homes of all those who were robbed in the past year; they will want to thank you generously. However, you will receive a natural punishment, having to listen to whining families as they curse the gods and swear at the authorities. It is tiresome and irksome work dealing with the public. I don't need to remind you that you will assure them of this: Rome takes care of its citizens."

Felicior turned to Anthony, "For leading your squad to capture the eagle standard, I appoint you as an instructor."

When the men had returned to formation at the camp, Felicior addressed the recruits. "Soldiers," he barked, "Instructor Anthony will teach scouting. Instructor Prosperus will continue to teach hand-to-hand combat and military maneuvers. Furthermore, a gang that has been robbing the wealthy citizens' homes has been captured, but a ringleader escaped. That thug must be captured."

COMMANDER FELICOR'S OFFICE, THE ACROPOLIS

Later, in the commander's office at the acropolis, Felicior

demanded, "Little Lion, only you talked with Taba, and you convinced him to trust you. Describe him."

"I think he is a professional soldier gone sour. He was apparently in charge of the men that we caught, and they told him that I had overheard the story about treasure. When he was trying to recruit me, he started to refer to making money from slaves."

"Selling slaves? Importing slaves? Making slaves revolt against their masters? What's all this about?"

"I didn't get any more information than that. May I say more, sir?"

"Yes, of course," answered Felicior.

"I may be imagining some things, some of which may not be correct, sir._I believe that Taba was a high-ranking soldier at some time because he had a way of giving orders that indicated an officer's position. I am sure that he came with instructions to enlarge this gang. However, these four we captured are unskilled men. Look at them! They delivered chipped stones for house mosaics and then hauled off the stolen things!

"But not Taba! He is a leader. He reports to a commander of sorts, called Craga. I am certain Craga was a professional soldier too. Sir, I think we have stumbled upon a rebellion in the making."

Felicior thought about this information for a few seconds. "Little Lion, you are to report back in one hour. I will have a scribe here to put all the details in a written report. You are dismissed."

Felicior waited for Little Lion to leave the room. He turned to Anthony and simply said, "How did you do it, soldier?"

Felicior's tone was not quite so harsh now. "I gave you a hard assignment: take possession of the eagle standard. When did capturing robbers become part of it?"

"Sir, you gave me an impossible task. Prosperus was well dug in, and I could not get past his guards. He had only to wait it out. I had to do something unexpected."

"How did you get the idea?"

"I said a prayer to my God and looked to the mountain."

"What god? What prayer?"

"I said a prayer right after you gave me the task, and just then, I saw the ledge on the mountainside. We set up camp on the ledge, and that night we looked over the edge. We expected to see a fire warming up Prosperus's camp, but we saw two fires. One of the fires led us to the gang that was arrested."

"That was a coincidence. You were there at the right time."

"I prayed again, sir. I asked, 'How can we fulfill the command to us without great danger to my recruits?' They were unprepared with only three weeks of previous training."

"I needed to prove your mettle, soldier."

"We had to obey you, but at the same time, I didn't want Prosperus to lose his instructor position. He has earned his position over fifteen years."

Felicior bristled. "I wanted a task as difficult as war!"

"Sir, if you will permit me, I wanted Prosperus to stay in his position, just as I wanted to be accepted as an instructor. I believe in agape love, which was taught to me by—"

The commander interrupted. "Impossible! There is no such thing! Foolishness! We are training men to serve under Domitian, and you speak of self-giving love! Love and war do not mix! Stronger animals eat the weaker ones. A soldier cannot speak of agape love. The word *compassion* must never cross his lips. Rome became powerful by subduing the weak, not becoming weak. The empire must forever expand. We are training men for a *victory* in Dacia."

Anthony leaned forward. "I, too, am a Roman soldier. I, too, want a victory in Dacia. My family has served in the army for five generations. Julius Caesar conquered my village, and our men became legionaries. Yet I believe in agape love...."

"You learned that from your Yeshua? The carpenter who was crucified as a criminal?"

"Yes, sir, I did."

"Crucifixion is for criminals, for insurgents. Yeshua the carpenter was crucified! No one can follow the teachings of a criminal."

"I would say the same thing, sir, except for two things."

"Which are?"

"Even the Roman governor who judged Yeshua said he was innocent, not a criminal. The governor submitted to political pressure. Secondly, Yeshua died on that cross. However, he rose again. He sent his followers to show love and kindness. He instructed his followers to live in righteousness and justice."

"Rubbish!"

"His grave was guarded by a detachment of four soldiers. The seal of Pontius Pilate across the stone could not hold him in that tomb."

Felicior was not convinced. "He was crucified! Enough! Do not speak about this to me again!"

He took a moment to begin breathing normally again. "Now for your assignment: As I told you on the mountain, I am dividing instruction. You are to teach scouting. Anthony, beware because you are no longer under house arrest. Soldiers watched you for months, but I am watching now! Do not spread tales about wandering criminal teachers who lived in Jerusalem. Put aside thoughts about this Jewish Messiah!

"Your beliefs are dangerous. What would happen in Dacia if half the soldiers in your legion wanted to be *kind* to the enemy? The other half would be fighting for *victory*! What confusion! Decide! Will you train them for the glory of a parade through Rome or give Decebalus the chance to fight another war?

"You have only one task: to train scouts for an impressive victory in Dacia. Now, I'm giving you a few days off. It will take time for all those stolen items to be correctly returned to their owners.

"I expect some difficulties when people hear that there is loot ready to be returned. Imagine the confusion! People will claim things are theirs, fabricating stories. When you return, training begins in earnest. I will let you know through a messenger when to report. Remember, I'm finished with this Yeshua talk!"

Chapter 26
October's Secrets

THE CITY OF SARDIS

Delbin, the banker's wife, hurried through her routine of dressing and putting up her hair. She had counted down the days until Monday, the fifteenth of October. No other day of the year brought her together with so many other Sardian women.

She looked out the window. Last night's moon shone brightly, almost a full orb. With the moon's full face showing early in the evening, the Festival of Thesmophoria would bring all her friends to the Temple of Demeter.

Delbin drew in her breath as her servant braided her hair. A thin golden thread matched her yellow tunic. White borders around the neck, the sleeves, and the hem set her off as the bank manager's wife. Breathing out slowly, she went over the story to be acted out. In her memory, she saw last year's theatrical performance.

The streets were filled with women walking to the Temple of Demeter. The story of Persephone, the Queen of the Underworld, touched married women from every social class.

"I'm going to be at the temple all day," she said to the wagon driver as they moved along Royal Road. "Mothers of large families and those having no children...everyone comes. Greeks and Romans, slaves and free...all proclaim their faith in Demeter, the mother of Persephone."

Panthea Tmolus, the mayor's wife, had already arrived. After hugging each other, Delbin commented, "You've put on your best clothing. I love your necklace, bracelets, and earrings. It all matches your orange-red clothing. And where did you get that beautiful perfume?

"So much has happened since last year's October festival," Delbin continued. "My personal slave lost her child. One of my servants watched her husband die slowly. He woke up one morning unable to move his left side. Worst of all, my father is not with us anymore. He fell over and only breathed a few more times. It has made my life exceedingly difficult. So many decisions on things I know nothing about."

Panthea gave her friend a hug. "How will you manage without your father? You always wanted to fill up those rooms in your home, but the gods never gave you children." The two friends joined in a tight embrace, and tears flowed freely.

"I decided to open my home to younger people," Delbin sighed. "A fine young man, Diotrephes Milon, has come to stay with us. I knew his mother when I lived in Pergamum. That was before I married Diodotus and came to live in Sardis."

"Look! The temple is filling up. Come! Here are other friends!" Panthea stepped back.

Delbin watched several younger women enter, many of them here for the first time. A friend explained in a high, excited voice, "This temple is truly special. After one or two years, you will all know the festival rituals by heart. We mothers understand the pains of life and death. Persephone's ordeal speaks to us, bringing all the women of Sardis together. Remember, you will never tell the details to your husbands.[42]

"That smaller building is the Temple of Demeter. She's our watchful mother, bringing abundance to the earth. In winter months, though, she suffers. Every year after Persephone disappears, Demeter stops supporting agriculture. Crops don't grow. That's why the winter winds blow. Life comes to an end."

Delbin and Panthea, friends for many years, laid gifts at the small building. Their plates would be joined with many more for the noon and evening meals.

Panthea, the most prominent woman present, gave a greeting, and the high priestess offered a sacrifice. Prayers followed, and women circled the temple grounds in a brief procession. A high wall protected them from prying eyes.

To the west, a golden sun slid toward distant hills. To the east, the full moon was already partway across the sky. "This is the part I

---

[42] A more detailed description of this event is found in *Through the Fire: A Chronicle of Pergamum: Heartbeats of Courage, Book 1.*

hate," Delbin remarked as the presentation began. "Look. That's Hades, the cruel brother of Zeus, ready to capture Persephone. I can't bear to look at her face when she sees him coming to take her to the underworld."

Panthea shuddered. "And he forces her to be his lover."

With more than a thousand other women, Delbin and Panthea sang mournful verses. Delbin's tears flowed freely as she remembered her father falling onto the floor.

I never even said goodbye to him.

Through her tears, Delbin watched Hades capture Persephone. The song continued, describing how the bounty of the earth waned. In the following stanzas, an angry Demeter went in search of her daughter. The autumn days became shorter, and trees lost their leaves. After the grape vines had shriveled, the land lay cold and barren.

Delbin kept watching the actress playing Persephone. The captured young woman remained in a small temple at the western end.

"I wish Hades had never found Persephone," Delbin sighed. "He's such a powerful god. He forces the young woman to stay there all winter."

At this point, the play stopped.

Delbin drifted into a trance-like moment, remembering her grandmother, so kind and loving. Two of her ancestors were crushed by the landslide from the acropolis. Her heart was racing as she recalled the suffering and hunger. Cold weather brought less food, and hunger had been a daily trial in her younger years.

Now, paying attention once again, the hairs stood up on Delbin's arms. A soft wind blew, and a single torch cast a flickering light. Darkness filled the temple. "Panthea," Delbin whispered, "I hate the dark. These last months have brought harsh words, worry, sickness, rape, and...my father's death."

Delbin knew most of the words by heart in the next few songs. These came during the middle portion of the play. The dismal winter continued when lesser gods complained to Zeus, the father of the gods. Aroused from his sleep, the father of the gods entered the underworld to bring Persephone back. After a long negotiation, Hades agreed with Zeus to let Persephone return to the earth with Demeter. She could leave the underworld but only if she returned to

Hades to live with him for several months each year.

A single torch was lit. Delbin mouthed the words the chorus was singing. Spring would return, but first Persephone had to be released. Although the two women had watched the drama before, tears again threatened. Once again, she felt the loss of her father.

Delbin closed her eyes, for the flicker of the torch had a cleansing action. Light coming into a dark place was like love and hurts experienced together in a single day.

I'm hoping for a life without pain, honor without shame, and forgiveness without a sense of guilt. I want our city to have many more births and far fewer deaths during this coming year.

"Panthea, don't you love it when the women's chorus begins? The best part of the evening has started! I love the sound of these harps and flutes. It's a promise to us. How we always wait for the return of the sun's rays!"

Her prayers made, she opened her eyes, praying for Demeter to return. That was how the spring weather would return.

Delbin hugged Panthea tightly before walking to her wagon, which was waiting outside the temple. A full moon, no longer bright yellow and emerging over the horizon but now a watery white and high in the sky, shone brightly. Delbin folded her hands in her lap, reassured that grapes would again be harvested. Yellow and red fruits would enrich her table. Of course the fertile plain along the Hermus River would come back to life. Love would bloom again. Many expectant mothers were going to their residences. Their babies would be healthy and grow up to begin their own homes.

"I'm home!" Delbin called to her husband, confident that she would enjoy another harvest next year.

SIMON AND JUDITH'S HOME

Miriam answered the door the next day when Eugene knocked. Isidoros and Hector, Eugene's grandchildren, came regularly since Hector was training under Anthony's instruction.

Eugene, claiming that the noon meal would never be ready unless he helped Lyris, darted into the kitchen.

A thought crossed her mind. *Eugene comes to this home with his grandsons, but he always "stays out of the way." Then I go into the kitchen, and I see him enjoying Lyris's company. Coming here with his grandsons is a perfect excuse to be in the kitchen with her.*

Miriam's smile became a laugh when someone else knocked at the door. "Anthony, you're home again! My dear, I'm so happy to see you! You're just in time for the noon meal."

Simon came in from his workshop. Nissa, who was chatting with Judith, stayed for the meal. Lyris was serving their noon meal, and Eugene was helping. He brought dishes to the small table in front of the family. Eugene was talking with Lyris. He had been telling her a story, and she had her head back, laughing.

Miriam came alive with a sudden thought. *When was the first time I threw my head back like that? Yes! It was after Anthony shared a joke with me. He came to visit me in Grandpa's shop. Hmm, I'm going to start making plans for a special event. I will need Uncle Jonathan in Thyatira to help me by preparing some wedding clothes.*

Miriam reclined at the table with Anthony, who took two small pouches from around his neck and handed them to Simon. "Here are the four eagle rings you loaned to Little Lion!" he said with a broad smile.

During the noon meal, the story spilled out. Anthony told about the contest between the two squads, the capture of the four robbers, and the successful capture of the eagle standard.

Miriam kept her hands tightly folded, fearful during each step of his story but now delighted at his safe return.

"How did you get the idea about using the rings?" Simon asked.

"My task was impossible. How could I capture the eagle standard? In my dream, I saw your rings, and I believe that dream came from God."

"It was Jehovah Jireh," said Nissa firmly. She rarely talked and was saddened that Ravid had withdrawn from the family. "Isn't that His Name? 'On the mountain of the Lord, it will be provided.'[43] I'm certain Adonai answered Anthony's prayer."

"What is the best part of coming back home, Anthony?" asked Judith.

Anthony stood up and walked behind Miriam, and then he pulled her to a standing position. Miriam was holding Grace. He put his arm around her, but he didn't need to say a word. He took Grace in his arms, and the eight-month-old baby responded, wanting to jump, stretch, and exercise her chubby little legs. The little girl gurgled and

---

[43] Genesis 22:14

laughed.

The family laughed with them. Nissa exclaimed, "I think she just said 'Baba,' 'Daddy.' Listen to that! It's the first time she said 'Daddy,' and he just came back home!"

Laughter sounded in Anthony's voice. "So to sum up, I am now an instructor, which means I'll be living with the recruits. Thank you, Uncle Simon, for the loan of these gold rings. You trusted me, and I am returning them with gratitude! I will also repay you for the loan to Little Lion. Families in Sardis that lost their possessions because of the robbers are going to be happy to get them back."

Miriam could not control her joy. She was bouncing little Grace, whispering in her ear, "Daddy is home!" She looked around the table. The two babies, Grace and Saulius, were developing normally. Grace's dark brown eyes and soft black hair were gorgeous.

Saulius was big and healthy too. His blond hair made people want to reach out to touch his head. Everyone laughed when soft gurgles came from Grace. Anthony's awkward attempts to wipe her little mouth while she pulled her face away from his big hands brought further laughter.

Nissa watched her family, and a frown pushed her laughter away. She lowered her hand to cover her lower abdomen. *Lord, Anthony is so happy to come back home. O God, Jehovah Jireh, please hear my prayer. Help me to conceive and bear a child. For eight years I've been waiting, and now Ravid is saying cruel things to me.*

SIMON'S LIBRARY

Simon meditated in his library. Since Diotrephes's destructive arrival, his deepest desire had become the pursuit of a righteous life. Two more families wanted to come to his home to keep up their worship with the God-fearers. They were friends he had known for years. Like him, they were distressed by the increasing assimilation of some of the Jewish families, especially the merchants, into the ways of Sardis. These families wanted more instruction in the Scriptures, and they asked Gaius and Simon to teach them more about Yeshua.

A year ago, Simon would not have conducted worship with other families in his house, but something was changing. Strengthened in his heart, he lifted his prayer shawl to cover his head. Thoughts about the sins of Israel and the mercy of God were woven into his prayers.

Lord, are these families prepared to withstand the pressures we are about to receive? I will teach your ways to these families, but we will need your strength.

SIMON AND JUDITH'S HOME

Anthony had two days before returning to the mountain training camp to resume recruit training. During this time, guards under the direction of Felicior were returning stolen treasures to their owners.

Hector met with Anthony both afternoons and ran on a course laid out behind the Ben Shelah home. Anthony made suggestions and gave encouragement to the young runner.

"You must develop a runner's instincts. You have chosen the long race, one of the most demanding, so you require both stamina and a strategy. When you run, you often look over your shoulder. Learn not to do that. Each time you do, it breaks your stride, slowing you down. Only one thing counts in a race: finishing well—winning.

"You have to know how much energy you have. How will you use it? I hear that Athan was almost beaten by one of the other runners even though he stayed in front most of the race. But when Athan was challenged at the end, he was able to outrun the final surge of his opponents. Like him, during those last few paces, you will need enough energy for the final surge."

As Hector started another grueling run around the training course, along the path from the house to the hill and back, Miriam clasped Anthony's hand. The next day, he would be returning to the military camp. She asked, "What chance does Hector have of winning the race next May?"

"Hector has good motivation. I think he will improve a lot, but is he able to outrun Athan? I don't know about that."

"I missed you so much up when you were on the mountain."

Anthony pointed to a dark spot near the top of the mountain. "See the ledge? It's made of black rock. You can barely make it out. That's where I took my squad. The whole time, I was praying that Felicior would not send me back to Pergamum."

He put his arm around her waist. "It's not dangerous for them here, but there will be intense danger for those recruits once they leave Sardis. They know nothing about Dacia. Domitian will send the army into battle by next spring, but no one knows the date yet."

"I can't stand it when you are away," said Miriam.

Hector returned gasping for air but proud of himself and feeling far more confident. Anthony pulled the young boy close. He wrapped his long arms around the slight, youthful shoulders and praised him for his hard work and youthful energy. The natural spontaneity of young boys reminded Anthony of living in Rome and running along the streets when his mother was still alive.

"Hector, you are growing stronger, and life is filling your head with lots of things. Make sure they are good things. You are going to face a demanding race next year. Go back and practice again. Take one more lap around the course."

THE WESTERN AGORA, MARKETPLACE IN SARDIS

Diotrephes faced a significant dilemma. The first problem lay in his lack of knowledge of the Jewish faith. How could he teach that to the God-fearers? He could persuade the families under his care to change their views about Yeshua. In Pergamum, while listening to Antipas talk about that subject, he had learned a lot. But now he needed much more help.

He selected three young men from the God-fearers, all with Jewish backgrounds. Each one had responded to the phrase "special knowledge." Next, a separate interview with each one made him feel they could be acceptable assistants.

Diotrephes invited them to a thermopolium for their noon meal. Nearby, at the image of Hera, animal sacrifices were offered, and the meat from sacrifices was sold in the market. Some of it was consumed in the thermopolium, providing the Temple of Hera with income.

"I want you to be part of my team at the God-fearers," he began.

The three guests were made to feel important. He appealed to their pride. "This is a significant group, and each of you is needed by this congregation. You can wield a considerable influence. I would like to invite you to be agents of renewal for our assembly. With Gaius leading the group and my weight in the city, each family associated with the Jews will be well accepted in Sardian society.

"I can teach things about Yeshua and the recent events in Judea. I was trained for that by Antipas. I will change some of what he taught of course. But when it comes to the Jewish holidays and special events, I don't know enough!

"A month ago, we celebrated the Jewish New Year. I still don't know why some Jews mark April as their first month of the year and why others say the new year begins in September. I need you to help me with Jewish backgrounds and things like that. All the ceremonial parts will be up to you as my designated assistants."

They nodded in approval, and Diotrephes called for dishes of roasted beef to be brought to the table. Wine flowed in abundance, good red wine made from the vineyards close by. He moved to the topic of his being an assistant to Gaius.

"Yesterday a man asked, 'Why do we need Diotrephes as an assistant to Gaius?' It is because I have both the social and political connections—far more than Gaius has. Few have my privilege of birth; my mother has influence in Pergamum. After only a short time here, I have made some valuable relationships with the authorities in Sardis. Where I am staying, I'm learning much about the city. Eventually I will be required to take over Gaius's leadership. You do know his health is declining, right?"

These three new friends understood the benefits of being well associated. The new teacher had arrived only six weeks before and had already become a talked-about figure in Sardis.

Diotrephes explained that instead of an inspirational message at their next Saturday evening, he would ask Gaius to give a short talk. He would then speak to the gathering about persons who had higher status in Sardian society.

"I need to speak about important aspects of life in Sardis. After all, several Jewish families are about to move into their new business locations. They will have a higher profile, and all will need to learn how to benefit from these new arrangements."

THE SYNAGOGUE PORTICO

At the Saturday night meeting, Gaius finished a short message and sat down.

Diotrephes spoke. "I will only add a word to all the things Gaius has explained tonight. During the ceremonies on the fourteenth of September next year, the eleventh anniversary of Domitian's reign, we will need your help as a congregation. I want the God-fearers to have an important part in the civic celebration. We will be a well-known group of supporters. This means that we have eleven months to prepare. Who would like to help in the preparations for this important event?"

His first task in making himself well accepted was easily solved. One comment, overheard as he left the portico, left a grin imprinted on his face. "Diotrephes is the new face of the God-fearers."

However, Diotrephes's second task was more challenging. He had not destroyed Anthony's credibility. Gossip going around the city had it that a band of robbers had been caught. When he asked for details, the name of the new military scout, "Instructor Anthony," came up. People were speaking highly of him.

He found it difficult to sleep. *Anthony is gaining influence. My mother's prayer against him hasn't yielded results. Getting Chrysa back to Uncle Zoticos will require me to find an unrestricted way to get into the Ben Shelah home.*

THE TRAINING CAMP

Contented with the way things had worked out in recent days, Anthony sighed. He would not be sent back to Pergamum. A new commission was his: to train scouts for Dacia. Ten of the new recruits were so limited. They could never fight on the front lines. Instead, they would become auxiliaries, moving stone-throwing machines into place, finding food, and cooking for legionaries.

Before mounting his horse, Anthony observed colored leaves that had appeared on some trees.

My help came from you, Lord. Thank you for leading me. I will not have to face Cassius in Pergamum. Not only have I been accepted as an instructor. Many families will get their belongings back.

Little Lion has stumbled onto a dangerous rebellion—more significant than we can understand for now.

Prosperus has been saved from shame. I prayed that no one would be harmed or shamed, and you have honored that. Felicior has prohibited me from speaking about your name. In all of this, help me to find a way to obey you.

Chapter 27
Gaius

SIMON AND JUDITH'S HOME

Once again, Simon and Gaius met for a conversation. Deep lines on Gaius's face told of his growing conflict with Diotrephes. "Every time I try to explain something, he turns my words around, Simon. I'm worn out by it all."

"Well, your health is a concern to me as well. What about your work in my store? Can you continue there?"

"Yes, I enjoy our customers and selling articles. What's better than watching regulars leave with a glow on their faces? I also enjoy visiting families in the insulae. Those apartment blocks seem endless. So many poor families live there. However, many days I only have enough energy to work at your store."

"Can you continue as a leader in the portico?"

"I would like to. However, there's a growing distrust. Some families want to know the truth about the covenant, but they don't trust Diotrephes. He twists the teaching of both Moses and Yeshua. Others, people with little knowledge of the Messiah or the Scriptures, are glued to every word he says. Much of what he teaches is totally false, and it is becoming more apparent all the time.

"Last week, for example, Diotrephes said, 'We're saved by mystical knowledge. We aren't sinners from birth but become sinners through the effects of others acting against us. More than that, sin results from conflicts between the soul and the body. My special knowledge enables all of us to overcome these difficulties. You need the special wisdom I can bring through my teaching.'"

Judith had been listening to Gaius and spoke for the first time. "Diotrephes is the director of the gymnasium history department here in Sardis. But I think he's come here to discredit Yeshua. From what I have heard and seen, he doesn't want anyone to be a follower of Yeshua Messiah. All he talks about is the ancient Lydian Kingdom. He praises riches and power. How he loves parades! He covets being in control and having status.

"Wait to see if he doesn't start teaching about Zeus, the father of the gods, instead of God, the Father of Yeshua. What does his name mean? His mother gave him this name 'sustained by Zeus'! He's declared that he wants our people to be better assimilated into the life of Sardis. Mark my words! He'll soon be trying to take over more than just the God-fearers!"

Miriam was upstairs, standing at the window and looking up at the dark mountain. She wanted to tell Judith, *Anthony is away at the training camp, and I'm so lonely when he isn't here. I keep imagining conversations with him. He was home for a few days, and I didn't remember to tell him some little things Grace had been doing. I wanted to tell him everything. I can't sleep, so I toss and turn all night. I'm so unhappy without him.*

A phrase quoted by her grandfather many times came back to her: "I did not come to be served but to serve."

Another phrase her grandfather loved came back: "Love your neighbor as you love yourself."

She started to argue with the Almighty. *I can't, Lord! How can I love people I don't know? I don't like the women I met at the mayor's home. I don't know anyone here enough to love them.*

My mother was killed by my own people. I can't even remember her face. I didn't have a mother all those years when I was growing up. I get so depressed and downcast trying to remember my parents. You must know that because you know everything.

Something else came to mind, a statement from one of her favorite psalms. She remembered it being quoted by Yeshua when he was crucified: "My God, my God! Why have you forsaken me?"

Sensing that she should submit and yield her sentiments to the Lord, she offered a prayer. *Do you want me to love others, people I don't know? Is that what you are telling me? O God, be close to me in the midnight hours. Show me how to live in this city.*

Starting to praise God, words came quickly for a new song.

In the night you are my song.
In the dark you help me see.
Though it's dim, the hours long,
Through this darkness, walk with me.

Two days later, Simon asked Heber to bring Gaius home from the shop. Gray clouds filled the sky. The sun was weak, and by mid-morning the clouds hid it all together. Haze over the mountain announced the coming rains. A light snow had fallen on the mountain peaks overnight. They sat in the great room of the house, Judith on one side and Simon on the other. Heber and Ravid were sitting on another couch. Miriam was also present.

Simon had given much thought and prayer to the situation. "Gaius, you need a rest, a change! We're concerned about your health, and we have a suggestion. You have been ill for almost half a year."

"Yes, since May. I haven't been feeling at all well."

Judith spoke up. "Gaius, I've been watching you, and I talked to Simon. I know you don't have the strength you need. It's clear from what I have heard that Diotrephes is going to gain control of that fellowship. He'll push you out, and he has the approval of the elders. They do not want more outbursts questioning Diotrephes's authority. Moreover, our family will not be going back.

"That's why I asked Simon to speak to you about your health. You can't work at our shop, live with the stress from Diotrephes, and do all the other work. We approve of your visiting and comforting others, especially the poor. Gaius, you have much knowledge, but you don't have the strength for all this."

Gaius was not offended. Instead, he nodded thoughtfully.

Simon addressed his good friend. "Judith and I think you should consider a move. In Pergamum, our friend Marcos Pompeius is pleading for someone to help in the teaching at their House of Prayer. That is the only work he needs help with. Marcos doesn't have sufficient knowledge to lead a congregation. He's a follower of Yeshua, but he was only with Antipas for a short time, not long enough to learn everything that Antipas wanted to impart."

"Go on." Gaius nodded, showing he agreed.

"Many new visitors have shown up in the Pergamum assembly, and guiding their group has grown more difficult. Gaius, save your energy. Use it only for the House of Prayer. Don't think of working in one of Antipas's workshops! Marcos has a place for you to stay in Antipas's house. You'll need time to rest and recuperate fully. Gradually take on the oversight of the congregation."

Simon was happy to see Gaius agreeing with the plan

Judith added, "We don't want to see you go, but you need a place where you can recover."

Heber, who had been silent during the meeting, leaned forward. "What will you miss most if you move to Pergamum?"

Gaius rubbed the side of his head. "I'll miss the friendship and love of all these people. I have grown to care for them. When I was a young man in Ephesus, I could keep up with Timothy, Titus, and Aquila. They bought wool cloth first thing in the morning and then worked until noon, making tents and carpets. Others in my family sold items in the agora. But I can't keep up that pace anymore."

"I think the move should be made right away." Simon got up and went to his writing desk. "With your permission, I will write a letter to Marcos. I'll tell him you will help with the teaching in the Pergamum House of Prayer. If he accepts, we should hear back from him within a week. However, considering what happened to Antipas, you must understand there is a risk to you in Pergamum."

Gaius straightened up. Simon saw a flash of determination in his eyes as he grasped the challenges of his new task. "Followers of the Messiah will never be safe. Those holding power feel threatened when our Master's ideas are put into practice. Can you imagine a senator in Rome standing up and saying, 'Love your enemies'? Rome doesn't teach people about compassion. Antipas suffered because he translated his beliefs into action.

"Yes, my talents are those of a teacher. If you are willing to release me from working at your store, I'm willing to go. One thing worries me though. Who will care for the poor people in the insulae? I've found it hard to interest others in doing this work. Few want to visit poor families. Yes, I am ready to move to Pergamum, but I'm going to miss each of you. You have become my family."[44]

Simon nodded. The meeting was over, and the decision was made. Judith, Heber, and Miriam left Simon to write his letter.

The next day, remembering the conversation with Gaius, Miriam broke off a piece of flatbread at breakfast. She went over her new thoughts.

---

[44] Both the Roman Catholic and Orthodox Churches record Gaius as the Bishop of Pergamum. Nothing is known of Gaius's date of birth or death.

I accept your leading, Lord. I seek to obey your voice. Take away my fears of being alone, the panic of being abandoned. Grandfather Antipas lived according to your kingdom. He sought justice and righteousness.

Here in Sardis, what can I do? Could it be that you want me to take over what Gaius has been doing?

After the meal, Miriam walked with Heber to the shop on the Royal Road. During a lull in the business, she asked for a moment to talk to Gaius. "You talked with Uncle Simon about your visits to friends in the city's poor districts. I'm sure they will miss talking with you. I think many still need the encouragement that you have provided them."

She paused before going on. Her jaw was set firmly. "Now that Anthony is teaching recruits, I have some free time."

As Gaius and Miriam continued to talk, she told him that she was interested in going on visits with him.

He nodded. It would be an excellent way to see if she had the gifts necessary for this challenging task. "I would like you to meet with my friends, but I must tell you, it is not safe to go alone. You need someone to go with you. I'll start by introducing you to some families who live in my building."

Miriam nodded. "Yes! If I continue after you leave, I will find someone to go with me."

I will need a companion if I go into the insulae. I'll invite Kalonice over for a heart-to-heart talk.

JACE AND KALONICE'S HOME

Kalonice sat with Miriam, having been invited to join Simon and Judith at the noon meal, and Miriam spoke directly. "Kalonice, remember the day you invited me to meet the women at the mayor's house? Well, this afternoon, I am asking you to please come with me. I'm going to visit Gaius, a friend of mine. We'll meet some of his friends. They live in the poorer section of town."

Kalonice's eyes widened. "I'll go but just once! I can't stand bad smells, and the insulae overflow with those."

Simon agreed that Miriam could go across the city in one of his small wagons. Gaius drove with Miriam on one side, and Kalonice sat on the other. The roads were filled with noisy crowds. Donkeys, horses, camels, sheep, and goats almost outnumbered the people.

Miriam learned that Gaius lived close to the storage barns where wheat, barley, oil, and other staples were kept for the winter. He described how his neighbors survived better than most other people since, like him, they earned small, regular incomes.

"Others, mostly day laborers in the Southeastern Quarter, are much worse off," he explained.

Gaius took Miriam and Kalonice to his apartment with two small rooms. "This is all I need!" he chirped happily.

Miriam looked around his place. Along one wall was a narrow single bed. A neatly folded blanket was placed at one end. The only other pieces of furniture in his bedroom were a table and one chair. Scrolls and writing materials were organized neatly on the table.

The other room provided space for cooking and storage. Standing on a stack of bricks was a small ceramic oven, and a basket of charcoal was in one corner. A pitcher on a table close by held clean drinking water. The room itself was simple yet clean. Two couches were set in the corner. The space was large enough for five visitors.

"I buy bread from the community bakery and use the oven to heat food. I also warm up the room in the chilly evenings."

"Isn't the fire in a charcoal brazier like that dangerous?" asked Kalonice.

"Actually, the oven is relatively safe. The oil lamps are the dangerous items. They are easily knocked over. If a fire spreads, the whole building could burn down. Tomorrow I will take you to the home of a family where a young child was burned in their previous apartment. That building went up in flames, and eight families lost all their possessions."

"I don't think I will be able to come tomorrow!" Kalonice observed, frowning.

They climbed the stairs to the third floor of an adjacent building. Gaius tapped on a door and introduced the two women to a family whose father was a stonecutter.

"Come in!" said the young mother. "Come, children! We have visitors! Cosmos! Learn to stand up when visitors come into our home!"

A bricklayer lived in another apartment. Eight children shared a small apartment with the mother and her father. The man was lying on a tiny, dirty bed in the corner, weak from hunger. The left side of his face was paralyzed; he made a futile effort to stand up but soon sank back down again.

The ground floor of the apartment building was owned by a businessman who formerly lived in Miletus. His small shop sold vegetables, oil, soap, and rope. "I came here to make money!" he said. "I was so happy when I bought this building. All the apartments are rented by good people, and of course they all pay their rent on time. They have to."

Gaius took them to the top floor of the next building, which was occupied by two families. One father was a carpenter, the other a blacksmith. Their wives were sisters, and the doors were open between the two apartments. A crisp autumn breeze blew through cracks in the window.

"My husband works for one of the best shops in the city!" said the younger sister. "Did you ever visit the hardware shops on the Royal Road? Well, my husband works at a forge at the back of one of them."

Miriam and Kalonice heard the names of their eleven children. They counted twenty-five children living in the four apartments they had visited. Some of the children belonged to other families.

Going home, Kalonice held Miriam's wrist. "My head is spinning! I can't remember which children belong to which parents!"

SIMON BEN SHELAH'S SHOP, THE ROYAL ROAD, SARDIS

A schoolboy took Cleon's message to the gymnasium. "Ask your new teacher, Diotrephes, to come as soon as possible. I need to see him right away."

Classes had just begun on Monday morning, and Diotrephes was irritated. He did not want to be interrupted during his lecture. However, he was curious what Cleon had heard.

Cleon explained, "I learned things that you were asking about. First, the guards who were watching the Ben Shelah home were dismissed. Second, Anthony will stay for a long time at the training camp on the mountain.

"Also, I heard that Miriam visited families in the insulae yesterday afternoon. Can you imagine a wealthy woman going into the insulae, visiting poor people? The baby girl wasn't with her. She must have been left in the Ben Shelah house."

"How long will the soldier Anthony remain in the military camp?"

"For weeks at a time."

"Is there anyone else in the house during the day?"

"Yes, lots of others: Simon and Judith, their daughter-in-law, her children, two lame people, their son, and two servants."

"Not a big help. That's not what I wanted to hear."

"Well, here is the big news! Simon, Judith, and Heber are sending Gaius to Pergamum. He'll be gone before the end of this week! Gaius will become the 'bishop' of the assembly there. It's called the House of Prayer. Marcos, a lawyer, wants help in teaching the people. Even after what happened to Antipas, Gaius isn't afraid to go to Pergamum. He's going to explain things to the followers of their Messiah!"

"Are you sure that guards are no longer keeping watch at the gate of Simon's house?"

"Yes, but the family has guard dogs. They don't want 'visitors.'"

"Hmm, what does it mean that Gaius is going to be a bishop? Atheists aren't organized like people in the Greek temples! They don't have supervisors, the people we call bishops! They can't be that prepared! Of course, they need someone to teach. But that group! It caused so much trouble in Pergamum. Thankfully, it's dying out!"

"No, Diotrephes, you are wrong. I heard it straight from Simon. by pretending to be interested. Here's what he said: 'Gaius will look after Antipas's followers in Pergamum. The group is made up of Jews, Gentiles, and Scythians.' They are all followers of that Messiah person. And that group is growing in number!"

Cleon noted the frown on Diotrephes's face. "That's not all! You might think that Gaius's leaving here means that the God-fearers group is falling apart. You would expect that to happen. No. They are meeting at Simon's house instead."

Diotrephes's voice was hardly more than a whisper. "The atheists may be harder to get rid of in Pergamum than I had thought. Antipas was killed, and I thought we had got rid of that group. Here in Sardis, I expected the Simon Ben Shelah family to gradually lose their influence. This is unwelcome news, Cleon."

"I'm sorry about that. You wanted to know everything about the Ben Shelah family."

"Cleon, there is a little girl living in that house, and I must find a way to get in and see her. Can you help me? I will pay you very well."

He reached into his leather bag and placed two silver coins in Cleon's hand.

"I'll find a way."

"What did you do with the silver coins I gave you?"

Cleon's words came out slowly. "I lost them."

"You...lost...them?"

"Well, I gambled and lost. Before the Games, I was told that the gladiators from Ephesus were a sure bet."

His statement hung in the air, with no comment possible. Lost wagers brought huge disappointments.

However, to Diotrephes, each bit of information was worth a reward. One day Cleon might be instrumental in helping bring Chrysa into his arms. Yet Cleon was a gambler, a loser. Who besides Cleon could bring him the information he needed? Walking back to his classes, he was grateful for a small success.

Hmm, I've hooked him! He needs money for his habit. From now on, I will control him at will!

The young schoolteacher scowled. This was unwelcome news about the Ben Shelah family. A dull fire burned inside him, but he was not sure why. The news that the sick man, Gaius, was going to Pergamum disturbed him greatly. Families from the God-fearers in Pergamum and Sardis were supposed to be intimidated. Instead, they were gathering. In Gaius, the man he had displaced at the meeting place of the God-fearers, they had a "bishop" to lead them!

The only good bit of news today was about Chrysa, but even that left him feeling a bit limp.

How do I write about this to Mother? Should I tell her about the assembly in Pergamum, that it's growing? What will she say when she learns that a bishop named Gaius is going to be there? Should I let her know that I can't simply march into Simon Ben Shelah's house and take Chrysa away?

THE INSULAE, SARDIS

On Tuesday, Miriam asked Gaius to take her farther into the poor section of the city. Simon's wagon bounced in the ruts, and the smells grew worse. Kalonice sat quietly but looked uncomfortable.

Three raggedly dressed little girls played on the dirt road, hopping from one flat rock to another. Raw sewage flowed along a small open ditch, only a step from where they were playing. An older child pushed a younger one, and one foot ended up in the ditch.

Kalonice gasped and pressed her fingers against her nose.

Further along, a child was rubbing dirt out of her eyes. Nearby, two boys fought over a piece of stale bread. After the smaller naked boy was pushed against the dirty wall, he slumped on his haunches. He put his head on his crossed arms and cried. His arms were thin, and Miriam could count his ribs.

The sound of a couple fighting in a nearby apartment reached them. A man was shouting ugly threats at his wife, and the high, shrieking voice of the woman came to them. "I don't have the money! You took it all! Why did you go to the tavern again last night?"

Miriam and Kalonice looked up to see where the shouting came from. Each floor of the apartment building was built a little farther out from the apartment's wall below. When people threw their garbage out, it landed on the street below. A pail of garbage fell behind them on the ground, splashing the children.

"I thought you weren't going to come today," said Miriam playfully to her friend.

"Well, you needed protection, didn't you?" Kalonice looked away, examining a broken door. "But do not count on me coming here again. How much of this punishment can I take?"

SIMON AND JUDITH'S HOME

That evening, after talking over legal matters regarding her inheritance, Miriam made some decisions.

"Uncle Simon, please write to Marcos. These are my ideas, but they must be written by you. First, thank him for coming to see you in Sardis during the Meeting of the Asiarchs last month and that you have explained the details to me.

"Second, say that he was right to challenge the city's action when they wanted to expropriate everything—the houses, the farm, and shops. Marcos's recommendations saved the city time and money and allowed many people to continue working.

"Next, his idea of taking the profits from all of Grandpa's businesses and dividing it ten ways with the Ben Shelah brothers is a good idea. It is the only way for Great-grandfather Eliab's will to be honored and yet keep the village intact.

"Fourth, tell him I understand how the court cases in Ephesus and Pergamum will be finalized. Eliab's final wishes will be fulfilled just as he wanted. That will happen before starting to execute the second will, my grandfather's. So, Uncle, will you please write all this in a letter?"

"I will do it, but why are you having me write the letter?"

"I could. However, I don't want a letter from me, as a woman, to be presented as evidence in court. If a wily lawyer ever stated, 'A woman wrote this letter to influence a court's decision,' he might request a stay of procedures.

"He could add, 'Miriam created a conflict of interest before the first will was fully executed.' I don't want that. But if you write it as one of the remaining brothers of the Ben Shelah family, then it's just your opinion, right? I want both of us to avoid future legal problems."

Miriam smiled at the surprised look on Simon's face. She had an idea of how things worked in the District Court of Pergamum.

She gave her uncle a little hug and looked around his library. All the scrolls were rolled up and placed in square boxes. On his desk lay several blank pieces of parchment and papyrus.

"Hearing you speak like this, Miriam, leads me to think that you have a plan of your own. What are you preparing for the future, my little niece?"

"I don't have a plan completely laid out yet. But I promise you this: When it is ready, I will need your help!" She smiled with satisfaction and hope.

Chapter 28
Cleon's Secret

THE INSULAE OF SARDIS

Miriam asked Kalonice to join her on another trip. "Just one more time please. I know you can't stand the place, but I want you to come with me today. Gaius said that the really impoverished families live farther in."

"I cannot go there! You know why!"

"Put on some extra perfume! Please, just this one time."

On their third day of visits, Miriam and Kalonice encountered more people. These insulae buildings were more dilapidated, and the roads were full of potholes. In one apartment, a deaf woman sat on the edge of her bed, rocking back and forth. Miriam saw a dried rose on the tiny table beside her narrow bed.

In another room, a blind man sat on the edge of a bed. It had no mattress. He was using his hands to twist out yarn from a pile of wool, trying to make something for his ten-year-old boy to sell.

A lame man was confined in another apartment. He had been injured in the Western Agora. A block of stone fell and crushed his ankle, so now his foot hung limply. His wife was making a little money by washing clothes, but there was not enough food for the nine children.

The woman was talkative. "We moved here because the rent is low. Neighbors say the building is full of evil spirits. Bad men lived here before us. A neighbor woman says those men went around to houses stealing things, taking what didn't belong to them."

Miriam asked a question. "When did you move into this place?"

"Only a week ago. Our landlord lives downstairs behind the shop. He is afraid those brothers might come back. Oh yes! He's scared of them."

"Where did they go?" asked Miriam. "If they're far away, then he doesn't need to be afraid of them."

The woman pursed her lips for a moment. "People downstairs heard the men say they would meet up in Hypaepe. I remembered the name because my mother was born there."

At their next visit, Kalonice did better than Miriam in communicating with a young deaf man. By speaking slowly and using her hands to talk, she understood. "He was born with good hearing, but his father kept hitting him about the ears as punishment. He can write well, but his hearing..."

As they were returning to Simon's house, traffic came to a standstill. A caravan of camels and donkeys made its way out of the city. As they waited for the animals to pass on the Royal Road, Miriam and Kalonice watched a family working in a dilapidated building next to the road. Women were weaving in a makeshift workshop, only partially restored after the earthquake.

Three women sat on the floor, surrounded by piles of wool, and preparing to form thread. A blind man worked in the corner, washing the yarn, and setting it on a rack to dry. Others were carding the dry wool into long strands. Miriam gazed at them, fascinated by the scene.

An hour later, they entered the main gate of Simon's house. "You are a real friend, Gaius. Thank you for blessing us by showing us where you were working. Did you ever get sick after visiting those people?"

"Yes, last winter. Someone must have given me unclean water to drink. I got sick several days later."

"Gaius, I will pray for you every day when you live in Pergamum." Miriam smiled and then turned to look up at the mountain.

Somewhere up there, Anthony was at his work. She prayed. *El Olam, Everlasting One, you keep showing us loving-kindness. Anthony is an army instructor, and amazingly, you provided for him. These three days visiting with Gaius opened my eyes to people who also need provision. They have so little, and I have so much.*

"Thank you, Kalonice, for coming with me," Miriam said. "It was good of you to spend your time this way. You used sweet perfume!"

Kalonice paused before climbing down from the cart. She turned her head away, but even so, Miriam saw tears in her eyes. "I'm sorry I said that about not going again. I want to help those people, but I just can't stand those horrible lanes winding between the houses. However, if you ever want me to help you in another way, call me again."

"You are a help, Kalonice. If I can think of something to help those families, I know you are willing to help make it happen."

"I have no idea what you are talking about. What could we do to help any of those people?"

"I don't have a plan yet, but I think we would work well together."

Kalonice walked quickly toward her home. She cringed, wondering if Miriam was pulling her into something that she did not want to be involved in. She walked into her house, asking why she had agreed to go to see poverty-stricken families.

SIMON AND JUDITH'S HOME

Miriam went over the events of the day. She could not sleep; too many ideas chased each other. One memory would not leave: the shabby workshop where the women were working at weaving and a blind man was washing wool.

After tossing and turning, she rose, reached for her cloak, and quietly went downstairs. A small lit lamp was kept in the kitchen. She went into Simon's library and found a scrap of papyrus and a quill. As she started to write, words flowed like a stream. A Sardian tune came back to her.

This morning several small children had been singing the same song as they played. And it was the song mothers often sang. She wrote, "I'll wait for you again," across the top of the sheet.

I face the cold against the night.
When nightmares come, they bring no fright.
I know, for you are my delight.
But you are not at home.

Farmers awake. I wash my face.
We sit for breakfast; first comes grace.
Animals munch in their green space.
They are all at home.

Children leave the table content,
Come back again with hot bread's scent.
At noon I hear of their events.
They enjoy their home.

Now evening prayers and funny jokes,
Familiar faces, same dear folks.
Laughter sounds, no one needs to coax
Them all to stay at home.

The sun has set with fading light,
The talk of war gives me a fright.
My God will keep you in his sight
And soon will bring you home.

As she finished, Judith came downstairs to the library room. She had heard a noise. Sitting down on the bench beside Miriam, she read the song. Miriam began to sing, then, halfway through, she choked up. Judith drew the younger woman to herself, and both women cried together.

Simon had agreed with Judith and Heber. Gaius should move to Pergamum to teach in Marcos's fellowship. Antipas's home at the village was waiting for him.

A new question emerged: Who would Simon hire as a replacement worker in his shop? At the same time, Miriam began talking with her uncle about ways to give gainful employment to some of the insulae's families. None had the skills to work in the Ben Shelah shop, but they could be productive by preparing wool and making cloth for clothing.

At first Simon was reluctant, but Miriam showed him that it would be a cheap source of winter items for his shop. Perhaps they could export new products to his brothers' shops in other cities.

Simon responded, "Several months ago, my brother in Philadelphia, Amos Ben Shelah, purchased an inn. To buy that building, Amos sold his shop. I might ask Zebadiah, a servant who worked in Amos's shop, to replace Gaius.

"I don't actually mistrust Cleon, but items have disappeared. Cleon is always asking for a pay raise, and he never looks straight at me when claiming that small boys stole merchandise."

"Do I know Zebadiah?" asked Miriam.

"No, but he's a distant cousin, part of our extended family."

Zebadiah was glad for a move to Sardis, a much bigger city. His wife and six children would come as soon as he could find a suitable apartment for them to live in. Zebadiah enjoyed sales but refused to brush down and care for the horses or donkeys.

Eugene was coming daily, arriving about mid-morning, helping in the kitchen, and leaving halfway through the afternoon. Miriam recalled how she and Anthony had similar meetings for months without anyone knowing their growing love for each other.

Her eyes were twinkling as she said, "Aunt Judith and Chenya, let's invite Eugene and his family for an evening meal!"

When Lyris heard about the invitation, she burst out, "I'm going to be busy day and night. I'll be making food all day long, washing pans, cleaning the griddle, and preparing cooking pots! Of course, I need an extra helper, a man's strong arms to lift the pots and put them on the stove!"

Afterward, Miriam and Judith took Simon aside. "If you will hear us out, I think we are going to need wedding tunics."

"Why?" Simon asked with a blank look.

Judith explained, and Simon replied, "Yes, I've noticed Eugene here during the past months, but I never gave it another thought."

Miriam leaned forward in her chair. "Well, I'm going to ask Uncle Jonathan to send one hundred wedding tunics to your shop. If they are needed for a wedding party, we can use them here. I will pay for them with the money I'll inherit from Grandpa Antipas. Of course, if we don't use them, there's sure to be another important event in Sardis. In that case, you can sell them and make a handsome profit!"

Simon rubbed his hands together. "Antipas could foresee business opportunities. You, too, have that ability."

"I received a letter from Zebadiah. He has a cousin, Elisha, in Thyatira who has been married for three years. Elisha cares for a wife and a baby and is an excellent carpenter. I would like him to come here for four months until the spring weather begins the agricultural season. Then he could return to Thyatira."

"Why would he come to Sardis?"

""Kalonice and I passed some broken down, empty warehouses

on the way home from the insulae. It gave me an idea. We should take a one-year contract on a damaged building, and Elisha could do some repairs. That would give us a usable workshop. We'll give people work and make money at the same time."

"Miriam! I really do see my brother in you! Antipas started workshops, and now you want to do the same!"

They laughed together, talking about wedding garments and the possibility of people working for Simon in what was presently an old building with a caved-in roof.

Elisha was delighted for the opportunity. Since the end of the harvest, he had been looking for work to keep him busy until spring. The young father enjoyed farm work but also took pleasure in carpentry and working with wool. He knew how to prepare wool and to weave. When people talked about craftsmen, Elisha's name often came up.

Simon wrote to Jonathan, asking for Elisha to bring one hundred garments suitable for a wedding. Most would fit adults, but some were for children. For four months, Zebadiah and Elisha were to stay in one of the little buildings behind Simon's home.

A week later, Miriam met Nikias and Elisha as they came through the front gate with the garments.

At the morning meal the next day, Elisha explained how Jonathan had transformed a useless piece of property in Thyatira and made his new home there. Building Jonathan's house took several years. "I helped him as that project was coming to an end," Elisha said.

"I'm glad you love to do carpentry work," said Miriam, "The renovation project I mentioned will take several weeks. Next we'll set up a weaving shop."

"How do you want me to help?"

"Five days ago, Uncle Simon found a weaving loom for rent. A friend of mine and I want to train people to do weaving. Your reputation arrived before you did! My friend, Kalonice, managed to negotiate an excellent price for the building that we need you to repair. Negotiating comes easily to her, I think. The loom will need to be installed, and then perhaps you'll have time to build us a new loom too."

"Congratulations! Another acquisition of the sprawling business of the family," laughed Elisha. "I am learning the ways of the Ben Shelah clan!"

SIMON BEN SHELAH'S SALES SHOP, THE ROYAL ROAD

Cleon was curious about the goods brought to the shop that afternoon. "What's all this?" asked Cleon as they unloaded a handcart full of clothing.

"These are wedding garments, one hundred of them!" replied Elisha, overflowing with enthusiasm. "Simon says to store them in the storage area. They aren't for sale yet."

"Who's getting married?" asked Cleon.

"I don't know. Miriam asked me to bring them from Thyatira. She said that they might be handy for a wedding or possibly some other purpose. Her letter said, 'You never know who might want to put on wedding garments at the Ben Shelah home.' Now, what do you think about that, Cleon? I also learned an incredible secret on my first day here! She told me not to tell anyone, but I'm sure you can keep a lid on things, can't you?"

"Of course. You can trust me. Completely. Fully!"

"Well, I learned last night that several bankers in Sardis approached Simon to ask him if he would be interested in being a partner in their bank. And at the same time, Miriam has asked that I bring these new tunics from Thyatira, one hundred of them. I don't know if there is a connection, but doesn't it sound interesting?"

Cleon put his index finger over his lips and then slid it across his throat to indicate that the information was safe with him and that it would not be spread.

THE WESTERN AGORA, MARKETPLACE IN SARDIS

Diodotus, the chief manager of the Bank of Hermus, had studied Simon's accounts and was pleased. He was convinced that he should take the next step in bringing Simon on as a partner. He set up a formal meeting at the bank to announce the decision.

The chilly winds of mid-November began blowing as Simon came with his family. Diodotus studied the family members standing in a semi-circle. All were dressed for the occasion, wearing light cloaks over their best clothes.

He watched Judith chat with his wife, Delbin, and the other wives.

However, Ravid, the young man who previously had made a rude comment, stood aside. Diodotus shifted his weight to the other foot, hoping there would not be a repeat of the bad manners.

The sun broke through the cloud cover, and the Western Agora marketplace shone brightly after the cleansing rain the night before. The first of the seasonal rains had come, leaving little ponds sparkling on the pavement. White awnings around the stoa swayed back and forth in the morning breeze.

The bank's offices occupied the second floor of one of the newly renovated marketplace office buildings. Fluted marble columns added an enchanting touch. Inside, the temperature was chilly, and a brazier was lit to add some warmth.

Diodotus escorted the family into the meeting area. An event like this brought several of the most powerful families together. He waited as men talked business. Women made small talk, mentioning children, or complaining about slaves.

The bank manager cleared his throat before making a short speech. "I am going to talk about the golden age of Sardis and how we still glory in those days."

In his speech, he explained how gold coins enriched the city and then repeated a fable from Aesop. The moral was how wealth was insecure in the hands of a sneaky person. A fox was used to characterize such a financial hazard. He then indicated that a reliable bank such as theirs was the better alternative.

Everyone laughed gingerly, hoping that the reliable reputation applied to them. Everyone quoted at least one of Aesop's fables each day.

Diodotus came to the main point of the meeting. "Simon Ben Shelah and his family have lived in Sardis for seventeen years. He is well known, and we admire his hard work as an importer and exporter. His shop on the Royal Road enhances the reputation of our city, and it consistently runs a profit."

For some reason, speaking of profitability brought out pleasant laughter in all those present.

"Therefore, we are pleased to formally announce that Simon Ben Shelah has been recommended as a director. This move will help us gain leverage over our competitors."

Cheers went up. Competition between the cities was a frequent subject around their dinner tables. "Now, Simon, will you grace us with a few words?"

Simon first spoke of Alexandria and his move to Sardis. Next, he presented his sons, Heber and Ezar, and discussed their roles in the family business. He did not mention Ravid, because his son-in-law had told Simon that he wanted to remain unmentioned.

The speech was received well, and the bankers nodded in satisfaction. "How wonderful to have the head of this Jewish family with such good connections, not only in Egypt but throughout Asia. He'll be confirmed as a new director!" Diodotus observed. "A sumptuous noon meal is awaiting us at the nearby thermopolium."

However, Diodotus was not prepared for what happened next. Simon called the bank manager aside. "Diodotus, as Jews, my family is restricted in what and where we can eat."

"What is this, my friend? We are inviting you to sit as a partner in our bank! Yet you refuse the most common courtesy of sharing a meal together. Many Jewish families occupy shops in this newly completed marketplace. I don't think any of them would refuse a meal with us! They would consider it an honor!"

The silence was broken when a woman's loud voice rang out. "These people think they are too good for us. Do we really want such a family to join our bank if they don't socialize with us?"

One man remarked, a little too loudly, "Simon wants the financial rewards of being a director in our bank, but he doesn't want the pleasure of our company! Imagine that!"

Judith murmured to Simon as they returned to their home. The light rain had started falling again, and the sky was gray under dark clouds. "Simon, I wonder if it is such a good idea to become part of the bank management. It will be difficult to participate without taking part in every social event."

SIMON AND JUDITH'S HOME

Ravid approved the arrival of the two new workers, Zebadiah, and Elisha. "We need more Jews like them," he said, talking with Nissa. "Zebadiah is hardworking. He's stayed with one family all his life, he shows stability, and he follows Moses's laws."

Nissa loved seeing her husband being more enthusiastic. She had reason to hope. Perhaps his long period of gloom was coming to an end.

That evening Ravid had a positive word to say about his father-in-law too. "You should have seen how he turned down the invitation to eat with those bankers! If he had done things like that every day since May, we would not have this tension in the home! It was good of him to feast at home rather than join in with the bankers according to their customs."

He walked to the front of the house and looked through a window, deep in thought. "Previously, I was planning to undermine your father's influence. But I have been softened because of the strong opposition he showed to the bankers. I can see that Simon is not going to 'walk in the counsel of the wicked, or stand in the way of sinners, or sit down to a meal, in the comfortable seats of the mockers.'"[45]

SARDIS GYMNASIUM

The next day, sure that this juicy tidbit was worthy of another coin, Cleon called on Diotrephes. "I have new information," he whispered. "Simon and Miriam brought a man from Thyatira to get workshops started. Elisha, that's the young man's name, is going to help Miriam. The family has rented an old building to give jobs to poor people. She visited the needy people that Gaius was friends with, and now she wants to find them jobs!"

"What kind of jobs?"

"Weaving cloth and working with wool, things like that."

"This is hardly worth anything," whispered Diotrephes, his face flushed. "Bring me real information. Help me get into their house! That's what I want. Remember that!"

As Diotrephes turned his back and left, Cleon had an idea. The plan he was hatching in his mind would yield him all the money he would need for placing bets during the last two weeks of the year. All Cleon needed was the right moment. He reckoned that the first week in December would be the best time for that.

---

[45] From Psalm 1:1

Chapter 29
Tremors of the Past

SIMON AND JUDITH'S HOME

Achim, the newly appointed leader of the synagogue, went to visit Simon early on Friday morning. The date for this visit was chosen with care. In less than a week, all Jews would be celebrating Chanukah. Achim straightened his shoulders as he left his house.

My responsibility is to correct what I believe has been an injustice, he thought as he knocked at the Ben Shelah gate.

"This is purely a social visit, Simon, a private visit," he stated enthusiastically. Then, being led to Simon's library, he added, "What a wonderful collection of scrolls you have here!"

Achim had been agonizing over the results of recent decisions. He believed that the disagreement with Diotrephes should not keep Simon from attending regular synagogue services. Several families had also been absent since the Ben Shelah family was barred from the God-fearers. Achim also noted that financial donations into the treasury were somewhat reduced.

"How can I help you?" asked Simon. They finished small talk after drinking new wine.

Achim answered, "I want you to come back and worship with us. All I ask is that you meet only with Jews. Stay away from the Gentiles. In a week, we will light the first candle of Chanukah. I also ask that you leave the beliefs of the carpenter aside."

Simon stood up and walked back and forth across the room. "Achim, the Holy One has given us a new purpose. 'Forget the former things; do not dwell on the past. See, I am doing a new thing! Now it springs up; do you not perceive it? I am making a way in the desert and streams in the wasteland.'[46] You often quote that promise in our scriptures. Well, I do believe the Messiah has come. In his kingdom, he gives us the freedom to worship with the Gentiles who fear God.

[46] Isaiah 43:18–19

He wants them to see his light."

He sat down close to Achim, and there was a light shining in Simon's eyes. "By allowing Diotrephes a voice in the God-fearers, the Synagogue of Sardis is like someone who unknowingly harbors a snake in his house. I do not want the poison of falsehood to bring death to anyone."

"So you are determined to stay away from Friday evening worship because Diotrephes has been permitted to help?"

"That is correct." Simon's fingers were intertwined on the table.

Achim came straight to the point of his visit. "Simon Ben Shelah, I came here to help you. I intended to restore fellowship for your family before the first night of Chanukah! However, by resisting my generosity, you also resist the elders' tradition. Look at you, frolicking with Gentiles! I saw several people in your house when I came in, and they all seem at home here. These non-Jews—the lame man and clubfoot woman and the old man, Eugene—will lead you away from our basic beliefs!"

Without warning, Achim burst out, not taking time to consider the implications of his words. "Until now, you have voluntarily stayed away from our fellowship. But now you are rejecting the Jewish leadership. I am forced to formally impose temporary exclusion. If you do not repent, you will suffer the maximum sentence, *hçrem,* just as Antipas, your brother, was cut off from fellowship!"

His hands were trembling, and he stood up to leave.

"Don't leave just yet my dear friend Achim. Let me understand. Usually temporary exclusion lasts thirty, sixty, or ninety days. You wish for me to immediately renounce my faith in the Messiah. That would satisfy you, and I would then be accepted. But if I do not reject Yeshua, you will utter the word *hçrem,* and I would be cut off permanently. Is this what you intend?"

"Yes, that is correct. Having people stay in the fellowship is important, but the purity of our beliefs is vital. How can we continue fellowship with a family that openly offers hospitality to non-Jews at their home?"

"Well, please know this. I will not renounce my belief in Yeshua. I believe that he came as our Messiah. Would you let me tell you why I..."

Achim covered his ears. He didn't want to hear the rest of the sentence. "Thank you for sharing a cup of wine with me, Simon. I do not want this to be our last. I must go now but know this: If you refuse fellowship with us, your name and the names of others who do not join us will be blotted out of our Book of Life.

"If Mayor Tymon Tmolus were to hear of a continuing division, he might question all the business arrangements Jakob worked on for months. After almost three hundred years, we are finally socially accepted in Sardis yet still able to keep our beliefs. I will not tolerate anyone who threatens the unity we desire by speaking of and teaching a Messiah we will not accept."

As Achim left the house, he called back, "Chanukah, the Feast of Rededication, will be here in just one more week. I do hope you will change your mind, Simon."

THE TEMPLE OF ARTEMIS, SARDIS

The next day was the seventy-fourth anniversary of the great earthquake. A light rain woke people up on November 17.[47] Ankara, the high priest, arrived an hour before the crowds came for the commemoration. He watched them coming to stand in front of the Temple of Artemis. Soon thousands of people would be weeping for the dead.

He turned to study the sheer cliff formed by the sudden plunge of tons of earth and rock from the acropolis. At that moment, the ancient street called Temple Avenue, the most well-to-do street in the city, had disappeared. Many affluent homes were covered in a dull brown rockslide of gigantic proportions.

Ankara stood on the top step of the Temple of Artemis. Alala, the high priestess, stood one step below him. Ankara watched twenty-four vestal virgins raise and lower their arms, each holding the end of a white linen sheet. Twelve cotton drapes were to be lifted upward and then drift downward slowly, imitating clouds. With the drizzle settling in, however, the fabrics did not fulfill their purpose. Instead, the sodden cloth was weighed down, and the heavy fabric

---

[47] When the Hermus Valley region was struck by an earthquake in AD 17, Sardis suffered the most severely. Architectural treasures from Hittite, Lydian, Persian, and Greek times were destroyed. The disaster struck the acropolis. The collapse may be behind the words of the revelation in which people 'cry out for the mountains to fall on them,' a quote from Hosea 10:8. The actual day of the year is unknown. For this novel, the commemoration takes place on November 17.

added to Ankara's sense of gloom.

With water dripping down his face, Ankara walked to the doors of the temple entrance. He knew that was the exact location of the first temple's construction almost three thousand years earlier. He closed his eyes, unable to imagine how many people had come to this spot. Opening his eyes, he saw thousands standing in the light rain. Covering their heads with straw hats, they were declaring their persistent devotion to their goddess.

The twenty-four virgins stopped raising the sheets, unable to lift the heavy fabric. Ankara walked along the rooms on the side of the temple. Scores of chambers were used by eunuch priests, but at this moment, all of them stood in the outer courtyard. These men had given their manhood to the goddess. All the priests were dressed in different-colored vestments. Ankara smiled and wiped the last drops of rainwater from his chin.

Now inside, he nodded at each division of the priesthood. The high priest was amazed that such a variety of functions within the priesthood had evolved over the centuries. His lips bent upward in a wet smile. More than two thousand people were presently employed at the Temple of Artemis.

He turned and faced the entrance. A white bull was led into the temple and up the steps. The animal almost fell on the wet steps but recovered its balance. A priest with a green turban tugged it gently, using the rope tied to its nose ring. The sacrifice had to appear as if it were going willingly. An unwilling sacrifice could make Artemis angry, and Ankara wanted the best for his city.

Ankara cut the bull's jugular vein, and a large bowl caught the draining blood. As life began to fade from the beast, it fell to its front knees. He could see the light of life fading from the bull's eyes.

Artemis would be grateful for this offering. She would accept it and keep the city safe. Indeed, this sacrifice would prevent another earthquake from happening.

Ankara offered his petition. "Artemis, Queen of Heaven, deliver us from earthquakes. May the damage our city sustained seventy-four years ago be kept far away from your children."

Crowds waiting outside gladly received the news. That bull had been sacrificed. These faithful mourners were descended from families that had died in the great earthquake. They stood patiently in the large, paved area in front of the temple.

The rain began to fall harder. Moments later, lightning flashed, and thunder sounded. Some started to run home, but Ankara nodded to Alala, the high priestess, and she called to the visitors, "Come under the roof for shelter!"

Hundreds rushed under the protection of Artemis's roof, shivering under the long portico.

Mayor Tymon Tmolus, his wife, Panthea, and their daughter, Cynthia, were present for the sacrifice. They walked through the long portico toward the Sacred Hall; as mayor, Tymon was permitted to enter the room at the center of the temple.

Cynthia saw her mother crying. "What are you thinking, Mother? We're here to hear Father's speech to the city counselors."

"We lost so many of our family in that earthquake!" wailed Panthea. Despair was imprinted in the dark lines on her face.

Mayor Tymon was to talk at the end of the ritual. As he surveyed the crowd, he saw that it was a smaller group than what he had hoped for. Puddles of rainwater formed on the polished stone floor around each visitor as they stood shivering.

The mayor spoke. "Hades was irritated many years ago, and he came to the surface of the earth, causing the ground to rumble. He could again become angry, so we must appease him by giving our best. Let's give gold to the goddess. We will continue to finish rebuilding her temple because this is what we learned from her: 'Never enough gold!'

"We grieve for many reasons. No longer may we marvel at Greek or Persian art. Even treasures of the Lydians, our actual ancestors, are lost forever, hidden beneath our feet. However, fragments of our past are still with us. So our heritage will remain alive but only in our memories. What a loss! We will leave a legacy to our children and to our children's children.

"Artemis has a message for us today: 'Preserve the living.' Our city was built in ages past with industry, vision, and drive. And we, the citizens of Sardis, will continue to develop far into the future!"

A weak cheer arose from the people. Grown men shivered as they stood in the wet and cold. They had welcomed the arrival of cold weather but wished they did not have to stand in wet clothing after the morning downpour.

The Temple of Artemis, the ancient symbol of Sardis's glory, still stood proudly.

MILITARY TRAINING AREA, TMOLUS MOUNTAIN

Four legionaries were seated at a table in Prosperus's tent at the mountain camp for a late afternoon meal. The purpose of the meeting was to review the training exercises for the recruits.

Anthony and two others, both from Laodicea, had been invited. Little Lion was Anthony's best choice for a future scout, and Dares sat beside Prosperus. It was hoped that Dares would make an outstanding army leader because his skills in forming strategies were truly exceptional.

The rain was now merely a drizzle resembling tiny diamonds falling from the sky. Water was drenching the land with much-needed moisture for the forest, fields, and pasture lands. After the rains stopped in late March, the region would survive through eight dry months until the heavy clouds once again returned.

A chilly wind caused all four men to clutch their cloaks tightly. The weather, which had been cold at night and warm during the day, was now chilly even at noon. In a few weeks, all the trees except the pines would be bare, and the ground would be completely sodden.

Anthony looked around, thinking about his family. Grace would soon be learning to walk, and he was going to miss her first steps. Miriam and the others in her family would be having a quiet little supper, safe indoors, where the rain could not come in.

Anthony and Prosperus's rigorous training brought constant groans. Prosperus put his recruits through endless exercises with swords and javelins. Anthony kept his recruits learning complex scouting actions. All learned how to stave off attacks. The instructors worked together, but a competitive edge between them was noticeable.

"I say the old ways of training are the best," said Prosperus, returning to a point he had debated before. "You go up against a city and place it under siege. Men dig under the foundations of the city walls. Auxiliaries bring in the catapults, and we throw great stones or flaming pots of oil over the walls."

"Where did you see that done effectively?" asked Anthony.

Prosperus boasted of past victories. "I fought with Legion X in the East. Those Persians are a real fighting force!"

"I have some questions about our assignment," said Anthony.

"What went through your mind when Commander Felicior said you were to stop me from taking the eagle standard?" After several weeks, he was finally inviting an analysis of that event.

Prosperus scratched his back. "We thought you would come with a frontal attack, so we placed our strongest men at the gate. You surprised us, even Dares. He stayed in the tent, guarding the standard, but I must say you used an unusual strategy."

Anthony spread his arms wide. "In the beginning, I had no plan. We were given an impossible assignment. However, you lost the eagle standard, didn't you?"

"What are you saying?"

Anthony ignored the irritation in Prosperus's voice. "Here we were, safe on the mountain, without a single idea of what to do to carry out Felicior's order. I prayed to my God. We just bumped into the bandits. I didn't mean to, but then an idea came of how to use them against you. However, in the end, a strange thing happened. Look, the bandits were a help to you! People call you 'the hero of Sardis.' You've returned the stolen items. Even Mayor Tymon Tmolus is calling you a star! And he invited you to come to his table with Lady Panthea and Cynthia. You told us how much you enjoyed the evening and the entertainment at the banquet!"

Anthony wanted to return to the purpose of training the recruits and for the need for extra caution in Dacia. "Yet, Prosperus, your men lost. In the end, who had the standard?"

"What are you trying to say? You have something deeper in mind, don't you?"

"Yes. When these young soldiers arrive in Europe, they will face situations you cannot imagine. Emperor Domitian knows that King Decebalus built his capital far away from the Danube River. How will Domitian's generals move their legions, maybe forty thousand men, including all the auxiliaries, all that way? How close must they come to the enemy's capital to bring about a victory? How well do you think our troops will fight?"

"Rome's strength lies in our numbers!"

"How will our army get close enough to Decebalus's capital to force submission? Do we know how many traps his forces will plant along the way? His men know where to hide on top of rocky crags as well as in valleys. They will kill ten or twelve of our soldiers at each cliff and then move away and not be hit once. Romans like to fight face to face. The enemy prefers to hide, hit, and run."

Prosperus no longer sounded irritated. He conveyed disdain with sarcasm. "Anthony, maybe you should ask your god to place you at the head of a battalion against Dacia in the coming fight."

Anthony smiled. "I am no longer fit for a battlefield. This scar would shine in the dark, giving me away!"

Little Lion had been listening quietly. "Seriously, Instructor Anthony, I want to know. What did you do? You don't use the same word when talking about a 'god' that we use at home. You make it sound as if you can talk to your god at any moment. Does your god really hear and answer you when you speak to him? Can you speak to him about other problems as well? Are you sure you don't have to go to a priest?"

Anthony spoke seriously. "Years ago, I thought I could never ask anything from the gods. I wanted to do that, to have my father and mother come back together again. Then, two years ago, I met an old man. He taught me this name: The God of Israel, Adonai. I believe he is the true God, the One and Only God. There are no other gods in the nations like him."

Prosperus pushed himself back from the table and tightly crossed his arms to put space between himself and Anthony.

However, Little Lion leaned forward to catch every word.

"Adonai created the world, the sky, the heavens, the sea, the land, animals, and birds. He is not far from us. Not like Zeus, who is supposed to live on Mount Olympus. I have stood at the foot of that great mountain near Thessalonica. And I have also seen more majestic, taller mountains, the Alps. We marched by them for days. The Alps are glorious. But God does not hide himself in far-off places like mountaintops."

"Where does this god of yours live then? I don't understand," said Prosperus, interested despite his scorn.

"God fills the heavens, but he also wants to come close to us, to establish his covenant in our hearts. There was a man named Jeremiah who suffered during a terrible siege. He lived in the kind of walled city you were talking about, Prosperus. Armies circled Jerusalem. Great engines of war bashed against the walls and gates. The city was eventually burned, and all its treasures were taken to Babylon. People boasted that their well-built city walls could protect them, but Jeremiah knew the walls would fail."

Prosperus leaned forward, anxious to hear about the war's success against a city with such strong walls. "I know much about mining under walls and climbing over them. That is my kind of warfare!"

Anthony prayed for wisdom as he talked to his fellow soldiers. "People are always going to boast! About what? Well, a strong man brags about his strength. He can run faster than others in a race. A rich man boasts about his riches.

"In the middle of the chaos, Jeremiah had a word from the Lord. People were boasting that they would survive the attack, but God knew they were about to be defeated.

"Jeremiah said true greatness is better than boasting because it comes from a life built on God. God said, 'Don't boast about your wisdom and strength. If people want to boast, let them boast 'that they know me. I am the Lord, who exercises kindness, justice, and righteousness on earth, for in these I delight.'"[48]

Prosperus pushed himself away from the table quickly. He stood up, shouting, "Foolishness!"

His voice was tense, and he was ready to demean Anthony. "Why not boast about being strong, rich, and wise? That is what it means to be victorious after all. The prize always goes to the strongest!"

Little Lion stood up, much shorter than Instructor Prosperus as they stood side by side. "I think you should listen, Prosperus. Because Anthony was given an impossible task—to take the eagle standard from you. He found a way to do it, even when you were well prepared. During these weeks, Anthony hasn't boasted once. Quite the opposite, he found a way for you to keep your honor. Did he shame you? No! Could he not have caused you to be the loser in the war game? Yes!

"And Prosperus, he showed you mercy! What was it that made it possible for you to meet Mayor Tymon and Lady Panthea? How did you come to meet their daughter, Cynthia, the one you could not stop describing last night at our evening meal? Don't you think that his words about fighting in the forests and mountains of Dacia make sense? And if they make sense, and he has the experience and the scar to prove it, then why should we not listen to him talk about his God?"

---

[48] From Jeremiah 9:23–24

"Do not talk about the God of Jerusalem in this camp!" shouted Prosperus. "Why didn't he care for a million and a half Jews when our legions marched against those triple walls? Where was this 'god' when we captured one hundred thousand Jews? We took them from Jerusalem. Marshall Titus made sport of them when ten thousand Jews were thrown to animals, five and ten at a time, in Caesarea Philippi. My father was there and said he never saw such sport in his life.

"The other ninety thousand imprisoned Jews were taken to Egypt to work in the mines.[49] I am a reservist, training men for war. In three years, I will be retired, and I aim to go to Pisidia Antioch. I plan to get a farm near the northern side of that beautiful lake."

Prosperus's words came out in an angry outburst. "Isn't a god supposed to protect his own city? But your god was powerless. Did he protect his city against Rome? What kind of god claims fame by saying people should boast about 'kindness, justice, and righteousness'? Those are qualities unknown to an army besieging a city!

"The Jews couldn't even bury their dead, and the stench was unlike anything anyone has ever experienced. Anthony, is this the god you want me to trust? Where was their god when our legions marched against Jerusalem?"

The instructor's voice was now loud enough to be heard by everyone in the camp. "You are an over-confident, wounded, lucky-to-be-alive soldier! You think you are superior, boasting about the victories of Legion XXI, the Predators, in Upper Germanica! But I think you twist everything to make yourself look good."

Little Lion wanted to hear more, but he knew this was not the time. He would come back to Anthony, talk with him personally, and learn everything he could. Little Lion longed to hear about a God who heard prayers, responding personally to his deep human needs. He had not told the others how he had to work hard to provide food for

[49] Josephus estimated 1.1 million dead and 97,000 captives because of the fall of Jerusalem. He estimated 2,700,200 purified worshipers had come to the Passover Feast. The Romans burned the outskirts of the city. They demolished the walls, not leaving any stone on top of another, except in one portion, the Western Wall of the Temple.

his infirm and lonely mother.

He began a quiet conversation. "I don't know anything about you, 'God of Jerusalem.' Perhaps I should say, 'God of Anthony,' but that does not seem right somehow. A god is the protector of a city, not a person. But he calls you 'Lord,' and that doesn't seem right either, because we are only allowed to say, 'Caesar is lord and god.' So I'm going to call you 'God of Anthony.'

"He says you are the 'One true God.' Please take care of my mother. I had to fight so hard for jobs to earn enough to bring home bits and pieces of food. She was so weak when I left her three months ago in Laodicea. She's all I have. I hated carrying wood, bringing charcoal in sacks, and having people make fun of me just because I'm small.

"If you can hear me and if I can speak to you like this, please take care of her. Mother always goes to the Temple of Apollo. She has never heard about 'Anthony's God.' If I can say a prayer to you, here in a forest, without taking a sheep to sacrifice, please take care of her. And 'God of Anthony,' I want to know who you are."

SIMON AND JUDITH'S HOME

Anthony, granted leave to go home for two days, was encouraged with the progress of his recruits. As he left his sandals in the porch area and came in through the front door, he saw Ravid slip out the back.

His arrival caused a commotion and noise. Miriam squealed with delight as she held Grace and ran to give him a hug.

Judith had been sitting on the couch talking with Kalonice, and Simon came from the workshop announcing, "Welcome! You arrived for the last day of Chanukah! See, seven lamps on the menorah are already burning!"

All the adults gathered on the couches, and Miriam passed Grace into Anthony's arms. He explained how the training had improved the recruits' abilities and that he had two days off while other activities were continuing in the mountain camp.

Out of the corner of his eye, Anthony saw Elaine watching Isidoros. He wondered if this would ever blossom into a lively relationship. Isidoros and Hector were sitting on the floor talking with Tamir.

Eugene came in to announce that Lyris would now be bringing

out food for the noon meal.

Afterward, when all the bowls and platters were taken back to the kitchen, the boys started asking questions about the army.

"Anthony, what do you train scouts to do?" Isidoros was almost the age of the young men he was training on the mountain.

A scene from his past came to mind. Anthony's squad had been cutting down trees in Upper Germanica, making an ample space where a wooden palisade wall would be built. Later, the first small fort would be upgraded into one of the many stone forts connected by a Roman road.

Scouts of another cohort had let down their guard. They had been assigned to keep a secure watch over the valley. Suddenly, a barbarian had come up out of a creek, running at them, and a fellow soldier screamed as an ax ripped open his left arm. The brute had been killed, but the soldier lost the lower part of his arm.

He put that scene aside as inappropriate and answered quietly, "A large part of training for scouts is learning to work together while gathering information. They are trained to look and then remember everything they see. They must be able to imagine what the enemy might do in any valley or on any mountain. They learn to put gathered information together so that their commander can use it. All that takes wisdom. If they don't work as a closely knit team, they get hurt. A common phrase is 'work together or die.'

"So I teach them to develop constant vigilance, endurance, flexibility, and strength but also to keep learning new skills. On top of all that, they receive the combat training that they need for survival."

"How long are you with us this time?" asked Elaine.

"I am here for two days, and then I have to return to the camp."

Kalonice and Miriam waited until the younger ones had finished their discussions with Anthony. After they went to another room to play, it was the adults' turn to talk.

"While you were away," started Kalonice, "something wonderful happened. Miriam and I also did some 'scouting.' Gaius took us to the insulae three times before he left to go to Pergamum.

"We are opening up a workshop to help the people there. I've bought two floor looms, and Miriam located a vertical loom. We're hiring some destitute people to do the weaving. They are a strange group. One man is blind, but his hands are sensitive. He has a good mind and can sort out the wool. Another is deaf, and he has a lot of children. He is learning to use the ground loom. They are not making good value woolen clothing yet, but they are learning and getting better."

Anthony's eyebrows went up, and his mouth had opened a little wider at each comment. "Wait a moment! Start at the beginning. How many are involved? How did you get this done so quickly?"

Miriam looked on with a growing smile while Kalonice talked. "We found a building that was partially destroyed. For the time being, we are renting it from month to month. Our workshop is called Closely Knit. It is like what you said when you explained the scouts' work to the children. Unless they work together, they will die. Some parents have so many children, and they don't have enough food. One man lost the use of his foot after a large block fell on him, so he can't work."

Anthony looked at the two women, so different in many ways yet friends. Both had come alive in a new way. This evening would mark the Sabbath return and the beginning of the last day of the Festival of Lights, Chanukah.

Everybody gathered as the sun was going down. Rich smells came from the kitchen where Lyris had been preparing food all afternoon. She needed extra help to cook for twenty-three people. Eugene went this way and that, fetching vegetables from the storeroom and then returning for more food. Zebadiah and Elisha, Ateas and Arpoxa, Anthony and Miriam, Kalonice's family, and the Ben Shelah family would share supper together.

Ravid took food to his home separately, so he and Nissa were by themselves.

Lamps and candles were lit. Tonight, Simon involved the youngest ones in the Sabbath teaching before the meal was served. They all washed their hands, each pouring the water from the decanter onto the next person's hands.

"Amath, when did the first Chanukah take place?" asked Ezar.

She spoke loudly and clearly. "Antiochus IV was his name! What he did was so bad that the people revolted and defeated his army. The temple needed to be cleaned and rededicated to the Lord. The Maccabees needed eight days for the rededication. The week would start on one Sabbath and end on the next; that's eight full days. They needed lots of oil to light the menorah lamps but only had enough of the special consecrated oil for one day.

"But even though they did not have enough oil, God made it last all week long. Each night they lit one more lamp. Finally, the last one was lit, and the temple had been cleansed. The miracle was that the lamps kept on burning for all eight days."

The family chuckled with pleasure, hearing the story once more, and continued their Sabbath readings and prayers. During the meal, Anthony realized how much he was missing when he was away at camp. Bathing in cold water, sleeping in a cold tent, and walking with wet sandals through the forest was different from being in a warm home with a close-knit family.

Miriam lay beside Anthony in the dark, happy to have him back with her for even two days. They couldn't seem to go to sleep, so they talked for a long time.

She discussed the changes in the people now working at the sales shop and the new workshop. "Zebadiah has taken over Gaius's job at the Ben Shelah shop on the Royal Road. Heber keeps track of inventory, the accounts, the banking, and shipping items to the other brothers. Elisha came to do some carpentry and then to train people in weaving. I have found a bigger warehouse if I can get a fair price to rent it. Elisha said he would do the repairs needed for us to move into it."

"This is what you do while I am at the training camp?"

Miriam giggled with delight. "It just happened! One thing led to another. I was so sad with you away. I thought I would never get out of that misery. Then I remembered some of my songs. I said, 'Why don't I do something for some disadvantaged people while Anthony is away?' Kalonice and I went with Gaius into the impoverished area of Sardis. He introduced us to people he had been visiting.

"Oh, I almost forgot. I learned some news from the insulae people that you might find useful," she said, suddenly remembering a critical detail. "It was two weeks after soldiers were bringing the stolen treasures back to their owners. One of the poor families that we visited told us about four brothers who moved in last spring. They designed and installed mosaic artwork on floors and walls.

"All summer long, they often got drunk, bragging too loudly

about 'our treasures.' They left suddenly after those robbers were captured up on the mountain. Remember how I told you about the rich women at that big party I went to? I remembered them talking about their homes being robbed."

Anthony frowned. "Why didn't the neighbors tell the soldiers about their suspicions?"

"Nobody in the impoverished section, men or women, trusts a soldier! When the men were leaving, they were telling each other to meet at 'Hypaepe.'"

After she had fallen asleep, Anthony stayed awake. Miriam might have possibly stumbled onto information about the much larger theft ring that Little Lion suggested might exist. His mind whirled from one question to another.

Where did those four men go? Were they directing the robbers who were caught? Were others from outside the city working with them?

MILITARY TRAINING AREA, TMOLUS MOUNTAIN

Anthony went back to the training camp and asked Prosperus to go with him immediately. At the garrison, Felicior looked surprised to see both his instructors barge into his office.

"Does this mean trouble?" Felicior asked, frowning.

"No, sir, but I may have information about who the others are in that gang of robbers. I wanted you and Prosperus to hear this at the same time. On the mountain two months ago, we captured four men. One got away. We never discovered how many others may have been involved. You have had soldiers looking into it, and you learned that all the robberies happened during the spring and summer.

"My wife told me that she visited some people in the poorer parts of the city. Some residents tell of squabbles and fights among four brothers who talked about 'hidden treasures.' Those men were 'mosaic artists.' They disappeared just after we captured the bandits, and I've heard that the last two mosaics they had begun were not finished. They were accomplished artists who designed beautiful floor mosaics for wealthy families.

"It seems likely that these four brothers were the artists who stole items from the homes. From questioning the thieves, we know they were bringing sacks of mosaic materials to those houses and taking stolen items away to the cave in the emptied sacks."

Felicior, on the other side of the table, narrowed his eyes. "You are saying that a woman found this lead?"

Anthony continued. "Yes. Suppose that those four men left Sardis when we caught the others. Could the man who got away from us that morning have gone to tell them to get out of town? If so, perhaps I know where they were living. The problem is this: We don't know where they are now. The woman in that apartment says she heard the men saying they would meet later in Hypaepe. Where is that?"

"Why, that's the name of a small village on the other side of the mountain," noted Felicior.

"May I have your permission to follow up on them, sir? I suspect that instead of just five men, there may be more working together."

"Do you have a suggestion?"

"I want some of our best trainees to search Hypaepe and the nearby towns. The brothers must have guessed that we would be searching for them here, but they will never dream of us looking for them in Hypaepe. They left shortly after we captured the four members of that gang."

Felicior warmed to the topic. "We learned through the torture of the robbers that they were working for four brothers. We have not been able to locate them. This is the first confirmation that four brothers, the mosaic artists, were indeed involved in the robberies. The man who got away is the mastermind, but we do not know if he is one of the four. I want to have him stand before me. Now we need a plan. Who has a suggestion?"

Prosperus shrugged, but Anthony leaned over with both hands on the desk in front of the commander. "Will those brothers abandon their way of life in the spring just because their friends got caught? No, they will likely go to another city to do the same thing. We need a way to deceive the robbers, to see if they can be located. Why not send two or three of our men to Hypaepe? Let them spend two or three months there. They can go from one tavern to another. They should spend time in each surrounding village or town. I think we can work out a plan to entrap the brothers if they are located."

Felicior could not hide his pleasure. He squared his shoulders, sure that he understood the most essential elements of Anthony's plan. "I'm sure your method involves Little Lion. I remember how he imitated me his first day here, and then he tricked Taba and those four thieves. Have Little Lion pretend to be a robber again, set them up, and apprehend them.

"Go! Execute your plan. May Jupiter be with you! Select your men and send them to Hypaepe, by way of Smyrna and then through Ephesus. No one can go over the mountain at this time as the deep snow makes travel on that road impossible."

Chapter 30
The Darkest Night

THE ACROPOLIS AND THE TEMPLE OF ARTEMIS, SARDIS

Early in December, a large section of the block wall around the top southern edge of the acropolis fell on the homes below. Any further erosion of the wall's foundation threatened an additional catastrophe. Suddenly the city was preoccupied with a single topic of conversation. Mayor Tymon Tmolus rested his head on his knees. "Oh, those unfortunate people who built their houses right under the south edge of the acropolis!"

"Why didn't Artemis protect them?" Panthea asked her husband, her face an ashen gray.

It took much longer to get from one side of the city to the other because Temple Avenue was now almost completely blocked off by rubble. One of the bankers, Diodotus's friend, threw his hands in the air. "No one knows how many people died." He had not only lost several relatives; he also lost their accounts.

Gradually the missing people were accounted for. Mayor Tymon Tmolus spoke to a group of the city supervisors. "Unfortunately, 139 people appear to have been buried under the debris."

Grief was felt by all: rich and poor, men and women, free and slaves. The destroyed homes would likely stay covered. Most people affected were either dead or did not have the funds to rebuild. Even if they could, why build another home where more rock and dirt could slough off the acropolis again?

Ankara, the high priest, and Alala, the high priestess, stared at the dreadful gash on the acropolis. Alala spread her hands wide and then placed them over her mouth. "We must have further sacrifices. Hades is angry again."

She groaned and bent over, her eyes closed.

After talking with Ankara, the Sardian priests decided that the next six weeks would be set aside for individual sacrifices. They would ask Artemis to be an overcomer in her struggle with Hades. They begged their goddess, asking that no additional rockfalls would take place. As an additional precaution, even the most ancient statues, those of Kubaba and Cybele, would be brought out and worshiped once again.

THE INSULAE OF SARDIS

The ferocious winter storm also caused another disaster. During the high winds, a fire broke out on the third floor of a building in the insulae. One survivor told how it started: "The fire began when the wind blew open a shutter and an oil lamp was knocked over. Eleven people were sleeping there. Three escaped alive, all little children."

The strong wind turned into a gale after midnight. The apartment building was ablaze, and there was no way to put it out. Five other buildings, those closer to the eastern wall, also went up in flames. Neighbors heard the screams of dying families but could not help.

After the fire died out, Mayor Tymon Tmolus walked by the ashes of the six buildings. A firefighter said that forty-two people had died. Over a hundred had suffered burns and were taken to the Asclepius Hospital in wagons to bathe in the hot springs.

The two disasters, the landslide, and the fire, set the mayor and city authorities on edge. It was winter, and there was no accommodation for the survivors. A small tent-town was set up outside the eastern side of the city.

A gloomy mood descended on everyone. Some angrily condemned the authorities but always in hushed voices. It was evident that deep, mysterious magic would have to be found to provide safety in the city. The longest night of the year was near.

SIMON AND JUDITH'S HOME

On Wednesday morning, two men came to the gate.

"We are from the Bank of Hermus," they said to Lyris, who had answered the door. "We want to speak to Simon Ben Shelah."

Lyris seated the men in the great room and went to get Simon from his workshop. When Simon entered the room, he recognized the men immediately and smiled broadly. "Welcome to my home, gentlemen. May we serve you a drink? Would you like bread and fresh, hot milk on such a cold day?" He knew that they had come to discuss his partnership.

"We can only stay for a short while." It was very unusual to turn down hospitality. The men were obviously in a hurry to convey their message.

"Well then, gentlemen, how may I be of service?" Simon asked. From the frowns on their faces, he knew instantly that the bank's partnership proposal had been revoked.

"Recently the directors of the bank recommended you for a partnership in the Bank of Hermus. Unfortunately, due to other considerations," he paused to find the right words, "we cannot accept the recommendation," one of the visitors said.

Expensive gold rings on fingers captured Simon's eye. "Are you free to tell me why?"

"We found that your name has been removed from the Synagogue Book of Life." Simon knew the banker, Diodotus, had sent the two men.

The other visitor answered, "You were excluded by your friends, your own people. You must have done something drastic to upset them like that. How can our bank trust you to give us a good name if you are not well received by your own people? We have to think of our reputation."

The rest of the day was a blur. Simon returned to his workshop but could not focus on making jewelry. All he could do was call on God's name for patience to deal with these painful exclusions, these significant events in his life.

In the evening, he explained the situation to Judith, Heber, Ezar, Ravid, Nissa, and Miriam. He gathered them together after sending the children out of the room.

"How much have we actually lost? Our name and personal integrity matter to us more than any partnership. I know my stubborn pride is being hurt because I had to leave the congregation. And now the bankers' community has cut us off.

"I suffered much pain today. But when I evaluate it honestly, being a partner at the bank is somewhat like outward glitter. My relationship with God is more important than membership in the Synagogue of Sardis. Becoming a partner at the bank would make me famous, but now I am more secure. I am making better decisions for the right reasons. This, my dear family, lets you know much been going on during these past months. Now, be patient while I tell you the whole story, bit by bit."

Miriam shivered violently as she tried to keep out the cold, her shawl drawn tightly around her shoulders. She was only going to be gone for a short time before returning to the house. She thought about the events of the day. Simon would not become a partner in the bank, but he had accepted rejection with a positive attitude.

Her mind came back to the growing bond between Eugene and Lyris. The wedding tunics in Uncle Simon's sales shop would be moved into storage at the new Closely Knit workshop next week. Arpoxa had become part of the workshop, where she taught several women to embroider. If a wedding were confirmed, doing finishing embroidery on the tunics would be a perfect project for them.

Miriam had discovered that the woman with the dried rose beside her bed possessed a creative mind. She was now making beautiful designs with her needle and thread. Miriam asked Elisha to pay the woman a bit extra at the end of each week.

For some reason, Arpoxa's physical disability brought about a bond with a deaf woman. Arpoxa also fit in well with other needy people. These workers were teaching songs to each other and telling stories while they worked.

Two deaf men were working on the two floor looms. They communicated using hand signals. A month before, when they received their first day's pay, they held out their hands, looked at the coin, and started to weep. For the first time ever, they were going to receive a regular wage. Never had they held a steady job.

The man with a leg injury explained that many men were injured at work every year. After an accident at work, he was rejected for other labor. Freemen often suffered more than slaves. Through the workshop's project, seven families with children and five widows were getting a living wage.

Miriam asked Zebadiah and Elisha to think about other jobs that could be created. The subject of joblessness, a hot topic at mealtimes, replaced talk about the bankers' visit.

The next day, Simon welcomed Friday, December 7, the commemoration of the Fast of the Fourth Month. He bowed his head, remembering the long siege against Jerusalem by King

Nebuchadnezzar's forces.

There was no food on the table when Simon spoke to his family. "Today we fast all day because 676 years ago the Babylonians began their siege. Think of how our people felt as they saw all escape routes being cut off. Our hunger during this fast should remind us about those in Sardis who now have little to live on.

"Yesterday Miriam talked to some men with artistic skills. We will keep them in mind, but we can't do anything to help them right now. Many are hungry, many who have no regular pay."

In the late afternoon, Miriam took her uncle aside. "Uncle Simon, had you saved money to become a partner in the Bank of Hermus?"

"Of course. Why do you ask? What an inquisitive person you are!"

"One of our lame workers heard of a man who wants to sell a vineyard. It's close to the place where the road to the Royal Cemetery meets the Post Road coming from Philadelphia to Sardis. I talked to the owner yesterday, and he wants to sell his land to a trustworthy family. He doesn't want to risk getting tricked when it's time for payments."

Simon looked at her with a new appreciation. "The Sabbath begins soon, my child. I cannot plan anything today—that would be work. But after the Sabbath is over, I want to hear about this vineyard."

He lowered his head in a moment of gratitude. *The money I was going to invest in becoming a partner in the bank may be more useful now—perhaps in ways I cannot imagine.*

SIMON BEN SHELAH'S SALES SHOP

Monday morning dawned with a dim gray light. Cleon had asked for Diotrephes to come to the shop before business hours. He was confident that the information he had to share with Diotrephes would earn him several denarii.

"What is it this time?" demanded Diotrephes with one eyebrow cocked.

"I am sorry to call so early, but I can only tell you this news when Heber, Ezar, and Zebadiah are away from the shop. This news will only take a moment, sir. What if I could get you into the Ben Shelah house without calling attention to yourself?"

"I'm interested. Tell me more!"

"I learned this late yesterday. Elisha said Miriam believes there's going to be a wedding. Lyris, a servant and a widow at the Ben Shelah home, may get married. Eugene is the father of Jace, a teacher at your gymnasium. Eugene pretends he's taking Hector, his grandson, to be with young Tamir. But the old fellow is there to spend time with the widow while working in the kitchen. Hector and Tamir are the same age. I also found out that Hector has been receiving special coaching from Anthony, the military instructor."

He looked around, making sure he was not being observed. "The wedding has not been announced yet, but Miriam is sure it will happen. She wants the banquet to be held at Simon's house. To go to the wedding, the guests will have to wear one of these." He held up a wedding tunic. It was one of the batch made in Thyatira.

"Are you sure? If I wore one of these, could I get into the Ben Shelah home?"

"Yes, you would simply wait until the guests are going in for the banquet and then enter along with them. All these gowns and tunics are identical in design. This is a small one for a child; this one will be worn by an adult."

"I'll take that one!" snapped Diotrephes, reaching for it.

Cleon pulled it away. "Not so fast! I'm not allowed to sell these! However, I could say that one was stolen. Later this afternoon, all these gowns are being moved to a workshop for safekeeping. Perhaps I could just say that along the way, one got lost or was taken from the wagon."

Cleon silently blessed Artemis, the goddess who protected Sardis. With Diotrephes's coins, he could win wagers during the Festival of Saturnalia. He allowed his mind to wander and dream of having his own shop.

Cleon whispered his dream: *"Never enough gold."*

Diotrephes left the shop, blessing Zeus, the father of all the gods. He now possessed a wedding tunic and had a way to get past the Ben Shelah gates. He took the wedding tunic to his room for safekeeping. He heaved a huge sigh, relaxing because he did not need to rush. A wedding would be held in the springtime, and that was when he would hold Chrysa, his niece, for the first time.

Diotrephes had found a way to walk through the gate of the Ben Shelah residence. He could wait for the opportunity to take the child, and no one would notice.

More importantly, Cleon had given him vital information about Jace. And he did not have to pay to learn what was happening in this teacher's home. Surely that information would come in handy.

Also, he knew Anthony was helping Hector prepare for the Games in May.

Further, Miriam was helping poor people and working with Kalonice, Jace's wife. Eugene, Kalonice, and Hector—the people in Jace's family were far too close to those of the Ben Shelah family!

Another event had brought him even higher hopes. He had met Cynthia at a social event in the lecture hall, and he had talked with her for a moment. He closed his eyes, smitten by her beauty. She had dark black hair, and her tunic was sewn with rich embroidery around the sleeves and neckline. As the popular new lecturer in the Hall of Karpos, he was soon to dine with her father, the mayor. That meant that a week from today, Diotrephes would be formally introduced to Cynthia in her home.

DIODOTUS AND DELBIN'S HOME, WEST HILL

A week passed by. Since this was a holiday at the gymnasium, Diotrephes took a pen to write to his mother.

December 21, in the 10th year of Domitian
From: Diotrephes, "Nourished by Zeus"

To my dear mother:

I trust you are well. May your spirit strengthen all you do.

I found out something useful. I made friends with a salesman at the Ben Shelah shop, Cleon. He told me a wedding is expected in the spring. I will be there.

I now believe that Marcos is behind our family's problems. He is cunning, and it appears that he worked out the schedule for Anthony and Miriam's marriage and Chrysa's adoption.

I have a plan to snatch the baby. Miriam rarely takes the child outside the property. According to Elisha, Gaius's replacement in the shop, she leaves Chrysa at home when she attends to needy families. Apparently, Miriam is afraid that the child will get sick from the people she visits. I must wait until all the adults are away from Simon's house.

I hope to visit the home of Mayor Tymon in one week. I remember you once told me that something unfortunate happened between our families several generations back. I am going to try to mend fences. A closer relationship between the Tmolus family and our Milon family might be useful, don't you think?

Diotrephes looked forward to the New Year's banquet. He had a few days to decide what he would wear when he visited the mayor's home. He closed his eyes and imagined himself walking with the governor. *My dream...to join the two families, the Milon family to the Tmolus clan. Two things altogether...taking my niece back to Pergamum and meeting Cynthia in her own home.*

THE CITY OF SARDIS

Cleon's favorite week of the year was the Festival of Saturnalia. The week-long event had arrived! Sounds of drunkenness filled the Royal Road starting early in the afternoon. Men and women flooded into the Eastern Agora, singing loudly and dancing in small circles.

Enchanted, Cleon gladly joined in the dancing. One man with a booming voice called out the verses of popular songs and encouraged the dancers, urging them on. When the dance party reached the East Gate, they turned around and slowly stumbled back to the West Gate. The man with the loud voice never seemed to tire. Cleon kept going for hours. He moved along, arms intertwined with strangers. Many dances involved walking two steps forward, turning slightly, then walking backward a step.

Thankfully for Cleon, Saturnalia would continue for several days. On the third day, he joined the followers of Dionysus. They lived for revelry and passion. In their songs, the words "death and immortality" rhymed with "drink and immorality."

Stories of the gods were incorporated into lewd plays. When the holiday ended, Cleon went back to his small apartment in the Southeast Quarter and slept for a whole day. The streets of Sardis were strangely quiet for several more days.

Chapter 31
The Sardians

JACE AND KALONICE'S HOME

As the end of the year drew close, Kalonice struggled to find the right moment to tell her husband about changes taking place in her heart. Finally, when Eugene and the boys were away at the Ben Shelah home, they were able to talk privately.

"Jace, I need to tell you some of my thoughts," she began.

He smiled. "We have the whole day! Hector and Isidoros are with Eugene, and it is cold outside. Here, come and sit down."

"You know that I have become good friends with Miriam."

"That's obvious! You spend lots of time together."

"In September, I invited her to come with me to meet some important women, remember? Well, the experience left me empty afterward."

"Why? What happened? I thought you enjoyed that gathering!"

"I have been going to the Festival for Women for sixteen years, and it never changes. I found it amusing at first, but stories of Sardis get stale. On the other hand, Simon's stories fit into the story of my mother. When he talks about Adonai or about my people's history, something tugs my heart in a new way.

"The story of Yeshua the carpenter is what began to attract me. I hear Miriam singing her songs, talking about Yeshua helping the poor, or saying, 'God wants to forgive our sins through what Yeshua did on the tree of sacrifice.' That's when I sense something new calling to me. She really believes that she should help the poor. Her strong beliefs drive her to action."

"What are you really saying?"

"Simon and Judith believe the truth. They have the truth, and I want it too."

Jace wrinkled his eyebrows. "Simon's whole family has been expelled from their congregation! What makes you think he has the truth while the others don't?"

She told him what had been happening. "Now that they are gathering in Simon's house with a few other families, I am discovering a treasure. The Jewish writers were not afraid to speak honestly. Their Scriptures bring conviction."

"I know Miriam enjoys visiting families in the insulae, but is it wise to go there?"

"Speaking honestly, I am being motivated by something new. I enjoy overseeing what happens at the Closely Knit workshop each day."

Tenderness filled his voice. "So that is why you're changing? You like helping people get ahead, people who have no hope."

Kalonice replied softly, "I am beginning to believe Yeshua really was the Jewish Messiah."

"That conviction cost Simon a lot of friends. I told you that."

"Well, here at home, I do not want conflict between us about my beliefs. That's why I am telling you honestly what's happening. I am feeling alive in a new way."

"I'm happy that you are learning these things. You are not the only one examining what is going on. Speaking of conflict, well, I have something to tell you that I have been hiding since October."

A shocked look of dismay showed in her eyes. "Tell me, my dear."

For the first time in many days, Jace spoke with complete honesty. "My problems with Diotrephes began the first day of October in my first class. Looking back on it, I remember the first moment. I felt nervous. Diotrephes walked in and stood at the back of the classroom, his arms folded, listening to me. At the end of the lecture, he left with a scowl on his face. That alarmed me.

"On my third day with the students, Diotrephes was in my classroom again. I asked the students, 'Yesterday I taught you about the beginning of Sardian history. Today I am going to ask you for answers to see if you are paying attention to what I teach. Whose tumulus is the largest in the Royal Cemetery?"[50]

"'The tomb of Alyattes II,' said one boy.

"'And who was the King of the Golden Touch?' I asked.

---

[50] The Royal Cemetery, a national park, contains more than one hundred large, man-made mounds. The cemetery is the final resting place of the Sardian aristocratic families. A few have been excavated. Priceless treasures found in the tombs are on display in museums in Ankara at the Museum of Anatolian Civilizations.

"'King Midas of Phrygia!' they all shouted at once. 'When he touched things, they turned to gold!' Everyone knew the answer. They had heard the story scores of times.

"Then I said, 'That story comes from a kingdom that even the old-timers, our grandfathers, cannot remember. The ancient Hittites had their capital northeast of here. Kingdoms were small, and languages were not united as they are today under Greek and Latin.' That brought a frown to Diotrephes's face. I didn't know why then, but I do now.

"I pointed out that most ancient kings were either crazy or died foolishly. Their descendants are still around, keeping their old family names, but people don't speak about their ancestors.

"For example, I told them about Atyads and his son, Lydus. I stated, 'From the name of this king came the name of our people, the Lydian Kingdom. King Lydus moved to the top of the acropolis and built it up as a secure area. Unfortunately, Lydus went mad one day and threw himself into a fire.' My students laughed, but that made Diotrephes scowl, not the first time I saw that expression come over him.

"I told them, 'All those ancient kings had strange deaths. Lydus's grandfather, Manes Tmolus, was gored by a bull and died a few days later. Now he's the god of our mountain!'

"Then I mentioned another Lydian death: 'Manes's brother offered his son as a sacrifice to the god Pelops as a feast for the gods.' I noticed that Diotrephes seemed upset hearing that.

"The only time Diotrephes did not seem distressed was when I told of the great King Alyattes II, who fought a great battle on the River Halys.[51] He was fighting against the army of the king of Persia to keep the Persians out of Lydia.

"Suddenly, during the battle, the bright day became as night. The armies declared a truce, saying, 'The gods of the sky have determined the western limits of the Persian Empire.' We repeat the same phrase: 'The god of Mount Tmolus determined the eastern limit of the Lydians.'[52] A miracle took place in the middle of the

---

[51] Much of this historical information comes from Herodotus. The Lydian Kingdom encompassed twenty-two kings over 505 years.

[52] Herodotus (*Histories* 1.73–74) stated that the eclipse of the sun was taken by both sides as a message from the gods. The date of the eclipse has been determined as taking place on May 28, 585 BC. This may be the earliest such

battle. The moon blocked out the sun in the middle of the day! Everything became dark. Then I told the students, 'That's all for today.'"

Jace went on to tell what had happened, summarizing other lessons Diotrephes did not appreciate. "I told them, 'King Candaules was murdered by General Gyges, who wanted to be king. Afterward, Gyges bribed the population with promises of riches, formed a huge army, and joined with Egypt to fight Assyria. He became the founder of a new dynasty.'[53]

Diotrephes liked that, but then I explained, 'The beginning of the Lydian Empire is full of blood and gore! I feel sorry for Candaules because General Gyges killed him.' I saw something like hatred reflected in his eyes.

"For Diotrephes, Lydia's greatness lies not in Gyges's killing King Candaules and marrying that man's queen. Honor came from his ability to spread his power from Sardis. His power reached as far as Jerusalem and Egypt. He was all about glory, power, and an expanded influence."

Jace kept his head back, gazing at the ceiling. *Looking back on it now, I saw Diotrephes's face flinch. Now I know why he was upset. He was dismayed because his hero, General Gyges, did not leave a lasting kingdom. Sardis was overtaken by Persian troops, and the Lydian language began to die out.*

Just then, Elisha came to their front door. He wanted Kalonice to go to the workshop, and she left the room. "I will be gone for just a moment. One of the blind men at the workshop fell and hurt himself. Elisha wants me to tell him what to do."

---

date to be calculated with precision. Amazingly, Thales, the mathematician of Miletus, had predicted this total eclipse. The defeat of Croesus set the stage for a long, bitter conflict lasting 150 years. The invasion of Alexander the Great from Macedonia led to the defeat of the Persian army. This changed the balance of power in favor of the Greeks (331–320 BC).

[53] Some commentators believe Ezekiel 38:39 refers to King Gyges, the Lydian, (reigned 716–678 BC). "Gog" and the Assyrian "Guggu" may have been intended by Ezekiel to describe him. Obadiah verse 20 is thought to refer to the existence of Jews in Sardis: "the captives of Jerusalem who are in Sephard" may be a reference to Sardis. A marble inscription found in Sardis and now located in the Manisa Archaeological Museum uses the word "Sfarda," in the Lydian language as the Lydian name for Sardis. (Manisa is less than one hour's drive from Sardis.)

Kalonice returned from her conversation with Elisha an hour later. "Fortunately, it was just a bad scrape on his knee. We will have him stay at his home for a day or two. Someone will check on him occasionally and prepare his meals. Now, where were you?"

Jace continued his story. "After Diotrephes heard my lessons, he told me that he needed to 'correct' my teaching. Those are his words. Nothing like this had ever happened in my sixteen years at the gymnasium. He took me to a table at a sidewalk thermopolium for a noon meal and instructed me, 'Clothe those kings with glory and honor. Make them come alive as wonderful leaders and kings!' However, I countered, 'But I would have to make things up!'

"You should have seen him. His face turned red, and his eyes almost popped out! 'Do not make *facts* the focus of your teaching,' he yelled. 'Make them feel *emotions!* They must feel jealous, longing for the past glories of our people! When they leave your class, they have to say, *'How wonderful to have been a Lydian! I want to learn to speak our Lydian language! I want to be a Lydian!'*

"My dear, at his core, the man is rebellious against Rome!"

THE TEMPLE OF ARTEMIS

On the last day of the year, formal public events were again held at the Temple of Artemis. The blood of a bull was required to bring back the sun to warm the earth again. Ankara disrobed, ready to be covered with liquids representing the three mysteries of life: blood, oil, and wine.

Blood was poured over his curly black hair. As it dripped from his head to his toes, he bowed his head again, and olive oil was spilled. The oil dripped, and it mingled with the rivulets of blood. A third time he bowed his head, and wine ran down to the ground. Blood, the force of life; oil, the symbol of agricultural health; and wine, the promise of friendship, covered his body.

Attendant priests then poured cold water on him, cleansing him from the three fluids. This symbolized the cold winds of the season. Next, he sprinkled salt into the flame of a small brazier.

The ritual elements of blood, oil, wine, and cold water were sure to bring back the warmer weather. Indeed, no more rockslides would happen. The acropolis was deemed reliable again.

NEVER ENOUGH GOLD

Part 3

January AD 92

Friends in Sardis

Chapter 32
A Change of Heart

SIMON'S LIBRARY

On the first day of the new year, Simon put down his scroll. He lay prostrate on the floor in front of his desk, his hands stretched out toward Jerusalem. The words still rang in his mind.

"I will signal for them and gather them in. Surely, I will redeem them; they will be as numerous as before. Though I scatter them among the peoples, yet in different lands they will remember me. They and their children will survive, and they will return. I will bring them back. They will pass through the sea of trouble. I will strengthen them in the LORD, and in his name, they will walk,' declares the LORD."[54]

He humbled himself in prayer. *O Holy One, you care for your people, but how can your promise be fulfilled? Romans destroyed our altar, and our animal sacrifices are no more. You know my shame, Lord, because I have been rejected by my own people. Yet my brother's granddaughter is married to a Roman soldier, and he loves you. He reads your Law, and now my own son-in-law refuses to have fellowship with us!*

He lay on the cold floor and then rose to read the passage again. He was reclaiming the promises of his word and was convinced that Zion would again be restored. God had promised it.

THE INSULAE OF SARDIS

As winter winds gripped the countryside, illnesses of many kinds became common. Coughs and colds were rife throughout the city. January 1 had arrived, and Miriam covered her face with her cloak, for a gusty wind took her breath away. She rode in the wagon, ready to visit the families she had come to know.

Some were in a weakened condition. Gina, a petite mother, was sobbing. She had six children, all small, and the oldest child, Cosmos,

---

[54] Zechariah 10:8–12

was nine, a bright little boy. The mother told how she had suffered at the hands of her brother, and Miriam felt a great love for this family. The baby was weak and ill, and Miriam wondered if she should take the child home to try to bring her to health.

With little food in the cold rooms, a lack of clean water, and thin, small blankets to cover eight people at night, how could this child recover from a fever? How could Felix, the father, provide everything his family needed? Even with the wages brought back from Miriam's workshop, he did not have enough money.

Hector was sick too. For the first time in weeks, he did not practice for the future races. In despair, Hector worried that he would not be able to make up for the lost time in his training.

Prosperus and the recruits shivered in the military camp, not used to such cold weather in Asia Minor. The instructor swore much of the time as he remembered his home in Syria, where the weather in January was much milder. He longed for Damascus and the gentler winds. There, Mediterranean storms were followed by pleasant, open blue skies after pelting rains. He even craved the summer heat, longing for the sunbaked streets of Parthia.

The trees in Sardis had lost their leaves and looked dead. Everyone longed for the enchantment of spring. No one could remember a winter when the winds were so cold. The soldiers shivered because the rains were so constant.

THE HOT BATHS OF SARDIS

"Jace, I have been following your teaching carefully," Diotrephes observed. He had confronted Jace several times since November. They were leaving the hot atmosphere of the *caldarium* and entering the warm waters in the *tepidarium* at the hot baths.

"Thank you," replied Jace politely, wondering what would come next.

Diotrephes scowled. "Now, about the Lydian language...when was it spoken?"

"Lydian was the local language from before the Persians until the arrival of the Roman army. I suppose Lydian co-existed with Greek. The Lydian Empire became intertwined with Athens and the Greek islands through trade. Why do you ask?"

"How many people still speak the Lydian language?"

"Only a few hundred, perhaps as many as a thousand people. I speak it a little."

"Do you have a desire to know the truth about the past?"

"I think we know far more now than we did then. Why all these questions, Diotrephes?"

After a while, they moved to a massage room. Jace lay on his stomach as a slave rubbed oil from his shoulders toward his spine.

"I have been in your classes." Diotrephes's repeated phrase was a warning signal to Jace.

"I know that. You often listen to me teach."

Breathing was difficult as the slave rubbed his back.

"And there are a few things you must change."

They moved to the *frigidarium*. The water was refreshing, and the two men waded in. The water reached up to their hips.

Jace's pulse was racing as he confronted Diotrephes. "Look at these floor mosaics. You walk into this grand room, and what do you see? Here is the picture of Apollo seducing Daphne. What is this 'picture' made of? Thousands of tiny stones form this 'picture,' and the mosaic tells a story. It takes months to draw it, find the right colors and shapes, and then place the stones into wet cement! Students must know the details that make the final picture. That's why facts, like tiny stones, are exact information. They're essential."

Diotrephes answered, "Fine. Take this mosaic! No one cares about just one tiny, colored stone! What they see is Daphne being seduced. But look! She escapes Apollo's attention because, at that very moment, she is being turned into a laurel tree! This is how the laurel tree came to be. The details are not important.

"You should convey emotion, not give students little fragments. Why? Ten years from now, when your students are grown men, all they will remember is the overall picture. Our students must remember that Lydia was a magnificent kingdom. Learning to speak the language will bring them back to the story of our ancient kingdom. That's more important than stories about how ancient kings died."

Jace let his breath out very slowly. "It is because of the details, the carefully placed stones, that a figure comes alive in a mosaic. Artists work hard to compose a picture."

He thought, *How did Diotrephes get his job? He is so tactless and obstinate! He tries to twist everything to his point of view!*

As they left, Diotrephes leaned close to Jace and said in a soft voice, "You are the only one in the department who has not accepted my guidance. Think about this. Be ready to change."

SIMON AND JUDITH'S HOME

Anthony returned from the mountain training camp. Several soldiers were sick and getting worse with coughs and fever. With Felicior's permission, he had come down to the city to ask Zebadiah, the new steward at the Ben Shelah shop, to find some remedies. At noon, he made a quick trip to see Miriam. "I have only an hour. Several men are down with high fevers. It is cold in the camp. When snow falls, we just stay in our tents."

Amath welcomed him with little shouts. "Where did you come from?"

Anthony took her to the door and pointed. "See that smoke rising in the woods on the mountain? That's where our camp is."

"You live in a camp in a tent? That must be so exciting!"

Miriam glowed with joy for having him home unexpectedly. She handed Grace to him, and his little daughter jumped up and down in his arms.

"Put her on the floor and see what she does!" boasted Miriam.

Grace tried to stand up. She held on to the first finger of Anthony's hands, taking wobbly steps and trying to step forward. It was an ungainly, awkward, beautiful moment. The family stood around, proud and thankful.

"That's enough now," said Miriam. "The floor is cold, and I don't want her to be sick."

Anthony's visit was over far too soon. Lyris prepared hot drinks for the family. Over the years, she had accumulated remedies for every sickness. She stacked them up for Anthony to take back to camp.

"How can I carry all that on a horse?" he asked with a grin. He had to leave quickly and return to camp, so he wrapped up the remedies in a large sack, said his goodbyes, hugged everyone, and left. He went by the shop to pick up the few items that Zebadiah was able to find and headed out of the city.

As he kept his face covered, hidden from the cold wind, he thought about the events in the three years since he had come to know Antipas.

Rome doesn't talk about a "transformation in the heart" or "repentance." Something is changing in me, like today. I really wanted to get herbs and medicines for these men. It wasn't just a task to be done. Just a few months ago, these recruits were strangers; now I care deeply for them. Philosophers like Cicero, hoping that "knowledge" and "'willpower" will provide the motivation for improvements, never understand that people seldom change, except in answer to a higher aspiration.

Anthony went back to camp, and his horse tossed its head, snorting from the effort of climbing quickly up the mountain road. He rubbed his hands on his horse's neck to warm up. The temperature was lower, and the winds blew harder upon the military training camp than down in the Hermus Valley. He pulled his cloak more tightly around himself and headed for the warming fire. Fortunately, surrounded by trees, there was always enough fuel to keep the fire burning.

JACE AND KALONICE'S HOME

Kalonice noticed a sudden change in her husband one day. He returned from the gymnasium withdrawn entirely. At meals, he became quiet and rarely laughed.

"Is everything all right?" she asked a week later.

"I can't get through to him. I think Diotrephes is planning something against me."

"Why would he do that, Jace?"

"I refused to promote his Lydian language as something all the boys should learn."

"So why are you concerned?"

"If I read him correctly, I think he wants me out of the gymnasium."

"But he can't do that! You have been teaching there longer than most teachers."

"Well..." He would not finish the sentence.

"What does it mean that Diotrephes is planning something against you?"

Her voice rose in volume, and she was ready to defend Jace. "If he is showing the other teachers how to polish the ancient Lydian life and requiring them to teach that way, then this news will eventually reach the ears of the mayor. Who is going to support a young man who wants to lead this city backward in time?"

SIMON AND JUDITH'S HOME

The next few days brought continued cold winds under blue skies. Hector, who was over his cold, came to the Ben Shelah home to spend time with Tamir. The boys confirmed their friendship by composing a secret language. Eugene also came but emphasized that he was "only there to keep an eye on my grandson" and ensure that he behaved properly.

Hector disagreed. "No, he's not here for me. He just likes to spend time in your kitchen with Lyris. It gives him something useful to do."

Judith came into the kitchen and saw Lyris and Eugene talking. They had just stopped laughing as if they had shared a little joke and as if they were still young. Lyris turned a bright red and Judith excused herself quickly.

At that moment, Miriam was walking by, and Judith took hold of her arm. "I think this is a sign that Eugene and Lyris have really fallen in love. Shall we confront them now?"

Miriam had been sure of it before, and now Judith was openly talking about it. Yes, it seemed as if these old people were falling in love!

The two women giggled and walked away from the kitchen. "The time has come to tell Chenya and Nissa!" said Judith. "I won't say a thing to anyone else!"

"For myself, I'm going to ask Arpoxa to teach a special embroidery symbol to the women in our Closely Knit group. I'll have her design a pattern that can be used on all the wedding tunics," said Miriam.

THE INSULAE OF SARDIS

Two days later, Miriam returned to the southeastern side of the city. As she passed by in her cart, beggars called to her in fearful, high-pitched voices. "Help us! Please! We're hungry!"

She went back to a partially burned building where she found a family that she had visited less than two weeks before. There was little food in the apartment, and the children were all sick. There was only one bed, and the five malnourished children sat in fear beside their mother. They held each other, shivering because of the cold. Words of sympathy would not help much. She had only five copper coins left to give. "Here," she said with tears in her eyes, "use this to get some food for your children."

A wave of love and compassion flooded over her. Miriam spontaneously pulled the hood of her coat over her head in reverence to Adonai. She recalled the prayers of blessing given by her great-grandfather. She decided to bless the family, speaking life through her words.

"I bless you and your children," she said. Raising her arms, she looked at the ceiling above. It was lined with watermarks. "I bless each of you in the name of Yeshua, our Messiah. I bless you with love and care for your little ones and wisdom to bring them up in the knowledge of what is right and wrong. May each of you be led along good paths, free from bitterness caused by anger and poverty. May each of you be touched by God, for he alone can heal life's scars. I bless you with God's forgiveness flowing into your hearts."

The children watched with awe as Miriam uttered these strange words. She left, and the room became silent. Cold air whistled through the cracks in the door. They stared at their mother.

"Why are you crying?" the oldest girl asked. "Mommy, what's the matter? What was she talking about? Is she a bad woman?"

"We never had anyone pray for us," said the destitute woman. "No one ever came to us like that or tried to understand. She was here to talk with us twice before. Remember when I told her that I hated my brother for taking all our family's money and not sharing with me? My brother made us poor. I haven't spoken to him for years. When Miriam came, I felt as if I could tell her everything. And if it weren't for her providing work for your father, we would not have any money."

Unashamed to be talking about such a private matter, she pulled her children close. Felix, her husband, looked on with wonder. His wife had not shown this intensity of feeling for years.

She continued, "Your grandpa and grandma were not wealthy people. Grandpa made things—leather bags, sandals, and pouches—and sometimes he made bread at the bakery. He could fix wagon wheels, and he once was a miller.

"He had a house and a little vineyard in a small village close to Philadelphia. At that time, there was no work there, so my brother and I came to Sardis to find jobs. It took us a whole day to get here.

"Later, I met your father in the Eastern Agora when I was shopping. We fell in love, but my brother didn't want me to marry him. My brother and I had a quarrel afterward, and we never forgave each other. When your grandpa died, my brother refused to carry out the terms of his will. He moved back to Philadelphia and kept everything for himself."

She looked around at her shabby apartment. Mold sneaked its way down the walls. Watermarks at the top of the walls formed random patterns. The wind blew the rain in on windy nights. The shabby shutters were unable to keep the room warm and dry.

"I did not get anything that should have been mine." She brushed her hand over Cosmos's tangled hair, and she held her eight-year-old daughter very tightly.

"Miriam talked to us the other day about forgiveness, remember? When she prayed just now, she said things that made me cry. I never thought I could learn to forgive another person, but she has put the idea into my heart. I grew to hate my brother. But can I forgive him? I know it is a sin, but I cannot forgive him."

She felt a touch of panic. She wanted Miriam to come back, to explain mysteries to her. She was willing to open doors and windows to places in her heart she had shut tightly ten years before.

Miriam left the family with a question going around in her mind. *How does a family become so weak? How can they suffer like this and still be alive? They are worse off than the first time I saw them. Where would one even start to help?*

She struggled with her thoughts, finding such poverty overwhelming. Each visit led her to witness further misery, and it was causing anxiety. She started to pray and then found herself composing a song about them. Miriam wrote about the children in one bed, the father who was so proud of his family, and the little girl who died during the winter.

Is it a sin to compose a song about such a poor family?

LYDIA-NAQ'S HOME, THE ACROPOLIS, PERGAMUM

As the weather improved, Diotrephes made a trip to his mother's home in Pergamum at the end of January.

He told his teachers, "I'll be away for about ten days to attend a series of meetings."

No one knew that he would talk with his mother, getting ideas on how to bring the baby Chrysa from Sardis to Pergamum. He would have to speak with Potitus Vinicius, the family's young lawyer, and have him draw up the necessary documents if he were challenged by soldiers at any of the military checkpoints.

THE GYMNASIUM, SARDIS

Free to teach without Diotrephes checking everything he said to students, Jace talked about Aesop's fables. Several copies were available in the library at the east end of the gymnasium. He started the morning by reviewing some of the famous man's 655 fables.

Jace loved making lists, and he could organize anything. He had written a partial list of the characters in the fables and said he would quiz the boys on their old Phrygian heritage.

"Do you know how many characters are found in Aesop's fables? There are ants, asses, bald knights, bats, bears, boys, blind men, bulls, chargers, cats, caged birds, dogs, eagles, flies, frogs, fishermen, geese, hares, Hercules, herdsmen, hounds, jackdaws, lions, oxen, masks, millers, mules, monkeys…"

He stopped for breath and added, "…also peacocks, ravens, roosters, shepherds, serpents, tortoises, woodcutters, and wolves. There are other characters too, but you don't need to know them right now."

One boy raised his hand. "Teacher, your order was not entirely correct. You got the oxen out of order, that is, if you were organizing everything alphabetically."

Jace looked at his list again. "That's what I like to see!" he said enthusiastically. "I want you to pay attention to details."

He was ready to introduce them to some of the greatest writers of the past. Next year, these same students would have advanced to the point of reading Greece and Rome's great treatises.

For Jace, a young man was a good citizen if he saw himself as one small stone making up the enormous, dynamic edifice that included all the peoples in the empire. Rome was a coastline with many shores, a mosaic that included thousands of different-colored stones.

THE INSULAE OF SARDIS

Learning to listen to families and learning to bless them, praying with them, and understanding their situations was a regular activity for Miriam. She left the house early in the morning with Elisha, who shared her concerns. At the workshop, she talked with Kalonice. They inspected the weavers' products, appreciating their pride in growing skills in carding the wool and weaving.

The first garments made by a new worker always went to family members; their store would not sell garments if they contained flaws. Within a short time, though, they would improve enough so that the clothing could be sold. Each family was earning a wage sufficient to pay for rent, food, and essentials.

People said it was the coldest winter they could remember, and while Miriam felt the cold around her legs, her heart was warmed. She wondered if this was anything like Grandfather Antipas's sentiments before he started building houses in Pergamum.

Grandpa's village, with all its houses, is going to be mine. With the inheritance money I'm already receiving, I can do a little for these people! It's a miracle of the oil of Chanukah all over again. The light keeps burning in the dark.

Miriam visited a mother who was concerned about her boy. He was five and still had not yet learned to speak. Miriam had no idea how to help, so she asked if she could pray in the name of Yeshua Messiah. The woman nodded in desperate approval.

"I bless you in the name of the Creator, God Almighty, who made the earth, the sky, the trees, and little boys and little girls. I bless you with patience for your son and with love to hold him close, even when you don't want to and even when you can no longer stand his lack of responsiveness. And I bless your son with listening ears, that he will learn to listen to God and understand his voice whispering words of hope. I bless him with ears to hear and a mouth to speak."

She had little faith to pray anything else for the child.

In another home, a mother was just as desperate, as if someone had died. It was Miriam's third visit to that home. When she knocked on the door and heard only crying inside, she pushed the door open. The woman was lying face down on the floor.

Previously the home had a few bits of furniture. "What happened?" asked Miriam, alarmed. Her heart pounded for she wanted to protect the woman stretched out on the cold floor.

"Men came an hour ago, taking away our furniture. I screamed, but no one helped. My husband loses everything when he gambles. He always says he is going to stop, but he places another bet and then gets drunk to forget what he lost."

Miriam felt compassion for these people, wondering where these feelings were coming from. A year ago in Pergamum, she could not have done visits like this.

SIMON'S LIBRARY

Simon's heart was beating faster as he began to appreciate the plans that Miriam had just laid before him. Simon caught himself, thinking that his wealth was being used in a kind of partnership. He wondered if he would have been this happy if he had been accepted as a partner in the bank.

With Miriam, he felt fulfilled. Yesterday they had found a job for a man who had many children. The previous week, Simon sat beside a blind man in a warm spot in the workshop, helping to comb out a wool pile.

He listened to Judith's stories of the day and knew his thoughts would keep him awake tonight. His recently completed purchase of the small vineyard brought a smile of satisfaction to Judith. He went over a conversation from the evening meal.

"Miriam has the same heart that my brother had! How could I have known that Antipas's granddaughter would show such creativity? She and Anthony… How could such a lovely Jewish girl marry a Roman? On that first day, when they showed up at our door, I wanted them to go away.

"Judith, a year ago, the thing I wanted most in my life was to be accepted. I wanted to be on the Synagogue Council and be a partner at the bank. But I've lost the desire to be in those circles."

She responded, "Oh! That's strange. Instead of that, you want the company of Anthony and Miriam?"

"Yes, things are changing. And I wonder what Miriam means when she talks about 'my plan for you, Uncle Simon.'"

Chapter 33
Grace's Birthday

SIMON AND JUDITH'S HOME

Miriam entered Simon's workshop, where he was working with Ateas. Feeling nervous about her request, she asked, "Uncle Simon, in a week, Grace will be one year old...."

"I think you are asking for a birthday, a celebration as a social gathering with friends! Am I right?"

"Yes, what do you think of the idea?"

"Ateas, you would like a happy evening, wouldn't you? I certainly would! Miriam, would you like me to send out invitations?"

"Oh, that would be wonderful!"

"Here's what I'm going to write: 'On Friday, February 8, Chrysa Grace Suros will be one year old. Please celebrate with us at the Ben Shelah home starting at one hour before sundown.' I'll send copies to our friends at the synagogue and to the God-fearers with whom we still share fellowship."

Miriam asked a servant to send a message to Anthony. He would need permission to attend his daughter's first birthday. When the reply came back that he would be coming, Miriam jumped for joy, swinging Grace around and lifting her high.

Early on Friday morning, Eugene came to help Lyris in the kitchen. Miriam went to the library and spoke to her cousin. "Ezar, are you expecting Kalonice today?"

"No," he said.

"Nor am I," said Miriam. "So why did Eugene come?"

At noon, Simon blessed the food. The talk was about crops and animals and the coming spring. Eugene brought small grilled squares of lamb meat and a special sauce.

Miriam asked, "Eugene, is Kalonice coming today?"

"No, she is at the Closely Knit workshop," he replied.

Judith nodded at Miriam, indicating that it was time to tease him and get it into the open. Miriam stood close to Eugene. "Eugene, have you started an extension of our workshop here?"

Lyris was bringing cooked vegetables and hot flatbread.

"No, what do you mean?" Eugene's face turned a bright red.

Miriam added, "I thought you and Lyris intended to start a similar group, perhaps also called Closely Knit."

The family broke into peals of laughter. Lyris was also red-faced and shy for a moment. "Well, you guessed our secret," said Lyris, "although I have no idea how. We've been talking about marriage for only a few days."

Miriam's face lit up. "God arranges things perfectly!"

"Yes, God looks after widows as well," Judith said, and everyone laughed. "God loves widowers too!" she added, looking at Eugene.

Heber asked, "Eugene, will you really feel comfortable being married to a Jew?" As usual, he was direct without being snobbish or nosy.

"I was married to a Jew," he said. "Jerusha was a Jew, but she didn't tell many people."

Miriam smiled. She hugged Grace, thinking, *I think all this will work out correctly. Uncle Simon has bought the vineyard. If Lyris and Eugene want a place for themselves, they can live in that little house in the middle of the vineyard as caretakers. They will be close to the city and can start their own lives all over again. Uncle Simon will have someone there he can trust.*

For Grace's birthday, the visitors were all friends from Simon's new home fellowship.

Anthony talked enthusiastically, walking with Grace in his arms. "It's been a long time since I've enjoyed the warmth of a home, a feast, and the sweet giggle of my daughter."

Before the meal, Miriam explained, "Chrysa Grace Suros is her full name. Chrysa, "golden", comes from Greek. Grace, her middle name, summarizes the history of God working in the hearts of all peoples. And her last name, Suros, comes down from the conquered peoples of France and Spain."

She bounced her finger on her daughter's nose. "My child, your identity came from three names and three backgrounds. You will grow and bless people from everywhere in the empire!"

TRIFANE'S HOME, PERGAMUM

In Pergamum, Trifane, a young woman, stood at her father's front door. The door was open just wide enough to peek out. The moon had been shining, but now it was covered over. A rising wind moaned as it tugged at window shutters and loose roof tiles.

Trifane felt used and taken in. Seeing Zoticos, the baby's father, earlier in the day, she darted onto a side street rather than face him in the marketplace. It was gossip from a shopkeeper that let her know that the Chief Librarian often took advantage of beautiful women. She learned that he was unable to settle down with just one.

Months ago, Marcos had informed Trifane that Chrysa was well taken care of. "Your daughter was adopted into a loving family. Not just a father and mother but also cousins, aunts, uncles, and a grandfather. In her home, children play and sing songs."

Trifane closed her eyes, listening to the wind.

God of Mercy, you gave me a precious girl. I held her for just two weeks and how I wept as I gave her away. I have only one request, Lord. Well, two. Before I die, let me see my daughter, and...if you have the right man for me, I am ready for him.

Trifane opened the door a crack, taking note that the sky was dark without a moon. No rain would fall since it was only a windstorm. Her meditations and petitions laid before the Lord had given her a fresh hope.

I will see you one day, my child. I believe I will hold you in my arms before I die.

Trifane tightened her arms across her chest, and her fingers dug into her upper arms. She was reliving her childbirth one year ago. Those pains seemed unbearable. During that long, terrible night, she feared her life would ebb out.

Closing the door against the wind, Trifane leaned against the wall. Those agonizing moments came back. She wiped a tear away, and her cheeks felt hot. She shuddered from shame and regret, and she wanted to talk to her daughter's new mother. If they were together... She thought of what she would say.

"Zoticos seduced me. No, I allowed him to take me to his house. He offered me a position in the Library of Pergamum. I fell for him...those constant advances after a year of study with the other twenty-three students. Why did I have to fall for him?

"Then the time came for my baby to be born. For hours, my mother encouraged me. It was a long, difficult labor. She kept saying, 'Breathe deeply. Don't push down yet.' What would I have done without my dear mother? And then my baby was born.... The morning when Chrysa was born, a dark storm had given way to a clear, bright dawn.

"Oh, where are you, Chrysa, my darling baby?

"Was it to Zeus, or Hera, or Demeter to whom I prayed? Who else did I have to pray to at that time? I whispered, 'If my baby is born healthy, I will give it to the family Marcos told me about. I want the family that talks about agape love to raise my baby.' Now I know how to pray to him who hears my thoughts.

"I don't direct my words to Zeus anymore. The people in the House of Prayer assembly are teaching me the truths that allowed me to live again. My father and mother are also attending meetings early on Sunday mornings, when we break bread at the Holy Meal."

CLOSELY KNIT WORKSHOP

Light-hearted laughter sounded throughout the workshop. Simon had bought two old, broken-down horse carts, and a man who had injured his eye due to a stone chip repaired one of them.

That half-blind man now drove for a completely blind man, taking him to and from work. He transported poor women in the morning and took them back again in the afternoon. He also picked up a man with an injured foot and brought him to the workshop.

These were some of the people who were learning how to weave woolen clothing on the loom.

At home, only Ravid seemed unimpressed by the things being accomplished. "Why are so many uncircumcised Gentiles being accepted into the Ben Shelah business?" he huffed, slamming his door in disgust.

No longer would he feel generous toward his father-in-law.

Chapter 34
Diotrephes

SIMON AND JUDITH'S HOME

Ten days passed, and once again, cold winter winds blew through the streets of Sardis. Late in the morning, the guard dogs barked, announcing a visitor. The children saw Anthony dismount quickly from his horse at the front gate. He led the horse around to the animal shelter behind the house and then ran to the house.

Judith yelled, "Oh, look, Anthony is back! Come over to the brazier. Come get warm!"

"Thank you! I've come for additional herbal remedies for the soldiers at the mountain camp. I had to make a quick visit." The winds made a low moaning sound.

Simon looked out the window and said, "Anthony, you can't go back in this rain. Stay here. Enjoy our company!"

As the rain pelted down, Miriam told stories about families in her grandfather's village in Pergamum. Arpoxa asked, "Can you sing some songs?"

Anthony and Miriam chuckled at how the day had turned out. Bad weather was keeping them together. "Let's have an adventure," said Miriam. "There is plenty of time before the noon meal. Nikias brought that big bag of Grandpa's scrolls from Olive Farm. We've never looked at them. Shall we peek at the scrolls that Grandpa never let me see?"

The sky was dark, and their room needed light. Miriam lit an oil lamp and opened a bag. It was made of black woven wool. For six months, it had remained in the corner of Nikias's house, together with other belongings. Miriam whispered, "I feel like a child examining a stolen treasure!"

Several scrolls, each tightly wound up and placed in a decorated leather container, lay inside. Each night, before he went to sleep, Antipas had taken time to write notes of the day's happenings and decisions.

"Look, this is about the three men he trained to go to his new shops up the coast!" exclaimed Miriam. "These are the notes for what he taught." She unrolled the scroll. Before them was a story of the care and preparation that Antipas put into training younger men, recorded years before.

She unrolled another scroll. "Here is a note that Grandpa wrote near the time when you came to Pergamum. Listen to what he wrote: 'As I went to the Upper Agora, I talked to Egyptian priests. They have come here to Pergamum to build a new temple for their gods. They confronted me today, and your word was in my mouth, sweeter than honey. They came to build a huge temple, but my purpose is to build lives, "to free those in bondage and preach the acceptable year of our Lord," as Yeshua said on one occasion. Lord, I love Egypt and Alexandria! It was there I learned to love your law.'"

Another entry had been written at an earlier time.

"On this day, he wrote prayers to God about men learning how to copy the scrolls. 'Thank you, my Lord, for the provision of four men who started studying with me tonight. They are not quick-witted or highly skilled, just ordinary craftsmen, stubborn and hardworking. They will have to be trained. With them, I can make four scrolls at a time. One will go to my brother Amos, another to Simon, and one to Joshua in Smyrna. The fourth copy will go to Assos.'"

Miriam put that scroll down. "I knew he had it planned out, how he was going to get the scrolls copied and sent to the different cities, but there is so much here I never knew. He also made plans for new leaders."

Anthony sat on the bed, rocking his daughter in his arms. The wind howled outside, groaning then growling.

Here, inside, Grace was safe, innocent, and well protected.

Miriam pulled another one out of the bag. It was older and told of her grandfather's struggles as he decided to go to the slave market for the first time.

"Listen. Here's the story of why he bought a slave each year! Here he wonders what will happen to the slave when the man has been set free. 'I concluded that if I free a slave, then a job must also be found for him. If I build a house and allow him to work for me, it will cost more. But in the long run, this will pay off. Father was disturbed by my decision and said, "How do you know if a slave will be a good worker after having been freed? Won't the slave go back to his own people? Don't you run the risk of losing your money?" Not only that but my brother Daniel is distraught. He wants a say in how to develop the property Father bought.'

"Isn't this interesting, Anthony? It's as though Grandpa Antipas is here with us telling his life story!"

Anthony did not say anything as he rocked Grace and nodded silently. She was teething and had not slept well the night before.

Miriam felt a bit sheepish, having never gone through her grandfather's personal things.

"Grandpa wrote this years ago! I was a child, and Grandma was still alive. This is wonderful! So much of his life is here! Anthony! Here is Grandpa's life story, and you are not giving me your full attention. You are just holding our daughter."

"Miriam, she is beautiful! You get to hold her every day. I only get to hold her when I am not at camp. Do you want me to divide my attention between Antipas and Grace?"

His voice sounded playful, but she knew he was giving her his full concentration.

She put her hand in the bag and took out another scroll. "Several younger men who started in Grandpa's class but didn't finish... 'One young man continued, but another fell away, his time dissolving in wine and his feet taking him on the road to the stadium instead of God's path. Save them both from their youthful errors, Lord.'"

Anthony listened, spellbound. "It sounds like he wrote those notes as a guide for his prayers."

"My dear, I remember when you started coming to the cave. Grandpa asked for more than just one person to pray for you," Miriam said, laughing. "It must have taken half the families in our village to cover you in prayer!"

She continued reading the scroll. "Here is more on training leaders. He placed some young men on a special list, called 'New Emerging Leaders.'" She pointed to one part of the scroll, where the word "Evaluations" was written.

"Talking about evaluations, I remember a man. Grandpa sent him to the coast to a new shop he had begun. This man spoke in public once, and a woman said to him, 'You started with one topic, but you never came back to it, and by the end, no one could understand what you had said at any time in your talk.' We all thought he would never meet with us again, but he did. He told Grandpa that he knew he needed help in organizing his thoughts. He wanted to learn. Grandpa talked about him at home that day. 'Now there's a man who's going to do good work in my shop. He will form a community because he's not afraid to ask for help. He is humble, and he is ready to learn.'"

Miriam had unrolled several volumes when she gave a startled sound. "This scroll has a wax seal. It must be special."

The wax seal on the scroll was soon broken. Miriam opened it, and she couldn't swallow. "This one is about Diotrephes!" She read the writing in round Greek letters. "It sounds as if Grandpa was worried about Diotrephes from the start. He wrote, 'The Milon family is considered part of the aristocracy in Pergamum. Demetrius had advised me against letting Diotrephes be a student. He is the son of the high priestess of the Altar of Zeus. At first, I dared to hope Diotrephes might get his mother, Lydia-Naq, to change her mind and turn against Zeus. From the time I learned about her, she has been against the followers of Yeshua.'

"'Diotrephes came tonight to his first class. He seems to be sincere, with a huge thirst for knowledge. He has a convincing, almost overpowering personality. He can sway listeners because of his authoritative speech. In a short time, he has devoured everything that I loaned to him. He asks how we came from Alexandria. He wants information on everything: Egyptian religion and ships, glass blowing, the Law of Moses, selling merchandise, and running a business. He wants to know how Roman taxes in Egypt are different from those in Asia. One day he asked for my scrolls on the Maccabees, but I wouldn't loan those to him.'"

Miriam looked up. "Did you know Diotrephes has such a hunger for knowledge?"

"No." said Anthony. "Maybe Diotrephes only wants knowledge but without seeking the One who gives understanding. That's why he talks about 'special knowledge' so much."

She read again. "'Diotrephes wants to be a future leader, to take over for me when I am too old to keep on teaching. February 21: Several weeks have passed by, and I said, "Soon I will be asking each student to give a lesson. Each of you will explain what you have learned and what you believe." March 21: Tonight I asked

Diotrephes to make the first presentation. This is a summary of what he said and my response.

"'Diotrephes said, "John's letter from Ephesus teaches about sin and atonement, love and mercy, and Yeshua as the Son of God. These are important topics; we all need to know about them. First, though, we know Yeshua will never be seen again. He died, and we are the ones left here to carry on his life. When some teachers talk about Yeshua returning, it means people see Yeshua in us. Right here. Right now. We carry his character in us. That's what resurrection means. In that way, we are sons of God.'"

"You should see your face, Miriam!" said Anthony in mock alarm.

"I can't help it," she said and kept reading.

"'Diotrephes explained, "I disagree with the teaching brought to us by Demetrius. Actually, it comes from John the Elder, who is from Jerusalem. He thinks he is the only one who has knowledge, but people should not be told to avoid special knowledge. We in Pergamum have always sought to know more. This is why the Library of Pergamum is such a treasure. Special knowledge is passed from one generation to another, coming to us from distant generations. In this way, the Jewish covenant is deficient. It does not show me how to find the knowledge I am looking for. If I ask, 'Where can wisdom be found?', the answer you gave me, 'The fear of the Lord: that is the beginning of wisdom,' is unsatisfactory."

"'I speak as a Gentile, as you like to call me. The Law of Moses that you follow is not adequate. A large part of the problem is that you cannot see the gods. Thus, everyone holds a different image in their mind. Take Zeus, for example. Simply walk around the Altar of Zeus, and you will know what he looks like! You need to see your god.'

"'John the Elder says, 'If we say we have no sin, we do not carry out the truth, and sin abides in us.'[55] I say we should be humble enough to confess. Yes, we do sin. We transgress the law, but that does not mean sin is shameful. We should sin intentionally and unintentionally. This is good. Repeated sin leads to a constant experience of forgiveness, and forgiveness rescues us from ignorance. Didn't Yeshua say mercy should be extended seventy times seven? Therefore, keep committing sin without fear. Sin

---

[55] 1 John 1:8

repeatedly. Both knowledge and forgiveness are suitable for the soul. Sinning is a good thing." At this point, I interrupted Diotrephes and asked him to leave. I had been too quick to include him in my class of new leaders.'"

The last part of Antipas's notes ended with firm, neat handwriting: "'I am horrified by this teaching. He doesn't understand the nature of God's grace or the subtlety of temptations. I told Diotrephes, "You may not be a leader in the Household of Faith. You can come and learn at the cave like anyone else, but you must put aside these Nicolaitan teachings.'"

The scroll was only one-third full.

Anthony said, "I remember it all. Antipas told him to not come back to that class. Diotrephes's face showed red, and he left, leaving a few threats behind. It was a tense moment."

"By the way, I think Lyris and Eugene are going to formally announce they want to get married." Miriam tossed the comment into the conversation casually.

Anthony responded as she thought he might. "We are talking about Antipas and Diotrephes, and now we suddenly switch to talking about Eugene and Lyris? He's a Gentile, and his first wife was a Jew! And now he's going to marry another Jew."

Miriam laughed, snuggling up against him. "For many months, Judith and I had suspected they had fallen in love, but then they admitted it on Grace's birthday."

Anthony knew that Eugene and Lyris spent much time together. "So he was not simply 'serving food and helping make the meals and clean up after meals.' They were actually enjoying each other's company, learning about each other, and no one knew about it!"

Miriam advised him, "Pretend to be surprised if you're here for an announcement!" Her mind was spinning. "I have a plan that no one, not Ravid, not Uncle Simon and Aunt Judith, and not even the children, will ever forget!"

"What's that? Tell me!"

"When Elisha came from Thyatira to help us in the weaving workshops, I asked him to bring one hundred wedding tunics. Remember? Well, my first thought was that Uncle Simon would be accepted as a partner in the bank. If so, we would need tunics for a great celebration for his 'promotion into Sardian society'!

"A little later, I thought I saw love blooming in the kitchen.

Anthony! Since Uncle Simon was rejected as a bank director, we can use the tunics for the wedding. And I'm going to invite the people working in the workshop. Them and their family members."

Anthony's face mirrored his disbelief. "The wealthiest people of this city won't be coming to this house for a celebration, but poor people will be getting invitations?"

"Yes." She continued explaining her ideas, and the more she spoke, the harder he laughed. Tears poured down his face. Miriam's proposal seemed so out of place.

Anthony saw Miriam in a whole new light. She was a constant delight, and he never knew what she would do next. Her involvement with the needy families in the insulae had been unexpected. He said something to her that he had heard a Jewish man say, but he knew it was true. "A wife of noble character, who can find? She is worth far more than rubies."[56]

The next day, when the weather had improved, Miriam asked, "Anthony, would you come into the city with me? I'd like you to meet a few families."

"Yes, if we don't stand and talk for a long time. I won't go into any of the homes, but I can drive Simon's cart. I'll take you there for an hour. Hey, what if I hold Grace while you talk to your friends?"

"How much time do you have?"

"I don't think Felicior and Prosperus will mind if I return by noontime. I'll take you there and bring you back."

Miriam asked Simon for the use of a cart to take some supplies to two families suffering from hunger. Anthony hitched two horses and loaded the food on the back. Miriam held Grace, and she explained a little bit about each family they were going to see.

---

[56] Proverbs 31:10

Chapter 35
Little Lion

THE VILLAGE OF PYRGION, ON THE LESSER MENDERES RIVER

As soon as the decision was made that Little Lion would help track down the four brothers, he started letting his beard grow. It spouted thin and spindly. Hardly anything grew on his cheeks, but a small goatee grew on his chin.

"Anthony, trying to find unknown men is going to be a difficult and stressful task," Little Lion observed. He put on a long coat. On cold days, he walked with his arms folded around his small body.

Little Lion welcomed the other two army men on this assignment. The hard feelings of October's adventure had been put behind them. The two brothers, Dares and Cohn, also wrapped borrowed, ragged coats around themselves.

Anthony sent them on their way, saying, "Go to the taverns. Avoid any mention of Sardis. Never tell about the preparations for war in Dacia."

Felicior's last words rang in their ears. "Don't say a word about your real assignment. Instead, speak about homes with rich mosaics. Explain, 'I dream of a house like this and this. Oh, how I would love to work in a place like that or, even better, be the wealthy owner."

Two long days on military horses took them from Sardis to Ephesus, with a night spent at the Garrison of Smyrna. From Ephesus, Little Lion and the brothers walked two days to reach Hypaepe, a regional town tucked between two mountain ranges.

As Little Lion, Dares, and Cohn searched for clues about the four robbers, they pretended to be laborers waiting for springtime.

They divided their time between Hypaepe, the central city in the area, and the nearby villages. These mostly unknown communities were tucked away in the Lesser Menderes River valley.

Little Lion suggested that they spend time in each community.

"Since we three are from Laodicea, many days away by foot, we can talk in taverns without worrying about someone checking up on our stories," Dares added.

After a month, Cohn shook his head. A week spent in Palaiapolis passed without meeting anyone who looked suspicious. "We've made no contact with the four brothers. I'm getting discouraged. Perhaps the brothers were not coming to the Hypaepe Valley area after all."

Little Lion suggested, "Let's spend some time in Pentakoma. It's a smaller village in this agricultural area. I hear there's a tavern there. Come on. Let's go!" They spent a week there, speaking loudly and telling stories of their home area: Laodicea, Hierapolis, and Colossae.

They remembered every detail of artistic work. Descriptions of homes they had visited spilled out. People especially enjoyed listening to Little Lion tell stories of wealthy families in Laodicea, the most prosperous city in Phrygia.

There was still one town that they had not explored, the small village of Pyrgion. They made their way to the south slope of Mount Tmolus. The village was about a third of the way up the road to the peak. They went when the weather began to improve.

"It would be a good spot where 'our people' might want to hide," suggested Dares. "It's more isolated than the others."

A half day's trip in the first week of February took them up the winding road to the isolated village. A light snow had fallen two days before, but now the road was passable. They found accommodations in an inn built with rough black stones.

Leaving their horses with the innkeeper, they went to the only tavern open at this time. The weathered back porch overlooked a swollen stream where water rushed noisily. They entered the town over graceful stone arches that supported the bridge.

The next morning, a thin blanket of snow sparkled in the dim afternoon sunlight.

COMMANDER FELICIOR'S OFFICE, THE ACROPOLIS, SARDIS

The days were slightly longer and more pleasant when Felicior called Anthony in for a conference. "At ease, soldier," said Felicior.

"We must talk about the end of our present training session. The sailing season is about to start. As soon as ships start to sail northward, leaving Smyrna, we will send these new legionaries to Dacia. Prosperus is going with them. Preparations have been made to travel through the Hellespont and up the channel, past Chalcedon.[57] These soldiers will disembark in Lower Moesia and join your old Legion XXI, the Predators. Then comes the real test."

"That's good news, sir."

"Are our recruits well prepared?"

"We have done our best. Dares, Cohn, and Little Lion sent a message. They haven't located the robbers yet."

"If they aren't back before the ships sail, I'll have them go after they come back. How long do you think it will take to form those tribes into a peaceful province?"

Anthony related experiences with Germanic tribes as barbarians came under Roman rule. "Most tribes on the west bank of the Rhine River are now incorporated into provinces," he explained.

"And the others? What about tribes that resist?"

"I witnessed some villages counterattacking. Their warriors would die rather than submit to Rome. Others adopt Roman manners willingly. Most give in grudgingly."

"And the reason for the differences? I thought all barbarians were the same."

"It depends on the leader. If the local chief accepts what Rome stands for and sees advantages for his people, there are few problems. Those are internal decisions. Human will is involved."

"Let's get back to our last four weeks of training. We need to discuss their final day with us, when we send them to Smyrna to the garrison there." Felicior was now going to keep their conversation to the business at hand.

THE VILLAGE OF PYRGION

For several days, Little Lion, Dares, and Cohn stayed in the tavern. They noticed a man listening to their conversations one afternoon. He had a long, scraggly beard, and his clothes had not been washed for weeks.

"This is the most beautiful village I have ever seen, outside of Laodicea, my home city," said Little Lion. He spoke with the accent of people in his native Phrygia. "The only thing needed, my friends,

---

[57] Chalcedon, modern-day Kadikoy, on the eastern side of the city of Istanbul in Turkey, was located at the southern end of the Bosporus Strait. It faced both the Bosporus and the Sea of Marmara, providing Chalcedon with two ideally located ports.

to brighten up this inn is a charming floor mosaic. You should see the family of three brothers who carry on the mosaic trade in Laodicea. They are completing a mosaic right now...."

"What do you know of the mosaic trade?" the stranger interrupted, speaking with a raspy voice. Leaving his place in a dark corner, and without asking permission to join in, he pulled up the fourth chair at their table. His breath smelled of rot, and two teeth were blackened.

"My name is Magnus. I am out of work right now and looking for jobs for my brothers and me. Who are you? Where do you come from? I haven't seen you around here before."

"My name is Titus Memmius. These are my friends, Dares and Cohn, two brothers. We're from Laodicea. We're also away from our regular jobs, like you. Pull your chair closer. I'll tell you all about how we do mosaics most profitably."

By the end of the day, they were convinced that Magnus was one of the brothers they were searching for.

"My brothers went to Ephesus to spy out the land, looking for new work opportunities," Magnus concluded, pushing himself away from the table. "I'm off to Hypaepe. Maybe I'll come back here."

Four days later, Magnus appeared at the tavern again, bringing his three brothers. The burly man spoke of his admiration for mosaic artwork. He introduced his brothers to the three younger men.

"These are my brothers: Kosmiadis, Leonidas, and Orestes. You need to know that I am an accomplished mosaic artist, even if I say so myself. I do the design and layout." Each of the men wore cloaks used in the day to keep them warm and as blankets at night.

"My brothers install the stone chips. They polish them when the cement is dry. In between, we relieve the house owner of items he won't miss until we are gone."

Little Lion leaped at the opening. "That's interesting. My friends and I scout out the homes interested in new mosaics, those wealthy enough to have us work for them. We are between 'jobs,' but I know a family in Philadelphia that wants a new floor," said Little Lion. "That's where we were planning to go next."

He talked with a sly smile. *I must give a man's name and make these crooks think I'm taking revenge. I can't provide the real name of Simon's brother, Amos Ben Shelah.*

Pausing, Little Lion scowled, remembering his worst tormentor in Laodicea. Memories came back of the rude names, endless buffets to the head, and being pushed while taking wood to the hot baths. Little Lion's explanation suggested a desire for revenge against Argus, the bully who had hurt him the most. He decided that real emotion would come out if he called the owner of the Ben Shelah home in Philadelphia Argus.

"Argus is his name, and how I would love to get back at him! He did so many bad things to me. His father makes gold rings and other jewelry. His library has some gold pieces in it, or so they say. They live in an old Greek house. The floor was damaged during an earthquake years ago. I heard last month that they were looking for someone to replace it."

Anthony learned more about Simon's family and mentioned the details to Little Lion when they were up on the mountain during training. The house in Philadelphia belonged to Amos Ben Shelah. The floors and upper story had suffered extensive damage in the Great Earthquake, although Amos had repaired it and made it his home.

Most of what Little Lion said was true. Argus was the bully who had hurt his feelings and called his mother a bad name. Only one thing was a lie: that Argus was the son of Amos Ben Shelah. The name Argus was Little Lion's single addition.

"Now there's a real job!" exclaimed one of the men. "Remember our motto? 'We come in, fix your floor, and leave a little bit richer.' That's our business." His unpleasant laugh ended with a snarl.

"Well then, I think we are onto a trial partnership!" Little Lion kept up his Phrygian accent. "Let's earn some money! We will divide the take equally: half for us and half for you." His proposal was offered as bait and was meant to provoke a strong reaction.

The four brothers bent toward the younger men, reaching for the throats of the recruits.

"Not at all," exploded Orestes. "Titus, we are four! You are only three men! Young men! We're older! No, it's four portions for us and three for you of whatever we earn."

"But we are leading you to a 'lucrative job'! That is worth extra."

They argued for a long time. Little Lion baited them on, making their greed more obvious. "Agreed! You win!" Cohn finally said, pretending exasperation.

In the process, they had learned a lot more about the brothers.

"Now, Cohn," Little Lion said, continuing the ruse, "you will go ahead of us tomorrow and spy out the land. Maybe you can find out if any more houses there need a new floor. If the weather's good, the rest of us should be there in three days. When we get to Philadelphia, you will be waiting for us at the Inn of the Open Door."

"Sounds like a good plan!" exclaimed Magnus. "It gives us time to get our tools together and move to Philadelphia. We'll need a small cart to get everything there." He had taken the bait and swallowed the entire fishhook. He had no idea how easily he was being reeled in.

All Little Lion had to do was wait and not appear too anxious. He let the brothers convince themselves that they would be in for easy money from looting homes in Philadelphia.

Little Lion and his two friends held back as the four thieves drank several more mugs of beer. They thanked the gods with loud voices, happy for the good fortune of having three new "friends."

Cohn went ahead of the others the next morning. Arriving n Philadelphia, he went to the commander of the garrison.

He showed the commander his authorizations and explained the operation. A letter was immediately dispatched to Sardis.

Before Little Lion and the others started their trip to Philadelphia, Commander Felicior in Sardis knew what was happening. He sent Anthony and other soldiers to apprehend the robbers who worked as mosaic artists.

THE INN OF THE OPEN DOOR, THE CITY OF PHILADELPHIA

Little Lion and Dares left Pyrgion and waited in Hypaepe. Two days later, the robbers brought a wagon filled with tiny stones used in making floor mosaics. Another cart contained their equipment. Near Ephesus, the robbers washed, cut their scraggly beards, and put on clean clothing.

Leaving the Lesser Menderes Valley, their horses strained to pull the extra weight. They went up a winding escarpment road from the floor Once on the higher plain, they followed the winding road between two lengthy mountain ranges.

With the extra weight the horses had to pull, it had taken three days to come near to Philadelphia, a smaller city snuggled against the side of a great mountain. The six men left the high ground and looked down on miles of soft green vineyards, where leaves were beginning to sprout.

The four brothers by now were completely at ease with Little Lion and Dares. Having them agree with each step of the plan, Little Lion found a way to hoodwink them at their own game.

Traveling by horse while bringing two wagons filled with tools and bags of colored stone chips, the two young army men chatted with the robbers. Dares described several wealthy families in Laodicea, leaving the impression that he had robbed treasures from those homes. By now, they had learned the name of each city where the thieves had carried out similar crimes.

By nightfall, they were close to their destination, the Inn of the Open Door. Unknown to the four brothers, Anthony and a dozen soldiers were waiting for them in Philadelphia.

Arriving at the inn, Little Lion, Dares, and the four brothers were met by Amos Ben Shelah's servant. He had been brought in on the plan. Their horses were taken to the stable at the rear section of the inn.

"Welcome to Philadelphia and the Inn of the Open Door!" he said, extending his hand in greeting. "I work for the owner, and I'm happy you came. Our rooms are usually full, but you are the only travelers tonight. We have excellent beer. Satisfy your thirst! I see that you have had a long journey! We will serve a meal shortly."

Cohn told the brothers that he had contacted the house owner, and they only had to go look at the floor and agree with the owner for a price to do the work. As they were finishing the meal, Little Lion declared, "Tonight we celebrate our arrival! Tomorrow we'll probably get started on a new mosaic floor job, but for now, let's hear some stories!"

Cohn had arranged with Anthony that the arrest would come as a complete surprise. No one wanted another escape like Taba's a few months before.

"I have stories you've never dreamed of," began Little Lion. He told of his theft of a vase, a true story from his past. "I was only fifteen. You should have seen how my poor mother responded when I gave her that lovely 'present'! She said, 'Oh, my son, you shouldn't have done it!' Of course she was right. I should not have done it!"

Warm camaraderie enhanced by mugs of beer and recalling conversations from over the last few days helped robbers gain a measure of trust. Kosmiadis, Orestes, Leonidas, and Magnus did not notice that their goblets were refilled several times. Little Lion and his two friends had only filled their cups twice.

Leonidas, the second oldest, lifted his cup to commemorate the last mosaic floor they had completed. It was the home of a wealthy family in Sardis.

Orestes added, "We were going to divide the spoils from that house, but our plans were thwarted. Our treasures were discovered. I would like to kill the soldiers who took our possessions!"

"Somehow we were betrayed to the authorities," Magnus added, cleaning a piece of meat from blackened teeth. "After the cave was discovered and our four helpers were arrested, we had to disappear and fend for ourselves."

Orestes belched loudly. "We used to be truthful men, doing an honest day's work. But we learned something from Taba. He claims that a rebellion is coming, and Emperor Nero will make his return with thousands of soldiers. He is coming to reclaim his position as emperor. Listen...why don't the three of you join up with us?"

Orestes's words were slurred, but his meaning was obvious. Taba, the gang leader who had escaped, had recruited four humble workers using the excuse of Nero's return. Taba had an advantage. The robbers were tempted to become rich quickly.

Magnus realized his brother was saying too much. He snapped, "Shut up, Orestes! Stop talking about our lives! We haven't worked with these guys yet. We don't know if they're trustworthy or not."

"No, it's not a lie. I'm telling the truth!" was the response from a stumbling, stuttering Orestes. He pushed his cup forward, ready for more. Then he leaned back, patting a full belly, thankful for delicious food and drink after a long winter of hunger and scarcity.

Little Lion kept probing. "If we had been with you, how would you have divided the treasures up for payments?" Orestes and Leonidas were only too happy to describe their treasure: tumblers, highly polished brassware, intricately woven carpets, and jewelry. They were too drunk to remember Little Lion's question about how the treasures were turned into money.

Anthony and the squad waiting outside had heard enough. The four burglars had incriminated themselves. Anthony's men were not dressed as soldiers when they entered. Outside, another small detachment of soldiers was prepared to come in to help with the arrests if needed. Not even one of the brothers was able to resist.

The next day, Little Lion wrote a simple report to Felicior: "They were so drunk they could not struggle."

The criminals were taken to Sardis. Commenting on the arrests, Felicior said, "Forced confessions may still be needed, not about the robberies in Sardis but about the man who escaped up on the mountain. Who is Taba? What kind of a rebellion is he planning?"

THE GARRISON OF SARDIS, THE ACROPOLIS, SARDIS

Spring arrived, and the first vessels would soon be sailing. Sailors were preparing the ships leaving Smyrna and traveling to northern ports.

Anthony had been thinking about Little Lion. Of all of the trainees going to war, Little Lion was the most agile. He could creep through the forest. The young man motivated others and, during training, had shown that he could lead a squad. Most importantly, he had the courage needed to penetrate enemy lines. How would he manage in Dacia? That would have to be learned during battle.

On the last Tuesday in February, just before marching out, Little Lion approached Anthony. "There is something different about you," he said, looking at Anthony's long red scar. "You have a hidden strength."

"What do you mean?"

"You were given an impossible job. We believed you would never snatch the eagle from Prosperus's men. Yet you marched right up to Prosperus, challenging him: 'Watch out! You are going to lose the eagle standard!' We knew then that we could trust you, that you would bring victory! We have been watching and noticed that you never used the word 'god' when talking about Domitian."

Anthony prayed for wisdom. Such a moment might not return. If he did not say enough now about the source of his confidence, he would lose an opportunity to confess what the covenant meant. But if he said too much, he might bring punishment upon his head.

"I accept our emperor and am loyal to him as the most powerful leader in the world. Yet he does not rule all lands. Nations far to the east, the lands from which silk and spices come, do not obey him. You are observant. I do not accept the emperor as a god. Instead, I worship God, who is above Domitian. God revealed himself in Yeshua, the Messiah."

For a few minutes, he spoke of Yeshua Messiah. He explained the Messiah's life and death and how Roman soldiers put him on the cross and then guarded his tomb. Anthony made the decision to teach Little Lion the words he had learned from Antipas.

"Sit down, Little Lion. In our family, we say that the Messiah is 'Lord of lords and King of kings.' We believe he is coming back someday. His kingdom is not of this world. It is not about political intrigue or obtaining riches at any cost. He makes us 'overcomers.' We give him glory by the way that we live."

Little Lion shot back, "But we all have to declare, 'Caesar is lord and god.'"

Praying hard, Anthony said, "Remember when I said God would show us how to win the contest between the two opposing detachments Felicior set up? Well, I prayed. Sometimes God speaks to me in a dream. Other times I remember God's guiding words written in a scroll. I think about Yeshua. God's Spirit is always close to me. I got an answer to my prayers that day. One thing led to another; we got the eagle, and more than that, criminals were captured."

Little Lion tried to understand. "You speak about the kingdom of God. You said our soldiers crucified Yeshua."

"Yes."

Little Lion knew he was scouting out new territory. "Was there something you could not say when Prosperus was there?"

"Yes."

"What is it? Please tell me."

Anthony spoke slowly. "Yeshua did not just die. He gave up his life, choosing to die on his own terms. There is a big difference. His death was intentional. While he was being crucified, he said, 'Father, forgive them because they do not know what they are doing.' He forgave his enemies, and three days later, he rose from the dead; he was then seen, talked with, and physically touched by his followers. He is the Messiah."

"This is extraordinary." Little Lion had never heard the story.

"It is not a myth, not like the ones made into mosaics on the floors of rich people. None of those stories are true. This is different. People witnessed Yeshua's reappearance, and he appeared at least ten times to people—for forty days. More than five hundred saw him alive. After that, he went up into the heavens."

Little Lion was listening intently. "How long have you known about this?"

"I first heard this twenty-three years ago. My mother became a follower. She was sick in her last days and died in Rome. Recently I met a man by the name of Antipas, and he told me many truths about the Messiah. I came to believe and understand all this only two years ago."

"Quick! I'm marching to Smyrna in a few minutes. Tell me everything you can."

Anthony explained, "Little Lion, Messiah taught us about the Kingdom of God. We must value justice and righteousness."

Little Lion said, "Felicior is calling us to fall in. My mother is sick. If you ever get to Laodicea, she lives below the big theater overlooking the valley. She's near the big theater, not the smaller one. Will you visit her?"

"Yes, I will, if I ever get to Laodicea. My wife is part of a business family. Stewards working for the family go back and forth between Sardis and Laodicea all the time. What is your mother's name? How can I find her?"

"Her name is Charmaine Memmius. Go into the insulae from the Hierapolis Gate. Turn left, down where painters mix their paints. There's a narrow street. It leads down toward the river. I'm going to Dacia, and our legion will be at war, so you will see my mother before I come back from the battles. Can you tell my mother something?" Little Lion looked away, across the valley.

Anthony raised an eyebrow at the tenderness in Little Lion's voice. "What is it?"

"Tell my mother, 'Little Lion told me to tell you he is part of an invisible kingdom. It's where love and justice have met.' Tell her about the two kingdoms, like you did for me. Tell her I believed..."

Felicior was approaching, and Little Lion spoke quickly. "Tell my mother that I want her to know this story. Tell her all about what happened on the mountain and how we captured the robbers. Can you give her that message?"

"If I can, I will find a way for your message to get through."

Felicior came close to them and heard Anthony's last comment. "Little Lion, you want your mother to know what happened on the mountain? No, Anthony cannot do that. What happens in the army only gets reported to officers and commanders. Remember that. The enemy has ears everywhere."

The commander turned and spoke to another young soldier.

Soon the new troops would leave for the port of Smyrna. They would sail north, past Bithynia, into the Black Sea. They would soon be fighting in battle, perhaps in two or three months.

It was time to go. Anthony sent Little Lion on his way with a blessing. "May the name of the God of Jacob protect you!"[58]

Anthony pointed to his scar, showing the full side of his wounded face. "Little Lion, when you are cut deeply, both outside and inside, pray this prayer: 'In you, O Lord, I have taken refuge; let me never be put to shame; deliver me in your righteousness. Turn your ear to me; come quickly to my rescue; be my rock of refuge, a strong fortress to save me.'[59] Keep trusting! I want to see you again. You will see terrible things in war. Later, we will talk, and you can tell me what it is like to be a scout."

They shook hands briefly before Little Lion turned and ran back to his squad.

Recruits who had trained for months were now being sent off as soldiers. The forest land above Sardis had provided them with the best conditions for preparation to face hostile forces in Dacia.

Prosperus shouted, "Attention!"

Young soldiers fell into line. A few minutes later, he led them onto the Royal Road. They marched westward toward Smyrna, a two-day journey. They disappeared over the hill where the Royal Road dipped into a small valley.

After they were no longer visible, Felicior called Anthony aside. "You have earned three days' leave, Anthony. Report back to me on Saturday."

"Yes sir. I will be at your office on March 1."

"I have other news. An unsuccessful robbery took place on the road close to the city of Aizanoi. One man was captured, the only one from a larger gang. Under duress, he told us the name of the man he reported to. Can you guess his name?"

"It wouldn't be Taba, sir?"

"Yes, it was, and interestingly, he told us of another name, Craga. He did not know more than that, only the name Craga. This means

---

[58] Psalm 20:1

[59] Psalm 31:1–2

they are part of the same gang we have been looking for. We did not learn anything about who is the overall leader. No name yet, but we'll discover who he is.

"The bandit who was captured said he deserted from the army in the Province of Moesia. He said a man by the name of Craga recruited him in Chalcedon. The gang he joined is called the Faithful, and he reports to Taba. What strange names! Never heard them before. That's all the army could learn about him. He was executed.

"Taba is the one we must find. He escaped when your training group captured the eagle standard, and that is not something you can boast about. However, you did succeed as an instructor and prevented those four brothers from further 'artistic endeavors.' I want you to continue as a reservist attached to the Garrison of Sardis. Come back on Saturday ready to train the next group of forty recruits!"

SIMON AND JUDITH'S HOME

By the end of the day, after laughing and joking around the table in the evening, everyone was tired. The whole family had stood at the gate, watching the newest soldiers marching off to Smyrna. The days were slightly longer now that spring was coming. Mixed emotions abounded. Watching army troops march made people feel uneasy, while the warmer weather brought happiness. Elisha had finished his repair work on the workshops and returned to Thyatira several days before.

Anthony held Miriam close. "I am only home for three days," he said. "I wish it were longer."

Miriam touched the long scar on his face and said playfully, "What are you going to do when you grow up? Amath wants to be like Queen Esther. Who do you want to be like?"

She was teasing him because he made so many social blunders in the Jewish home. "Oh, there are so many things I will never understand. Your family celebrates feasts and fasts! One day you overeat and the next day nothing!"

She chuckled at how little he understood about her ancient Jewish customs, but she wanted to say something serious. "Ravid will never be satisfied with you here."

Anthony did not want to talk about that topic, so he asked about something else urgent. "Is Uncle Simon going to accept your idea of inviting your new friends to a wedding party?"

Miriam knew how difficult it could be to get both families to agree to hold a unique marriage reception.

Miriam and Anthony asked for a private conversation with Simon the next morning. "Eugene and Lyris's wedding is set for the beginning of June, just four months away. What if we did something never done before in Sardis?"

"What are you thinking of?" Simon felt slightly uncomfortable.

A gleam shone in Miriam's eyes. "Grandpa Antipas said we must obey Yeshua's teaching. One of the things he instructed his followers was 'Give a party, but not for the rich or friends. Instead, give one for those who never receive an invitation: the lame, the blind, and the sick. And afterward, do not expect to receive rewards on earth.'"[60]

"Let me think about it," Simon said. The responding twinkle in his eyes gave them hope. They left, laughing, and he wondered how younger people could enjoy life so much.

Simon found Judith, and he confided in her. "Miriam has a new request. What a strange idea! If the lame and sick come, oh my! What would Ravid think? My biggest fear is losing him. He will declare me a complete pagan if I host a wedding like Miriam wants.

"Yet these are Yeshua's demands about showing consideration for others. I'm at a crossroads. If I were to be loyal to Rome, I would always be looking for what I could get. But the kingdom of God teaches something else."

---

[60] Luke 14:21–24 and Matthew 6:1

Chapter 36
Jace

DIODOTUS AND DELBIN'S HOME, WEST HILL

Diotrephes sat down to write his weekly letter to his mother, and he had much to tell. "The God-fearers are going to participate in all the social activities of Sardis this year. There is hardly a vestige of Gaius's influence left."

He clenched his fist in a victory signal after writing the opening part of his letter.

But then a frown took away the look of pleasure. Yes, four of Diotrephes's five teachers were prepared to start classes with a renewed emphasis on the Lydian culture and language, but he had not had total success.

I would love to tell Mother that I could redirect Jace's thinking, but he is stubborn. Simon is influencing Jace's family, and Anthony is too by training Jace's boy for the races!

The letter to his mother was one of the shortest since he had come to Sardis. His burning anger, something he omitted from his letter, was directed against Zebadiah, the new steward at the Ben Shelah shop. The steward had recommended that Cleon be discharged. Immediately.

Two days before, Zebadiah had found Cleon walking out of the shop with some jewelry. He claimed that he was taking it to a customer. Still, it had become clear to Simon that Cleon was responsible for most of the "lost merchandise," including one of the wedding tunics.

So Cleon could not provide further communications about Miriam. Diotrephes felt cut off from the Ben Shelah family's inner life, and silver coins could no longer bring him the information he longed for.

THE WESTERN AGORA, MARKETPLACE IN SARDIS

Flowers carpeted the meadows, and trees were in blossom when Diotrephes called Jace for another meal. Almost immediately, they were arguing.

Jace began where their previous conversation ended. "You have been telling me to teach differently, but I want to challenge your assumptions."

Diotrephes was ready to debate. "Go ahead."

"It's about the influence of the Lydians. I do not agree with your fundamental convictions. Ancient Hittites, Phrygians, Lydians, and Persians—all those civilizations died out. Now we study Greek and Latin, and our laws are made in Rome."

"Your point is? I don't get what you are driving at."

"What happens to ancient languages?"

"What are you trying to say?"

Jace made his point with care. "Languages die out! Lydian was spoken for a thousand years, and then Persia took over this area. That kingdom dominated Sardis, and the Persian language was heard on every street.

"But who speaks Persian now? It dominated for 230 years. Think about what happened when the Greeks came. Their language replaced Persian. Today you and I teach young boys in Greek and Latin. Face it, Diotrephes, languages come along and then disappear!"

"So?" Diotrephes had assumed that he was going to have a simple dialogue. Instantly, he knew he was facing a determined teacher who had a reason to refuse to submit to his demands.

Jace kept talking. "Think about it. Can a dead language be resurrected? I believe you came to Sardis to bring back a language that only a few speak. You are not able to make Lydian the third language after Greek and Latin.

"A language conveys layers of complex meaning. It expresses countless relationships. A culture, from the richest to the poorest person, depends upon thousands of words. And one word will mean different things to different people. At most, your efforts will meet limited success. You will never see our youth using Lydian in business or social events. Why? Because that old language will not convey current subtle ideas. These concepts did not exist back then.

Lydian is a dead language!"

The words crashed about Diotrephes like lightning flashing in a storm. He knew he faced a foe with skills equal to his own. But Jace would not rob him of the success he wanted. His reply came in a soft voice.

"Sardis was the heartland of the Lydian Kingdom. Jace, there is a pure spirit still alive here. The wise are those who have kept the Lydian language alive. You still know a little bit of the language."

Jace was ready for that argument too. "Yes, my grandmother spoke it, but I can only understand a little bit. My sons don't know any words, and we don't speak Lydian at home. You will soon be in trouble with Rome if you push your ideas too far. Who do you think will argue on your behalf if someone criticizes you for your concepts?"

THE GYMNASIUM

Two weeks went by. Jace was still holding out, not giving an inch to the demands first given to him in October. One day, when the boys were entering the gymnasium for classes, Diotrephes waited for him at the main gate.

"I want the ancient language and culture of Lydia restored to its rightful status. You need to agree with me."

"You have other teachers who are teaching as you wish. And if I do not comply, Diotrephes, what then?"

Something deep within Diotrephes snapped. "Your job depends on it. I am the head of this department, and I'm giving you an order. Carry out the teaching as I require. This must be your concern. I will tolerate nothing less. For instance, your sons must be coached only by teachers who work here at the gymnasium. You are too close to the Ben Shelah family. Any relationship with that family will have to be put aside. If you want to continue teaching here, you must comply."

All morning, Diotrephes's unwelcome words rang in Jace's mind. He was only half present as he mechanically taught his lessons. At noon he called his sons to him. "Hector, you will not have Anthony training you anymore. Isidoros, I want you to stop visiting the Ben Shelah house. Something happened. None of us can have anything to do with Simon's family."

He hung his head, afraid of other consequences. *And you, my father-in-law...you will have to cancel your marriage with Lyris.*

Later that afternoon at home, Jace's pronouncement became the reason for a lively discussion. Eugene spoke first after the initial flareup. He was disappointed with his son-in-law. "I do not usually say very much. My words are only those of a father-in-law. Jace, I think something serious happened. Is there a problem you haven't explained to us?"

Jace's eyes searched the floor for an answer but found none. *Shame! The same feeling that came over me when Diotrephes first started hounding me. Only it's worse now. By giving in to Diotrephes, everyone is going to lose out. Kalonice won't be able to work with Miriam. Isidoros will lose good friends. Hector will probably do poorly in the Games. And do I really have the right to prohibit my father-in-law from getting married?*

SIMON AND JUDITH'S HOME

Hector ran to the Ben Shelah house as soon as he learned he was to stay away from there. He found Tamir and exploded. "I'm not permitted to come here again! And Father says Anthony is not allowed to train me anymore."

Tamir's voice rang out throughout the house. "What about Isidoros? Can he come?"

"No, he is not allowed to come either."

"And Eugene? Surely he and Lyris can see each other!"

"I don't think so. Father was adamant. Something is eating at him. We had a nasty argument in our house. He will not speak a nice word to anyone, not even to Mother!"

Hector left quickly, running away, hurt and disappointed.

Tamir told Elaine the news, and she ran to her room and refused to come for the evening meal. Tamir repeated the story again at the evening meal. No one believed that Jace would forbid all contact between the two families.

Lyris wiped her eyes in the kitchen. She did the cooking and washing up by herself.

Concerned for her daughter, Chenya went to sit beside Elaine. Miriam went to see her as well. She could understand something of Elaine's grief. Her feelings of rejection had overflowed like this when Antipas was persecuted and killed in Pergamum.

Miriam knew only one person in Sardis who could force Jace to act this way. She guessed that Diotrephes had caused the division. Tossing and turning, she was unable to sleep.

After an hour, Miriam wrapped her coat around herself, went down the stairs to the kitchen, and lit an oil lamp. Judith heard her get up and went downstairs too.

"What are you doing, my child?" asked Judith.

"I am writing a song. It's about the breakup of young love."

Judith said, "Miriam, you have your grandfather's sensitivity. When overcome by events, the covenant has always sustained you. The covenant is like a foundation, and our emotions are like the building blocks. Sometimes we sorrow because people act faithlessly and don't keep their word. Other days, we are joyful, rejoicing because the Lord is faithful.

"Now write your song and reflect your emotions and those of my granddaughter as well. She needs understanding and support."

Miriam composed words that matched a tune she had heard a mother singing at the workshop. The original Sardian song was called "A Thousand Friends." It told the story of someone enjoying friendship and losing it because the person moved to another city. Despite the song's name, the tune was set to a minor key, and people sang it mournfully. Another version had words about a family member who died due to sudden illness.

Miriam called her song "A Thousand Smiles." She imagined a harp, a flute, and a lute playing together. Between the next to last and the last verse, she imagined just the harp playing.

Early the day, Miriam went to Elaine's room to sing the new song.

"I wrote a love song to encourage you," she said at the door.

There was no answer. Elaine had turned over, hiding her face in the pillow. Miriam came in, sat down on the bed, and placed her hand on Elaine's cheek. It was wet. Miriam sang softly to not wake up the rest of the household. She wanted to comfort her niece.

My heart beats fast. My breath comes short.
For other girls, this had been sport.
His gaze, so sharp, has stormed my fort.
I am so sure; he will be mine.
A thousand visions fill my mind.

The sunshine's bright. White blossoms burst.
Spring fragrance fills the air. Love lurks
In spring, and no one dreams of hurts.
He wants me! See, I'm just his kind!
A thousand dreams will turn out fine.

My tunic's clean, woven with wool.
Excitement's like first day at school.
Bracelets, nose ring, my curls combed full.
Within his arms, I'm sure to find
A thousand smiles. His face will shine.

Then sudden shock! My hope is drowned.
Love is denied. My ship's gone down.
No special feast, or guests, or gown.
His father said he cannot be mine.
A thousand tears will leave me blind.

Elaine placed her hand on Miriam's hand. "You understand, don't you?" she said with a soft voice. "You understand because you are a Jew and married to a Roman. Your husband is an army man, hardly ever here with you, and you must miss him so much." Elaine paused then said again, "You really do understand, don't you?"

Their friendship was sealed with the song, and Miriam went back to her bedroom. Her cheeks were also wet.

Elaine will sing my song a thousand times.

Later that morning, when Miriam was getting ready to go to the workshops, Kalonice came to Simon's home carrying an extra bag. "What's that for?" asked Miriam.

"Have you heard what my husband said?" asked Kalonice sharply.

"Yes, Hector ran in at noon and told us. Everything has been disrupted. Elaine refused to join us at mealtime last night."

Like Miriam, Kalonice showed a fighting spirit. Courage was a common characteristic drawing the two women together. "In this bag, I have some food. Remember the woman with the hungry children?"

"Which family are you talking about?" Miriam asked. "How many women have hungry children?" The question amused them.

"The last family we visited. Listen, I have no intention of obeying my husband! And my father...imagine Jace telling Eugene that he can't marry Lyris! I don't know what has gotten into my husband, but I suspect it has to do with that director at the school! We'll talk about that on the way to the insulae."

"Do you mean to say you are coming with me?"

"Yes, absolutely. It's the right thing to do!"

Once again, they laughed, ready for more unexpected events in the homes of humble people.

MARCOS AND MARCELLA'S HOME, PERGAMUM

In Pergamum, Trifane spent hours with Marcos and Marcella in their home. During the past year, she had increasingly realized her weakness for flattery.

"I told you that I saw your daughter," Marcos said to Trifane. "The couple who adopted Chrysa is taking good care of her. They gave her a second name. I received a letter telling me about her first birthday party. Chrysa Grace is safe with them, but they live far away."

"I am asking God to let me see my baby at least once before I die."

"Perhaps you will see her one day."

Marcella wrapped her arms around Trifane, and the young woman started to cry. "I am ready to live, ready to love, ready to have my own family, but I can't do it on my own. I need the strength I get from all of you at the assembly at the House of Prayer. Every day I feel my spirit growing stronger. I feel myself thinking more clearly."

"That's the Spirit of God talking with your spirit," Marcos said.

"Please continue to help me," said Trifane. "I don't want to make another big mistake in my life."

She knew that she was gaining a second family, a wider circle of people who would be with her through her joys and sorrows.

Chapter 37
Festivals in April

SIMON AND JUDITH'S HOME

The Ben Shelah home had been in preparation for a week before Passover, the Feast of Unleavened Bread. Any food that might have yeast in it was discarded, but a tiny amount was placed below the front window. The women worked hard washing rooms to clean the house. Anthony received special permission from Felicior to be home for one day for a "special party."

Simon completed the job of cleaning the house, and he "accidentally" found the offending piece of leaven. He always knew where to look for it, and the final task of declaring that the house was free from contamination was part of the fun in preparing for Passover.

"What if he didn't find it?" asked Lyris. Everyone laughed, but their hearts were deeply concerned. Eugene hadn't said anything about going through with the wedding.

Monday, April 7, dawned. Under a dawn streaked with orange clouds, Simon went to his library to prepare for the Passover seder meal. Prostrated in prayer, he stayed there many minutes. He rose and read the familiar passages he would quote during the evening meal. It was the *Haggadah*, the written order.

That evening, the family gathered, the candles were lit, and the sun had set. Simon stood before them and recited the *maggid*, the story of the Exodus from Egypt.

When the story was over but before the seder meal began, Ravid stood up to make a declaration. He left the entire family stunned and Nissa speechless.

"Simon, my dear father-in-law, you missed one part of the story, important in my way of thinking. This is what our Law says: 'No foreigner is to eat of it. Any slave you may have bought may eat of it after you have circumcised him. An alien living among you who wants to celebrate the Lord's Passover must have all the males in his household circumcised; then he may take part like one born in the land. No uncircumcised male may eat of it. The same Law applies to the native-born and to the alien living among you.'[61] I do not think you ever intend to follow the Law of Moses's instructions. I cannot be part of this family when instructions in our covenant are not supported. Moses made things so clear."

He got up and walked to the door. "Come, my wife. You and I will celebrate the meal alone in our home. Finally, all must know my decision. I cannot remain in Sardis."

During the week following Passover, a tense atmosphere hovered over the home. Ravid worked alongside Simon in the workshop but refused to stay in the main house.

He sullenly greeted his mother-in-law and took long walks into the city.

Jews finished the seven-day Feast of Unleavened Bread on April 15. Everyone in the Ben Shelah home returned to their daily schedules.

THE TEMPLE OF ARTEMIS

April 15 also marked the first day of the Festival of Artemis. Farmers came in large numbers, and flocks of sheep were left in the care of older shepherds. Publicans and winemakers celebrated, drinking at taverns and pubs. All bars had extra vats of beer as many parties would last long into each night during the next two weeks.

The holiday was celebrated across the whole province. Fresh scents of spring filled the air. Spring flowers were at their best, and trees exploded in bright displays of reds and yellows, mauves, and pinks. White petals blossomed where crab apples would soon appear. Nature had dressed the hillsides in floral beauty.

Thousands participated in the inauguration of the festival, starting in the large gymnasium square. Young men climbed onto tree branches to get a better view of the procession. Crowds on either side of the Royal Road were five or six people deep.

Along that wide avenue leading southward to the Temple of Artemis from the Royal Road, crowds jostled for space. People spread from sidewalks up the gentle lower slopes of the acropolis. People from every profession in the city took advantage of the

---

[61] Exodus 12:48–49

holiday atmosphere, as thousands loudly cheered the procession.

The procession began with Ankara, the high priest, leading the way. Dressed in bright colors, the high priest stood out from the others. He wore a red cape over a white tunic. His red and white turban was made from a long linen cloth twisted around a soft conical piece. It was secured with bronze clasps.

Trumpets blared as the throng turned left from the Royal Road onto Artemis Way. Another priest followed behind Ankara, leading a sacrificial ox. Behind him, 150 priests walked in groups of three, each group leading a sheep to the temple for sacrifice. The priests' white tunics were spotless, and small red capes hung behind their shoulders. The procession left the gymnasium and turned south. Guards, lawyers, bakers, and physicians called out as they moved by. Loud words of support echoed for their favorite deity.

The procession passed along the Pactolus River. A mile later, the procession stopped in front of the Temple of Artemis. The high priestess, Alala, was waiting at the temple gate as the parade came toward her. She wore a brilliant white linen tunic trimmed with intricate black and gold threads.

Behind her, the other priestesses stood tall, their tunics showing fine, shapely feminine bodies. These were the vestal virgins who guarded the purity of Artemis. Narrow leather belts around their waists were made from the skins of white sheep. The young women stood in pairs. Each pair held one end of a long white linen cloth. The strips of fabric were lifted and lowered while the vestal virgins were chanting songs praising Artemis. As the white materials descended softly, one could imagine showers tumbling to earth. When this had happened this several months ago, the rains had been falling relentlessly. Today, under a bright blue sky, the effect was stunning.

Next the virgins greeted Artemis, the great queen of heaven. Her statue had been placed on the platform that formed the entrance to the temple. As priests and priestesses entered the sanctuary, a great shout went up from the crowds standing around the large entrance area.

One by one, animals were led to the altar at the eastern end of the temple. Their blood would guarantee the goddess's power to bring health, fertility, and prosperity.

During the night, as the moon faded away on the second day of the festival, Ankara and Alala met with older men and women. In the darkness, the elders called upon the old gods. Ancient magic was required, magic older than the mountains. If their city was to be spared further destruction from earthquakes, they must say the right words and perform the correct rites.

Perhaps, they reasoned, the ancient gods worshiped before the Lydian Kingdom should also be appeased during the festival. They pleaded earnestly for the gods to prevent further erosion of the acropolis. No one could bear the thought of more agonizing deaths.

On the second day of the festival, Ankara and Alala were happy to proclaim to the city that Artemis had accepted the people's sacrifices. They announced that all the trials of the winter were over. Artemis could now bring abundance and blessing to the land.

DIODOTUS AND DELBIN'S HOME, WEST HILL

Diotrephes broke the red seal on the scroll as quickly as he could. He had just received another letter from his mother.

April 20, 10th year of Domitian
From: Lydia-Naq
To: Diotrephes, my dear son

Peace and health. If you are well, then I am well.

Reading your many letters, I see that you are increasingly worried about Anthony's success. Here is my advice: Write a letter to his commander. Say, "Anthony is known to be an atheist, and this news is reaching the public." Make it sound as if he is a threat to the city. You must imply that it would be a pity if the news got out that the atheists from Pergamum had escaped to Sardis and were being protected by the garrison.

Chapter 38
Hector's Race

THE STADIUM OF SARDIS

In the week before the Games, Jace spent several hours by himself. He saw the fallen expressions on his sons' faces. Pursing his lips, Jace contemplated the demands made on everyone following the confrontation with Diotrephes. He walked back to his home after classes one day with his head held high and asked for a quiet moment with Eugene.

Jace wanted forgiveness for his outburst. "I am sorry," he said. "I should not have said things like that. I was under pressure, and I responded shamefully, taking it out on my family members."

Eugene smiled with his characteristic quiet grin. "Thank you for saying that, Jace, but I wasn't going to pay attention to you anyway, Jace. Lyris is soon going to be my wife."

"Of course I want you both to be happy together. I told Hector he should run the race, and I've invited Tamir to watch. It hurts to admit these things as a father, but I made a big mistake. Strangely, I was trying to protect Hector, but I can't go into that. Someone has been trying to hurt me. It's too complicated to say much more for now."

Anthony wanted more time with Hector in preparation for the race, but that was difficult. He was going to be limited by his work at the garrison during the month before the competition. He had new recruits to train.

A month before the Games, Anthony had explained to Felicior that he had been helping a young runner. "I would like to spend several afternoons a week with him," he said.

Felicior was sympathetic to the request and released Anthony to have the time to coach Hector. In the days before the race, he helped the boy stretch his legs, making sure his tendons and muscles were supple but not overworked. He noted with satisfaction the growing stamina and the sparkle in the young man's eyes.

The day of the big race arrived. Hector had formed his winning strategy. He would take the lead and keep it to the end. On the first day of the games, Hector came in first in his qualifying run and was listed for the final competition. He was confident of victory, not permitting the prospect of second or third place to enter his mind.

Anthony wondered if Hector really would run faster than Athan. The previous year's winner had become the talk of the city. It was a long shot.

Hector is learning how discipline influences the formation of his character. Wanting to win this race has helped him focus on his energies, but it does not guarantee success.

Trumpets blared, and runners entered the stadium. Anthony looked down from his place in the spectator seating. He was with Jace, Eugene, and Tamir, with a good view of the finish line and the entire running track.

This race was known as the "Under Sixteen's," one of the most popular competitions of the Games. The winner would be entered the following year in Ephesus in the "Under Nineteen's" race. As the young men lined up on the track, Hector looked around the stadium. The sun was shining brightly, and the warm temperature favored the runners. Other races, those for older age groups, would be run later, when the sun's rays penetrated even more.

Gambling men would sweat for different reasons. Their talk centered on speculation about which athlete would compete in the coming years, and they stood to lose money if they made the wrong choice.

Hector's everyday tunic was hung up on the wall at the entranceway to the track area. Now naked, he turned to the racetrack, his jaw clenched. His pursed lips held a secret. *I was trained by a Roman soldier.* Anthony had instructed him how to hold his head when he ran, maneuver the sharp corners at each end of the stadium, and keep his balance. More than that, he had developed his own strategy.

The runners were now lined up at the west end of the stadium. Hector was ready. Last year's race, the one in which Athan had become the hero of Sardis, filled Hector's mind. *I am not going to think about that event. I must concentrate on my strategy.*

He looked left and right, taking in the crowds. Spectators filled the seats all around him and were sitting in the grassy areas above the stadium.

All around him, he heard Latin words of encouragement: *"Citius! Altius! Fortius!* Faster! Higher! Stronger!" These were words continually shouted by spectators as they urged athletes to victory.

Hector intended to outdistance the others by the end of the first lap. He had raced up and down the hill at the back of the Ben Shelah farm so often, and now he was confident of his endurance. His first move was to get out in front quickly.

However, he knew all the others also wanted to win. He was not the only one who longed to be known as a hero, but his special secret gave him extra confidence.

Who else has put himself through such a rigorous training program? To walk beside the mayor of the city as an overcomer, dressed in a new white linen tunic! I am going to be the hero of these Games!

That was his dream. Hector would run along the length of the stadium seven times. That meant a race of three and a half laps around the oval track. He dreamed about it at night. When he woke up, he was still thinking of every move. He saw himself leading from the beginning of the race, outrunning them all, and then keeping ahead of his opponents. At the end of the race, his heart would be pounding with pain at every stride.

The signal that the race was about to start was given. With shouts from spectators, the runners were off. Hector adjusted his pace, running in the middle of the pack. He turned his head, glancing up, hoping to see his father. Shouts from the crowds were deafening, and he could not see his father, but amid the screams, he heard, "Hector, Hector!" but it was impossible to see who had called out.

Halfway along the first stretch, he spurted and ran ahead of three boys. He ducked outward to pass a fourth then swerved inward to avoid another. He would be disqualified if he made someone trip and fall.

Athan was just ahead of him now, and Hector was in second place as they reached the first bend. Negotiating the corner demanded balance and skill. He had practiced breaking to the outside, then swiveling slightly on his foot. Suddenly Athan was beside him. He felt the extra strength he had gained during his year-long training and rejoiced in his strong muscles as he pulled ahead in a sprint. Dashing forward, he was three paces ahead of Athan.

Leading the race, his legs pumping and his arms in the smooth motion that Anthony had taught him, Hector pulled farther ahead. He felt a sense of elation, a sense of victory. He must have gained a little more because voices in the crowd began to chant his name: "Hector! Hector!"

He was ahead of Athan on the second stretch. Determined to be a victor, his legs pumped as fast as he could run. He wanted to—no, he needed to—do his best; he was going to win! The discipline learned from Anthony was paying off, and he did not look back, convinced he would be the hero of Sardis.

I will make Anthony proud of me.

Just thinking about winning gave him more strength. This would make his father come out of the depressing funk that had permeated their home for the last month. If he became the hero of Sardis, it would bring happiness to his house. His father would smile again, and he envisioned his mother bursting into tears of joy.

Athan was six strides behind him as he reached the west end of the stadium for the second turn. He completed the corner while the other runners were just entering it. Glancing at the wide-eyed competitors on the other side of the long divider, Hector formed two fists. He wanted to sprint so the others would never be able to catch up to him at the end of the race.

On the third stretch, he was twenty strides ahead of Athan and one other boy. The other runners were ten paces behind them.

Those fifteen runners have only a faint chance, and the two stragglers behind them have no chance at all. I'm one of twenty, and I'm going to win!

Extending his lead, he was suddenly concerned that his legs might not have the power he needed on the final stretch. Mentally, Hector went over his plan for the race. He sensed Athan behind him as he rounded the third bend. Athan had slightly closed the distance between them, but the crowds were chanting, "Hector! Hector!" Perhaps the hero of the Games the previous year might be outdone by a younger athlete.

As he began the fourth stretch, he felt his left leg lighter than his right one. It had bothered him when he was training on the hills behind the Ben Shelah house, but he always had said, "It is only the uneven ground. It will be all right in the real race."

He quickly glanced down at his leg, but he brought his head up immediately. He did not want to give anything away to the competition.

If anyone saw me flinch or admit pain, they would know I was fearful of not winning.

His father and brother stood as they watched him. For an instant, he saw them waving from where they said they were going to be, above the finish line. They were shouting, putting their hands to their mouths, and waving their arms. Beside his father was his best friend, Tamir, which spurred him to sprint ahead. He gained several more paces over Athan as he approached the middle of the fifth stretch.

The final stretch was to be the most difficult.

Because of this, he wanted to finish the sixth stretch at least ten paces in front. He was determined to keep Athan and the other three runners behind him until the finish line, so he sprinted briefly.

Confident of victory now, he felt his heart pounding. He slowed down, ready to make the turn, beginning the last, the seventh, stretch, and saw the sight he longed for.

There! The finish line!

He was around the sixth corner. He had turned smoothly on his toes and was racing toward the finish line.

Now it's only this last stretch!

He realized he was still in front. However, Athan was no longer ten paces behind. His dreaded opponent had almost caught up on the sixth length. He heard Athan's breathing only a few paces back! The distance was too close for comfort.

Hector knew it was too soon to begin his final sprint. Still, his entire strategy depended upon being able to stay ahead until the end. He sprinted, slightly angry at himself for having to start the final push early. He knew from conversations with Anthony and coaches at the gymnasium that he should not have exerted himself so much on the third and fourth lengths. They had warned him to save that final strength for the last strides when the race would be won or lost.

The race was not won by who was ahead at the end of each lap. The first runner across the finish line won the crown. He felt his arms and legs getting heavy, but he was able to keep the lead. Halfway down the last stretch, his heart soared.

My sprinting early on paid off! My plan worked! I am still in front!

Suddenly, he felt like he had been struck by an evil magic spell.

His arms became heavy. His legs seemed weighty, and he had trouble lifting them. He put his head back to suck in more air and closed his eyes against the pain. Every muscle hurt. The crowds to his right, up the hillside, were on their feet. Some were yelling, "Hector, Hector!"

He closed his eyes to the pain and then opened them immediately. Others were screaming, "Athan, Athan!" He realized that his worst nightmare was happening. He forced himself to lift each leg. He wanted to run at the same speed, but his attempt to sprint changed nothing.

His face was lined with pain as he realized he was losing strength with only thirty-five paces left. Now he was twenty-five paces away from being a victor.

This is what I wanted, what I've trained for since last summer. I ran in the rain and in the sun. I ran in the early morning and late at night.

The sound of a runner behind him—puffing, running, puffing, striding ahead—caught his attention. He refused to turn his head, knowing it had cost him a position or two last year. He kept his eyes on the finish line and gritted his teeth with the pain. Only another twenty paces, and then he could rest. The screaming from the stands, from the theater, and from the hillside was so loud he could not make out what was happening. He forced himself to run smoothly, not to lose his stride. The pain in his right side became intense, and his left leg felt off balance.

Still he ran. Athan was beside him now, and the finish line was rushing toward them.

Athan passed him, charging ahead with a strength Hector did not possess. A different strategy had been part of Athan's race. He had let Hector use his best energy in the first part of the track while he kept the distance between them the same on the second and third long stretches, knowing that he could pass Hector at the end.

It was a daring move, one Athan had used in Pergamum only two weeks earlier. No wonder men all over the province were talking about him. He would run in Ephesus next year, and then Athan would be going to the races in Corinth. Perhaps he might even run in Athens!

Two other boys passed Hector in the final moments. They had shadowed Athan. In the last strides of the race, they claimed second and third positions. After all his efforts, Hector could only claim fourth place.

I put in all that effort for a whole year! I lost the race in the last few seconds! Last year I placed fifth, this year fourth.

He was too old to cry. Only little boys could cry. Hector was too tired to do anything more than fall to his knees with his face to the ground. He looked up and saw Athan at ease, talking with the important men of the city. At that moment, he knew deep in his heart that he could never beat Athan.

After such a totally draining experience, Athan still has energy left to walk around, laugh, and enjoy the victory!

The crowd chanted, "Victory to the Overcomer! Athan is the winner!" They gave credit to the goddess Nike, the goddess who granted speed and victory to the one she chose to become close to her. Her name symbolized victory, and Nike was Athan's goddess.

Hector stood up. His left leg shook a little bit. The pain in his right side was worse. His father, his brother, and all his friends from school were waving.

Slowly, Hector left the running track area and claimed his tunic from the wall. He climbed the steps into the spectator stands to join Jace, Anthony, Eugene, and Tamir. He was grateful for his family and his friends.

He knew that his name would never be among the winners carved in marble above the massive entrance to the stadium. He winced at the thought: Athan's name would be forever read and always commented on. Athan, he was certain, would run in Ephesus, and most probably in Athens. Hector had done his best, and he knew he would have to follow other dreams. Running could never be more than just a pastime for him.

SIMON AND JUDITH'S HOME

The postal courier from Pergamum finally pulled himself away from the stadium. It was just his good luck to have arrived in Sardis in time to watch the races. He rode his horse to the Ben Shelah home, delivered the letter he carried in his saddlebag, and received the payment.

A few minutes later, Miriam ran out of the house to bang on Simon's workshop door. Ravid opened the door, and Miriam burst in.

"Guess what, Uncle Simon!" she called out. "It's a message from

Marcos. The Imperial Court in Egypt agreed fully with the proposed settlement of Great-grandpa Eliab's estate. The first payments are on the way and will be here by the end of the month. We are both going to receive our portion of my great-grandfather's inheritance. Oh, and we will be able to keep paying the people we have hired in the workshops!"

SIMON AND JUDITH'S HOME

"Miriam, I need to talk to you."

"Yes, Uncle Simon."

"My dear niece, we have only enough of your money to last until the end of May—that is, if you and Kalonice don't dream up any more projects. There is only a little left for the wedding in June, but never mind. Lyris has been with us for many years; she is almost part of the family. I will cover all the costs of the wedding. But after that..."

"Do not worry, Uncle Simon. 'On the mountain of the Lord, He will provide.'"

"Miriam, there is a big difference between you and Antipas. He earned money and then spent it. You don't earn anything, and you are spending all of the inheritance from your grandfather's estate."

Chapter 39
Garments of Splendor

SIMON AND JUDITH'S HOME

Preparations for Lyris and Eugene's wedding continued. Anticipation was building, and the wedding garments were ready.

Lyris wore a smile on her face, but her heart almost exploded when she saw what Arpoxa had accomplished. The younger woman had taught embroidery work to many women. Now each tunic had symbols of eagles sewn onto the edges around the neck.

Lyris's excitement grew when Miriam told her, "You should see how the invited families in the insulae are acting. They brag to their neighbors, and the children strut about. I heard one say, 'Our section of the city has been chosen for special treatment.' Of course, that's causing some neighbors to be jealous."

Miriam went to Jace and Kalonice's house to make sure everything was ready. She observed, "Kalonice, your father-in-law needs a wife, and Lyris needs a good husband. The good hand of God brought them together. Tomorrow the conditions are going to be perfect! Look how the colors of this sunset forecast tomorrow's gorgeous weather!"

Kalonice had come to use the name of God as Miriam and Simon did. Like Anthony, she had become a follower of Yeshua Messiah. She commented, "Wagons and carts are going to bring the guests in the late afternoon. I am so excited about each person coming from the insulae. None of them have ever experienced an event like this! God bless them, even if it is just this once!"

Ravid had come to accept the inevitable. He was determined to leave Sardis peacefully, so he chose to be civil. Having decided to not attend any meetings or events, he entered the house. "Please excuse me from the Bridegroom's Dinner this evening. I am not hungry. Oh, and tomorrow evening, I'll leave before the guests arrive. I'll spend the evening at the home of one of my friends, and I'll come back before midnight."

He looked for Lyris, but she was nowhere to be seen. She had gone to her new place in the vineyard with Miriam and Kalonice. Lyris and Eugene would live there after the wedding, and the women were busy getting things ready.

Tonight was the men's night, the Bridegroom's Dinner. Simon and his sons, Heber and Ezar, poured the best wine while servants brought in the meal. The children had already eaten and were curious to hear the men's talk. Elaine and Amath giggled at the top of the stairs but controlled themselves, straining to hear every word.

Only Tamir, now considered to be a "man," could participate with the men.

The men relaxed on the three dining couches, savoring the experience. Simon, Eugene, and Heber reclined on the center couch. To their right were the men of their home: Ezar and Tamir. To the left was Eugene's family: Jace, Isidoros, and Hector.

Anthony had received permission to come to the city late on the next day. He was to return the morning after the wedding.

As the meal progressed, Eugene told stories of his life. Most events recounted parts of his life the others had never heard. Relaxed and talkative, he spoke of his marriage to Jerusha and the birth of their only daughter, Kalonice.

Hector's recent race was a topic of conversation. He had outpaced everyone for almost the whole race. Eugene commented, "It was such a shame that you couldn't stay in the lead during the last fifty paces." Hector grinned, happy to be part of the men's evening.

Thursday was the day of the wedding. Amath jumped, sang, and ran up and down the steps. Elaine marched around the house, humming in Grace's ear. The little girl was teething again and was looking tired and crying with pain. Miriam had dark circles under her eyes and was exhausted from caring for her daughter.

"It must hurt so much to get your teeth," said Elaine softly. She sang songs to comfort her little cousin, but Grace refused to be comforted. Miriam looked for soft food to ease the pain.

Elaine took Saulius and played with him. She could hardly stand the hours passing so slowly. She longed for the wedding banquet to begin.

Wagons formed a line outside Simon's gate on the Royal Road as the sun bent toward the mountain peaks. Three wagons belonged to the Ben Shelah family. The others were rented. Directions were given to the drivers to guide them to the pickup places for the guests.

The wagon drivers could not believe that out of the squalor, dirt, and sleaze of smelly buildings, wedding guests could come dressed in new white linen garments. One by one, they climbed onto their wagons, singing and cheering. They looked as if they came from wealthy families, but their speech linked them to the city's most unfortunate situations.

For many weeks, Arpoxa had brought her memories from Scythia to life. Her love of the Scythian landscape, her city, and her people from north of the Black Sea was evident in the beautiful embroidery on the marriage tunics for the guests. It was an artful Scythian link that brought a Jewish home and a Sardian slum together for a joyous wedding celebration.

One wagon driver looked carefully as two families piled into his wagon. Finely sewn birds soared silently on the collar of each tunic. It was as if an artist was inspiring them to rise far above their present social situations.

"We embroidered these tunics with our own hands!" boasted a woman. Several front teeth were black and diseased. "Thanks to Miriam and Kalonice, we have these new garments. Arpoxa taught me a new skill."

"I have a new tunic too," exclaimed the widow's young daughter. "Mommy got a big tunic, and I got a little one. She says I must not spill food. I must be nice. And I cannot swear at anyone. I must be polite to big people. Oh, so much to remember!"

In another carriage, young Cosmos spoke up. "We all had to get washed really good, so we smell nice. Miriam gave each family perfume from her shop. She said, 'Use it before you get on the wagon.' I love the smell, don't you, Mr. Driver? Do you put perfume on when you go to weddings?"

Cosmos had such a natural way of talking, and he made people laugh. Happy comments continuously poured out of him, and people loved his cheerful, engaging chatter.

Wagons came through the city along the Royal Road, and heads turned, as they always did when people passed by going to a wedding. On this occasion, though, people stopped and stared. Gossip about the wedding guests spread along the Royal Road.

"Are those *poor* people dressed in such *fancy* wedding clothes? You can tell from their speech."

"Who would spend such a large amount on poor people?"

One man lamented, "Such a waste!"

The wagons began to arrive at the Ben Shelah home just as the sun was going down. Fortunately, it was a beautiful evening as guests were to wait outside the gate until everyone arrived. They were instructed to enter only after Eugene and his family members had gotten settled.

The din of excited voices grew as the wagons continued to drop off guests at the entrance to the Ben Shelah residence.

For months Ravid's patience had been stretched to the limit. And now uncircumcised Gentiles had come for an important event, not only at the family table, like last night, but now for a wedding.

Similar gatherings over the last months had confirmed his decision to leave Sardis and return to his father's home in Smyrna.

While the wagons were picking up the guests, he talked with Nissa. "A year ago, I made my objections known for Passover. Your father had made up his mind to walk away from the Law. I prayed, hoping for a sign from on high. If there was another violation after Passover, that would force me to leave."

"No, my dear! Please!"

"Yes, more than a month has gone by, and in this event, I have found my answer! Tonight my father-in-law is drifting even further away from the covenant. He has invited ninety-nine guests.

"Not only are these the uncircumcised but these low-brows are from the dregs of society. My love, I am leaving this family. I want you to return with me to my father's home in Smyrna."

"I don't want to leave here. Oh!" Nissa sat down on the bed. She bent down and buried her face in the pillow, not bothering to wipe away the tears.

"When I arrive, I will tell my father that he was right to be strict in the observance of the Law and follow the elders' tradition. I will become like him."

Ravid had delayed his exit from the property until it was almost dusk, determined to have nothing to do with the wedding festivities. Eugene and Lyris would be united in marriage, but he could not bless such a union. He wanted nothing more to do with Simon, his father-in-law.

He closed the door of his home, frustrated that Nissa had not agreed with him about guests coming to the house. He told his wife that he would avoid the wedding, but she would probably not notice his absence because she had to be busy with the arrangements.

Ravid walked past the large tent set up beside the creek on the eastern side of the property. Carpets were spread on the ground. A blue wedding canopy had been placed in the middle, where Eugene, a Gentile widower, and Lyris, a Jewish widow, would be blessed by the King of the Universe.

He made his way to the front gate and was surprised that the wedding guests had already gathered outside. He paused since he would have to walk through the noisy crowd. The people were waiting to come in together.

Ravid opened the gate, and the throng cheered. They thought he was opening the gate for the grand entrance to the wedding celebration. He looked at the crowd.

Instead of the filthy clothing the poor usually wore, he saw the same lovely soft linen that he and Nissa had worn when they were married. What a change the new raiment made! He could hardly believe it. Embroidery on the collars, carefully sewn, showed blue eagles soaring into an imaginary sky. A faint perfume came to him.

Someone has gone to great lengths to transform them, to make them presentable with a beautiful garment. Is this another surprise that Miriam, Kalonice, and the family have been up to?

As he looked around at the crowd, he noticed a man whose collar was not embroidered—a strong young man. He looked again.

All the other guests had two eagles soaring upward, each one with their wings stretched out, gliding on the wind's unseen power.

What's this? Everyone is wearing an identical garment. All have the same two eagles soaring into the sky, but this man hasn't got the right apparel! He is taller than most and certainly better fed. His arms are thick. And look at that...a slight paunch. He looked at me just now, and then he looked away. Why did he turn his back?

Intrigued by the possibility of an imposter among humble

people, Ravid made an instant decision. *That looks suspicious! I'm going to stay. If there is an imposter here, I'll find out.*

Heber arrived at the gate. "Hello, everyone! In just a few minutes, we will be opening the gate. Has everyone arrived?"

"We're all here!" said Cosmos in his high, loud voice. "Where is your white tunic? Why are you wearing yellow?"

People laughed at the spontaneous comment from a young boy.

Ravid looked closer. Some families were standing together, the little ones hanging onto the bottom of their mothers' tunics. This family, standing close to him, had six children. Cosmos reached out to shake Ravid's hand. Ravid moved away so that he would not have to touch a little boy from the insulae.

He looked for the man who had the right wedding gown but lacked the delicate embroidered eagles. He had moved to the back, behind the others, and no longer seemed to be taller. He blended in with them, apparently hiding. His black hair was the same color as that of the other guests.

Ravid entered the property again and closed the gate, determined to solve the mystery outside.

That man's intense eyes... What did that strange expression on his face mean?

Diotrephes stood at the back of the crowd. He was thankful that he had avoided the stare of the stranger who had just appeared at the gate. During the previous minutes, he had been able to learn the names of several people. He was stunned and chagrined to learn that he was amid a crowd of destitute people. Their speech gave them away. He looked around and could not see the wealthy people that Cleon had promised would attend.

One man was blind and was being led by another, a cripple. Several were maimed, apparently because they had suffered accidents on the construction sites of the public buildings. He said to the crippled man, "Here, let me slip in here and help this blind man."

Focusing on the purpose of his being at the party, he grimaced at having to put up with the "scum of the earth," as he called these people. He could hardly wait for the right moment. *I will sneak into the Ben Shelah house.*

In just a few minutes, he would hold his cousin, little Chrysa-Naq, for the first time. Zeus would provide him access to the house and help him get out of the home with the baby girl. Uncle Zoticos would soon have his daughter, and then Chrysa would be appropriately brought up in Pergamum.

Ravid walked back into the property. He found a place beside a corner of the tent. From his vantage point, he would observe everyone coming up the walkway after Heber opened the gate. He could also see anyone going into the house. He stood in this dark corner where he would be out of sight of the unknown stranger.

Who is this man, and what does he want? Why is he here? Oh! Perhaps he came to steal jewelry from the workshop.

Heber opened the gate, and people entered quickly.

"Welcome to the wedding supper, everyone!" called Simon above the noise. The men in the Ben Shelah family were all wearing yellow, and his face was glowing. Children ran up the path to the tent, their mothers calling, "Slowly, children!"

Eugene stood beside the wedding tent, unsure how he should conduct himself at the home of a wealthy Jewish family and with so many poor people present.

It took Simon a while to get all the people seated on carpets. Lyris walked out of the house, turning to the left toward the little creek. She walked gracefully, dressed in an elegant white wedding tunic made of linen. It matched those of all the guests, but the bodice was sewn with fine brown and black threads. Instead of eagles flying upward, toward each other, her eagles flew together toward the right side. Serving in the kitchen, she had soared to the heights of love. Lyris had found her new husband, Eugene, as they prepared and served together. Arpoxa's artful embroidery illustrated this.

Behind her walked the Ben Shelah women, all wearing matching light-yellow dresses. Judith held pink oleander flowers bound together in a large bunch. Elaine and Amath followed.

Nissa walked behind them. She saw Ravid and smiled, waving to him. She felt elated, believing Ravid had decided to stay for the wedding after all. He had adamantly stated he would not eat a meal with so many uncircumcised non-Jews. Was he beginning to change? Was he about to become more patient with her father?

Miriam ran down the steps and out of the house just in time to see Lyris and Eugene step under the marriage canopy. She had finally been able to get Grace to sleep. The child had cried for hours but now was sleeping. At last she could concentrate on the wedding. She hoped Grace would sleep all night. She looked so sweet when she was laid in her little crib.

The wedding was carried out with the words of Scripture, the ageless commitment to the covenant. The couple walked around the blue canopy and then stood under it to make their commitment to each other. They broke a cup, and Simon, the family's patriarch, led the service, using the words repeated from generation to generation. He had to explain each part of the service to the guests. A Sardian judge had already conducted the civil ceremony earlier in the day, and people cheered when Eugene held up their wedding certificate.

Ravid kept his eyes on the stranger as the wedding continued. He sat quietly where the candlelight was dim, waiting and watching. Eugene and Lyris were standing under the wedding canopy as Simon spoke. Ravid kept thinking, *Why is that man here? Who is he?*

Diotrephes leaned over to a neighbor and whispered a question. Then the man walked over to Ezar, who pointed toward the house. The man went back, sat down on the carpet, leaned over, and looked at the home. Diotrephes got up slowly and walked toward the house as though he were going to use the latrine. Night had fallen, and torches were lit along the path toward the house.

A servant occasionally poured oil on the torches to keep them burning. The fresh oil prevented the rags from being consumed. Diotrephes entered the house, and Ravid watched him go in. When he had not come out after a reasonable amount of time, Ravid moved towards the door. *Just as I thought! The man is a thief! He's come to steal something!*

Ravid entered the house, but the lamp that lit the way into the toilet was missing. The stranger must have taken it as he scouted the house. He searched the lower part of the house quickly and noiselessly. The only noises he heard were coming from the kitchen, where servants were finishing the supper preparations.

He looked up and saw a lamp flicker through the stairwell. It came from a light in Elaine's room.

He's gone upstairs while everyone is at the wedding!

Ravid moved up the stairs quietly. While on the stairs, he would remain in the dark. He watched the intruder enter the second bedroom and waited for the robber to come back down the stairs with something in his hands. However, the dim light of the lamp lit the way to the next bedroom. The stranger was entering one room after another, looking for something. He stood for a long moment in the doorway of each room and then moved to the next room.

Ravid was on the verge of confronting the man and yelling at him when the stranger entered Anthony and Miriam's room. A strange sound came from his throat, and then, in a soft whisper, he said, "I've found you, my baby!"

Ravid, standing at the head of the stairs, close by, heard the strange words and wondered what it was all about. Suddenly he realized the man's search was not concentrated on gold, rings, ornaments, or bottles of perfume.

He's after Miriam's baby!

He crept along the hall to where the stranger had pushed open the door. The burglar's right hand held the lamp. Ravid, using all his strength, grabbed the man's left arm and swung it backward until it was behind the man's back. He pushed upward with all his might. The action was completed in a second because Ravid had the advantage of the surprise attack.

"Who are you, and what do you want?" Ravid snarled in a low voice. "How dare you sneak into our property!"

Diotrephes almost dropped the lamp. The pain of his arm pinned behind him and Ravid's chest pushed against his shoulders caused intense agony, but he recovered instantly, as he had done so often during many arguments won over the years.

"I am a friend of the family. I was invited to the wedding. I have known Anthony and Miriam for a long time. I'm from Pergamum. That's where I knew them."

Temporarily taken aback by the stranger's self-confidence but still holding the arm in a wrenching position, Ravid asked, "Then why are you sneaking around in our house?"

"I am making sure their little girl is sleeping well. See, there she is!"

"You came to kidnap the little girl, didn't you?" Ravid pressed upward as hard as he could. Diotrephes suppressed a yell. "I watched you at the gate. All the people who came in are poor. All have a special gift, a tunic made of fine linen cloth. Your tunic is different. You don't have the same embroidery that's on the others."

"I told you that I am a longstanding friend of the family."

"Why did I never hear about you? How did you get the tunic?"

"It came from their shop."

"How did you get it?"

"I bought it from Cleon."

"Cleon was a thief! Just as you are! Where did you first get to know Anthony and Miriam?"

"I knew them in Pergamum. We were friends there."

"But you never showed up to talk to them here?" Ravid suddenly understood who the stranger was. "Say, aren't you the man who took over the group called the God-fearers and made sure that my family was expelled? Now I remember you!"

As he said this, Ravid pushed the helpless man's arm up toward the back of his neck. The pain was now unbearable.

Diotrephes thought of dropping the lamp and fighting off the unknown man who had caught him kidnapping Grace, but he knew that the noise would attract the attention of the wedding party. He would be in an impossible situation if he had to face Miriam and her family.

Ravid had enough of this encounter. He pulled Diotrephes backward, turned him around, and marched the intruder down the stairs one step at a time. He made sure that each step downward was accompanied by a sharp pull upward, inflicting the maximum pain.

"Go toward the front door! I am going to report you as a thief!"

Diotrephes felt the strength of his position. "I have not taken anything from this house. What have I done wrong? Besides, I am friends with Mayor Tymon Tmolus. You can accuse me of nothing."

"I should have broken your arm instead of being so merciful!" Ravid was angry with himself. He could not prove anything against the young, confident, quick-talking man. It was his word against that of Diotrephes.

They walked onto the front courtyard, and Ravid forced the stranger to walk to the front gate. He demanded that the intruder place the lamp onto the ground and had Diotrephes open the gate with his free hand.

Ravid heaved Diotrephes into the night, pushing with all his might into the darkness of the evening. He heard a dull snap in the man's left side. Diotrephes screamed through clenched teeth at the pain of a dislocated shoulder. He tried to conceal his wailing by covering his mouth.

Walking back to the tent, Ravid heard singing and dancing. These spoke of much joy. Once again, he took up his place at the dark corner and saw people enjoying an evening like they had never experienced before. He saw Miriam talking to her husband.

While I was in the house, Anthony must have returned from the training camp, perhaps while I was upstairs. Anthony can only be home for an evening and must be returning early in the morning.

Miriam turned to her guests and talked to the crowd. "In a few minutes, we are going to have the most wonderful meal. Our servants have been preparing it all day. But first, I want to sing a song. In this city, there is a common saying. Do you know what it is?"

A man shouted out, "Never enough gold!" Miriam nodded.

Several others echoed, "Never enough gold!" For all of them, gold was only a dream, an impossible vision, something others boasted about. None of these guests would ever become wealthy.

"I heard that phrase many times, so I took a little children's song from the marketplace and wrote some words to fit the tune. After each verse of my song, tell me who I am singing about. Here's a hint: All the people in this song are real people who live in Sardis." She grinned, "Maybe even some of you!"

Miriam looked around. These guests, gathered for the wedding party, were her friends. A year ago, she did not know any of them by sight or by name. Now she and Kalonice were working with them. Some of the women had embroidered these wedding tunics, learning how to do fine craftsmanship.

"My song is called 'Never Enough!' Now, everyone, stay seated and listen to the words."

The Ben Shelah children took their places with instruments. Elaine played the lyre. Tamir had trained well and could carry the melody on the flute. Amath accompanied with cymbals, coming in just before the fourth and sixth lines of each verse.

Hair done up in braids, locks with fancy curls,
Eyes enhanced with black, necklace hung with pearls,
Reddened lips in smiles, tunics swirl in twirls.
Olive skin is glowing. Their perfume's stored in glass.
Greek gods dance on pots, smiles reflect in brass.
"Never enough! Please add to my supply."

"That's about all the rich women on South Hill!" yelled one woman excitedly. The rest took up the cheers. Miriam had described the ladies that lived there!

Animals and birds, decorated rocks,
High ornate stairs carved from marble blocks.
Peacocks, camels, sheep—count my wealthy flocks.
A treasury of gold brought him variety!
Words inscribed in stone hide his jealousy.
"Still not enough! I can't imagine why."

"I know who that is," yelled nine-year-old Cosmos. "I saw my Daddy with a rich man who had those kinds of things. He wanted inscriptions for a pedestal. Daddy used to do that work."

People laughed, trying to imagine a wealthy man's estate.

Nissa looked around and saw Ravid standing where he had been. She had become worried when he had been absent during Simon's talk. He had spoken for a long while about the real meaning of a wedding. Her husband had been gone for such a long time she was about to go after him, but he was back again. Miriam continued:

Faces carved in stone; work is ceaseless toil.
Working extremely late, lamps run out of oil.
Plowing fields, sowing seed, caring for the soil.
Hauling wood, lighting fires, shaping dough for bread.
Loaves are ready now. Try to get ahead!
We earn a copper coin, but only if folks buy.

Again, people shouted. One man called, "That's me! I'm a baker!" A woman commented, "No, it's about all of us. We work hard at many jobs but never get paid enough!" They were proud to be recognized in Miriam's song for their hard work.

Auxiliary soldiers bringing food from farms.
Trumpet blasts are heard, calling men to arms.
Danger straight ahead, the leader sounds alarms.
"Grab the breastplate, javelin, helmet, and the shield!
Though foes outnumber us, we will never yield!
One more victory! Honors multiplied!"

The crowd was quieter. Everyone had heard that Miriam's husband was a soldier. And they knew that he trained men for the battle against Dacia. He was here with them, the first time most of them had seen him, although two families had seen him bring them food when he came with Miriam. Anthony was the legionary people talked about, the one who discovered the robbers!

One little boy, Cosmos, yelled, "It's about your husband!" This little boy called out often and usually had the right answer—no one needed to say more.

Matted hair, empty plates, only crusty bread,
Broken pots, baby's cries. Help! Our sister's dead!
A father's pride: six children in one bed.
Loud, constant crying from the hungry little one.
A boy asks, "Dad, will we ever have some fun?"
When is it enough? How often shall we cry?

The group sat in momentary silence, for Miriam had captured their lives in the words of a song. She had come to their homes, and she knew their pain of hunger, even if she had enough food for herself. She was not alarmed when talking with poor people, and she cared that energetic little boys like Cosmos longed for fun just as other boys did.

Cosmos called out loudly, "We're having fun tonight, aren't we, Mommy?" Hearing him, people laughed until tears poured down their cheeks.

Judith also had tears, not because of Cosmos but because the simple gesture of giving people a tunic and inviting them to a party brought her and others such joy.

Enjoy clean clothes, turn over a new page.
Lives can be changed, no matter what their age.
Leave lust aside and put away that rage.
Cast off envy, deceit, and dishonesty.
Do not tell that lie. Cast off idolatry.
This is enough: live and love with dignity.

A hush came over the party. Miriam had not only come into their homes, but she had also entered their lives. Their friend knew how quickly gossip spread from one home to another and how easily chin-wagging damaged reputations and relationships.

Live a new life; Yeshua is your friend.
Find time for love, forgiving without end.
Speak kindly words; find others to befriend.
Gentle thoughts help us bear with one another.
Share compassion; treat others as your brother.
'That's enough!" Selfless love will satisfy.

Cosmos immediately called out, "Mommy, can we all sing that song? Let's all sing it together!"

They sang the song again and then a third time. Then the meal was served. Servants went back and forth between the kitchen and the large tent. Laughter and light-hearted comments flowed with the wine.

People asked Miriam to sing more songs, and music filled the night air. The party lasted for hours, but reluctantly, it had to come to an end. Grudgingly, people piled back onto the wagons, and all the guests headed home.

Cosmos was on the last wagon to leave the Ben Shelah home. He sat between his mother and his father. For months, his father's broken leg had kept him home, but now he was working in Miriam's workshop.

He said in a loud voice, "Mommy, that lady whose feet are twisted worse than Daddy's foot...she helped us make these fancy clothes, didn't she? She's hurt bad, but she knows how to make poor people like us look nice."

"Yes, Cosmos, Arpoxa embroiders and weaves. She understands beauty. She cannot walk, but she's teaching many of us how to make beautiful clothing."

They rode along the Royal Road, now passing the gymnasium on their left and shortly afterward, the stadium to the right. Cosmos looked up at the band of stars across the sky.

"Mommy, you said that when people die, they become stars, isn't that right?"

"Yes, that's what I said."

"Is one of those stars my little sister who died last winter?"

"I think so."

"Do you think she is looking down and seeing us?"

"Yes, she probably is."

"Will she be singing as nicely as Miriam?"

The woman pulled her bright-eyed son close to her bosom. Such moments with her children were so precious. "I am sure of it, my child. After Miriam came, our roof was fixed, and we have enough food. Your father started to work. Your daddy and I learned how to weave."

Cosmos bounced on the seat, leaned toward his father, and said, "Daddy, I had a lot of fun tonight. I think Miriam loves our family."

"Why do you think that, Cosmos?"

"Because she sang about us. She told everyone about our family. She said we were six children in a bed, and the little one was now dead. She told everyone about our crusty bread. She sang about us to all those people."

The parents exchanged glances, their fingertips touching in the darkness. The tragic loss of a daughter merged with the joy of a nine-year-old discovering how unexpected love had enriched their lives.

Cosmos looked up at the sky again. "When I grow up, I want to be like Miriam."

He wanted to say a lot more, but he was tired. In a few minutes, Cosmos stumbled up the dirty steps to the tiny apartment, holding his sister's hand to keep her from falling, and he was soon asleep.

Innocent observations wove in and out of conversations like the warp and weft of a weaver's loom. Precious love had brought them beautiful linen tunics, and the family had been guests at a delightful wedding supper.

Chapter 40
The Aftermath

SIMON AND JUDITH'S HOME

Ravid woke up first, having lost most of the night tossing from one side to the other. He was sleeping on one of the three couches in the big room. Nissa was on another one because the couple had given their place to Eugene and Lyris for the night.

Nissa woke up. "Come on. Sleep a little bit more," she said lightheartedly.

"No!"

"What's bothering you?"

"You know what I'm upset about!" Ravid answered in a loud voice.

"No, I don't! Why are you in such a bad mood this morning? Didn't you enjoy the wedding last night?"

They argued for several minutes, their voices gradually increasing in volume and waking the other members of the family as they wondered what was happening so early downstairs.

Judith took command of the situation as she descended the stairs. She tried to humor her irritable son-in-law. "What a wonderful wedding!" she said. "Shall we all be cheerful today?"

Eugene and Lyris came in, smiles covering their faces and his arm around her waist.

For breakfast, warm milk filled their cups, and white goat cheese was spread over hot flatbread. Ravid pushed his mug aside, and his voice had an icy edge. He was going to teach these imprudent relatives how wrong it was to let strangers into their house.

"I suppose you know the dangers of inviting the uncircumcised into your home." He looked around, waiting for a reaction.

Miriam knew of his disapproval toward her plans and his objection to the wedding, so she kept quiet. No one wanted a quarrel. Last night had been such a remarkable event.

"What did you think of the stranger who came here last night?"

asked Ravid. This second strange comment let them know he was aware of something important about which they were ignorant.

"What stranger? Who are you talking about?" answered Simon, slightly alarmed.

"I am talking about the man without the right wedding gown, the man who tried to steal your daughter," said Ravid, looking directly at Miriam and Anthony. He knew Miriam was the one behind the idea of the wedding party.

"What are you talking about? Who tried to take my baby?"

"None of you noticed, did you? See, you trust people too easily. You think you are doing good and helping people. You invited the blind man, many lame people, and poor families. But who else came last evening?"

"Who?" Miriam slowly put down her flatbread and her cup.

"A man came last evening, and I spotted him right away. I was going to walk around the streets until your guests left. At the gate, I noticed a man who did not have eagles embroidered on his collar. I thought he was an imposter, so I stayed to watch him. He was clever and fit in, helping the blind man. To avoid my gaze, he kept his head down and pretended he was bending over to help. Did anyone else notice him?"

He waited for an answer, but everyone was speechless.

"When he came into the house, I followed him. He looked around the downstairs and then went upstairs. I followed, watching what he was doing. He went from one room to another. When he came to your room, Miriam, he made a soft, satisfied noise. He had found something. Until that moment, I thought he was here for gold or something that could easily be sold for money."

The effect of his story was just what Ravid wanted. Anthony could not say a word. He looked as if someone had just slapped him on his face.

"I came behind him and twisted his arm behind his back. Surprise was on my side, so I had that man in a solid grip. He wanted your baby. The stranger was going to take her."

"How can you be sure?"

"He said, 'I came to see my cousin.'"

Everyone started to speak at once. Simon put his hands up, palms facing outward. "Let's listen to each other—one at a time!"

Miriam started. "I'm certain I know who it was." She described the stranger, and Ravid nodded. She said, "So Diotrephes came to our house. But why would he want to take Grace?"

Judith remembered news of a stolen tunic. "I think Diotrephes planned this months ago."

Ravid added, "He said he bought a wedding garment from our shop."

Heber gave his opinion. "The tunic taken by Cleon! That salesman is a thief. I'm glad Zebadiah confronted him."

Ravid's face was becoming flushed. The whole conversation was moving away from the announcement that he was bursting to voice, and his words came out quickly. "For the past year, Anthony, Ateas, and Arpoxa have been here with their children. This family, Father Simon, continually moves further away from the covenant given to our fathers, away from the tradition of the elders. Non-Jews are living in your house. All these people were supposed to be guests for only three days, and a whole year has passed....

"Listen! When you asked your Jewish friends to come for the birthday of Chrysa Grace, only a few came. But last evening you invited ninety-nine non-Jews, and one hundred came. So, tell me, who are your true friends? Father Simon, I respect you as a son-in-law should, but your friendship with Gentiles and the wedding last night—all of that is a disgrace!"

No one gave an answer.

Miriam shut her eyes and a shiver shook her shoulders.

Ravid continued, "Simon, for almost twelve months, I have asked you to lead as the head of this house, to ensure that everyone here keeps the Law as it was intended to be followed. However, the Law continues to be broken.

"Someone needs to leave, either these aliens or those who intend to fulfill the requirements of the Law." He stopped, and now it was not just Miriam whose heart was beating wildly. Everyone felt anxiety filling the room.

"I will be leaving the Ben Shelah family circle on Monday. This place is no longer my home. I will not be forced into fellowship with these people."

He got up, turned his back on them, and walked out of the house. Suddenly he was not sure how to pack up his belongings. His home was being used by Eugene and Lyris. Changing his mind, he walked to the stable and saddled a horse. He would return later to prepare for the move. He needed more than just today to get ready.

In the main room, the family sat in complete silence, stunned that the recent joy of a harmonious wedding could end with an abrupt reaction. Anthony had his arm around Miriam's shoulder, comforting her, but then she went to their room to wake up Grace.

Nissa had not moved. Instead of reclining, she lay prostrated on the couch. Tears poured out, and in her heart, words tumbled around that no one could hear.

I love you so much! Ravid, you have such strong opinions. You have always been observant. If you hadn't noticed that man last night, we would be crying now because Grace would have been abducted. You saved us from a huge disaster. But, Lord, what about me? I face shame every day. And only I feel the shame. When will I have a child? And now he will take me from my family!

THE WESTERN AGORA, MARKETPLACE IN SARDIS

Diotrephes knew the news of his botched plan would be circulating in the Ben Shelah home. The grim look on his face showed he urgently needed to confront Jace about their ongoing feud and force a resolution.

"I must take you to a noon meal again," he said, trying to keep the stabbing pain from showing on his face. He had no idea who the man was who had injured his shoulder. Pain pierced every muscle down the small of his back and around to his collarbone.

"What happened to you?" Jace asked, looking at the sling supporting Diotrephes's arm.

"Nothing much. Just a little accident last night. I fell down in the dark."

The marketplace throbbed with life. In the early summer weather, merchants were unloading camels. Some animals stood drinking from the magnificent nymphaeum, a water fountain. The ornately built fountain provided water for households and animals. Part of the space was occupied by women gossiping as they filled water jugs for their homes.

The enormous monument was two stories high. Water flowed down a white marble face and splashed down over five sculptures of the water nymphs. A tired merchant's caravan of almost forty camels drank from the large pool at the base of the fountain, seemingly unable to quench their thirst. Many more camels awaited their turn.

"That's the camel train of the famous merchant, Flavius Zeuxis," said Diotrephes, trying to start a conversation. "He lives in Hierapolis and has made many trips to Rome. I hear this is his second trip this year. He is one of the richest men in Asia, and his family comes from a famous family who ruled here three hundred years ago. He came from Persia and learned the Lydian language."[62]

He had found a way to make his point, that people do learn languages not their own.

"No wonder he's famous! Has anyone ever made that many trips to Rome?"

"None. This merchant has contributed to many public buildings in Hierapolis, so his name will be forever remembered. His daughter, Maximillia, is one of the most beautiful young women in that city."

"Why are you telling me this?"

"Would you like to be rich and famous like Flavius Zeuxis?"

"There must be a reason why you ask. You have never talked about my becoming rich and famous before. Instead, you've threatened me."

"Believe me, I want an agreement so we can work together. I need your cooperation."

"Diotrephes, something tells me you are in real pain. Exactly how did this happen?"

Diotrephes put his right hand under his left elbow, trying to stop the aching in his shoulder. He did not want to reveal any details to Jace.

Jace didn't see me when he came to the wedding with his family because he and his two sons were the last ones who came in. Therefore, Jace doesn't know I was there. That's fortunate! But that unknown man destroyed my plan, and he tried to break my arm! Who was he? Was he the man who helps Simon Ben Shelah make gold jewelry?

"I tripped in the dark coming back from the gymnasium to the house where I stay. It's nothing, only a sprained shoulder. I'll be careful not to fall in the dark again."

Jace continued. "So it's only a sprained shoulder? All right then.

---

[62] Titus Flavius Zeuxis was a famous merchant in Hierapolis. He went to Rome, Italia, seventy-two times and was well-known for his exploits. Inscriptions from his tomb are found in the Museum of Hierapolis.

I've wanted to talk about your demands for my teaching. I've given it a lot of thought, even talking it over with members of my family. Let me be blunt. I cannot fit into your program. And I will not. I do not believe in what you want me to do.

"Last night a lot of things became clear to me. A wedding took place between two old people, and Miriam sang a song. In no time, she had the whole party participating. She cares about other people. I watched everyone sing, old and young, rich and poor, and then something hit me. I realized that I often put my own wants and needs before those of others. Kalonice has been telling me that for years, but I ignored it.

"I've watched a change take place in my wife. She believes in God now. She says he is close to us, not far away, and I believe her. You see, Zeus is a distant god. He cannot feel our pains. But the Lord understands us, and that changes us. It makes us want to be sensitive to the needs of others. Miriam and Kalonice care for others because they see how God cares for each one of us."

Diotrephes wanted to slap Jace. *How can Jace speak like this against Zeus? My name— "Nourished by Zeus." This man has wholly rejected my beliefs. Jace has fallen for the ignorant teaching taught by women! He'll be bringing these ideas into his schooling at the gymnasium! And I will not permit that. I cannot trust him.*

"Jace, instead of spending time on these new ideas, let me ask you something. Don't you want to be rich? Wouldn't you like to be famous? Think of your name being written on an important sarcophagus one day. You, like Zeuxis, could be buried in a small funerary temple. Think of how proud your family would be!"

Jace countered, "No, I'm not interested in having my name written on stone. I've watched Kalonice. The best way for people to remember someone is to recall their character while they're alive. 'Living honestly, putting away jealous feelings'—Miriam sang about many things last night, and my heart was stirred in a new way."

Jace noticed that Diotrephes listened carefully, so he told his superior about the party at Simon's house. "Let me tell you what happened. My father-in-law was married last night. There was so much joy and laughter at this wedding! The widow is Lyris and her employer is wealthy, but he invited many poor people. Folks came from every background you can imagine. I left with a song in my heart. Suddenly, it made sense to me, what those people mean when they talk about 'the covenant.' God wants us to be part of something so much bigger than our own little lives.

"So, Diotrephes, here's what I believe. Learning Lydian is fine if it is to better understand the past. However, I will not cooperate in attempts to revive an ancient language to be spoken every day. I intend to continue with the courses I've been teaching for a long time."

Jace examined the face across the table. Diotrephes had never talked about his family circles, not once. He had only talked about his mother and an uncle and mentioned his age when it was his birthday. "May I ask you a few personal questions, not about your program for classes but about your family?"

Diotrephes bent forward and rested his elbow on the palm of his right hand. "A few—that's all."

"How many people are there in your family?"

"I told you about my mother, the high priestess of Zeus, and her brother, my Uncle Zoticos, the Chief Librarian of the Library of Pergamum."

Of course, there is my cousin too, my uncle's daughter, but I won't tell you about Chrysa.

"Three persons: you, your mother, and your uncle. And you are a family with ancient roots, descended from a family in the time of King Gyges."

Diotrephes nodded. *Yes, Jace, you know about my ancestry!*

Jace said, "Your mother will probably not give birth to another child. Your uncle, you told me once, is forty years old, and you are not married, right?"

"What is your point?" Diotrephes did not like questions that dug into the details of his life.

Jace pushed on. "Look at the families in the insulae. They have many children. At the same time, your 'noble family name' is dying out. Your family is like the Lydian language. You don't have children, so perhaps teaching the Lydian language is like a family legacy you want to leave to pass on to others."

Diotrephes's face turned red, and his breath came in little spurts. "Jace, I will not tolerate you trying to worm your way into my personal family life!"

I cannot let this man work in the gymnasium any longer. I do not trust him! He is a threat to everything I stand for.

He let his breath out slowly. "You are going to be looking for a new job. Let me be clear. The last day for you to receive a wage is June 15."

Jace's complexion turned a creamy color, a lighter tone than his usual olive skin. "Are you firing me?"

"Yes. You refuse to accept the new program agreed to by everyone else in our department."

"This makes no sense! I will request a meeting with the administration."

Diotrephes's patience had run dry. The pain in his shoulder took his strength away from any further desire to argue. "The administration will not listen to you, Jace, after they learn that you are being influenced by the teaching of Antipas, who spoke of a crucified Messiah. Antipas, Simon's brother, was eliminated for disrupting the city of Pergamum. His beliefs are dangerous to society. Your contribution to the teaching program is over."

He glared at Jace. Without thinking it through, he added, "And you showed disloyalty by not demanding that a gathering must be opened with 'Caesar is lord and god.'" Unable to control himself, Diotrephes burst out, "You, as a teacher, are always to acknowledge the authority of our emperor at a—!"

The words were no sooner out of his mouth than Diotrephes wanted to take them back. *I promised myself to be more self-controlled at this meal. Self-control is the one characteristic that I most lack at crucial moments in my life!*

For a long moment, neither man spoke. Then Jace leaned forward and asked again, "How would you know what I say or don't say on my own time?"

Jace's mind raced as he attempted to put all the things Diotrephes had said into a coherent storyline. Did the light in Diotrephes's eyes suggest that perhaps the man was talking about what happened last night?

"Are you talking about what was said or not said at the wedding last evening? No, you could not have been there. You certainly could not sneak in. Only those with a special wedding tunic were there."

Once warm and inviting, the meal was now almost cold. Jace no longer felt like eating. The fingers on his hands had gone numb, and his legs were shaking.

I've been teaching for years, and now, in less than two weeks, I will be without a job. What am I going to do? How will I support my family?

The food remained unfinished. The waiter did not know if he should clean the table or not as the two customers sat silently looking at each other but not eating. After a while, Diotrephes got up slowly, awkwardly pulling money out to pay for the meal.

They left the thermopolium in different directions. The two men would never speak cordially again.

Jace knew that his words had cut deep into Diotrephes. Something he had said had wounded the young man from Pergamum who was so full of himself, but he was not sure what had offended Diotrephes.

Although his home was close to the gymnasium, Jace stopped along the Royal Road several times, delaying his arrival. He did not go to the hot baths as was his custom.

He planned what he would say to Kalonice. The words were on the tip of his tongue. *He got angry and fired me after I asked about his family. He wants me to teach the Lydian language but got upset when I belittled the idea that it could be used in daily life. I don't understand what caused such a reaction, but he fired me!*

Kalonice met him at their door. "You're home early! Oh, I can tell something happened. What is it? A problem with some of your students?"

"I was fired from my position. I'm without a job."

"What? You're fired?"

"Yes, after another conversation over a meal."

Jace explained his attempts to make peace with Diotrephes. "I never imagined things had gotten this bad! I told you about him before and you got upset, so I decided not to tell you anymore. Two months ago, he demanded, 'You will have no more to do with the Ben Shelah household.'

"I thought that by accepting his commands, I could keep my job, but it became clear that I could not destroy our family's relations just to make him happy. Today I plainly told him that I would not agree to his demands. I can teach Lydian but not to revive it in as a spoken language. Then I asked him a question about his family. He became very agitated and fired me."

Kalonice could not find the right words to console him.

His eyes took on a faraway expression. "Diotrephes made a

strange statement: 'And you didn't even demand that a gathering must be opened with "Caesar is lord and god."' My dear, I think Diotrephes knows about what happened at the wedding party."

"How could he know? He wasn't there."

"No, but I'm sure that one of the guests is feeding him information. Did someone in our midst come there to infiltrate us? Did Cleon have others spying on the Ben Shelah family? Has someone come to learn how to get into Simon's workshop, perhaps to take his gold?"

"Well, if there is, we should tell Simon right away! Let's go to their house. They have to know about this."

Jace splashed cold water onto his face and felt slightly refreshed. "I'm ready. Let's go."

At Simon and Judith's house, they found the whole family shocked and dismayed. They were met at the door by a servant and entered. Nissa was crying in the great room.

Simon and Judith sat on either side of her, holding their daughter. "I don't want to leave Sardis! Mother, I don't want to go to Smyrna! Ravid is leaving next week!"

Jace looked around the room. Grace, utterly unaware of what was going on, was walking from one adult to another with faltering steps. Anthony had left and was away, training the next group of recruits. Arpoxa was not there so that meant she was taking care of her little boy upstairs.

Simon was stroking his daughter's hand. "Nissa, my dear child, when you married Ravid, we all knew he was a strict man, guided by high principles. You loved his sense of beauty and his strength. His arms are strong, and his fingers are skilled. He is a wonderful jeweler and a good provider for you."

Jace and Kalonice turned to leave because it did not seem to be the time for a visit, but Judith beckoned them in. She explained, "At breakfast, Ravid said he will no longer stay with us. You know that he does not accept Gentiles. He does not even want them at a meal. He's distraught, and he's returning to his father's house."

Kalonice could not contain her news any longer. "We're here to tell you that Jace was fired! In two weeks, he will not have a job! Tell them what happened, Jace."

Judith and Simon expressed their surprise and dismay. "Oh, we are so sorry, Jace!" they said. "Can't you do anything about it?"

"I was invited for a noon meal with Diotrephes. He has been after me for months to change the way I teach. I told him I would not agree with his ideas. Then I asked him about his family, and he became angry. It was strange! Diotrephes, with his arm in a sling, dismissed me from my job. He said he tripped in the dark last night and hurt his shoulder, but something funny happened. He stated, 'You don't insist on the usual declaration, Caesar is lord and god.' Someone at the wedding must have told him how things went last night. I think someone among the visitors was here to spy for Diotrephes."

Jace saw family members look at each other. They did not act surprised but instead nodded their heads as if they knew about it already.

He continued, "I asked about his personal life, hoping to find common ground and something more agreeable to talk about. He got really offended and fired me on the spot. We left and didn't even eat the meal!"

Simon listened carefully, and he understood. "Here is what I make of it. Several months ago, the shipment of wedding tunics must have allowed Cleon to 'earn some extra money.' Diotrephes bought the tunic from Cleon. They probably thought it was for a celebration party that was planned if the bank had accepted me.

"Then different plans were made. It became a wedding with invitations given to the poor people. Diotrephes entered our property wearing the wedding tunic so no one would notice him coming in. Ravid spotted the imposter before he entered the gate, and after it was dark, he came into our house.

"We must thank God for Ravid being so alert, able to take in details such as the missing flying eagles that were embroidered on all of the other tunics.

"Finally, we understand, Jace. Diotrephes came here to take Chrysa Grace. We do not know why, but apparently, he has had his eye on her for some time. Diotrephes's arrival last night had evil intentions. Adonai helped Ravid to keep us safe."

With this explanation, Jace understood more. "So he did come here! That's how he knew that this wedding began without an oath of loyalty to the emperor. He was here to take the baby girl."

Deep lines were etched in Judith's forehead. "A year ago, we lost friends when we were asked to leave the God-fearers' group. Today my son-in-law said he is going away and will take Nissa with him. We almost had a child abducted last night. Now Jace has lost his job. Haven't we had enough losses?

"But we have lived through hard times before, not only the destruction of Jerusalem but also two pogroms in Alexandria. God has protected us as his covenant people."

Judith's faith took them beyond the immediate circumstances, back to their belief in the everlasting faithfulness of the God who had called Abraham from a distant land.

Simon said, "We will call upon the Almighty. Jace lost his job and can no longer support his family. Remember the story of Balaam, when the Almighty said to him, 'You must not put a curse on those people, because they are blessed.'[63] Now the Messiah has added to that, saying, 'Love your enemies and pray for those who persecute you.'[64] Let's do that."

He lifted his voice and his hands. The women pulled up their shawls to cover their heads for prayer. "Almighty Lord, you promised that a little child would lead them, that a young child would put his hand into the viper's nest and not be harmed or destroyed.[65] You promised that the earth would be full of the knowledge of the Lord's glory as the waters cover the sea.[66] So we call on you for your mercy and grace, for Kalonice and Jace; for Miriam, Anthony, and Grace; and for Ravid and our dear daughter, Nissa. Amen."

Jace noticed something as he listened. For the first time, he drank in every word. He found himself agreeing with everything Simon said.

Simon's voice cracked ever so slightly as he hugged Nissa, for she would soon live far away. "You made a covenant promise to Ravid, my daughter. You must stay with your husband."

Once again, Nissa's cheeks were wet with tears. Elaine and Amath hugged their dear Aunt Nissa. Little Amath turned to Chenya and said, "Mommy, if I ever get married, will I have to leave you too?" She tried to speak it in a low whisper, but everyone heard the question.

---

[63] Numbers 22:12

[64] Matthew 5:44

[65] From Isaiah 11:6–9

[66] Habakkuk 2:14

Elaine sat down beside Kalonice. In a quiet voice, she asked, "Auntie Kalonice, does all this mean that Isidoros can keep coming to our house in the future?"

Kalonice saw what she was getting at. "My dear Elaine, this is what it means. My husband lost his job. He has no reason to avoid this family. If he can come here now, then all four of us can as well."

Elaine did not respond, but the shine in her eyes said it all. During the hugs, tears, and laughter at Amath's question, Miriam moved closer to Kalonice and gave her a big hug.

"Kalonice, I just had another idea," said Miriam. "I need to think a bit, but I'll talk about it to you and Jace very soon."

DIODOTUS AND DELBIN'S HOME, WEST HILL

June 6, in the 10th year of Domitian
From: Diotrephes-Naq Milon
To: Commander Felicior, Garrison of Sardis

Peace and health. If you are well, then I am well.

As Director of the Department of History of the Gymnasium in Sardis, I wish to bring to your attention a matter of concern about one of your instructors. I speak of the character and actions of Anthony Suros. I know that he is an atheist. I believe that he has infiltrated the army with his teaching and is encouraging a rebellion. He teaches that followers of Yeshua, a deceased carpenter in Judea, should be loyal to another kingdom, not to Rome. Consequently, like similar atheists, he does not pledge unreserved loyalty to the emperor.

I know that he and his Jewish wife are having a corrupting influence on civic life in Sardis. Their rebellion is beginning in this city.

Last night, under the pretense of a wedding at the Ben Shelah home, they sowed the seeds of a rebellion. They include the poor and sick in their uprising, knowing the discontent that always is close to the surface among the neediest of our city.

I leave it to your discretion whether the Governor needs to know or not.

Diotrephes left his home with an unfamiliar feeling running through his veins. The sensation was something like the fever he had suffered earlier in the winter. He felt a fever spread down his body as he contemplated revenge. He hoped that Commander Felicior would report Anthony to the governor.

The authorities would then lose no time in sending Anthony back to the Army Reservists' Office in Philippi. That would inevitably result in a court martial, with the maximum punishment being meted out.

At the right moment, with Anthony out of the way, he would make a surprise announcement: Zoticos, his uncle, was Chrysa's father. Since Miriam could not show any reason for keeping the child from her father, the courts would take control. He no longer needed to kidnap the child.

Furthermore, he would have Uncle Zoticos write a letter to ensure Chrysa's release from Miriam's custody, consistent with the Roman law on adoptions.

It would help if Zoticos could find Chrysa's real mother to affirm that he was the father. A few bribes in the right place could make that unimportant. He offered up a prayer.

Thank you, Zeus! In the worst moment of my life, in the depths of deep shame, I know enough about the Ben Shelah family, so I will use what I learned against them. Now I will be able to take Chrysa to her rightful family.

JACE AND KALONICE'S HOME

On Friday afternoon, Miriam found a quiet moment with Kalonice. "How is Jace now?"

"Overcome with grief and anger. He doesn't know what he will do when his job ends."

"What if he kept on teaching?"

"Impossible! How could he? Don't hurt him by suggesting Diotrephes was only fooling him."

Miriam laughed. "No. I've had some serious thoughts! Ezar and Zebadiah are running the sales shop, so they do not have enough time to look after the Closely Knit workshop. And remember, we have a second workshop we will be starting soon. Who will manage the work and teach skills to the workers? Managing the people we have is hard work. Each one needs individual time and attention.

Kalonice's mouth had fallen open. "Miriam, are you describing a new project? I have heard you talk like this before."

"Not new, only a little expansion of what we are already doing. Here is the idea: Jace is out of work, and he is an excellent teacher. What if Jace were to supervise the weaving and sewing taking place in the workshops? We need someone to handle scheduling the work and inspecting the results. Look how fashionable the wedding tunics were, the ones Arpoxa's women embroidered! We are going to need more of those tunics to sell at the store. Each day our workers are making fewer mistakes and getting more work done. "They need a competent supervisor, and Jace is capable and gets along well with others; as a teacher, he knows how to be strict. Profits made from the workshop with better products could become part of his salary, completing what he needs to support your family. I'm suggesting that Jace could supervise in the shops part time and teach."

Kalonice began to smile, starting to put the whole story together.

"There's more, Kalonice. I am also thinking of the children. Look at boys like Cosmos. What a smart child! He needs to learn, but his family is so poor. They will never be able to afford to have him studying at the gymnasium. He begs to help feed the family, and he comes home late almost every evening. We want more for him in life than being a beggar!"

Miriam's eyes glistened. "So what if Jace worked full time with the Ben Shelah family? I'm sure he would earn about as much working for Uncle Simon and Aunt Judith as what he made teaching in the gymnasium."

Kalonice's mind was whirling as she thought about explaining all this to Jace. She imagined she was already seeing him smile. And there, in front of her, was Miriam with an amused look on her face.

SIMON AND JUDITH'S HOME

Miriam, Kalonice, and the servants helped Lyris as they lifted her household possessions up to the men who placed them gently in the wagons. They were soon filled with all the things Lyris and Eugene were taking to the house in Simon's new vineyard. The newlyweds were going to have their own home as caretakers in the vineyard.

The whole Ben Shelah family walked with them to the gate, but Miriam and Kalonice climbed onto the wagons to go help with the unloading. The three carts were stocked with food, furniture, kitchen supplies, pots, pans, and bedding. Their new house was in good shape considering that it was usually used only during the summer months, from spring until late harvest. It was a perfect solution for them and was close to the city so they could come and go freely.

The wagon drivers slowly made their way along the Royal Road, past the Eastern Agora, through the massive Eastern Gate, and then north toward the low foothills. All around, vineyards spread out on the dark fertile soil of the plain. Farm laborers walked along the roads, some pulling animals by a rope and others carrying rakes, hoes, or other farm implements. Merchants marched with their camels, horses, and donkeys. Sheep crossed the road in search of pasture.

The vineyards filling Hermus Valley spread to distant horizons. Grapes were beginning to fill out, and deep green vegetation promised an abundant harvest for both wine and raisins. The sun was shining warmer each day.

After the wagons were unloaded, Eugene and Lyris promised to come to the city from time to time during the next three months, until the harvest was finished in September.

On their way back to the city, Miriam took Kalonice's arm. "What does Jace think of our plans for the future? This is his last day at the gymnasium."

"Miriam, you are a clever little woman! He is thrilled to leave his job at the gymnasium and that nasty Diotrephes. We told Nissa about it before she left, and she liked the plan too."

Miriam started to laugh. After managing the stress of bringing all those poor people together to the wedding, each with the right size wedding garment; learning that they almost had lost Grace to a kidnapper; and then moving the newlyweds, they could relax as they were bouncing down the road on the way home.

From time to time, each would mention other funny events that happened during the last week, and both would spontaneously explode in peals of hilarity.

Their wagon driver looked behind him to see what was making them laugh. He wondered if they had a jug of wine hidden under their bench.

Kalonice asked, "Can you picture Jace at the workshop in a few more days? One minute he'll be guiding a blind man to where he will comb raw wool. Then he'll be helping another man get down from the wagon; he'll make sure he doesn't injure himself, but just then, he will have to give instructions to a deaf man. He will then organize a meal for the women and later teach many bright little lads! It will be a job that constantly changes from day to day. And for that, the Ben Shelah family business is going to pay him. He'll love it."

"I think you have a pretty good picture of his future," Miriam said confidently.

The thought sent them into another round of giggles. "I imagine he'll come home very tired and very satisfied," said Kalonice.

Chapter 41
Felicior's Decision

COMMANDER FELICOR'S OFFICE, THE ACROPOLIS

Commander Felicior stood up again and walked around his office. Four letters lay on his desk. The contents of three of them would test his leadership as much as anything in his past. Each of the three small scrolls brought disquiet. Taken together, they spelled potential disaster for Anthony Suros. The fourth letter, oddly, seemed to possibly provide a solution for clearing Anthony's name.

On one corner of the desk, lay the message from Diotrephes with a worrisome accusation about Anthony. He shook his head, unsure how much truth, if any, lay behind the malicious words.

Does Diotrephes know all this for sure or has he merely been listening to too much gossip?

The second "letter" was an incomplete scrap, and it lay beside Diotrephes's scroll. The note had come from Little Lion. Felicior re-read the letter written from a camp behind the enemy's battle lines in Dacia. He was prepared to show it to Anthony.

A letter from Commander Maro had been there for a week.

June 1, in the 10th year of Domitian

From: Commander Cassius Flamininus Maro, Garrison of Pergamum

To: Commander Felicior Priscus, Garrison of Sardis

Peace and health. If you are well, then I am well.

The Army Reserves' Office in Philippi has not answered my request seeking clarification about the assignment given to Anthony Suros. For the time being, he should be kept under your command. Assign him for duties for one more year.

This letter from Commander Maro was concerning for two reasons. The way it was stated implied that Maro believed he could call Suros back to the Pergamum Garrison. What possible reason could Maro have for doing that? The second concern was the army's lack of reply about the assignment. Very strange.

Commander Servius Callistratus at the Garrison of Soma sent the fourth letter, and it had arrived this morning. Felicior knew the young officer in Soma had a reputation for being ambitious. It was apparent to all when any of the younger officers were anxious for sudden advancement.

June 6, in the 10th year of Domitian
From: Commander Servius Callistratus, Garrison of Soma
To: Commander Felicior Priscus, Garrison of Sardis
Peace and health. If you are well, then I am well.

I recently received notification from Aizanoi about the murders of slave merchants between Prusa and Cotyaum.[67] *Two bodies were found in a state of decomposition, and it is believed that their stolen slaves were sold in Aizanoi.*[68] *This happened without the soldiers at inns or waystations noticing anything amiss.*

For now, every caravan of slaves coming from Prusa will need additional soldiers for protection. The garrison commander in Aizanoi believes that the murderer, or murderers, will attempt further robberies of this nature.

As the westernmost garrison controlling the Postal Road, we have been requested to send a squad to Aizanoi. I am understaffed and lacking sufficient qualified soldiers. I request that the best six soldiers from the Garrison of Sardis be temporarily placed under my command. Their task: to pursue and arrest those responsible for the two murders.

I request your immediate approval.

Felicior sent a message to the training camp: "Call Suros. I want him here right away."

---

[67] Ancient Prusa is known as Bursa, a large industrial city in Turkey. Ancient Cotyaum is the central Turkish city of Kutahya, widely known for the production of ceramics.

[68] Aizanoi was a large and important city between Kutahya and Usak. Today the village is known by its Turkish name, Cavdarhisar.

Anthony arrived mid-morning, and Felicior did not waste a word. "I received a written accusation specifically naming you."

Anthony studied his commander's face. Who could be bringing such a charge? He knew of no one who had shown dissatisfaction with his work in training recruits for the army.

"At ease, soldier. A teacher at the gymnasium by the name of Diotrephes wrote an accusation. He is rapidly becoming an important personage in the city and wants me to forward this letter to the governor. Remember this: Emperor Domitian executed our previous governor of Asia Minor for rebellion. Governor Ceriales was required to raise troops to counter a threat of invasion from beyond the Euphrates River. He did not respond quickly enough. Diotrephes's accusation is serious. He says you are organizing an uprising."

After reading Diotrephes's letter, Anthony handed it back to Felicior.

The commander placed the letter on the desk and looked at Anthony. "What is the relationship between you and the teacher at the gymnasium?"

"Not a good one, sir. We knew each other superficially in Pergamum. He studied for six weeks with Antipas, the old man who was burned to death there. Our paths crossed a few times last September, mostly with unpleasant words. I have not seen him since."

Felicior studied the letter for a few moments. "What do you have to say to the accusation?"

"I have not undermined the emperor's authority. These charges are not true."

"Are you inciting poor families to rise up against the State?"

"No...oh, I see! This must refer to a wedding held a week ago in the home of Simon Ben Shelah. One of Simon's servants, a widow, was married to a widower. A celebration was held for them."

"Why would Diotrephes say that event was intended to incite revolt?"

"I don't know his motives, sir, but I guarantee they are intended for an unpleasant purpose. It was a very normal, quiet wedding party. There was no evidence of rebellion. None. Quite the opposite."

Felicior took up the scroll from Commander Servius in Soma. "Word has come from Soma. The garrison commander wants me to contribute soldiers to his command so he can conduct a search in Aizanoi to dig out the person or persons who murdered two merchants near Prusa. They were taking slaves to the market from Prusa. The slaves disappeared, and the slave traders are dead. This is very strange, so I am thinking of sending you to Soma as part of the investigation team, but there are other matters first."

"What matters, sir?"

"These other letters on my desk. One states that no further news came from Philippi about your previous days in Upper Germanica. I wanted to know about your injury and secondly about your appointment as a reservist. There seems to be a permanent delay about everything associated with the Predators."

"That's my legion! Why the delay, I wonder."

"It *was* your legion."

"Pardon me, sir. Did you say, 'was'?"

Felicior passed him the letter from Little Lion. "This arrived this morning. Read it." Anthony unfurled the small scroll and read.

May 3, in the 10th year of Domitian
To: Anthony Suros, Garrison of Sardis
From: Little Lion

We crossed the Danube River, invaded Dacia...defeated. The first battle...we lost. I am severely wounded.... I will not live...too much blood.... We approached...the order to march was given before we scouts finished surveying a canyon.... It narrowed in one place and then opened into a wide valley. We did not spy out the valley sufficiently before our commander gave orders to march in and capture it...would have permitted him to circle to the left behind the Dacian army. We were to divide their forces, leaving our other legions to enter through the forest, but we were forced against a fortress...crushed between their army behind us and their stronghold ahead.... They held the high ground.... Almost all our horses, carts, machines, knights, and battalions destroyed...in the two-day battle...Legion XXI, the Predators...no more. I am bleeding...two arrow wounds to my left side. Few of us made it out...only those who had made it to the top of the canyon and...were gathering

information as scouts. I always remembered your teaching. You taught... to wait for the right moment to value victory over immediate impulse. You also taught me... the two kingdoms. I am ready... meet my king of...
{Nothing further – Scribe Flavius Lilivicus}

Anthony's face had turned ashen as he slowly rolled up the scroll and handed it back to Felicior. He blinked back a tear. "Sir, this is very unexpected. I am deeply saddened to know that my entire legion is...gone! All those soldiers and auxiliaries..."

"I felt the same when I read it. You fought as a scout for that legion. Now the Dacian army has destroyed it. Your eagle standard is lost. Most, if not all, of those soldiers, have perished. However, read the last line in Little Lion's letter again. Do you see the predicament that I am in? Does it confirm Diotrephes's accusation?"

"Please explain, sir."

"Little Lion was dying, losing blood, and he made it back to a tent. Somehow, he had the strength to dictate a letter to you. He describes the battle, the place where the defeat took place. The most important part is at the end. He confirms you were teaching him about another kingdom."

"Yes, it was only with him that I explained about Yeshua Messiah. He asked questions."

"So you disobeyed my command! I have to wonder if you talked about this troublesome Messiah to others as well!"

Anthony looked at each of the four letters on Felicior's desk. Two of them, for sure, spelled trouble for him. Diotrephes had denounced him, and Little Lion's last words confirmed that he had disobeyed Felicior. In his dying breath, the young man had confessed his belief in another kingdom.

Felicior looked at Anthony, weighing his possible decisions.

Is this soldier, marked for life with a scar on his face, a true legionary? He displays the leadership needed for training men destined for Dacia. Of all the men I know, he can hunt down the bandits behind these two murders. However, a severe accusation of disloyalty cannot be dismissed. I must be meticulous here.

"Soldier, I have decided on several things. Commander Cassius in Pergamum wants you to remain under my authority, and I am going to comply with his request.

"Second, I will send you to Commander Servius's garrison in Soma, along with the five best men in my garrison, to assist in the murder investigation. Soma is strategically placed, a small military post between Thyatira and Pergamum. The road narrows there; a high mountain is on one side and, on the other, a shallow river. A high mountain range rises farther north. In the next couple of days, you will say your goodbyes to this city."

"I understand, sir."

"You are to learn who the bandits are. Capture them all. I want each one brought in for questioning. We may already know two of their names: Taba and Craga."

"Is that all, sir?"

"No, the Simon Ben Shelah family is indirectly implicated. Rebellion is a terrible word."

"It is a totally fabricated charge without any foundation, sir."

"Nonetheless, you and your wife have been denounced. You will be staying out of this city during this assignment, but I think your wife must also leave Sardis for her safety. I want to determine how much truth there is to the allegations about Simon Ben Shelah. You say it was only a wedding party. I will investigate what is meant by 'stirring up rebellion among the poor people of this city.' Do you have a place for your wife to stay outside of Sardis?"

Anthony closed his eyes for a second, struggling to understand why the commander was speaking this way.

Miriam should not return to Pergamum. Marcos said Miriam should not go there, but that was almost a year ago. Miriam's Uncle Jonathan lives in Thyatira. That large city is close to Soma. What other choice do we have? If she went to Philadelphia, she would be too far away from Soma to see me when I have a day off. Perhaps she should go to Thyatira for a few days until we learn what is best for her.

Anthony leaned forward, hopeful because of this new idea. "Sir, my wife has a relative in Thyatira. She could stay with her Uncle Jonathan Ben Shelah."

Felicior seemed to mull over this possibility for several seconds. "I approve. She may stay with her relatives in Thyatira until you finish the task. If she moves to somewhere else, I want to be informed. I will authorize a military wagon to carry your gear and supplies. Your wife can ride on the wagon as far as Apollonius. Once there, she will have to switch to a commercial cart carrying goods to Thyatira. The five soldiers of your squad will meet you at the Apollonius Inn. Go directly to Soma from there."

"I understand, sir."

"I have another instruction, Suros. You are not to go to Thyatira until this assignment is complete. For your information, I don't...trust...the guilds in Thyatira."

For the first time, he stumbled on a word. He had trouble saying the word "trust."

Anthony wondered if Felicior was intending to protect Miriam and Grace by sending them away. *Could Felicior be using the trouble in Aizanoi as a means of getting both of us out of the city? Is there something that I do not know about Thyatira? Is there something that he doesn't want me to know?*

He put such thoughts out of his mind. "Is that all, sir?"

"Do you know the terrain around Soma?"

"Yes, I do. A year ago, I stayed at Forty Trees at a farm owned by my wife's uncle. His Olive Grove Farm is close to the Postal Road."

"Good, that may come in handy. It's always important to understand the lay of the land. I will select the five others in your squad this afternoon. Go up, claim your belongings at the training camp, and prepare yourself and your family for your journey. You are dismissed."

Anthony saluted and left. He claimed his horse at the gate of the garrison and walked down the acropolis's initial steep incline. The peaceful river basin spread out in every direction. The leaves of early spring were a lush carpet of bright green vegetation promising a coming harvest. Pine trees spread out below, down to the stadium. Several people, many panting from the effort of climbing the acropolis road on foot, passed him on their way up to the top. He mounted the horse and rode the rest of the way, reaching Royal Road.

He came to the bottom of the acropolis and pulled on the reins before crossing onto Royal Road. He passed children playing near the guards at the entrance to the Mint. Miriam's song about the soldiers at war came back to him. The tune was known to everyone in the city, but only a few knew the words she had composed. He sang her song to himself.

Before going back to the training camp, he turned to gaze at the splendor of the acropolis. From this position, the ragged edge caused by the avalanche at the south corner was hidden entirely. However, one portion of the rock ledge showed a small crack under the protecting wall. The mighty fortress was not as safe as the citizens of Sardis might hope.

Anthony thought of the recruits trained in Pergamum and Sardis. How many of them were dead after having been trapped in a canyon in a faraway land? His final conversation with Little Lion came back. Both wanted Dacia to become a peaceful province. He thought of Upper Germanica, where he had left newly pacified villagers four years earlier.

COMMANDER FELICIOR'S OFFICE

Felicior reread the four parchments and turned to the window, wondering if what he was doing was the best thing. Birds flew above the city, but from his position on the acropolis, he looked down on them. He followed a black hawk, its feathers spread out, down below as it soared in circles.

Picking up Diotrephes's parchment, he scowled. The charges could lead to a court martial. Their previous governor had been executed three years ago because of disloyalty. He talked to himself, a habit that came with his being slow to speak to others.

"Is Anthony insubordinate or not? I must know where his loyalties lie. If Suros is rebellious, then I, and not Diotrephes, will lay charges. I foresee that this soldier has a long road ahead chasing down these killers. I want him to search from Thyatira to Prusa and the Sea of Marmara close by. He'll have to travel about 420 miles.[69]

"Success in arresting the murderers of the slave merchants will almost certainly spell an end to Diotrephes's charges. If Anthony ever comes to a court martial for allegations of disloyalty, I will say that I responded by testing his loyalty to Caesar. I explain that I sent him on a mission to search out criminals and bring them to justice. He trained recruits well. He discovered the gang robbing the citizens of Sardis. But taking the eagle standard from Instructor Prosperus is nothing compared to finding brigands in those

---

[69] About 670 km.

godforsaken stretches of land. Good-bye, Suros. May Jupiter protect you."

Felicior warmed up the red wax, placing his seal on all four scrolls. Someday those seals might be opened. Until that time, these documents were for his eyes only. The letters were bound together with a cord and tied, and the knot was sealed with wax.

I need tough-minded and capable men around me. Anthony must locate the murderers of those two merchants. That's the kind of discipline I need, but why does he insist on accepting that false teaching?

Chapter 42
Sent to Serve

SIMON AND JUDITH'S HOME

Saying goodbye to Simon's family was one of the hardest things Miriam had ever done. They had arrived in Sardis a year before, not knowing if they would find safety. Anthony had not been sure if he would be accepted in the garrison or be returned to Pergamum. They had arrived as strangers. Now they were leaving family and friends.

Anthony looked around the room, which had become completely silent. "I've just been told that I have to leave tomorrow morning. Miriam and baby Grace will be coming with me."

Judith, who had been mainly silent during the ups and downs between Ravid and Anthony, was the one who broke the silence.

"Well, if we only have this afternoon and evening, then I will serve the best meal since you came."

The rest of the day remained as a haze in their minds. Each one went over the past year's events. The family called friends from their home fellowship group to come and say goodbye. Even some of the families from the insulae were brought in for the meal.

The next morning, when the sun had barely risen, it was time to get on the road. All Anthony would say to Simon's family about his future was that he had been given a "special assignment."

Miriam had promised Anthony that she would not tell anyone about his new task: capturing bandits on the Postal Road.

"You are so lucky, Anthony," said Tamir, trying to keep Anthony in the house a little longer. "Being a soldier must be a lot of fun! Tell me more about what you're going to do!"

Anthony replied, "Tamir, the army is no place for boys like you. You never know what is going to happen."

The thought of Little Lion's death would not leave him.

Elaine would always remember the joy of performing in front of so many guests. "Miriam, when you come back, will you teach us more songs? Thank you for letting us play instruments as your song unfolded during the wedding and thank you for your song. I'll sing it a thousand times."

Their smiles secretly acknowledged to each other that Elaine was still interested in Isidoros.

"I promise to teach you new songs and teach you the old songs again if you have forgotten them! Maybe I'll have a hundred more to teach you."

"We'll never forget the songs you taught us!" Elaine hugged Miriam, not letting go. "You let us play with Grace, a real live baby, not just with our dolls! We are going to miss you so much. Grace is so sweet walking now and trying to talk. She sings with us and tries to play our games. Anyway, I'm too old for dolls now."

Simon and Judith stood close to each other. Simon was always self-controlled, but his lower lip was trembling a little bit.

"So much happened in such a short time," he said. "We have been rejected by the Synagogue of Sardis. The Assembly of the God-fearers is completely assimilated into the life of the city unfortunately. There seems to be no difference between their worship of God and their reverence of Artemis!"

He found that studying the roof kept the tears from forming. "Oh! And we've started teaching our own group of true God-fearers here." He lowered his gaze, taking in the beauty of his niece's face. "When you arrived, I didn't know how to cope with a Roman legionary coming into our home. I thought I was too old to have crying babies being passed around from one person to another at the table. But Grace and Saulius are one-year-olds now."

He let out a great sigh. "Your coming to live with us has helped me understand my father's blessing for me at the time of his death. He specifically told me that there is more comfort and warmth in providing for others than providing for myself. You have shown me what is profoundly important in living.

"Now I don't know how I will cope without you being here! The house will be too quiet. I have a blessing for you, my niece, from the Scriptures: 'Surely you will summon nations you know not and nations that do not know you will hasten to you, because of the Lord your God, the Holy One of Israel, for he has endowed you with splendor."[70]

Anthony was trying to hurry up the goodbyes. He called out, "Miriam, I can't hold up the military carriage anymore."

Goodbyes to Ateas and Arpoxa were shorter than Miriam wanted them to be. Arpoxa stayed on her chair because her feet hurt so much. The activities of the last days of getting ready for the wedding were going to require some extra rest.

"I have to tell you a secret," Arpoxa whispered as Miriam bent down to kiss her on both cheeks. "I'm expecting another baby. By the end of the year, I'll have two little ones."

Blinking rapidly, Miriam hid a twinge of jealousy. "Arpoxa, I'm so glad for you! We must see each other again soon!"

Miriam looked at her friend, recalling how they became so close. Arpoxa, born with clubbed feet, had grown to young womanhood, and was sold as a slave to pay for her brother's gambling debts. She was married to Ateas in Chalcedon when they left one slave ship to be transferred to another. Antipas had ransomed Ateas and Arpoxa in the slave market of Pergamum.

"Thank goodness you are teaching embroidery and sewing. The poor women love you," Miriam whispered, bending down and giving her friend a hug. There was so much more she wanted to say.

Arpoxa is a talented artist who uses thread and needle, and she's expecting her second child. Uncle Simon has offered for them to stay in the little house that Ravid and Nissa have left. Ateas is being asked to take over Ravid's work as Simon's assistant in the jewelry shop. He is going to further develop his skills in gold working. They will do well here.

Kalonice and Jace arrived just as Miriam was about to get into the four-wheeled wagon. She held Jace's hand on one side and placed the other hand around Judith's plump waist.

Kalonice blinked back the tears. "Miriam, you encouraged me so much. I never knew what it means to be 'a people belonging to God.' You simply burst into my life."

"Well, we had lots of laughs along the way, didn't we?"

"I remember the day you talked to us at the workshop. People were learning to weave. You said, 'Once you and Jace and your family were not a people, but you are now the people of God. Once you had

---

[70] Isaiah 55:5

not received mercy, but now you have received mercy.'[71] No one ever told me that before."

"And Kalonice, you've become such a dear friend. I'm so sorry that I have to leave like this. It's what happens, I guess, when you're married to a military man!"

"You're going, and I'm staying. When we bought the first looms for the workshops, you taught the workers, 'Weave your lives in the right way so you don't have to undo stitches in the future. Abstain from all the things that war against your soul, like wasting money, anger in the home, and gambling away funds that the little ones need for food.' Another day, you instructed, 'Live such good lives among the pagans that, though they accuse you of doing wrong, they may see your good deeds and glorify God on the day he visits us.'[72] Miriam, my dear friend, you have shown me how to live."

Judith turned to Kalonice. "We're all going to miss them, aren't we?"

Kalonice squeezed Jace's waist on one side and Judith's arm on the other. "Yes, we are going to miss them," she replied. Kalonice would not cry now, but later in her house, the tears would flow.

Simon's entire family and all the servants waved goodbye as the wagon rumbled through the gate. Heber was standing with his brother Ezar, waving as much as Tamir and Amath.

ON THE ROAD TO APOLLONIUS AND SOMA

Before noon, Anthony and Miriam passed the military checkpoint at Marmara Lake. Anthony talked with the soldiers and guards checking credentials, showing them the commission signed by Felicior. After a noon meal, they began the all-afternoon trip to the Green Valley Inn, where they would stay the night. It was halfway between Sardis and Apollonius, the Honeybee Keepers Village.

As they were approaching Green Valley Inn, Miriam held Grace so that the child could see. "Look, dear! Watch the birds swimming on the water!"

Then, to Anthony, she said in a whisper, "Now tell me why I have to go to Thyatira, and you cannot come to visit me! I don't want to stay in Thyatira all by myself, even if it is with my Uncle Jonathan. I

---

[71] 1 Peter 2:10

[72] 1 Peter 2:12

think it's a cruel plan. Honestly, I don't think I like your Commander Felicior! Of course, he didn't send you back to Pergamum, which earned him a few points." She grimaced and smiled grimly.

Anthony answered with a whisper, "At least we have tonight together in this lovely spot. Then tomorrow..."

They had arrived at their destination. He left his thought unfinished but pulled her close to him. They would not have many more hours together.

The next morning they were on their way, and Anthony returned to Miriam's thoughts the previous day. "You married a soldier, my dear. Many soldiers never get permission to marry. In fact, most soldiers don't survive the kind of injury that almost killed me. My scar reminds me of how fortunate I am to be alive. When I am away from you, I will remember you and think of you every day."

"But you still haven't told me why you can't stay in Thyatira with me. And how long is your new commission going to keep you away from me?"

"Apparently something is happening in Thyatira that Commander Felicior doesn't want to speak about. I don't know if he suspects an individual or an entire guild. There's something that has attracted his attention, though. He won't say a word about it; he only told me what my next assignment is. I'm going after bandits, but I can't explain to you much more than that. All I can say is, there are treacherous criminals along the Postal Road. Cheer up! We have one more day together."

"And you expect me to be satisfied with that?"

"Yes. Felicior is a good leader, always training his soldiers and giving them impossible things to do. He did it to me when I had to lead twenty young men on the mountain. He said, 'Soldier! You have an impossible job. Take the eagle standard from Instructor Prosperus.'

"He believed that we couldn't do it, but when we did, all of us working together, the success was shared by the entire squadron. That is probably what led to this assignment for me."

Miriam's face took had a puzzled look. "But you are going to be far away! You will be in danger going up and down the Postal Road. What do you say to criminals? 'Ready or not, here I come!' No! That's a game to play with Ezar and Chenya's children, and it doesn't work for crooks! Oh, Anthony, I am so worried for you!"

"I'm worried too. But I believe God will see us through this rough time. Uncle Simon kept saying the things your grandfather used to read from the scrolls. I learned how to call passages to mind when stressful situations come along."

She was comforted by the strength of his commitment. He had promised to remain faithful to her.

The second verse of a song mixed love, disappointment, and worship. It came as she watched the landscape slowly going by. Miriam was afraid of what the next days would bring, so she was comforted by remembering the blessings and struggles of the previous year. She would write down the words later, filling one of the unfinished sheets of papyrus that were in a pouch inside her grandfather's bag.

You trained young men, keen to fight, in the ways of war.
Then they left, the empire's best, bragging of their strength.
Scouts and soldiers, now just names, they will fight no more.
A legion smashed. Whose stories will be told at length?

You trained an athlete to run a long, hard race.
Tried his best, but winded, he could not keep up the pace.
Scandalous lies kept being told about our child.
Our enemy was stopped, his motives fierce and wild.

Needy folk now have jobs, Lord, from poverty set free.
I thank you for hope, when troubled beyond degree.

Later that day, they arrived at the Inn of Apollonius,[73] the only inn in the small town. The owners, Alyssa and Xenophon, remembered them from a year before and warmly welcomed them to Apollonius, the Honeybee Keepers Village.

"I remember you. Friends of Nikias!" Xenophon bellowed. "My hearing hasn't become better, even after my steady diet of honey! Speak louder! A *home* for you? Yes, of course! No? Oh, we'll arrange a *room* for you! Take your horses to the stables over there."

---

[73] Apollonius, an agricultural town, is known today as Ballica. It is five miles (9 km.) west of Akhisar, which was known as Thyatira in the first century.

Donkeys brayed, and horses swatted flies with their tails. Dogs barked, and chickens ran cackling everywhere. It was just a small village on the plain where little happened each day. Carts from the distant villages came to Apollonius, unloading vegetables and fruit to be transported the next day to Thyatira.

The five soldiers sent by Felicior had arrived earlier in the day. It had only taken a day for them to come from Sardis, unlike Anthony and Miriam, who rode more slowly in a military wagon.

Anthony would be the leader of this squad for the next few months until those responsible for the deaths near Cotyaum were brought to justice. Their horses were taken to the stables at the rear of the building, brushed down, watered, and fed.

After a full day of traveling, Anthony and Miriam found it hard to shake the jolts and bumps of the wagon from their bones. This was their last evening together for a long while. Miriam didn't know when she would see Anthony again.

Fear, like the night coming on, threatened her with future loneliness. She kept such thoughts away by focusing on her husband, not on herself.

Their last night together seemed too short. Miriam went to their room, thinking, wondering, and praying.

Cosmos's mother had six pregnancies, and she's my age. When will it be my turn? What if I am expecting a baby while Anthony is far away on his new assignment?

The next day, Miriam would be riding in a wagon to Thyatira. It would be filled with vegetables going to the market there.

THE INN AT APOLLONIUS

Their early breakfast was over, and it was time to say goodbye, the hardest moment in their fifteen months of marriage. The produce wagon going to Thyatira was almost ready to leave, but Miriam was desperate to keep him with her a little longer.

Anthony's soldiers, handpicked for this challenging assignment, stood beside their horses. They were dressed in their full soldier's uniforms, ready to leave for Soma.

Miriam asked him one more time, "How long will it take to find the criminals?"

"I don't know. Maybe a few weeks or a few months."

"Where will I send letters when I want to write you?"

"Give your letters to Nikias when he comes to Uncle Jonathan's. He can keep them for me at Olive Grove, a farm near Soma. In turn, I'll send letters to you through Nikias. He'll be our go-between. After I come back, I'll just fix wagons," he declared, joking.

A serious look came over his face. "I trained Hector for the Annual Games and legionaries for Dacia, but I wasn't entirely successful. Hector didn't win the race, and our legion is no more!

"Miriam, when I was at camp missing you and little Grace, I started to make notes. They are in your bag in the wagon. I will send you some notes on my observations of how Grandfather Antipas trained men. I have been thinking, and I have a plan for training men like Little Lion. I only wish that I had more time with him."

Miriam held onto his arm. "Write to me, and I'll write to you too. I will pray for you every day. I love you so much. I want you to make the highways safe quickly, but that's because my motives are selfish!"

The wagon full of vegetables and fruit was ready to pull onto the road to Thyatira.

Miriam was ready to hop on the back for her ride, sitting beside the two young women who had already taken their places. In a few minutes, her wagon would start to roll down the little hill, pass over the narrow stone bridge, and climb the incline on the other side of the slow-moving creek. She would pass beside the cemetery and then turn right, disappearing behind the tall green cypress trees lining the graveyard. She would be in Thyatira by late afternoon.

Anthony took Grace in his arms and kissed her, snuggling up against the soft skin under her chin and blowing little bubbles. She laughed, wanting more.

"Miriam, there will always be us!" He repeated the phrase again, thanking God for his family.

He repeated their secret phrase again. "There will always be us!" He added, "Never enough love!"

She poked him in the ribs, content to bask in the moment. He helped her up onto the back of the cart, which was filled with fresh vegetables.

When Miriam was seated, Anthony passed the baby up to her. Two horses started pulling, and Anthony walked beside them onto the busy road from Apollonius to Thyatira.

Now he had to let them go, and he stopped walking. He waved, and Miriam waved back. She waved Grace's little hand.

Anthony continued waving as the wagon reached the bridge and started up the other side. He did not mind if people stared at him, a soldier waving to a slow-moving wagon that was now bumping along on Thyatira's plains.

In the morning traffic, Miriam and Grace were swallowed up in the crowds. He waited for a while, keeping his gaze on the tall cypress trees. Her wagon might be visible, even for an instant. He would be with her again when his assignment was concluded.

That could never be soon enough.

*Never enough love!*_He repeated their secret phrase they had come to enjoy, and he waved one last time.

"Thank you, Miriam," he breathed. "Thank you for all you have ever given to me and to others. How can I tell you that? You make it all worthwhile."

Miriam's wagon had disappeared, and she was gone. As Anthony turned to his fellow soldiers, ready for his new task, he whispered a thought, wanting her to hear his voice across the space that now divided them. "Since I have been with you, everything, even trials and problems, has a joyous side. I will see you again, my dear. With you, life is precious, and riches count for little. For me, your love will always be more than enough. You changed my life.

"Never too much love."

MAKING SENSE OF THE NOVEL AND THINKING ABOUT

NEVER ENOUGH GOLD

The following questions are intended to encourage the reader to consider how each character in the novel fit into the overall story. Some characters will continue throughout the seven books, and it is helpful to consider the motives and experiences that drive them.

1. What kind of **suffering or grief** did each person experience in the past?

    Simon Ben Shelah and his wife Judith
    Miriam and Anthony
    Trifane, Grace's mother
    Impoverished families in the slum area of Sardis
    Commander Felicior

    What kind of **suffering or grief** have you experienced?

2. As the novel opens, what is the **motivation or outlook on life** of each person?

    Simon Ben Shelah and his wife Judith
    Miriam and Anthony
    Diotrephes
    Cleon

3. Each character lives in a city where **wealth, property, and social status** are key elements. Compare the characters considering the Sardian expression, "Never enough gold."

    Mayor Tymon and his wife, Panthea
    Banker Diodotus and Delbin
    Jakob Ben Shelah and his friend Achim
    Simon and Ravid
    The robbers

4. Earthquakes frequently rattled Sardis and the surrounding region. How did Ankara and Alala **respond to the threat** of further damage to the city?

How do you respond to threats of forest fires, earthquakes, floods, or other natural disasters?

5. Characters respond to situations, and as the novel ends, what **changes have taken place** in these persons?
  Simon Ben Shelah and Judith
  Nissa and her husband, Ravid
  Little Lion
  Commander Felicior
  Jace and Kalonice
  Trifane, Grace's mother

6. Significant pressure is placed on **the God-fearers gathering**. What motivates Diotrephes? Describe the changes Gaius had to make. How did Marcos in Pergamum deal with changes forced upon him by the death of Antipas?

7. How does each person in Simon's family respond to Diotrephes?

Have you lived through a "take-over," either at work, in your family, among your friends, or at your church? How did you respond?

8. A large part of the novel deals with **giving or receiving training**. How are skills and knowledge passed on and received in these groups?
  In the army: Commander Felicior, Prosperus, and Anthony
  Among the recruits: Little Lion, Dares, and Cohn
  Antipas, the deceased Christian leader in Pergamum, and Diotrephes?

9. Gaius, Miriam, and Kalonice share an interest in **visiting and helping needy people.** What were your thoughts as you traveled with them into the homes of these families?

Have you ever crossed a cultural or economic divide to form a relationship with a needy family?

10. Another theme in this novel explores **success and failure**. What responses take place in these characters as they either succeed or fail?

Simon Ben Shelah aim to be a partner in the Bank of Hermus
Rabbi Jakob's plans to obtain favorable results from the city
Prosperus's intent to keep the eagle standard in his tent
Little Lion's task of identifying the robbers
Diotrephes's attempts to gain Jace over to a Lydian worldview
Hector's training and wanting to win first place in the race

11. How was **the gospel made clear** to each person, and how did it affect their lives? How did the character move away from the demands of being a follower of Yeshua, the Jewish Messiah? And have you, like these persons, either moved further away or closer to the Messiah?

Jace and Kalonice
Little Lion
Instructor Prosperus

12. Who are the persons in the novel that made the deepest impression on you?

If you enjoyed this book,
please consider ranking it on Amazon or another book site
and posting a brief review.
You can also mention it on social media.

Please contact the author at:
Century One Chronicles
PO Box 25013
255 Morningside Avenue
Toronto, ON M1E 0A7

If you would like a Zoom visit to your book club
or an interview for your blog, email at
centuryonechronicles@gmail.com.

Website:

https://sites.google.com/thechroniclesofcourage.com/chroniclesofcourage/home

SARDIS IN THE BIBLE

Revelation 3:1–6

To the angel of the church in Sardis write:

These are the words of him who holds the seven spirits of God and the seven stars. I know your deeds; you have a reputation of being alive, but you are dead. Wake up! Strengthen what remains and is about to die, for I have not found your deeds complete in the sight of my God. Remember, therefore, what you have received and heard; obey it, and repent. But if you do not wake up, I will come like a thief, and you will not know at what time I will come to you.

Yet you have a few people in Sardis who have not soiled their clothes. They will walk with me, dressed in white, for they are worthy. He who overcomes will, like them, be dressed in white. I will never blot out his name from the Book of Life but will acknowledge his name before my Father and his angels. He who has an ear, let him hear what the Spirit says to the churches.

DIOTREPHES, GAIUS, AND DEMETRIUS IN THE BIBLE

3 John 1–14

The elder, to my dear friend *Gaius*, whom I love in the truth.

Dear friend, I pray that you may enjoy good health and that all may go well with you, even as your soul is getting along well. It gave me great joy to have some brothers come and tell me about your faithfulness to the truth and how you continue to walk in the truth. I have no greater joy than to hear that my children are walking in the truth.

Dear friend, you are faithful in what you are doing for the brothers, even though they are strangers to you. They have told the church about your love. You will do well to send them on their way in a manner worthy of God. It was for the sake of the Name that they went out, receiving no help from the pagans. We ought therefore to show hospitality to such men so that we may work together for the truth.

I wrote to the church, but Diotrephes, who loves to be first, will have nothing to do with us. So if I come, I will call attention to what he is doing, gossiping maliciously about us. Not satisfied with that, he refuses to welcome the brothers. He also stops those who want to do so and puts them out of the church.

Dear friend, do not imitate what is evil but what is good. Anyone who does what is good is from God. Anyone who does what is evil has not seen God. *Demetrius* is well spoken of by everyone—and even by the truth itself. We also speak well of him, and you know that our testimony is true.

I have much to write to you, but I do not want to do so with pen and ink. I hope to see you soon, and we will talk face to face.

Peace to you. The friends here send their greetings. Greet the friends there by name.

Purple Honors

A Chronicle of Thyatira

Part 1

June AD 92

Guilds and Gods

Chapter 1
Slave Traders' Plans

COMMANDER SERVIUS CALLISTRATUS'S OFFICE, SOMA

Servius Callistratus, the commanding officer of the Garrison of Soma, leaned forward, one hand half forming a fist. Late afternoon shadows darkened the small military office where Commander Servius interviewed six road-weary Roman soldiers.

He stared in disbelief as Anthony finished telling how, one year ago, the leader of a band of robbers had escaped. Servius, bent forward as if to better convey his irritation with the newly arrived soldier. A sneer framed his face, expressing his outrage.

"Suros, you are supposed to be an experienced scout! But look how you have disgraced yourself!"

The legionary being addressed was Anthony Suros, a veteran of many wars in Upper Germanica. The muscular soldier repeatedly blinked at the harsh words, and he reached his hand up to touch his right cheek. A long scar indicated a harrowing encounter, but Anthony never talked with anyone about how he came to survive that painful encounter.

Servius Callistratus turned to look at the other five soldiers in the room, and then he turned to address Anthony. Red-faced and with his eyes blazing, he stared in disbelief. Anthony had finished telling how, one year ago, the leader of a band of robbers had escaped.

He turned back to Anthony again, "You were leading twenty others, and still, you let him get away...running down the mountain in Sardis! What complete incompetence! Commander Felicior wrote me saying that there was a problem during the gang's capture, but I did not know it was this bad. I am glad you gave me the details. It will help me to know how to deal with you."

Anthony looked straight ahead. He dropped his hand to his side, and his face was blank. He suspected from this display that Servius, who had a slight build and was shorter than most commanders, felt insecure and needed to impose his will.

"We caught eight of the nine thieves. All were punished, sir."

"But their leader!" Servius stopped to glance at the scroll in his hand, "Taba escaped!"

The tone of his voice conveyed firm military discipline. The six legionaries could expect no tolerance if they failed in their new assignment in searching for outlaws, smugglers of slaves, and murders.

Servius pulled a chair away from his desk and motioned to the squad. All sat down. "Omerod, Menandro, Sextilius, Bellinus, and Capito: there must be some reason why Commander Felicior ordered Anthony to be your leader, but I have yet to find it.

"Suros, what happened to the scouts you trained? Part of Commander Felicior's note to me says that the scouts you trained were surrounded and killed by troops loyal to King Decebalus! You let a criminal escape, and the scouts you trained failed miserably! Do you have anything positive to say for yourself?"

Anthony bit hard before answering. "Sir, three days ago, I learned from an army dispatch that the scouts we trained died. They were with 5,000 other soldiers. Our army engaged the Dacian army. Unfortunately, my Legion XXI, The Predators, is no more. I know that Emperor Domitian is greatly distressed by the news. As we all are."[74]

Anthony knew his reputation was badly tarnished.

"Inexcusable! And as a reward for your ineptitude, Commander Felicior has named you the leader of a squad? Two bodies were discovered near Cotyaum, prompting Commander Diogenes Elpis in Aizanoi to believe a gang is operating along the Interior Road. The murdered men were slave merchants, and their slaves disappeared without a trace. All are to be brought to justice. He called the six of you together to work under my direction. What I don't know is what Felicior saw in you."

Before answering, Anthony glanced out of the window where late afternoon sunlight cast long shadows. He knew that he was not the failure that Commander Servius was suggesting.

Breathing deeply so that he could control his thoughts, he winced. *What I don't know, Commander, is how long this assignment*

---

[74] Emperor Domitian sent Legion XXI 'The Predators' against Dacia in AD 91 or 92, but it was wiped out. All legionaries were killed in action. Dacia, conquered between AD 101 and 105, was a large kingdom, covering present-day Romania and Moldova and smaller portions of Bulgaria, Serbia, Hungry, Poland, Slovakia, and Ukraine

will keep me away from Miriam and my little daughter. I owe no apologies for my actions.

Anthony stood up high. "May I give you some relevant details, sir? Here is what we know as we begin our search for the criminals."

"Yes, speak."

"The leader of these criminals is named Taba. Before his escape, he confided in Little Lion, a young army recruit. Little Lion wormed his way into their gang and learned that Taba was enlisting more rebels. Commander Felicior believes that they are carrying on an illegal trade in slaves, so he assigned us to find Taba and all those working with him."

"There is no excuse for failing to capture this enemy, Taba!" Servius spoke rapidly, a bitter note sounding in his words. Examining each member of the squad before him, Servius handed Anthony a scroll. "Here is your commission to begin this operation.

"Prepare your horses and supplies for a long trip. You begin the day after tomorrow. Expect to travel long distances every day.[75] You'll travel 350 miles from here to Prusa, and then seventy more miles to another garrison beyond that. Every commander along the way must be informed to prioritize the capture of these bandits. That is all."

The commander stood at attention, ending the meeting. "Caesar is lord and god!"

When Anthony came to the words "and god," he held his hand to his mouth and coughed.

Servius glared at the legionary with a red scar on his cheek. He noted that detail

A week before, Commander Servius had been slightly drunk in Soma's largest tavern, where he had consumed too much cheap beer. Talking too much, he cursed his bad luck. Being assigned to Soma, a small but strategic garrison halfway between Pergamum and Thyatira.

He had boasted, "I'm a capable officer; I can handle the toughest assignments. It's a shame that nothing demanding could ever happen here in this insignificant place!"

---

[75] Post houses, or relay stations, were located every seven to ten miles on the main roads. Horses traveling at a fast trot managed eight to nine miles an hour. When on urgent assignments, riders covered about one hundred miles in a day.

Now, his sentences were short and abrupt, and he would not repeat a drunken visit to the tavern. He intended every word to convey authority. Earlier in the afternoon, he had returned from a meeting in Pergamum. He was determined to show his authorities in Smyrna and Ephesus that because he was remarkably talented, he deserved to be assigned to a larger garrison.

In this squad of six soldiers lay his opportunities for advancement and prestige. Servius, longing for a tough challenge, saw this mission as an opportunity to prove himself.

He was posted to an insignificant garrison, but he knew his talents were equal to any commander in a larger city. He felt he deserved a greater responsibility.

Word had it that Commander Felicior in Sardis was going to be promoted to a southern city within a year, perhaps to Miletus. Servius saw this as his chance to move up.

Leading a successful operation against bandits on the Postal Road might finally bring the needed recognition of his abilities to headquarters and improve his chance of getting the Sardis assignment. Then, after two years in Sardis, he would be recognized more widely. His persistent dream of an assignment in Rome might be within reach!

Before asking the six legionaries to leave, Servius wondered if Anthony deliberately did not complete the oath. Was the man with the scar on his face disloyal as well as incompetent?

In his opinion, the leader of the squad might prove to be a bigger problem than he first thought.

"You are dismissed," he said, and the six members of the newly formed squad left his office.

ON THE ROAD FROM APOLLONIUS TO THYATIRA

While Anthony was encountering hostility in Commander Servius' office, Miriam, his wife, was riding on a vegetable cart. The young woman with a smooth forehead, black hair, and clear olive skin had left Apollonius,[76] the Honeybee Keepers Village early in the morning.

Nearing the manufacturing city of Thyatira, the cart bounced on

[76] Ancient Apollonius is known today as Ballica, or 'Place-of-Honey". The distance from Ballica to Thyatira, modern Akhisar, is 9 miles (15 km).

a cracked paving stone, and she reached out a hand to balance herself. She would not let her one-year-old daughter slip and fall. Her lips quivered, as they often did, whether from either excitement, joy, or anticipation. This afternoon, she was hungry, having spent hours with the tantalizing scents of fruits and vegetables all around her.

Miriam looked again at the vegetables and fruits. Boxes held melons, cherries, almonds, apples, peaches, figs, and apricots. And vegetables, too: celery, green beans, mint, cabbage, artichokes, lettuce, radishes, spinach, cucumbers, and herbs.

Tears in her eyes indicated sorrow and disappointment. She did not want to be separated so soon after her marriage from Anthony, the soldier she had married. Once more, the heavily laden wagon jolted on the uneven paving stones of the Roman road.

"It's a rough ride," called the wagon driver as he turned his head to the back of the wagon. "The road to Thyatira always needs repairs! But of course, no one comes to do the job. As a result, we all suffer."

The young mother grimaced, holding her one-and-a-half-year-old daughter Grace with one hand. She clutched the wagon with the other, while the little girl giggled, unaware of danger. "She thinks it's fun, but I'm petrified!" Miriam explained, speaking to one of the younger women riding with her.

Passing Grace to one of the two sisters, Miriam rearranged herself. Her lips quivered again, happy to have a more comfortable position. Taking Grace back on her knee, she strained her head to see how much further they had to go before arriving in Thyatira.

Jonathan Ben Shelah, Miriam's uncle, lived in Thyatira, and he was expecting her to arrive mid-afternoon. She tried to relax but could not. Her stomach was churning. She composed a letter in her mind, wishing she could send it to Anthony.

June 18, in the 11th year of Domitian.
From Miriam.

To Anthony, my beloved husband. I already miss you. One year and two months ago, we were married. Our time in Sardis went by so fast. Last year you were away so much of the time instructing army recruits at the training camp. Oh, Anthony, I love you so. How will I stand it? Not knowing where you are or when I will see you again?

A TAVERN NEAR PRUSA, ASIA MINOR (BURSA, TURKEY)

Curses sounded as Craga, a disgraced Roman soldier, pulled out a chair to sit down with his three friends. He fingered the damaged muscles of his left leg. Stress lines showed on his forehead.

The four men had paused at a tavern overlooking the Marmara Sea. Blue water reflected a cloudless sky. Each of the four Roman soldiers used armor and weapons stolen when they had deserted the army. The sun had begun to lose its biting heat, and they welcomed the breeze that would soon be cooling them.

"Taba, Maza, and Harpa!" Craga greeted them cheerfully, forcing a smile. "So good to see you! How was the sailing from Chalcedon? I had guessed you would be here by yesterday, but the trip is hard to predict with these variable winds. Were there any difficulties with security at Port Chalcedon? No? Me neither. I showed my 'credentials' and quickly got waved through."

Taba, who had recruited Maza and Harpa, two new members of the gang, during the winter months, smiled. A broken tooth, the result of a victorious fight against a barbarian warrior, marred his beam.

"The authorities only glanced at our papers. Who really wants to march with slaves for days on end? They're happy for older guards like us to be assigned to escort dirty, smelly slaves on their way to Aizanoi."

Craga glanced around to ensure that there were no eavesdroppers. "We have today and tomorrow to discuss my plans. Two days from now our next 'shipment' should be arriving."

He spoke quietly, confident of coming wealth. Their plan was to kill the owners of slaves being escorted and then take their "merchandise" to a lucrative market. All this had already been done right under the noses of the Roman authorities.

He leaned back, a huge smile indicating his pleasure. "Isn't Prusa a wonderful city?[77] We're staying there tonight! Look at that massive

---

[77] Ancient Prusa is today known as Bursa, a large industrial city in western Turkey with a population of about 2,000,000. In pre-Roman times, this city was the capital of Bithynia. It became the first capital of the Ottoman Empire (1535–1563) and today is known for specialized industrial production of vehicles.

mountain, the protective home of Zeus rising high above the city![78]

"A chest full of treasures awaits us. In the slave market, one male slave brings in close to five hundred denarii. In the army, it took us a year and a half to earn that much! And a female slave can sell for many times more if it looks like she will have lots of babies.

"Occasionally we'll also be handling wild animals to sell to arenas in Asia and Rome. Wild animals make us a lot of money, but they are troublesome to handle and expensive to feed.

"Eight weeks ago, we conducted two slave merchants who had twenty slaves going south. We sent them to an early death on an isolated section of the road and then took over their 'cargo.'"

Craga chuckled. "The slaves never knew what happened. They just thought we were sellers working on behalf of the merchants. All those unfortunates ended up in the mines and brought us lots of money.

"Now let us discuss the plans that involve the three of you. How will we all become rich? Two merchants and a caravan of slaves are going from Prusa to Aizanoi in two days. You'll go with the caravan as a military escort.

"At the beginning of the trip, the slaves will be conducted by the merchant, a slaver master who starts out with us, but when the slaves are put up for the auction at the other end, he'll be on the other side of his grave. His merchandise will belong to us. No one will ever learn what happened. The slaves won't even be aware. In a few more days, we'll have disappeared."

Laugher flowed easily as they dreamed of such easy riches. "The profits, less expenses, are divided by the sum of the sharing members in our 'army.' Mithrida, our general, gets a double share, but then each of us 'soldiers' get one share. Our auxiliaries[79] get a quarter share. If Zeus is pleased with our work, we'll each have enough in two years to buy a farm and maybe one or two slaves and settle down as..."

Maza's eyes bulged with excitement, and he leaned forward in anticipation, completing the sentence: "...as honest owners of lands

---

[78] Uludag Mountain, which affords visitors majestic skiing runs, was sometimes known as one of the homes of Zeus.

[79] Auxiliaries were the non-soldiers of the Roman army. They performed non-fighting, menial roles, such as cleaning, food preparation, transporting equipment, and, in this case, tending the slaves being moved.

and properties!"

Craga explained the size of their gang. "For now, our army includes ten soldiers and about twenty auxiliaries, but our army will grow. The more we have, the more 'projects' we can start. That means more money for us all."

Harpa, the quiet one, had not completely lost his senses despite several mugs of beer. "We can get the best farmlands in Scythia, far away from Domitian's long reach." He raised his mug again. "Cheers!" His three companions responded with gusto.

Several others in the simple tavern heard them laughing loudly and remarked, "Those soldiers! Drunk again!"

Craga, holding his sore leg with one hand, came back to his main task. "Keep your eyes open for suitable recruits. Remember our code names and how they came to be. If anyone is caught, the others will be protected. Always be careful to not draw attention to yourselves. A legionary may be remembered, and some might remember your name, but no one ever remembers the face of a slave! Don't they all look alike? That works in our favor. We are guaranteed success."

Taba agreed, nodding his head. "I gave myself the name Taba in Sardis a year ago, and it has worked great! Easy to remember. I'm sure I can find the eight men I recruited for our little army. I can hardly wait to get back there." As the others laughed with delight, he pondered questions that kept coming to mind.

Last year in Sardis was not a success; it was a disaster. I wonder what became of Little Lion, the young man I wanted to join our gang. He probably got caught with the first four men I recruited for our gang; I was lucky to escape. The army isn't too gentle with bandits. Bad judgement on my part to fall into that trap!

I'll never tell these guys how I lost everything last year. I escaped only by running downhill in the early morning light. I later heard that the other four men I trained were also caught. A disaster but I'll never let something like that happen again.

Delighted that they had found a way to pass undetected from one Roman garrison to another and seeing that the sun would soon be setting, they walked to the nearby city of Prusa. Each one was certain that they were going to be rich beyond their wildest dreams. Each used a false name. No guard along the Postal Road would bother to question the forged papers of soldiers conducting slaves to market.

Craga, Maza, and Harpa were laughing loudly as they neared the main gate of the city, where a soldier approached them. "Hail, soldiers! New to Prusa? I haven't seen you men before."

Craga answered, "We are conducting slaves." He introduced his three companions to the guard, who took them into the barracks beside the garrison.

"Welcome!" said the guard. "You can stay here in the garrison barracks. There's plenty of room. Every available soldier we had was rushed to Dacia after Legion XXI..."

He paused, not wanting to mention the death of legionary friends. "Such a sad event! Trained soldiers were killed like flies, just like that!" He snapped his fingers and cursed the army who served the king of Dacia. "Emperor Domitian has suffered a grievous setback with the loss of five thousand soldiers."

"Yes, the worst possible news!" said Taba sadly.

His thoughts, however, were of a somewhat different attitude.

If I hadn't deserted four years ago, I would certainly have been one of those fallen on that battlefield. They were my friends at one time. But no longer. They're dead and I'm alive. And to think that last year I was almost captured in Sardis!

After the terrible loss of personnel in Dacia, many soldiers from Asia Minor had been reassigned to help maintain security in the area still held by Rome. In provinces bordering Dacia, most military outposts were below minimum strength, so army officers in Pontus, Bithynia, and Asia Minor were on the lookout for additional legionaries. Thus, they welcomed retired soldiers as guards in cities and as patrols on the Postal Road.

The new recruits to Craga's illegal band were deserters from Dacia who had been disillusioned by the lack of leadership on the battlefield. Resentment against the army burned in their hearts, hot embers waiting to burst into flame.

These four criminals had their fill of danger from being thrown into battle against barbarians for the glory of Rome. Now each wanted his own riches.

The quicker, the better.

AFTERWORD

How did a tiny group of followers of Yeshua Messiah not only survive persecution in the Roman Empire but continue to grow in number despite pain and suffering? How did their faith in a Jewish Messiah spread, reaching both rich and poor, men and women, Jews and non-Jews, slaves and free?

Such thoughts intrigued me while living in Turkey, with its 5,600 archaeological sites. My teenage interest in the Roman Empire as a boy in Kenya returned. Later I was blessed with other teachers who made history come alive.

Turkey's unique geographical features are enhanced with the unending beauty of changing seasons. The visual attractiveness of the land is deeply satisfying. The country is famously known for its millions of tourists that arrive each year.

Seeing this opportunity, I joined others in promoting faith tourism, which is important to the country. Tourist groups I hosted wanted to spend time at the sites of seven ancient cities. At the end of each day, we relaxed and often engaged in questions and discussions.

Having explored Troy with a tour group, we sat down for a fish dinner. We searched our imaginations to describe people who might have lived there three thousand years ago. What were their professions? What happened at the port every day? Who built the buildings? Out of that conversation came a strong impulse to go beyond the stones strewn over the ground to imagine an ancient city throbbing with all sorts of people.

From this came the idea of Antipas being the central character of a novel. I wanted readers to travel in their imaginations, to walk up and down steep streets, to learn to shop in markets, and to receive invitations to come for a meal in ancient homes. It was important to meet living, breathing people. What were their hopes and fears, their politics, and religious beliefs? I wanted to understand their conflicts and difficulties, their victories, and defeats.

At first, I thought a single book would do. It would include seven sections, one for each ancient city.

But as I thought further about each city, it became clear that a single novel would not do justice to the geography, history, civic functions, Roman government, and Greek culture in each case.

Three years passed before the story spanning seven novels had jelled in my mind. The seven novels would weave elements of the seven letters of the Revelation into the cultural background.

It was important to employ names in use during this historical period. Most names may not be familiar to some readers.

Consequently, the names appearing in this book may be a difficult aspect for some readers to absorb the story. I used contemporary Scythian, Lydian, Greek, Roman, Persian, and Jewish names, some of which reflected usage centuries old.

Unlike the order of the seven churches that appear in the first chapters of the book of Revelation, the narrative in this saga begins with the first book in Pergamum and the last brings the reader to Ephesus.

At the conclusion of the long narrative, many characters from the earlier novels are brought face to face for a climactic ending in Ephesus.

ACKNOWLEDGEMENTS

For years, my wife Cathie and I were privileged to live in Turkey, where we learned to appreciate the commitment of present-day believers in Jesus Christ. We have friends who live in the same region as these seven novels. Our Turkish friends encouraged me in ways they will never know.

During those years in Turkey, many Turkish citizens offered us friendship and hospitality. They not only helped me to enjoy their country, but they made us feel safe. My thanks to them for helping us to learn about their way of life and the history of their land.

Archaeologists continue to uncover numerous ancient cities in Turkey. Findings by these researchers supplied dates, names, and details for cities and towns mentioned in these seven novels.

Museum staff were delighted for interested visitors to examine their displays. They passed on much helpful information. I am grateful to the countless scores of people who enriched my life in all the locations mentioned in these novels. Without their help, none of this would have been written.

During my high school years, I was blessed by capable history teachers at Rift Valley Academy, Kenya. Dr. Ian Rennie at Regent College, University of British Columbia, guided me in historical research at an important time in my life. He demanded accuracy, which was character forming.

Several friends provided the impetus for the effort needed to create the storyline and bring it to a conclusion. Blair Clark worked with me for several years, especially in coordinating faith tourism. Raye Han, a Turkish tour guide of boundless enthusiasm, taught us about her country, giving endless details and sharing a spiritual passion. Visitors to Turkey were amazed at her professionalism, as well as that of other tour guides.

Friends at the City of David Messianic Synagogue in Toronto, Canada, contributed much to the Jewish aspect of the novels. I am thankful to each one in this Messianic congregation. Through them, I became aware of various aspects of Jewish life and thought, and they helped to build me up in my faith.

Without the help of Jerry Whittaker as an editor, these volumes would not have made it to the press. No one could wish for a more capable and discerning friend. His creative suggestions and analyses improved the storyline and character development at each stage.

Friends and family members enriched the story through their comments. Robert, Elizabeth, Samuel, and Aimee Lumkes offered unique intergenerational feedback. Pearl Thomas, Anne Clark, Magdalena Smith, John Forrester, Susan and Max Debeeson, George Bristow, Noreen Wilson, Frank Martin, Ken Wakefield, Lou Mulligan, George Jakeway, and Michael Thoss provided helpful opinions as early readers. Other support came from friends and churches; their names are found in the Book of Life, and my appreciation extends to each one.

Daphne Parsekian graciously became my final editor, and I am grateful for her careful reading and her willing spirit in going through the final steps before sending this manuscript to the printers. She helped me immensely.

My wife Cathie has been patient with me through the many ups and downs while working on these manuscripts. No words can express my appreciation for her unending encouragement.

History and Dates in Sardis

(Based on accounts by Herodotus, Dionysius of Halicarnassus, Strabo, Euripides, and Livius)

BC ATYADS DYNASTY

1300 Ruled from Ephesus (Abasa); language: Luwain

HERACLID DYNASTY (approximate dates)

1185 Included 22 kings during 505 years

1100 Collapse of the Hittite Empire

1100 Tantalus, the mythical primordial ruler of Maionia

1050 Niobe, daughter of Tantalus, and husband Zethos make commercial links with Thebes (These may have been mythical persons.)

1000 Omphale, daughter of Iardanos, ruler of Lydia (may be mythical persons)

1000 Heracles (god Sandon), mythical Greek traveler, carried out heroic exploits

960 Diodorus Siculus, son of Omphale and Heracles

900 Pre-Heraclid kings of Lydia: Atys, Lydus, Tyrrhenus, Alcaeus, Belus, and Ninus

776 Alyattes, King of Lydia; Lydian widely spoken

687 Murder of King Candaules (King Myrsilos) by General Gyges

MERMNADE DYNASTY

687-652 Reign of King Gyges; overthrew the Cimmerians; built his capital in Sardis and fought with Egyptians against Assyria; killed by the Cimmerians; buried at Lydian royal cemetery (Or other dates: earlier: 716-678 BC; later: 680-644)

652-621 Reign of King Ardys II; first to mint gold coins?

621-609 Reign of King Sadyattes

609-560 Reign of King Alyattes II, one of greatest kings of Lydia; captured Smyrna in the west; captured Gordius in the north, putting Cimmerian threat to an end; against Medes to the east; May 12, 585 - Battle of the Eclipse, formal treaty between Lydia and the Persian Empire

560-546 Reign of Croesus, the end of the Lydian Empire under Cyrus II, also known as Cyrus the Great

ACHAEMENID (PERSIAN) EMPIRE

546-545 Period of Persian satraps; satrapy of Tabalus; revolt of the Sardians in 545; formation of the Royal Road to Susa, the longest road in the world at that time

545-544 Satrapy of Mazares; suppression of the revolt

544 Satrapy of Harpagus

530-520 Satrapy of Oroetus; conquered island of Samos

520-517 Satrapy of Bagaeus

517-513 Satrapy of Otanes

513-492 Satrapy of Artaphernes I; 499 - Sardis sacked by the Greeks in Ionian rebellion

494 Artaphernes dealt with rebels in a moderate fashion; Greeks given estates; many Persians settled in Sardis; Jewish forced migration from Susa

492-480 Satrapy of Artaphernes II; invasion of Greece

490 Persian defeat at Marathon

480 Persian defeat in Greece

480-440 (Few historical records about Sardis; most records tell of Athens and Greek cities after the victories against the Persians)

440-415 Satrapy of Tissaphernes; Persian struggles against Greek island

408-401 Satrapy of Cyrus the Younger

401-395 Satrapy of Tissaphernes; invasion of Lydia by Greeks with Tissaphernes killed in Sardis by Spartan King Agesilaus II

395-365 Satrapy of Tribazus; extensive revolts against Persia; restored Sardis to Persia and signed treaties between Persia and Greek city states. Extensive revolts of Sardians took place against Persia in 370 BC.

365-? Satrapy of Autophradates

334 Satrapy of Spithridates; killed by Alexander at the battle of Granicus

GREEK EMPIRE

334 Alexander the Great's victory over Persia at Granicus Sardis surrendered
330-301 Governed by Antigonus Monophthalus
301-281 Governed by Lysimachus

SELEUCID EMPIRE

281 The former Lydian Empire was governed by the Seleucid Empire based in Antioch
222-187 Under Antiochus III, 2,000 Jewish families brought to Sardis from Babylonia
189 Under the Peace of Apamea, imposed by the Romans after this important military victory, Sardis was to be administered by Pergamum.
133 BC Death of King Attalus III (138-133) in Pergamum

ROMAN EMPIRE

133 BC When the Kingdom of Pergamum was bequeathed to Rome by Attalus III, Sardis became an important regional city in the Province of Asia.

Dates AD

16 The Great Earthquake in the province of Asia with major damage in Sardis
20 A gradual rebuilding of Sardis, attempting to recover its former glory and reputation
55 Initial formation of the church in Sardis under the leadership of Epaphras
295 The leader of the church in Sardis was promoted to Metropolitan Bishop of the Province of Lydia. At that time, the church was the third in size, after Ephesus and Smyrna. (As written by Constantine Porphyrogentius – about AD 950). Sardis's importance slipped as Magnesia-upon-Sipylum to the west and Philadelphia to the east gained importance as bishoprics.

BYZANTINE EMPIRE

1071 Selcuk Turks captured the city and imposed Islam.

1097 John Doukas reconquered Sardis, establishing authority under the Comneni family.

1204 Sardis came under the Empire of Nicaea, with influence from Venice.

1261 The Byzantine Empire retook Constantinople, and Sardis was neglected. With the rising power of the Ottomans, a family called Ghaz pressured Constantinople for control.

1306 A treaty signed between Constantinople and the Ottoman family gave Sardis to the new rulers, the Ottoman family based in Prusa, today Bursa.

1402 The Mongol warrior Timur destroyed what was left of Sardis.

Made in the USA
Monee, IL
19 January 2021

57431829R00246